W9-AEN-675

The Law of Nines

The Law of Nines

TERRY GOODKIND

G. P. PUTNAM'S SONS

NEW YORK

PUTNAM

G. P. PUTNAM'S SONS
Publishers Since 1838
Published by the Penguin Group
Penguin Group (USA) Inc., 375 Hudson Street, New York, New York 10014, USA •
Penguin Group (Canada), 90 Eglinton Avenue East, Suite 700, Toronto, Ontario
M4P 2Y3, Canada (a division of Pearson Canada Inc.) • Penguin Books Ltd,
80 Strand, London WC2R 0RL, England • Penguin Ireland, 25 St Stephen's Green,
Dublin 2, Ireland (a division of Penguin Books Ltd) • Penguin Group (Australia),
250 Camberwell Road, Camberwell, Victoria 3124, Australia (a division of Pearson
Australia Group Pty Ltd) • Penguin Books India Pvt Ltd, 11 Community Centre,
Panchsheel Park, New Delhi–110 017, India • Penguin Group (NZ), 67 Apollo
Drive, Rosedale, North Shore 0632, New Zealand (a division of
Pearson New Zealand Ltd) • Penguin Books (South Africa) (Pty) Ltd,
24 Sturdee Avenue, Rosebank, Johannesburg 2196, South Africa

Penguin Books Ltd, Registered Offices: 80 Strand, London WC2R 0RL, England

Library of Congress Cataloging-in-Publication Data

Goodkind, Terry.
The law of nines / Terry Goodkind.
p.   cm.
ISBN 978-0-399-15604-5
I. Title.
PS3557.O5826L39   2009   2009017214
813'.54—dc22

Printed in the United States of America
1   3   5   7   9   10   8   6   4   2

BOOK DESIGN BY AMANDA DEWEY

To Jeri, the love of my life, who is always there for me.
She gives me her strength when I'm weak and her special smile
when I'm strong. No one knows as well as she everything that
has brought me to this place, this book, this new road. I could
never be who I am, or accomplish all that I do, without her
at my side every step of the way. She completes me.
This one is for her.

ACKNOWLEDGMENTS

At Putnam I wish to thank the publisher, Ivan Held, and my editor, Susan Allison, for their boundless enthusiasm and support.

I would like to give special thanks to my friend Andrew Freeman, not only for all his help, but for bringing his remarkable vision, talent, enthusiasm—and unfailing sense of humor—into my life.

My thanks also to Heather Baror for coming up with great ad copy as if it were the easiest thing in the world. It is not, believe me.

The Law of Nines

1.

I T WAS THE PIRATE FLAG flying atop the plumbing truck that first caught his attention. The white skull and crossbones seemed to be straining to keep from being blown off the flapping black flag as the flatbed truck, apparently trying to beat the light, cannonballed through the intersection. The truck heeled over as it cut an arc around the corner. White PVC pipe rolled across the diamond plate of the truck bed, sounding like the sharp rattle of bones. At the speed it was traveling the truck looked to be in danger of capsizing.

Alex glanced to the only other person waiting at the curb with him. With his mind adrift in distracted thoughts he hadn't before noticed the lone woman standing just in front of him and to the right. He didn't even remember seeing where she'd come from. He thought that he saw just a hint of vapor rising from the sides of her arms into the chill air.

Since he wasn't able to see the woman's face, Alex didn't know if she saw the truck bearing down on them, but he found it difficult to believe that she wouldn't at least hear the diesel engine roaring at full throttle.

Seeing by the truck's trajectory that it wasn't going to make the corner, Alex snatched the woman's upper arm and yanked her back with him.

Tires screeched as the great white truck bounced up over the curb right where Alex and the woman had been standing. The front bumper swept past, missing them by inches. Rusty dust billowed out behind the truck. Chunks of sod and dirt flew by.

Had Alex hesitated they both would have been dead.

On the white door just above the name "Jolly Roger Plumbing" was a picture of a jovial pirate with a jaunty black patch over one eye and a sparkle painted in the corner of his smile. Alex glared back as the pirate sailed past.

When he looked up to see what kind of maniac was driving he instead met the direct, dark glare of a burly passenger. The man's curly beard and thick mat of dark hair made him look like he really could have been a pirate. His eyes, peering out of narrow slits above plump, pockmarked cheeks, were filled with a kind of vulgar rage.

The big man appeared infuriated that Alex and the woman would dare to be in the way of their off-road excursion. As the door popped open there was no doubt as to his combative intent.

He looked like a man stepping out of a nightmare.

Alex felt a cold wave of adrenaline flood through him as he mentally choreographed his moves. The passenger, who seemed to be getting ready to leap out of the still-moving truck, would reach him before the driver could join in, making it one against one—at least for a brief time. Alex couldn't believe that it was happening, but it was and he knew that he was going to have to deal with it.

Calm fury filled him as he prepared himself for the unavoidable.

Everything slowed until each beat of his heart seemed to take an eternity. He watched the muscles in the man's arm bulge as he held the door open. In response, Alex's own muscles tightened, ready to meet the threat. His mind was cocooned in silence.

Just as the passenger's stout leg swung out the open door, flashing lights and the sudden wail of a siren made the burly man turn his attention away. A police car, tires squealing, launched across the intersection in a way that suggested the cops were angered by the truck's stunt. The police car had been parked beside a hedge to the side of the drive into the parking lot across the street. As they had sped past, the men in the truck apparently hadn't seen the parked police car watching traffic. Lost in his own thoughts, Alex hadn't, either.

The loudspeaker crackled to life. "Pull it over!"

The world seemed to rush back in.

The white plumbing truck, trailing a fog of dust, slowed as it rolled off the curb up ahead, the black-and-white police car right behind it. As the truck stopped, two policemen leaped out, hands resting at the ready on their guns as they approached from both sides of the truck at the same time. They yelled orders and both men carefully emerged with their hands up. In an instant the officers had them out and leaning on the front fenders of the truck.

Alex felt the tension drain out of his muscles, leaving his knees feeling weak.

As he turned his glare from the men being frisked, he found the woman's gaze fixed on him. Her eyes were the luscious color of his finest sable artist brushes. It was clearly evident to him that behind those sensuous brown eyes she appraised the world around her with an incisive intellect.

She glanced deliberately down at his big hand still tightly gripping her upper arm. He had intended to toss her back out of harm's way so that the passenger couldn't hurt her, but the police had shown up first.

She looked up at him in silent command.

"Sorry," he said, releasing her arm. "You were about to be run down by pirates."

She said nothing.

He had meant his comment to be lighthearted, to ease the fright of what had nearly happened, but by her calm expression she didn't appear to be the least bit amused. He hoped he hadn't hurt her arm. He knew that sometimes he didn't realize his own strength.

Not knowing what to do with his hands, Alex combed his fingers back through his thick hair as he stuffed his other hand in a pocket.

He cleared his throat, changed his tone to be more serious, and started over. "I'm sorry if I hurt your arm, but that truck would have hit you if I hadn't pulled you back out of the way."

"It matters to you?"

Her voice was as captivating as her eyes.

"Yes," he said, a little puzzled. "I wouldn't like to see anyone get hurt in an accident like that."

"Perhaps it wasn't an accident."

Her expression was unreadable. He could only wonder at her meaning. He was at a loss as to how to respond.

The memory of the way she'd been standing at the curb still hung in the shadows in the back of his mind. Even lost in distant, dejected thoughts at the time, he had noticed that her body language hadn't been quite right. Because he was an artist, a person's balance, either at rest or in motion, stood out to him. There had been something out of the ordinary about the way she had been standing.

Alex wasn't sure if, by her answer, she was simply trying to do the same as he had been doing—trying to lighten the heart-pounding scare of what had nearly happened—or if she was dismissing his chivalry as a presumptuous line. He imagined that a woman as attractive as she was had to deal with men constantly trying clever lines in order to meet her.

The satiny black dress that hugged her curves looked to be either high fashion or oddly out of time and place—he couldn't quite decide which—as did the long, deep green wrap draped over her shoulders. Her luxuriant fall of soft, summer-blond hair could have gone either way as well.

Alex figured that she had to be on her way to the exclusive jewelry store that was the anchor of the upscale Regent Center across the street. The slanted glass façade was just visible beyond the shade of ash and linden trees spread across the broad grounds separating the upscale shops from Regent Boulevard.

He glanced over at the plumbing truck sitting at the curb. The strobing lights from the police car made the white truck look alternately blue and red.

After getting handcuffs on the passenger, the police officer pointed at the curb and told the man to sit beside the driver. The man sat and crossed his legs. Both wore dark work clothes covered with grime. While both men quietly did as they were told, neither looked to be the least bit cowed.

One of the officers started toward Alex as the other spoke into the radio clipped to his shirt at the shoulder.

"Are you two all right?" the man asked as he approached, his voice still carrying an adrenaline edge. "They didn't hit you, did they?"

Both of the cops were young and built like weightlifters. Both had bull necks. Black, short-sleeved shirts stretched over the swell of their arms served only to emphasize the size of their muscles.

"No," Alex said. "We're fine."

"Glad to hear it. That was quick thinking. For a minute I thought you two were going to be roadkill."

Alex gestured toward the men in handcuffs. "Are they being arrested?"

With a quick glance he took in the woman, then shook his head. "No, unless they come back with warrants. With guys like this you never know what you've got, so we often cuff them for our own safety until they can be checked out. When my partner is finished writing up that ticket, though, I don't think they'll be in the mood to pull a stunt like this again for a while."

That two cops this powerfully built would be worried about the guys in the truck to the point of cuffing them made Alex not feel so bad for being spooked when he'd looked into the dark eyes of the passenger.

He glanced at the badge and extended his hand. "Thanks for coming along when you did, Officer Slawinski."

"Sure thing," the man said as he shook Alex's hand. By the force applied to the grip Alex figured that the man was still keyed up. Officer Slawinski turned away, then, eager to get back to the pirates.

The driver, still sitting on the curb, was thinner but just as mean-looking as the burly passenger. He sat stone-faced, giving brief answers as the officer standing over him asked questions while writing the ticket.

The two officers spoke briefly, apparently about the results of the warrant check, because Officer Slawinski nodded, then uncuffed the passenger and told him to get back in the truck. After climbing back in, the passenger rested a hairy arm out the side window as the other cop started uncuffing the driver.

In the truck's big, square side mirror, Alex saw the man's dark eyes glaring right at him. They were the kind of eyes that seemed to be out of place in a civilized world. Alex told himself that it had to be that in such a newly built, luxurious part of town the work-worn construction vehicles, despite there being a lot of them, all seemed to be out of place. In fact, Alex recalled having seen the Jolly Roger Plumbing truck before.

Alex's small house, not far away, had once been at the outskirts of town among a cluster of other homes built in the seclusion of wooded hills and cornfields, but they had long since been swallowed by the ever-expanding city. He now lived in a desirable area, if not exactly on a desirable street or in a desirable house.

Alex stood frozen for a moment, staring at the grubby, bearded face watching him in the truck's mirror.

Then the man grinned at him.

It was as wicked a grin as Alex had ever seen.

As the black flag atop the truck lifted in a gust of wind, the skull also gave Alex a grim grin.

He noticed then that the woman, ignoring the activity, was watching him. As the light turned green, Alex gestured.

"Would you allow me to escort you safely across the street?" he asked in a tone of exaggerated gallantry.

For the first time she smiled. It wasn't a broad grin, or a smile that threatened to break into laughter, but rather a simple, modest curve of her lips saying that this time she got the lighthearted nature of his words.

Still, it seemed to make the world suddenly beautiful on what was otherwise a rather depressing day for him.

2.

'D LOVE TO PAINT YOU SOMETIME—if you'd be interested, I mean," Alex said as they made their way across the broad boulevard.

"Paint me?" she asked, her brow twitching just a little. It was an achingly feminine look that invited an explanation.

"I'm an artist."

He glanced at the traffic stopped across the intersection to his left, making sure that no rogue construction trucks were about to make another run at them. With the lights flashing on the police car sitting at the curb, everyone was driving cautiously.

He was glad to at last be away from the pirate plumbers. They looked to have developed a grudge. Alex felt a flash of anger at the injustice of their belligerent attitude toward him.

"So you paint portraits?" she asked.

Alex shrugged. "Sometimes."

Portraits weren't his specialty, although they did occasionally bring him some income. He would work for free, though, just for a chance to paint this woman. In his mind he was already analyzing the curves and planes of her features, trying to imagine whether he could ever get such an enchanting face right. He would never start such a work unless he was confident that he could get it perfect. This was not a woman he would want to render in anything less than perfection. Changing her in any way would be unthinkable.

He gestured to the low, elegant structure peeking through the shimmering leaves. "I have a few pieces at the gallery."

She glanced to where he had indicated, almost as if she expected to see the gallery itself standing there.

"I'm headed there now, as a matter of fact. If you'd like to see some of my work, the gallery is down a little ways from Regent Jewelry . . ."

His voice trailed off. He suddenly felt a little foolish at his presumption. He imagined that a woman like her would be interested only in the exclusive jewelry store or the boutiques. Since she wasn't wearing any jewelry he wasn't sure why he assumed such a thing, but he guessed he feared that she probably wasn't interested in art—or his art, anyway.

"I'd like to see your work."

He looked over at her. "Really?"

She nodded as she pulled a wavy lock of blond hair back off her face.

Alex felt his cell phone vibrate silently in his pocket, letting him know that another text message was being delivered. He sighed inwardly as he cut a straight line across the nearly empty parking lot. It was only midmorning; most people didn't arrive until closer to lunchtime. A few dozen expensive cars, glittering in subdued shades of silvers, reds, and ambers, were parked in a cluster around the main entrance.

Message delivered, his phone finally stopped vibrating. Bethany, he was sure, was responsible. He hadn't even known that his phone was capable of receiving text messages until after he'd met her several weeks back. After he'd gone out with her a second time she had started sending him text messages. They were painfully petty. He rarely read them anymore. She usually asked things like if he was thinking of her. He hardly even knew her. What was he supposed to say? That she hadn't entered his mind?

He ignored the phone as he opened the center-pivot glass door for the woman. It wasn't the kind of shopping area that lent itself to the financially timid. She glided through the doorway with the kind of grace and confidence born of being used to such places.

Before the door closed Alex glanced back across the lot, between the linden trees lining the edge of the street, to the white truck still sitting at the curb in front of the police car. He couldn't make out the men inside.

As they passed into the hushed, grand seclusion inside, he was a little surprised to see the woman only glance at the alluring glimmer of Regent Jewelry. As they strolled through the halls, her cool gaze took in each exclusive shop in equal measure. The dress shop, Alex knew, didn't sell anything, except maybe a scarf, for less than four figures. The woman scanned the outfits in the window with no more interest than she took in the shoes in the next store window, or the purses in the next.

Alex saw other women cast appraising glances her way. She looked at the other women, but in an altogether different manner. They were evaluating her socially. She was assessing them . . . spatially, checking their distance before briefly taking in their faces as if to see whether she recognized them.

"Down here, around the corner," Alex said, drawing her attention.

When he spoke to her she met his gaze with a focused involvement that was respectful and interested. He couldn't imagine this woman ever sending him a text message.

She allowed him to direct her around the curve of the corridor decorated with sweeping inlaid metal lines in the speckled pink granite floor. Cast-stone arches stood at a branch of halls. The one Alex took led into a sunlit corridor. Skylights overhead let streamers of light play across the planters overflowing with philodendron and an assortment of salmon-colored hibiscus.

Alex drew them to a halt before the gallery window surrounded with ornate gold molding. The molding, meant to resemble a picture frame, showcased some of the more expensive and sought-after works just inside.

Alex gestured through the window. "This is the place."

A twitch of disapproval ghosted across her features. "Do you mean to say that you . . . painted this?"

She was looking at the large piece displayed in the center of the crowded floor just inside the window. It had been done by R. C. Dillion, a midwestern artist who was becoming a national figure. It was said of him that R. C. Dillion was at the forefront of a new reality in art.

"No, not that one," Alex said. He leaned closer as he pointed beyond the nonobjective works crowding the window to a small landscape displayed on an easel near the back. "That's one of mine back there. The mountain scene with the pines in the foreground to the left."

Alex was relieved to see that Mr. Martin, the gallery owner, had at least put a small spotlight on the painting rather than setting it on the floor, leaned against a wall, as he sometimes did. The small light made the sunlit clearing, within the hushed cathedral of trees, come to life.

"See the one I mean?" he asked as he glanced over at her.

Her mouth opened a little in surprise. "Alexander, it's beautiful."

Alex froze.

He knew that he hadn't yet mentioned his name. He knew because he had been waiting for the right time to do so without sounding like he was coming on to her.

It finally dawned on him that she'd probably been to Regent Center before and she must have visited the gallery. That only made sense; wealthy women knew the gallery, after all—they just didn't tend to take note of his work. Alex's bio, with his photo, was posted beside his paintings. He signed his name in the longer form—Alexander—and that was also the way it was shown on his biography. She must have known his name from that.

She looked up to study his face intently. "Why did you paint that?"

Alex shrugged. "I like the woods."

Her eyes began to look a little more liquid, as if what she saw in that painting had some hallowed meaning to her. "No, I mean why did you paint that particular place in the woods?"

"I don't know. I just made it up from my imagination."

She looked like she wanted to say something, but she instead turned back to stare through the window, looking too taken for words.

Alex was about to ask why that particular scene seemed to matter so much to her when his cell phone rang. He didn't want to answer it, but the woman was staring through the window, absorbed in gazing at his painting, so he turned aside and opened the phone.

"Hello?"

"Alex, it's me," Bethany said.

"Uh, hi," he said quietly as he hunched over the phone.

"Didn't you get my text messages?"

"I'm sorry, I haven't read any of them today. I told you, you should just call if you have something to say."

"You're so silly, Alex," she said in a lilting voice that he found grating. "Who doesn't use text? Don't be so ancient. Everyone does it."

"I don't. So, what is it?"

"Well, if you would have read the messages that I took the time to send you, you'd know. I made plans to take you out tonight and get you good and drunk for your birthday."

She sounded miffed. Alex didn't really care. Nor did he care to get drunk or do anything else to celebrate such a somber day. He was even more annoyed at her presumption.

Bethany was beginning to assume that there was far more between them than was actually there. He'd taken her out a couple of times—enough to find out that they didn't really have anything in common. The dates had been relatively short and unremarkable. He didn't know what she saw in him, anyway. They just didn't click. She liked expensive things and Alex wasn't wealthy. She liked to party and Alex didn't.

And, his art bored her.

"I'm sorry, Bethany, but let me read your messages and I'll get back to you."

"Well—"

He flipped the cover closed and turned back to the woman. She was watching him again in that way that he couldn't quite figure out.

"Sorry." He briefly held up the phone in explanation before stuffing it back into his pocket.

She glanced back over her shoulder to his painting. "Me too. My time is up," she said as she turned away from the window to face him. "I have to go for now."

"Really? Well can I at least—"

The phone rang again. He wished he had shut it off.

The woman's small smile returned, curving her lips in a way that was bewitching. She arched an eyebrow as she gestured to his pocket. "You'd better talk to her or she'll be even more angry with you."

"I don't really care."

But Alex knew that Bethany wasn't going to give up, so he finally pulled the ringing phone from his pocket. He held a finger up toward the woman. "Give me just a moment, please?"

The woman took one last look through the window and then turned back to him, considering. The way her expression turned serious made him pause in place.

The phone stopped ringing as it went to message.

"Be careful of mirrors," she said at last into the quiet. "They can watch you through mirrors."

Goose bumps tingled up Alex's arms.

He almost dropped the phone when it rang again.

"What?"

She only stared at him with that bottomless gaze.

"Please," he said, "hold on for just a second?"

She melted back into the shadows between the shops, as if to give him his privacy on the phone.

He turned away and flipped open the phone. "What?"

"Alex, don't you ever—"

"Look, I'm right in the middle of something important. I'll call you back."

He flipped the phone closed without waiting for Bethany to agree and turned back to where the woman waited in the shadowy nook.

She was gone. Simply . . . gone.

3.

ALEX CRANED HIS NECK, looking around at the well-dressed shoppers strolling the hushed hall. Most were women. He didn't see the one he was looking for.

How could she have vanished so quickly?

He trotted to the archway, looking back toward the massive Regent Jewelry, but he didn't see her there, either. It was not simply startling that she had left so quickly, it was maddening. He had wanted to get her name, at least.

He hadn't expected that he would so abruptly run out of time. He had missed his chance.

But maybe not. She had said that she had to go "for now."

He wondered what she'd meant by that.

He let out a long sigh. Probably nothing. She was probably only being polite. She'd probably wanted to be rid of him the same way he'd wanted to be rid of Bethany.

Somehow, though, it didn't seem like that was it. Something else was going on, he just didn't know what.

In the hallway filled with the whisper of footsteps and soft conversation sprinkled with light laughter it began to feel like he had just imagined the whole thing.

That was a thought he truly didn't want to have, especially not on this day of all days.

The Regent Center suddenly felt very empty and very lonely. His mood, which had only started to lift, sank back down.

He pressed his lips tightly together in agitation at Bethany and her mindless text messages and phone calls. They were never important, but they had just interrupted something that was.

Letting out another sigh of disappointment, he finally made his way back through the clusters of women out for a bit of shopping. He scanned the faces, absently looking for the one who had vanished. He eventually ended up back at the gallery without seeing her, somehow having known that he wouldn't find her.

Seized by a sudden idea, he peered in the window, wondering if maybe the woman had actually gone inside to look at his painting while he was answering the phone. Maybe he simply hadn't noticed. Maybe she'd just wanted to see it up close. After all, she had seemed to be taken by the painting.

Peering in the gallery window, he didn't see the woman, but Mr. Martin saw him and flashed a polite smile.

Hand-wrought Tibetan bells hung by a knotted prayer cord on the door into the small shop rang their simple, familiar chime as Alex closed the door on his way in. He only glanced at the featured pieces on his way past. He had trouble calling them "works."

The slender Mr. Martin, dressed in a dark double-breasted suit, had a habit of nesting his hands one atop the other. He usually reversed the order several times before their arrangement suited him. A bright pink tie flared from his collar just below his prominent Adam's apple.

"Mr. Martin, how are things today? I just stopped by to see if—"

"Sorry, Alex. None of your pieces have sold since the one last month."

Alex drew his lower lip through his teeth. "I see."

He guessed he would have to walk whenever possible until he could get his truck fixed. Fortunately the places he needed to get to were close enough, now that shops and stores had opened in the last year. His grandfather's house had always been within walking distance. Ben, in fact, was probably waiting for Alex to stop by.

Mr. Martin drew on his thin smile again as he leaned in patiently. "If you would let me guide you, Alex, I know that I could make a name for you—along with a lot of money." He lifted a hand, waggling his lithesome fingers toward the painting displayed in the center view of the window. "R. C. Dillion is making himself a fortune with his striking works. His all too obvious anguish and distress over the ruination of the planet is not just heartbreaking, but sought after. Collectors want an artist who can bring such meaningful emotion to the canvas. It gives them a certain sense of pride to let others see the important concerns they so obviously share with the artist."

Alex glanced at the angry slashes of red paint. It certainly did represent ruin. "I hadn't been aware that that was what R. C. Dillion was trying to portray."

"Of course not, Alex, because you won't take my valuable advice and open your mind to the essence of other realities, as important artists do."

"I like painting the essence of our own reality," Alex said as civilly as he could. "If you think that the buyers are so interested in the planet, why don't you show them my paintings of it?"

Mr. Martin smiled in that tolerant way he had. "I do, Alex, I do, but they're more interested in true artistic vision than . . . than what you do. You show nothing of the rapacious nature of mankind. Your work is charming, but not important. It's hardly groundbreaking."

"I see."

Had he not been so dejected, Alex likely would have gotten angry. Through his gloom, though, the slight didn't lift his hackles. Instead it only served to weigh him down further.

"But I assure you, Alex, I do display your work as favorably as possible, and we have had some minor success with it." The smile became fawning as Mr. Martin remembered that occasionally one of Alex's paintings did sell, and that his gallery took a forty percent commission. "I'm hoping for better sales of your work when the holidays come around."

Alex nodded. He knew that arguing his beliefs about art was pointless. It only mattered if he could sell his work. He had success with a few people who appreciated his landscapes. There were still people who wanted to see works like his, paintings that crystallized the beauty of a scene. There were people who appreciated a vision that uplifted them.

The woman, after all, had liked it, and she easily appeared more intelligent than any of Mr. Martin's collectors. She knew what she liked and wasn't afraid to say so. Most of Mr. Martin's clients depended on him to tell them what they should like. They were willing to pay handsomely for such erudite guidance.

Still, Alex needed to eat.

"Thanks, Mr. Martin. I'll check back—"

"Don't worry, Alex, I'll call you right away if one of your pieces sells, but please think about what I said."

Alex nodded politely before he headed for the door. He knew that no matter how hungry he got he would never throw paint at a canvas and pretend it was art.

It was turning out to be an even more depressing birthday than he had expected. His grandfather might cheer him up, though.

He paused, then turned back. "Mr. Martin, I need to take this one with me."

A frown creased Mr. Martin's brow as he watched Alex lift the small painting from the easel. "Take it? But why?"

Taking one painting left the gallery with six of his pieces to sell. It wasn't like there was a run on his work.

"It's for a gift—for someone who values it."

A cunning grin overcame Mr. Martin. "Clever, Alex. Sometimes a small gift can be the seed that starts an expensive collection."

Alex forced a brief smile and nodded as he tucked the painting under his arm.

He didn't know if he would ever see the woman again. He realized that it was rather silly to think that he would.

But if he did, he wanted to give her the little painting. He wanted to see her smile again, and if it took only a painting then it would be more than worth it.

4.

THINK THE MIRRORS ARE WATCHING ME," Alex said as he stared off into distant thoughts.

Ben shot him a look back over his shoulder. "Mirrors tend to do that."

"No, I mean it, Ben. Lately it feels like they're watching me."

"You mean you see yourself watching you."

"No." He finally focused his gaze on his grandfather. "I mean it feels like someone else is watching me through mirrors."

Ben gave him a look. "Someone else."

"Yes."

Alex wondered how she knew.

He was beginning to seriously doubt that she had been real. Was it possible that he could have imagined such a thing?

Was it beginning to happen to him, too? He fought back a ripple of panic at the thought.

"Don't let your imagination get the best of you, Alexander," his grandfather said, turning back to the work at his bench.

Alex's gaze again wandered off into gloomy memories.

"Do you think that I'll end up crazy, too?" he murmured after a time.

In the dead silence he turned to see that his grandfather had halted his tinkering at his timeworn workbench to stare up with an unsettling look, a kind of hard glare that could have been born only in dark and angry thoughts.

Alex found such a look frightening in that it was so unlike his grandfather, or at least the man Alex knew.

A wrinkled smile finally banished the forbidding look. "No, Alex," the old man said in a gentle voice, "I don't think that at all. Why would you come up with such depressing thoughts on your birthday?"

Alex leaned back against the paneling covering the stairwell nook so that the mirror on the wall to his left couldn't see him. He folded his arms.

"I'm the same age, you know. Today I'm twenty-seven, the same age as she was when she got sick . . . when she went crazy."

The old man stirred a long finger through a battered aluminum ashtray overflowing with a collection of odd screws. Ben had had that ashtray full of used screws for as long as Alex could remember. It wasn't a convincing search.

"Alexander," Ben said in a soft sigh, "I never thought your mother was crazy then, and I still don't."

Alex didn't think that Ben would ever come to grips with the sad reality. Alex remembered all too well his mother's inconsolable, hysterical fits over strangers who were supposedly after her. He didn't believe that the doctors would keep the woman locked in an institution for eighteen years if she wasn't seriously mentally ill, but he didn't say so. Even having the silent thought seemed cruel.

He had been nine when his mother had been institutionalized.

At such a young age Alex hadn't understood. He had been terrified. His grandmother and Ben took him in, loved him, took care of him, and eventually became his legal guardians. Living just down the street from his parents' house kept continuity in Alex's life. His grandparents kept the house clean and in shape for when his mother got better and was released—for when she finally came home. That never happened.

Over the years as he grew up Alex would go over there from time to time, usually at night, to sit alone in the house. It felt like his only connection to his parents. It seemed to be another world there, always the same, everything frozen in place, like a stopped clock. It was an unchanging reminder of a life that had been abruptly interrupted, a life suspended.

It had made him feel like he didn't know his place in the world, like he wasn't even sure who he was.

Sometimes at night, before he went to sleep, Alex still worried that he, too, would end up falling prey to insanity. He knew that such things ran in families, that insanity could be passed down. As a boy, he'd heard other kids say as much, even if it had been in whispers behind his back. The whispers, though, had always been just loud enough for him to hear.

Yet when Alex looked at the way other people lived, the things they did, the things they believed, he thought that he was the sanest person he knew. He often wondered how people could be so deluded about things, like the way they would believe it was art if someone else simply said it was.

Still, there were things when he was alone that worried him.

Like mirrors.

He studied the side of the old man's gaunt face as he searched through all the odd bits of junk littering the workbench. His gray stubble showed that he hadn't shaved that morning and possibly the morning before that. He had probably been busy in his workshop and had no idea that the sun had come and gone and come again. His grandfather was like that—especially since his wife, Alex's grandmother, had died. Alex often thought that his grandfather had his own difficulties dealing with reality after his son and then his wife had both passed away.

No one thought the old man was crazy, exactly. Most people thought that he was merely "eccentric." That was the polite word people used when a person was a little loony. His grandfather's impishly innocent outlook on life—the way he always smiled and marveled at everything, and the way he became distracted by the most ordinary objects, along with his utter lack of interest in the business of others—reassured people that he was harmless. Just the neighborhood nut. Most people regarded Ben as a meaningless old man who tinkered with the likes of tin cans, tattered books, and odd assortments of mold that he grew in glass petri dishes.

It was an image that Alex knew his grandfather cultivated—being invisible, he called it—and was quite different from the kind of man Ben was in reality.

Alex never thought that Ben was crazy, or even eccentric, merely . . . unique, a singular, remarkable individual who knew about things that most people could not even imagine. From what Alex gathered, Ben had seen enough death. He loved life and simply wanted to investigate everything about it.

"What are you doing here, anyway?" Ben asked.

Alex blinked at the question. "What?"

"It's your birthday. Shouldn't you be with a young woman, out enjoying yourself?"

Alex let out a deep breath, not wanting to get into it. He forced a smile. "I thought you might have a present for me, so I came by."

"A present? What for?"

"My birthday, remember?"

The old man scowled. "Of course I remember. I remember everything, remember?"

"Did you remember to get me a present?" Alex chided.

"You're too old for a present."

"I got you a present for your birthday. Are you too old?"

The scowl deepened. "What am I to do with, with . . . whatever that thing is."

"It makes coffee."

"My old pot makes coffee."

"Bad coffee."

The old man shook a finger. "Just because things are old, that doesn't mean they're of no use anymore. New things aren't necessarily any better, you know. Some are worse than what came before."

Alex leaned in a little and lifted an eyebrow. "Did you ever try the coffeemaker I got you?"

Ben withdrew the finger. "What is it you want for your birthday?"

Alex shrugged. "I don't know. I thought you'd get me a present, that's all. I don't really need anything, I guess."

"There you go, then. I didn't need a coffeemaker, either. Could have saved your money and bought yourself a present."

"It was meant to show respect. It was token of love."

"I already know you love me. What's not to love?"

Alex couldn't help smiling as he slid onto the spare stool. "You have a funny way of making me forget about my mother on my birthday."

Alex immediately regretted his words. It seemed inappropriate to even suggest that he might want to forget his mother on his birthday.

Ben, a tight smile on his lips, turned back to his workbench and picked up a soldering iron. "Consider it my birthday gift."

Alex watched smoke curl up as his grandfather soldered the end of a long, thin metal tube to the top of a tin lid.

"What are you making?"

"An extractor."

"What are you trying to extract?"

"An essence."

"An essence of what?"

The old man turned in a huff. "Sometimes you can be a pest, Alexander, do you know that?"

Alex lifted one shoulder in a half-shrug. "I was just curious, that's all." He watched in silence as solder turned to liquid metal and flowed around the end of the tube.

"Curiosity gets you into trouble," his grandfather finally said, half under his breath.

Alex's gaze dropped away. "I remember my mother saying—back before she got sick—that I got my sense of curiosity from you."

"You were a kid at the time. All kids are curious."

"You're hardly a kid, Ben. Life should be about being curious, shouldn't it? You've always been curious."

In the silence of the basement room, the only sound was the "tick" made each time the plastic tail of the black cat went back and forth, marking each passing second on the clock in the cat's stomach.

Still hunched over the bench, Ben turned his dark eyes toward his grandson. "There are things in this world to be curious about," the old man said in a soft, cryptic voice. "Things that don't make proper sense, aren't the way they appear. That's why I've taught you the way I have—to be prepared."

A shiver tingled up between Alex's shoulder blades. His grandfather's chilling tone was like a doorway opening a crack, a doorway into places Alex could not begin to imagine. It was a doorway into places that were not the realm of lighthearted wonder that usually seemed to make up Ben's life. It was the flip side of lighthearted, seen only during training sessions.

Alex was well aware that, for all his tinkering, his grandfather never really made anything. Not in the conventional sense, anyway. He never made a birdhouse, or fixed a screen door, or even cobbled together lawn art out of scraps of metal.

"What essence are you extracting?"

The old man smiled in a curious fashion. "Oh, who knows, Alexander? Who really knows?"

"You must know what you're trying to do."

"Trying and doing are two different things," Ben muttered. He looked back over his shoulder and changed the subject. "So, what is it you want for your birthday?"

"How about a new starter motor for my truck." Alex's mouth twisted in discontent. "Not all old things are so great. Women aren't much impressed with a guy who has a Jeep that won't start half the time. They'd rather go out with a guy with a real car."

"Ah," the old man said, nodding to himself.

Alex realized that, without meaning to, he had just answered the question he'd avoided when he'd first come down into Ben's workshop. He realized that he hadn't remembered to call Bethany back. He supposed it was more avoidance than forgetfulness.

"Anyway," Alex said, leaning an arm on the bench, "she's not my type."

"You mean she thinks that you're too . . . curious?" The old man chuckled at his own joke.

Alex shot Ben a scowl. "No, I mean she'd rather be out going to clubs and drinking than doing anything with her life. In fact, she wants to get me drunk for my birthday. There's more to life than just partying."

"Like what?" Ben prodded softly.

"I don't know." Alex sighed, tired of the subject. He slid off the stool. "I guess I'd better get going."

"A date with someone else?"

"Yeah, with a junkyard to try to find a cheap starter motor that works."

Maybe if he did ever see the strange woman again, and his Cherokee would start, he could take her for a drive in the country. He knew some beautiful roads through the hills.

He considered his memory of the woman, the way she walked through Regent Center as if she belonged in such places, and dismissed his daydream as unrealistic.

"You should get a new car, Alex—they work a lot better."

"Tell that to my checking account. The gallery hasn't sold one of my paintings in nearly a month."

"You need money for a car? I might be able to help out—considering that it's your birthday."

Alex made a sour face. "Ben, do you have any idea what a new car costs? I'm doing all right but I don't have that much money." Alex knew that his grandfather didn't, either.

Ben scratched the hollow of his cheek. "Well, I think you just might have enough for any new car you could want."

Alex's brow twitched. "What are you talking about?"

"It's your twenty-seventh birthday."

"And what does that mean?"

Ben tilted his head in thought. "Well, as near as I can figure, it has something to do with the seven."

"The seven what?"

"The seven . . . in twenty-seven."

"You lost me."

Ben squinted off into the distance as he journeyed into distracted thoughts. "I've tried to figure it out, but I can't make sense of it. The seven is my only real clue, the only thing I have to go on."

Alex heaved a sigh in irritation at Ben's habit of wandering off down rabbit holes. "You know I don't like riddles, Ben. If you have something to say, then tell me what you're talking about."

"The seven." Ben looked up from his essence extractor. "Your mother was twenty-seven when it came to her. Now you're twenty-seven, and it's come to you."

The skin of Alex's arms tingled with goose bumps. By her twenty-seventh birthday insanity had come to his mother. The familiar basement was beginning to feel claustrophobic.

"Ben, stop fooling around. What are you talking about?"

Ben paused at his work and twisted around on his stool to study his grandson. It was an uncomfortable, searching gaze.

"I have something that comes to be yours on your twenty-seventh birthday, Alexander. It came to your mother on her twenty-seventh birthday. Well, it would have . . ." He shook his head sadly. "The poor woman. Bless her tortured soul."

Alex straightened, determined not to get caught up in some fool word game with his grandfather.

"What's going on?"

His grandfather slipped down off the stool. He paused to reach out with a bony hand and pat Alex on the shoulder.

"Like I said, I have something that becomes yours on your twenty-seventh birthday."

"What is it?"

Ben ran his fingers back over his head of thin, gray hair. "It's . . . well," he said, waving the hand in a vague gesture, "let me show you. The time has come for you to see it."

5.

ALEX WATCHED AS HIS GRANDFATHER shuffled across the cluttered basement, kicking the odd cardboard box out of his way. At the far wall he moved rakes, hoes, and shovels to the side. Half of them fell over, clattering to the floor. Ben grumbled under his breath as he used a foot to push the errant rakes away until he had cleared a spot against the brick foundation. To Alex's astonishment his grandfather then started pulling bricks out of a pilaster in the foundation wall.

"What in the world are you doing?"

Holding an armload of a half-dozen bricks, Ben paused to look back over his shoulder. "Oh, I put it in here in case of fire."

That much made sense—after a fashion. Alex was perpetually surprised that his grandfather hadn't already burned down his house, what with the way he was always using matches, torches, and burners in his tinkering.

As Ben started stacking bricks on the floor, Alex turned to check. Just as he'd suspected, his grandfather had forgotten the soldering iron. Alex picked it up just as it was starting to blacken a patch on the workbench. He set the hot iron in its metal holder, then sighed in exasperation as he wet a finger with his tongue and used it to quench the smoking patch of wood.

"Ben, you nearly caught your bench on fire. You have to be more careful." He tapped the fire extinguisher hanging on the foundation wall. He couldn't tell if it was full or not. He turned over the tag, squinting, looking for an expiration or last inspection. He didn't see one. "This thing is charged and up-to-date, isn't it?"

"Yes, yes," Ben muttered.

When Alex turned back, his grandfather was standing close, holding out a large manila envelope. Traces of ancient stains were visible under a layer of gray mortar dust.

"This is intended for you . . . on your twenty-seventh birthday."

Alex stared at the suddenly ominous thing his grandfather was holding out.

"How long have you had this?"

"Nearly nineteen years."

Alex frowned. "And you kept it walled up in your basement?"

The old man nodded. "To keep it safe until I could give it to you at the proper time. I didn't want you to grow up knowing about this. Such things, before the right time, can change the course of a young person's life—change it for the worse."

Alex planted his hands on his hips. "Ben, why do you do such strange things? What if you'd died? Did you ever think of that? What if you'd died and your house got sold?"

"My will leaves you the house."

"I know that, but maybe I'd sell it. I would never have known that you had this hidden away down here."

His grandfather leaned close. "It's in the will."

"What's in the will?"

"The instructions that tell you where this was kept and that it's yours—but not until your twenty-seventh birthday." Ben smiled in a cryptic fashion. "Wills are interesting things; you can put a lot of curious things in such documents."

When his grandfather shoved the envelope at him Alex took it, but only reluctantly. As strange as his grandfather's behavior sometimes was, this ranked right up there with the strangest. Who would keep papers hidden in the brick wall in his basement? And why?

Alex was suddenly worried about the answers to those questions—and others that were only beginning to formulate in the back of his mind.

"Come on," his grandfather said as he shuffled back to the workbench. With an arm he swept aside the clutter that covered the work surface. He slapped his palm on the cleared spot on the bench. "Put it here, in the light."

The flap was torn open—with no attempt to be sneaky about it. Knowing his grandfather, he would have long ago opened the envelope and studied whatever was inside. Alex noticed that the neatly typed address label was made out to his father. He pulled a stack of papers from the envelope. They were clipped together at the top left corner. The cover letter had an embossed logo in faded blue ink saying it was from LANCASTER, BUCKMAN, FENTON, a law firm in Boston.

He tossed the papers on the workbench. "You've known all along what this is?" Alex asked, already knowing the answer. "You've read it all?"

Ben waved a hand dismissively. "Yes, yes. It's a transfer of deed. Once it's executed, you become a landowner."

Alex was taken aback. "Land?"

"Quite a lot of land, actually."

Alex was suddenly so full of questions that he couldn't seem to think straight. "What do you mean, I'll become a landowner? What land? Why? Whose is it? And why on my twenty-seventh birthday?"

Ben's brow creased as he paused to consider. "I think it has to do with the seven. Like I said, it went to your mother on her twenty-seventh birthday—because your father had died before his twenty-seventh birthday when it would have gone to him. So, the way I figure it, the seven has to be the key."

"If it went to my mother, then why is it mine?"

Ben tapped the papers lying on the workbench. "It was supposed to go to her, because your father had passed away, but the title to the land couldn't be transferred to her."

"Why not?" Alex asked.

His grandfather lowered his voice as he leaned closer. "Because she was declared mentally incompetent."

The silence dragged on a moment as Ben let that sink in before he went on.

"The stipulations in this last will and testament specify that the heir to whom the title is transferred must be of sound mind. Your mother was declared not to be of sound mind and has been in that institution ever since. There's a codicil to the will that stipulates that if the heir in line isn't able to take ownership of the title to the land because of death or mental incapacitation, then it remains in abeyance until the next heir in line becomes twenty-seven, whereupon it is automatically reassigned to them. If there is no heir, or if they are likewise declared in violation of the stipulations—"

"You mean crazy."

"Well, yes," Ben said. "If for any reason the title can't be transferred to your father, mother, or any of their issue—that means their descendants, and you're the only one of those—then the land goes to a conservation trust."

Alex scratched his temple as he tried to take it all in.

"How much land are we talking about?"

"Enough for you to sell it and buy yourself a new car. That's what you ought to do." Ben shook a cautionary finger. "This business with the seven is nothing to fool around with, Alex."

For some inexplicable reason beyond his grandfather's admonition, Alex didn't feel at all fortunate at the windfall.

"Where is this land?"

Ben gestured irritably. "Back East. In Maine."

"Where you used to live?"

"Not exactly. It's farther inland. It was land that has been in our family forever, but they're all dead now, so it goes to you."

"Why not to you?"

Ben shrugged. "Don't know." He suddenly grinned and leaned in. "Well, actually, it's probably because they never liked me. Besides, it's just as well—I've no desire to live there again. Blackflies and mud in the spring, mosquitoes in the summer, and endless snow in the winter. I've spent enough of my life hip deep in mud and bugs. The weather here suits me better."

Alex wondered if the people who made up the will had discounted Ben because they didn't consider him of sound mind in the first place.

"I've heard that autumn is beautiful back East," Alex said.

Autumn would soon arrive. He wondered if there was enough land to get away and be alone for a while to paint. From time to time Alex liked to hike into wilderness areas to be alone and paint. He liked the way the simplicity of primeval solitude allowed him to lose himself in the scenes he created.

"How much land are we talking about? Is there at least a few acres or so? I've heard that some of the land in Maine is pretty expensive."

"That's on the coast," Ben scoffed. "This is inland. Inland the land isn't worth nearly as much. Still . . ."

Alex gingerly lifted the cover letter, as if it might suddenly bite him, and scanned the legal jargon.

"Still," his grandfather went on, "I'd venture to say that this is enough to buy you a car." He leaned closer. "Any car you want."

Alex looked up from the papers. "So how much land is it?"

"A little under fifty thousand acres."

Alex blinked. "Fifty thousand acres?"

His grandfather nodded. "You're now one of the largest private landowners in Maine—other than the paper companies. At least, you will be once the title is transferred."

Alex let out a low whistle at the very thought. "Well, I guess I very well might be able to sell a piece of it and buy me a car. I might even sell enough to build—"

Ben was shaking his head. "Sorry, but you can't."

"Can't what?"

"Sell a part of it. The covenants to the deed say that you can't sell any part of it. If you ever want to sell, you have to sell the whole thing, all in one lot, all together and intact, to the conservation trust that's holding the land. They own the surrounding land."

"I'd have to sell it all—and just to this one group?" Alex frowned. "Are you sure I couldn't just sell some of it if I wanted to? Just a little?"

Ben was shaking his head. "Back when the papers first came your father and I studied the documents. We even went to a lawyer friend your father knew. He confirmed what we thought from what we'd read. It's airtight. Any violation of the stipulations will result in the title reverting permanently to the conservation trust.

"It's a very tricky document. It's drawn up in a way that ensures that any deviation from the stipulations will cause the land to go to the trust. There's no wiggle room. It's constructed so as to tightly control what happens to the land. You might say that it doesn't grant an inheritance so much as it offers choices among very limited options.

"With your father's premature passing, and then your mother getting sick, the transfer of title wasn't able to go forward, so it was put in abeyance, in limbo, until you were twenty-seven."

"What if I don't want to decide right now what I want to do?"

"You have the year you are twenty-seven to decide to take title or not. You don't have to take the land. You can refuse it and then it goes to the trust. If you don't act while you're still twenty-seven, title to the land automatically transfers to the trust—except under one condition: your heir.

"You're presently the last heir in line, Alex. You aren't allowed to will the land to anyone other than a direct descendant. If you never have children, then, when you eventually die, the land goes to the trust."

"What if next week I get hit by a bus and die?"

"Then the title immediately transfers to the trust—permanently— because you don't have an heir, a child. If you become a father, even if you don't act to claim rightful ownership during the time you're twenty-seven, then that child becomes part and parcel of the will. It waits for them to come of age. In fact, that's how you came to this place. If you're hit by a bus it doesn't affect any offspring's rights, just as your father's death didn't negate your rights.

"You can take title and enjoy the land all you want and if you ever have children you can pass it on to them, providing you haven't sold it to the trust. Once sold to them it's theirs forever."

"If I can only sell to the trust, then they can set the price cheap."

Ben flipped through the pages, searching, until he found what he was looking for. "No, look here." He tapped the page. "You have to sell it to the Daggett Trust—that's the conservation group—but they must pay fair market value. You can name your own appraiser to ensure that the price is fair. And I can tell you that at fair market value that much land, even being inland, is worth a fortune."

Alex stared off in thought. "I could paint all I want."

Ben smiled. "You know that I think a person should prepare for the worst but live all they can of life. You could sell the land and then paint the rest of your life and never have to sell one of them. I hate to see you having to sell your paintings. They hold such love of life. I hate to see you part with them."

Alex frowned as he came back from imagining. "Why would this trust want to buy this particular piece of land?"

Ben shrugged. "They already own all of the surrounding land. None of it has ever been developed. Most of it is virgin timber that's been in trust for ages; they want to keep it that way. Our family's piece is the last remaining part to the puzzle.

"The land owned by the trust is closed to people. No one is ever allowed onto the land—not even hikers. The Nature Alliance is a little miffed that they aren't allowed in. They think they should have special access since they're so devoted to preserving nature and all. I guess they went along, though, since the conservation group's purpose seems so high-minded."

"Well, what if I decide I don't want to sell it? What if I want to keep it and build a house on it?"

Ben tapped the papers again. "Can't. The deed comes with a conservation easement. That's why we've never had to pay any property taxes. It's some kind of special state wilderness area act that exempts land from taxes if it has a conservation easement constructed in the way this one has been drawn up."

"So, then, the land is of no use to me. I can't use it for anything?"

Ben shrugged. "You can enjoy it, I suppose. It's your land if you want it. You can walk it, camp on it, things like that, but you can't build any permanent buildings on it. You also must abide by the trust bylaws that you won't allow strangers—hikers, campers, and such—on the land."

"Or I can sell it."

"Right. To the Daggett Trust."

It was all so unexpected and overwhelming. Alex had never owned any land, other than the house that had been his parents'. The house, just down the street, the home where he'd partially grown up and now lived, was now in his name. In a sense it still felt like it belonged to the ghosts of those long gone. With his home on an ordinary lot Alex had a difficult time imagining how much land fifty thousand acres was. It seemed enough land that a person could become forever lost there.

"If I can't really do anything with it, maybe I should just sell it," Alex said, thinking out loud.

Ben pulled his soldering project closer. "That sounds wise. Sell it and buy yourself that car you want."

Alex suspiciously eyed the back of his grandfather's head. "I like the Cherokee. I only want a starter motor."

"It's your birthday, Alex. Now you can buy yourself a proper present. The kind none of us could ever afford for you."

"I never really wanted for anything," Alex said in quiet protest as he laid a hand gently on his grandfather's shoulder. "I always had everything I needed, and what I really needed the most."

"Kind of like my coffeepot," his grandfather muttered. "Never wanted anything better." He abruptly turned back, looking uncharacteristically stern. "Sell the land, Alex. It's just trees and rocks—it's good for nothing."

Trees and rocks sounded good to Alex. He loved such places. That was his favorite thing to paint.

"Sell it, that's my advice," Ben pressed. "You've no need of Castle Mountain."

"Castle what?"

"Castle Mountain. It's a mountain that sits roughly in the center of the land."

"Why's it called Castle Mountain?"

Ben turned away and worked for a time bending the tubing on his essence extractor to some plan known only to him. "People say it looks like a castle. Never saw the resemblance, myself."

Alex smiled. "I don't think Indian Rock looks much like an Indian."

"There you go. Same thing. People see what they want to see, I guess." Ben didn't look back as he handed the papers over his shoulder. "Get the deed transferred, then sell the place and be rid of it, that's my advice, Alex."

Alex slowly made his way to the stairs as he considered it all. He paused and looked back at his grandfather.

A dark look shadowed Ben's face. "This is one of those things that I mentioned before, Alex, one of those things that doesn't make proper sense."

Alex wondered at seeing such a forbidding look for a second time that day. "Thanks, Ben, for your advice."

His grandfather turned back to his soldering. "Don't thank me unless you take the advice. Unless you heed it, it's just words."

Alex nodded absently. "I'm going to go see my mom."

"Give her my best," Ben murmured without turning.

His grandfather rarely went to visit his daughter-in-law. He hated the place where she was confined. Alex hated the place, too, but his mother was there and if he wanted to see her he had no choice.

Alex stared down at the envelope in his hand. It seemed that such an unexpected birthday present should make him happy, but it didn't. It only reminded him of his dead father and his mother lost to another world.

Now this unknown connection to the past had found him.

Alex ran his fingers lightly over the age-dried label made out to his father. A faded pencil line ran through the name. Above, in the same nearly vanished, ghostlike pencil, was written his mother's name. Her name was stricken through with a dark, angry line drawn in black ink.

Above that, in his grandfather's handwriting, it said "Alexander Rahl."

When Alex reached the landing on the stairs he thought that he saw someone out of the corner of his eye.

He turned only to see himself looking back from a mirror.

He stared for a moment; then his cell phone rang. When he answered it, he could hear only weird, garbled sounds, like disembodied whispers churning up from somewhere deep on the other side of the universe. He glanced at the display. It said OUT OF AREA. No doubt a wrong number. He flipped the cover closed and slipped the phone back in his pocket.

"Alexander," Ben called.

Alex looked back, waiting.

"Trouble will find you."

Alex smiled at his grandfather's familiar mantra. It was meant as a world of love and concern wrapped in a call for vigilance. The familiar touchstone made him feel better, feel resolute.

"Thanks, Ben. I'll talk to you later."

Alex picked up the painting that he had brought from the gallery and headed up the stairs.

6.

ALEX HAD BEEN FORTUNATE. His Jeep Cherokee had started on the first try.

After the long drive to the older part of downtown Orden, Nebraska, he parked near the end of a side street that sloped off downhill. That way, if his Jeep wouldn't start, he could let it roll to get the engine to turn over.

In this older section of town there wasn't much parking other than on the tree-lined streets. The needs of a hospital, parking being only one of them, had long ago rendered the facility obsolete and so it had been converted to a private asylum: Mother of Roses. The state paid for patients, like Alex's mother, who were placed there by the order of the court.

In the beginning Ben had tried to get his daughter-in-law released into his and Alex's grandmother's custody. Alex had been too young to understand it all, but the end result had been that Ben had eventually given up. Years later, when Alex had pursued the same course, he had likewise gotten nowhere.

Dr. Hoffmann, the head of the psychiatric staff, had assured Alex that his mother was better off under professional care. Besides that, he said that they could not legally give him the responsibility of caring for a person who in their professional opinion could still become violent. His grandfather had put an arm around Alex's shoulders and told him to come to terms with the fact that while there were those who went to Mother of Roses to get help, to get better, his mother would likely die there. It had felt to Alex like a death sentence.

The mature trees on the streets in that part of town and on the limited grounds of Mother of Roses asylum made the place look less harsh than it was. Alex knew that the somewhat distant hill where he'd parked made a convenient excuse to delay walking into the building where his mother was imprisoned. His insides always felt like they knotted up when he went into the place.

On the way over he had been so distracted by scattered thoughts competing for attention that he'd nearly run a red light. The thought of Officer Slawinski scowling at him had dissuaded him from trying to make it through the yellow. As it turned out, the light had switched to red before he'd even reached the crosswalk.

For some reason it felt like a day to be careful. Staring up at the glow of a red light that had come quicker than expected had felt like cosmic confirmation of his caution.

Walking beneath the enclosing shade of the mature oaks and maples, Alex headed around the side of the nine-story brick building. The front, on Thirteenth Street, had broad stone steps up to what he supposed was a beautiful entrance of cast concrete meant to look like a stone façade of vines growing over an ornate pointed arch framing deep-set oak doors. Going in the front was a lot more trouble because it required going through layers of bureaucracy needed for general visitors. Close family were allowed to go in through a smaller entrance at the rear.

Grass under the huge oaks in back thinned to bare dirt in patches where the ground was heaved and uneven from massive roots hidden beneath. Alex glanced up at the windows all covered with security wire. Flesh was no match for that steel mesh. The back of the building was more honest about what it was.

The sprawling lower floors of the hospital were for patients who went to Mother of Roses for treatment for emotional disorders, substance abuse and addiction, as well as rest and recovery. Alex's mother was imprisoned on the smaller ninth floor, a secure area reserved for patients considered dangerous. Some of them had killed people and had been found to be mentally incompetent. Several times since Alex's mother had been confined at Mother of Roses there had been serious attacks on other patients or staff. Alex always worried for her safety.

He scanned the top row of almost opaque windows, even though he had never seen anything more than shadows in them.

The steel door in back had a little square window with safety wire crisscrossed through it. When he pulled open the door he was hit by the hospital smell that always made him resist taking a deep breath.

An orderly recognized him and nodded a greeting. Alex flashed a wooden smile as he tossed his keys, pocketknife, change, and phone in a plastic tub on a table to the side of the metal detector. After he passed through without setting off the buzzers, an older security guard, who also knew Alex but didn't smile, handed over the phone and his change. He would keep the knife and keys until Alex left. Even keys could be snatched from a visitor and used as a weapon.

Alex bent at the steel desk beyond the metal detector and picked up a cheap blue plastic pen attached by a dirty string to the registry clipboard. That string was the most lax security in the entire building. The woman at the desk, Doreen, knew him. Holding the phone to her ear with a shoulder, she flipped through a ledger, answering questions about laundry deliveries. She smiled at Alex as he looked up from signing his name. She'd always been nice to him over the years, sympathizing with him at having to visit his mother in such a place.

Alex took the only elevator that went to the ninth floor. He hated the green metal doors. The paint had been scratched off in horizontal patches by med carts hitting into it, leaving dirty metal to show through. The elevator smelled musty. He knew the tune of every clunk and clatter it made on the way up, anticipated every shimmy in its labored travel.

The elevator porpoised to a stop and finally opened before the ninth-floor nurses' station. Locked doors led to the women's wing on one side, the men's on the other. Alex signed his name again and put in the time: three p.m. Visitors were carefully monitored. He would have to sign out, with the time, when he left. The elevator door at the top was kept locked and no one would unlock it without a completed sign-in-and-sign-out sheet—a precaution against a patient talking his way past a gullible new employee.

An orderly in white slacks and smock came out from a small office in the back of the nurses' station, pulling his keys out on a thin wire cable extending from the reel attached to his belt. The orderly, a big man who always hunched, knew Alex. Just about everyone working at Mother of Roses knew Alex Rahl.

The man looked through the little window in the solid oak door and then, satisfied that the way was clear, turned the key in the lock. He yanked open the heavy door.

The man handed over a plastic key for the buzzer on the other side. "Ring when you're finished, Alex."

Alex nodded. "How's she doing?"

The man shrugged his rounded shoulders. "Same."

"Has she caused you any trouble?"

The man arched an eyebrow. "She tried to stab me to death with a plastic spoon a few days back. Yesterday she jumped a nurse and would have beaten her senseless if another orderly wouldn't have been ten steps away at the time."

Alex shook his head. "I'm sorry, Henry."

The man shrugged again. "Part of the job."

"I wish I could make her stop."

Henry held the door open with one hand. "You can't, Alex. Don't beat yourself up over it. It's not her fault; she's sick."

The hall's grayish linoleum floor was struck through with darker gray swirls and green speckles, presumably meant to add a little bit of interest. It was as ugly as anything Alex could imagine. Light from the sunroom up ahead reflected off the ripply floor, making it look almost liquid. The evenly spaced rooms to each side had varnished oak doors with silver metal push plates. None had locks. Each room was home to someone.

Cries coming from dark rooms echoed through the hall. Angry voices and shouts were commonplace—arguments with imaginary people who bedeviled some of the patients.

The showers at the rear of the bathroom were kept locked, along with a few of the rooms, rooms where patients were placed when they became violent. Locking a patient in a room was meant to encourage them to behave and be sociable.

The sunroom, with its skylights, was a bright spot in a dark prison. Varnished oak tables were neatly spaced throughout the room. They were bolted to the floor. The flimsy plastic chairs weren't.

Alex immediately spotted his mother sitting on a couch against the far wall. She watched him coming without recognizing him. On rare occasions she did know who he was, but he could tell by the look in her eyes that this time she didn't. That was always the hardest thing for him—knowing that she usually didn't have any idea who he was.

A TV bolted high on the wall was tuned to *Wheel of Fortune.* The gaiety and laughter from the TV struck a stupefying contrast with the somber dayroom. A few patients laughed with the TV audience without comprehending what they were laughing at. They only knew that laughter was called for and so they laughed out of a sense of social duty. Alex guessed that it was better to laugh than cry. Between the laughter, some of the younger women glared at him.

"Hi, Mom," he said in his sunniest voice as he approached.

She wore pale green hospital-issue pajama pants and a simple flower-print top. The outfit was hideously ugly. Her hair was longer than the other residents'. Most of the women had their hair cut short and curled. Alex's mother was protective of her sandy-colored, shoulder-length hair. She threw fits if they tried to cut it. The staff didn't feel it was worth a battle to cut it short. Occasionally they would try, thinking she might have forgotten that she wanted it long. That was one thing she never forgot. Alex was glad that she had something that seemed to matter to her.

He sat on the couch beside her. "How are you doing?"

She stared at him a moment. "Fine." By her tone, he knew that she didn't have a clue as to who he was.

"I was here last week. Remember?"

She nodded as she stared at him. Alex wasn't sure if she even understood the question. Sometimes she would say things that he knew weren't true. She would tell him that her sister had visited. She didn't have a sister. She would say that she had gone shopping. She was never allowed to leave the confines of the ninth floor.

He ran his hand down the side of her head. "Your hair looks pretty today."

"I brush it every day," she said.

An overweight male orderly wearing shiny black shoes that squeaked rolled a cart into the sunroom. "Snack time, ladies."

The top of the cart displayed a few dozen plastic cups half filled with orange juice, or something that resembled orange juice. The shelves in the cart held baloney-and-lettuce sandwiches on wheat bread. At least, Alex assumed it would be baloney. It usually was.

"How about a sandwich, Mom? You're looking kind of skinny. Have you been eating?"

Without protest she rose to take a sandwich and glass from the man with the cart when he rolled it near. "Here you go, Helen," the man said as he handed her a plastic cup of orange juice and a sandwich.

Alex followed as she shuffled to a table off in the far corner, away from the other residents.

"They always want to talk," she said as she glared at the women clustered on the other side of the room, where they could see the television. Most of the people in the place talked to imaginary people. At least his mother never did that.

Alex folded his arms on the table. "So, what's new?"

His mother chewed a mouthful for a moment. Without looking up she swallowed and said under her breath, "I haven't seen any of them for a while."

"Is that right?" he asked, playing along. "What did they want?"

It was hard to make conversation when he didn't know what she was talking about half the time.

"What they always want. The gate."

"What gate?" He couldn't imagine what she imagined.

She suddenly looked up. "What are you doing here?"

Alex shrugged. "It's my birthday, Mom. I wanted to spend it with you."

"You shouldn't spend your birthday in this place, Alex."

Alex's breath halted for an instant. He could count on the fingers of one hand the times she had called him by his name except when prompted.

"It's my birthday. It's what I want to do, Mom," he said quietly.

Her mind seemed to drift away from the subject. "They look at me through the walls," she said in an emotionless tone. Her eyes turned wild. "They look at me!" she screamed. "Why won't they stop watching me!"

A few of the people on the other side of the room turned to look at the screaming woman. Most didn't bother. Screaming in the institution wasn't an uncommon occurrence and was usually treated with indifference. The orderly with the cart glanced over, appraising the situation. Alex put a hand on her arm.

"It's all right, Mom. No one is looking at you now."

She glanced around at the walls before finally appearing to calm down. In another moment, she went back to her sandwich as if nothing had happened.

After she took a sip of orange juice, she asked, "What birthday is it?" She put the sandwich up to her mouth.

"My twenty-seventh."

She froze.

She took the sandwich out of her mouth and carefully set it down on the paper plate. She glanced around, then seized Alex's shirtsleeve.

"I want to go to my room."

Alex was a bit puzzled by her behavior, as he frequently was, but

47

he went along. "All right, Mom. We can sit in there. It'll be nice, just the two of us."

She held his arm in a tight grip as they walked back down the depressing hall. Alex walked. She shuffled. She wasn't an old woman, but her spirit always seemed broken.

It was the Thorazine and other powerful antipsychotic drugs that made her that way, and made her shuffle. Dr. Hoffmann said that Thorazine was all that kept her functioning as well as she did, and that without it she would become so violently psychopathic that she would have to be restrained twenty-four hours a day. Alex certainly didn't want that for her.

When they went into her simple room she shut the door. The doors didn't lock. She opened it and checked the hall three times before she seemed satisfied. Her roommate, Agnes, was older. She never spoke. She did stare, though, so Alex was glad that she had stayed in the sunroom.

The TV, bolted high on the wall, was on, but the sound was muted. He rarely saw the TV turned off. The sound was usually muted, though. He'd never seen his mother change the channel. He didn't understand why she and Agnes wanted the TV on without the sound.

"Go away," Alex's mother said.

"After a while, Mom. I'd like to sit with you for a time."

She shook her head. "Go away and hide."

"From what, Mom?"

"Hide," she repeated.

Alex took a deep breath. "Hide from what?"

His mother stared at him for a time. "Twenty-seven," she finally said.

"Yes, that's right. I'm twenty-seven today. You had me twenty-seven years ago, nine in the evening on the ninth of September. That's the date today. You had me here, at this very place, back when it was a regular hospital."

She leaned close and licked her lips. "Hide."

Alex wiped a hand across his face. "From who, Mom?" He was tired of the pointless, circular conversation.

His mother rose from where she sat on the edge of the bed and went to a small wardrobe. She pawed through the items folded on the shelf. After a brief search she came up with a shawl. At first, Alex thought that she was cold. But she didn't put the shawl around her shoulders.

She stood before the small dresser and draped the shawl over the polished metal square, bolted to the wall, that served as a mirror.

"Mom, what are you doing?"

His mother turned back with fire in her eyes. "They look at me. I told you. They look at me through the windows in the walls."

Alex was starting to feel creepy.

"Mom, come sit down."

His mother sat on the edge of the bed, closer, and took one of his hands in both of hers. It was an act of affection that unexpectedly brought a tear to Alex's eye. She had never done such a thing before. Alex thought that it was the best birthday present he could have gotten, better even than fifty thousand acres of land.

"Alex," she whispered. "You must run and hide before they get you."

It was startling to hear his name from her lips for the second time in the same day. It took a great effort to summon his voice.

"And who is it that I should hide from, Mom?"

She glanced around and then leaned closer so he could hear her whisper.

"A different kind of human."

He stared at her a moment. It made no sense, but something about it sounded serious, sounded sincere.

Just then something on the TV caught his eye. He looked up and saw that it was the local news. A police spokesman was standing before a cluster of microphones.

A news crawler moving across the bottom of the screen said "Two Metro officers found dead."

Alex reached over for the remote and turned up the sound.

"Do you know why they were there, in behind the warehouses?" a reporter asked through the clamor.

"The Center and Ninetieth Street section was within their patrol area," the official said. "Alleys throughout there provide access to loading docks. We check them often, so there was nothing unusual about them being there in that location."

Alex remembered when Ninetieth Street, about ten or twelve miles from his house, used to be the outskirts of town.

Another reporter shouted the others down. "There are reports that both officers were found with their necks broken. Is that true?"

"I can't comment on such stories. As I've said, we will have to wait for the coroner's report. When we have it we will release the findings."

"Have the families been notified?"

The man at the microphone paused, obviously having trouble getting words out. Anguish shaped his features. He kept swallowing back his emotion.

"Yes. Our prayers and sympathy go out to their families at this difficult time."

"Can you release their names, then?" a woman waving her pen for attention asked.

The official stared out at the tight knot of reporters. His gaze finally dropped away. "Officer John Tinney, and Officer Peter Slawinski." He started spelling the names.

Alex's whole body flashed as cold as ice.

"They break people's necks," his mother said in a dead tone as she stared at the TV. He thought that she must be repeating what she'd just heard. "They want the gate."

Her eyes went out of focus. He knew; she was going back into that dark place. Once her eyes went out of focus like that she wouldn't speak again for weeks.

He felt his cell phone vibrate in his pocket. Another text message from Bethany. He ignored it as he put an arm tenderly around his mother's shoulders.

7.

ALEX SAT FOR A WHILE just holding his mother, trying to imagine what madness haunted her. She no longer seemed to know that he was there.

The worst part was that he had no hope. The doctors had said that she would never get better, never be her old self again, and that he needed to understand that. They said there was brain damage that couldn't be reversed. While they weren't exactly sure what had caused the damage to her brain, they said that, among other things, it caused her to sometimes become violent. They said that such damage was not reversible. They'd said that she was a danger to herself and others and always would be.

After a while Alex gently laid her back on her bed. She was as limp as a doll—just a bundle of bone and muscle, blood and organs, existing often without conscious awareness, without anything other than a vestigial intellect. He fluffed up the pillow under her head. Her empty eyes remained fixed on the ceiling. As far as Alex knew, she didn't know where she was, or that there was anyone there with her. She was for the most part dead to the world; her body just hadn't fully caught up with that fact.

He pulled her shawl off the mirror, folded it, and replaced it in the wardrobe before sitting again on the edge of the bed.

When his phone rang he pulled it out and answered.

"Hey, birthday boy," Bethany said, "I have a big surprise for you."

Alex made an effort to keep the annoyance out of his voice.

"Well, I'm afraid that—"

"I'm sitting outside your house."

He paused a moment. "My house."

Her voice turned flirtatious and lilting. "That's right."

"What are you doing there?"

"Well," she said in an airy, intimate whisper, "I'm waiting for you. I want to give you your birthday present."

"Thanks for the thought, Bethany, but I really don't need anything, honest. Save your money."

"No money involved," she said. "Just get your tail home, birthday boy. Tonight you're going to get yourself laid."

Now Alex was really getting annoyed with her. He thought it easiest not to say so, though. He didn't want to have a fight with a woman he hardly knew. There was no point to it.

"Look, Bethany, I'm really not in the mood."

"You just leave that to me. I'll get you in the mood. I think you ought to get lucky on your birthday, and I'm just the girl to make it special."

Bethany was an attractive woman—in fact she bordered on being voluptuous—but the more he got to know her the less and less attractive Alex found her to be. She had nothing more than a superficial allure. He couldn't talk to her about anything meaningful, not because she wasn't intelligent enough, but because she didn't care about anything meaningful. In a way, that was worse. She was a living, breathing example of superficial, and willfully so. She seemed to have no interests other than that she had a kind of odd, narrow focus on him and the two of them having a good time—or, at least, what was a good time by her definition.

"I can't, right now," he said, trying not to sound angry, even though he was getting angry.

She let out a low, breathy chuckle. "Oh, I'll make sure you can, Alex. Don't you worry about that. You just get yourself home and let Beth take care of everything."

"I'm visiting my mother."

"I think I can throw a better party. Promise. Just come give me a chance to make your birthday something you'll never forget."

"My mother is in the hospital. She's ill and not doing well. I'm going to be sitting with her."

That finally threw Bethany into silence for a moment.

"Oh," she finally said, the sexiness gone from her voice. "I didn't know."

"I'll call you later," Alex said. "Maybe in a few days."

"Well," she said, sounding uncertain and reluctant to end the conversation so quickly, "I'm sure your mother is going to need to get her rest. Why don't you call me later today, after your visit?"

Somehow, it didn't sound quite like a question. It sounded more like an instruction. He hadn't wanted to have this conversation— not at the moment, not sitting there with his mother—but Bethany was giving him no choice.

"Look, the truth is I don't think I'm the guy for you. You're an attractive woman, you really are. There are a lot of guys who like you. I think you'd be better off with one of them instead of me. You'd have a lot more fun with them, with guys who are interested in the same things that interest you."

"But I like you."

"Why?"

"I don't know." She paused a moment. "You get me hot," she finally said, falling back on her lusty voice, as if lust was magic that could banish any objections. He imagined that it very well might with most men, but he wasn't most men.

"I'm sorry, Bethany. You're a nice enough person, but we're just not right for each other. It's as simple as that."

"I see."

He didn't say anything, hoping that she would leave it at that and not decide to make it ugly. It wasn't like they'd been seeing each other for any length of time. There was no reason to make a big deal out of it. It had been a couple of dates, nothing more. He'd kissed her a few times. That was it. She'd made it clear that he was welcome to go farther, to go as far as he wanted, but something had made him keep her at arm's length. Now he was glad he had.

"Alex, I've got to go. I need . . . I need to think about this."

"I understand. You think about it, but I think it's best if we go our separate ways."

He could hear her breathing for a moment; then, without a further word, she hung up on him.

"Good," he said under his breath as he used his thumb to push the phone back into the pocket of his jeans.

He glanced over at his mother. She stared unblinking at the ceiling.

Alex picked up the TV remote when he saw another report about the two murdered Metro officers. The place they'd been found was a good dozen miles from where he had met Officers Tinney and Slawinski earlier that day.

It shook Alex to realize that the two men were dead. If he found it shocking, he could only imagine how horrifying the news had to be for those close to them.

Both men had seemed so competent, so in control. He'd seen them for only a few minutes, but it seemed impossible to think that both of those men could be dead. The swiftness of such a thing left Alex feeling shaken and even more depressed.

He envied people who enjoyed their birthdays.

Just then his phone rang again. He was reluctant to answer it, thinking it would be Bethany with a list of grievances over her hurt feelings and wanting to rant at him, but when he checked the small exterior display window it said OUT OF AREA.

Alex flipped open the cover and put the phone to his ear. "Hello, this is Alex."

Weird, garbled sounds and disembodied whispers crackled through the receiver. The sounds made his mouth go dry.

Alex immediately flipped the cover closed. He stared at the phone a moment, then finally slipped it back in his pocket.

The sounds had been so unusual, so haunting, that he distinctly remembered hearing them before. It had been the call he had gotten earlier, just as he had been about to leave his grandfather's house, just after he had learned about the land that came to be his on his twenty-seventh birthday.

He remembered that he'd gotten the call right after he had thought that someone had been looking at him through the mirror. It had also been shortly after he had asked if Ben thought he would end up crazy like his mother.

Alex glanced at the polished metal mirror before looking around at the mint-green room. He wondered if he was destined to end up spending the rest of his life in a place like this, like his mother.

He wondered how he would know if he had gone crazy. He didn't feel crazy.

He bet that his mother didn't feel crazy, either.

8.

WHEN MR. MARTIN CALLED out of the blue, Alex could hardly believe the news. All six of his paintings had sold.

Holding the phone to an ear with a shoulder, Alex had swirled his brush in a jar of murky water and then wiped it on a paper towel as Mr. Martin asked him to come collect his money. Alex had been deeply absorbed in the work of painting an eerie evening mist along a shoreline of a mountain lake and didn't want to stop, but Mr. Martin had seemed unusually anxious that Alex get there as soon as possible. He wouldn't say anything about the person who had bought the paintings, only that they had paid cash and he wanted to give Alex his portion. He had made a weak excuse that he knew Alex needed the money.

Alex hadn't talked to Bethany since she'd called him while he had been visiting his mother two days before. Things seemed to be looking up in more ways than one. His truck even started on the first try.

When he pulled into the parking lot at Regent Center it was early afternoon. The gray sky looked to be a harbinger of an approaching storm. The air had an unusual chill to it, a first breath of the coming change of season.

Alex parked next to a new Jeep, hoping that his would start again later without a lot of difficulty. With the sale of the six paintings he could certainly afford to get the starter fixed. He had thought to replace the starter himself but he reconsidered; he would need to finish up the painting he was working on when Mr. Martin had called. The gallery would need to have more of his paintings if the buyer should decide to return and collect more of Alex's pieces, or if another buyer came along. It was far easier to sell paintings and get commissions if there was something on display.

Before he locked his truck, Alex picked the small painting wrapped in brown paper off the floor of the back seat. He didn't want to give it back to Mr. Martin to sell or display, but he was afraid of it being stolen out of his truck. He'd brought the painting with him because he wanted to give it to the woman if he ever saw her again.

The halls of Regent Center were more crowded than they had been the last time he'd been there, the day he had seen the woman. With the painting tucked under his arm he quickly made his way toward the gallery, checking the faces of people along the way just in case she was there. He thought that it was a baseless hope, even a silly hope, but he couldn't help himself from hoping to see her. When he caught sight of himself in a mirror displayed in the window of a boutique, he stepped a little quicker to get out of sight of it.

As he walked in front of the gallery window Alex spotted Mr. Martin pacing near the rear of the shop. He had on a dark suit with a bright orange tie, an odd choice that on Mr. Martin somehow worked. The bells on the door softly rang their familiar strain as Alex went inside. Mr. Martin, dry-washing his hands, stepped briskly among the pieces on easels.

"Ah, Alex, thank you for coming so quickly."

"It's been a while since my last payday," Alex said with a smile as he tried to figure out why the man wasn't smiling.

"Indeed," Mr. Martin said without catching Alex's attempt to lighten the mood.

Alex followed the gallery owner to the rear of the shop, where Mr. Martin sat on a rolling swivel chair and nervously worked a key to open a locked drawer. Once he had the drawer open he unlocked a metal box inside and pulled out a thick envelope. Inside was a stack of cash. He stood to count out the payment.

"Wait a minute," Alex said, holding up a hand. "You usually give me the story, first. I've never sold six pieces at once before. It must have been an unusual sale. Who was the buyer? What happened? How did you convince them to buy six paintings? Did they just love the paintings and have to have them all?"

Mr. Martin gazed into Alex's eyes for a moment as if overwhelmed by the barrage of questions. Alex realized that he was probably spooking the man. Alex frequently found that he made people nervous with his questions.

"Well," Mr. Martin said at last, seemingly trying to recall it in exact detail, "a man came in. He glanced around but I soon realized that he wasn't looking at the things that were on display—wasn't looking at different pieces the way people usually do. He seemed to be searching for something specific. I asked if I could show him something special.

"He said yes, that he would like to see the work of Alexander Rahl. Naturally I was only too happy to show him your paintings.

Before I could begin to talk you up, he said that he would take them. I showed him that I had six of your paintings and asked which of them he would be interested in. He said he would take them all. I was momentarily stunned.

"The man asked how much he owed. He never even asked the price. Just asked what he owed."

Mr. Martin licked his thin lips. "I was overjoyed for you. I knew how much you need the money, Alex, so as I regained my wits I took the opportunity, as the gallery owner and your representative, to get the best possible price for you. I quickly considered the dated, low price we were asking and then, in view of the man's interest, added some to it."

Alex was slightly amused at his good fortune, and Mr. Martin's quick thinking. "So how much did you add?"

Mr. Martin swallowed. "I doubled the price. I told the man that they were four thousand apiece—and a good investment in an up-and-coming contemporary artist."

"That's twenty-four thousand dollars," Alex said in astonishment. "You certainly earned your commission, Mr. Martin."

Mr. Martin nodded. "That makes your portion, after commission, fourteen thousand four hundred dollars."

Without delay he started counting off hundred-dollar bills. Alex was a bit dumbfounded and just stood there as the man counted out the money. When finished, the gallery owner took a deep breath. He seemed to be glad to be rid of the money. Alex straightened the thick stack of hundred-dollar bills before returning them to the envelope. He folded it in half and stuffed it all in the front pocket of his jeans.

Alex couldn't understand why the man seemed so nervous. Mr. Martin often sold paintings for a great deal more than Alex's work. One of R. C. Dillion's paintings would have gone for well over what

Alex had just earned for six. Maybe it was just that it had all been in cash.

"What then?" Alex asked, his suspicion growing. "Did the man say anything else?"

"There's a little more to the story." Mr. Martin straightened the orange knot at his throat. "After he had paid—in cash, the same cash I just gave you—he said, 'These are mine, now, right?' I said, 'Yes, of course.'

"He then picked up one of his paintings, pulled a fat black marker out of his pocket—you know, the indelible kind—and started writing all over the painting. I was stunned. I didn't know what to do. When he had finished, he did the same to each in turn. Wrote all over them."

Mr. Martin clenched his hands together. "I've never had such an experience. I asked the man what he thought he was doing. He said that they were his paintings and he could do any damn thing he wanted to with them."

Mr. Martin leaned closer. "Alex, I would have stopped him, I swear I would have, but, well, they were his, and he was very . . . insistent about what he was doing. By his change in attitude I was beginning to fear what would happen if I were to interfere. So I didn't. I had the money, after all—cash at that."

Alex stood with his jaw hanging. He was overjoyed to have the money from the sale but at the same time he was incensed to hear that his work had been defaced.

"So he finished marking all over my work and then just took his ruined paintings and left?"

Mr. Martin scratched his jaw, his gaze turning aside. "No. He set them down and said that he wanted me to give them back to you. He said, 'Give them back to Alexander Rahl. My treat.'"

Alex heaved a sigh. "Let me see them."

Mr. Martin gestured to the paintings sitting against the wall in the corner of the office area. They were placed face-to-face, and no longer in frames.

When Alex lifted the first one and held it out in both hands he was struck speechless. In fat black letters sprawled diagonally across the painting it said *FUCK YOU ASSHOLE*.

The painting was covered with every other hateful, vile, vulgar name there was.

"Alex, I want them out of here."

Alex stood, hands trembling, staring at his beautiful painting covered with ugly words.

"Do you hear me, Alex? I can't have these in here. What if a customer should happen to see them? You have to take them with you. Right now. Get them out. I want them out of here. I want to forget all about this."

Through his fury Alex could only nod. He knew that Mr. Martin didn't fear a customer seeing them. Many of Mr. Martin's artists routinely spoke like this in front of customers. The customers took the artist's "colorful" speech as an indication of social sensitivity and artistic introspection. The more times an artist could drop the F bomb in a sentence the more visionary he became to them.

No, Mr. Martin was not offended by the words—he was used to hearing them in the gallery—he was frightened by the man who had written them, and by the context of those words: raw hatred.

Mr. Martin cleared his throat. "I've been giving the matter a great deal of thought, and I think it best if for now we don't display any of your work."

Alex looked up. "What?"

Mr. Martin gestured to the painting. "Well, look at it. This kind of man could get violent. He looked like he was ready to break my neck if I dared lift a finger to stop him."

Alex's first thought was that it was Bethany's doing, but he dismissed the idea. He was pretty sure she didn't have that kind of money to spend on a grudge.

"What did this guy look like? Describe him."

"Well," Mr. Martin said, taken aback a little by the heat in Alex's tone, "he was tall, and good size—about like you. He was dressed casually but not expensively. Tan slacks, some kind of bland shirt, not tucked in. It was beige with a vertical blue stripe of some sort down the left side."

Alex didn't recognize the description.

He felt sick with anger. He ripped the canvas off the stretcher, then did the same with the other five. He only briefly saw the insults and obscene words desecrating the scenes of beauty. The range of profanity turned his stomach, not so much because of the words themselves, but because of the naked hate they conveyed.

They were just paintings of beauty. That's all they were. Something to uplift people who looked at them, something to make people feel good about life and the world they lived in. To harbor hatred for beauty was one thing, but to go to great expense just to express that hate was quite another.

Alex realized that Mr. Martin was right. Such a man could easily become violent.

Alex hoped to meet him.

9.

WITH THE ROLLED-UP RUINED CANVASES under one arm and the painting that he'd carefully wrapped in brown paper tucked under his other arm, Alex left Mr. Martin's gallery without an argument. Despite how much he was fuming, there wasn't any point in arguing. Mr. Martin was afraid.

Alex couldn't really blame the man. Alone as he was most of the time, he was a sitting duck in the gallery. The stranger could come back at any time. What was Mr. Martin supposed to do? Alex couldn't expect the gallery owner to have it in him to be able to handle an altercation that could become violent.

Conflicting emotions raged through Alex's thoughts as he made his way out into the elegant halls. He was depressed, he was furious. He wanted to run home and lock himself away from a world where such people roamed free. He wanted to find the guy and shove the black markers down his throat.

When Alex looked up, the woman was standing not far off in front of him, watching him approach. He slowed to a stop.

She was in the same black dress, with the same green wrap draped over her shoulders. He thought that he saw wisps of vapor—a hint of steam or smoke—rising from her fall of blond hair and her shoulders, but as soon as he focused on it, it was gone.

As impossible as it seemed, she looked even better than he remembered.

"You come here often?" he asked.

Her gaze never left his as she slowly shook her head. "This is only my second time here."

Something about the serious set of her features gave him pause. He knew that she wasn't there to shop.

His grandfather's old mantra, *Trouble will find you,* echoed through his mind.

"Are you all right, Alex?" she asked.

"Sure." The sound of her voice made him all right. "You know my name, but I don't know yours."

A small smile softened her features as she glided a step closer. "I am Jax."

Her name was as unusual as everything else about her. He could hardly believe that he was really seeing her again.

"I'd give anything to paint you, Jax," he said under his breath to himself.

She smiled at his words, smiled in a way that accepted them as a compliment, but didn't reveal her view of them or her willingness to be the subject of a painting.

He finally pulled his gaze away to check around, to see if anyone was close. "Did you hear the news on the TV?"

Her brow twitched. "News? No. What news?"

"You remember the other day when we first met out on the street? When that truck nearly ran us over."

"The pirates, as you called them. I remember."

"Well, later that same day those two cops who stopped the truck were found dead."

She stared at him a moment. "Dead?"

He nodded. "The news said that both men had been found with their necks broken."

The method of murder registered in her eyes. She let out a long sigh as she shook her head. "That's terrible."

Alex suddenly wished he hadn't started the conversation with grim news. He gestured to a bench set in among a grouping of large round planters.

"Would you sit with me? I'd like to show you something."

She returned the smile and at his bidding sat on the small mahogany bench. Huge split-leaf philodendrons created a green roof over the bench. The planters overflowing with plants to either side and behind made it resemble a forest retreat for just the two of them. The planters and vegetation blocked them off from most but not all of the shoppers strolling the halls.

Alex set the rolled-up canvases on the bench to his right, on the side away from her. He placed the painting on her lap.

"What's this?" she asked.

"A gift."

She stared at him a moment, then pulled off the brown paper.

She looked genuinely stunned to see the painting. She lifted it reverently in her hands. Her eyes welled up with tears.

It took her a moment to find her voice. "Why are you giving me this?"

Alex shrugged. "Because I want to. You thought it was beautiful. Not everyone thinks my work is beautiful. You did. I wanted you to have it."

Jax swallowed. "Alex, tell me why you painted this particular place."

"Like I told you before, it's from my imagination."

"No, it's not," she said rather emphatically.

He paused momentarily, surprised by her words. "Yes it is. I was merely painting a scene—"

"This is a place near where I live." She touched a graceful finger to the shade beneath towering pines. "I've spent countless hours sitting in this very place, gazing off at the mountain passes here, and here. The views from this hidden place are unparalleled—just as you've painted them."

Alex didn't know what to say. "It's just a painting of the woods. The woods can look much the same in one place as another. A species of tree all look pretty much the same. I'm sure that it simply reminds you of this place you know."

With the edge of a knuckle she wiped a tear from under an eye. "No." She swallowed and then pointed to a spot he clearly recalled painting. For some reason he'd put extra care into the trunk of the tree. "See this notch you put in this tree?" She glanced up at him. "I put that notch there."

"You put it there," he said in a flat tone.

Jax nodded. "I was testing the edge I'd put on my knife. The bark is thick there. I sliced paper-thin pieces of it to test the edge. Bark is tough, but is easier on a freshly sharpened blade than other things, like wood, might be."

"And you like to sit at a place like this?"

"No, not a place like this place. This place. I like to sit at this place. This place is Shineestay."

"Shineestay? What's that mean?"

"It's an ancient word that means 'place of power.' You have

painted that exact place." She looked again at the scene and tapped a spot to the side of the sunlit glen. "The only minor difference is that there is a tree, here, near the side of this open area, that you have not painted. This is the exact same spot, except for that one tree that's missing."

Alex felt goose bumps tickle the nape of his neck. He knew the tree she was talking about. He had painted it.

He had originally painted it exactly where she was pointing, but while it might have been right in such a forest, it had been compositionally wrong for the painting, so he had painted over it. He recalled at the time wondering why he'd painted it in the first place, since it didn't fit in the composition. Even as he looked where Jax was pointing, he could see the faint contour of the brushstrokes of the tree beneath the paint that now lay over it.

Alex was at a loss to explain how it could be the place she knew. "Where is this place?"

She stared at him a moment. Her voice regained a bit of its distant, detached edge. "Alex, we need to talk. Unfortunately, there is a great deal to say, and like the last time, I can't stay long."

"I'm listening."

She glanced at passersby. "Is there somewhere not far away that's a little more private?"

Alex pointed down the hall. "There's a restaurant down there that's nice. The lunch rush is over, so it would be quiet and more private. How about if I buy you lunch and you can tell me what you have the time to tell me?"

She pressed her lips tightly together a moment as she considered the place he'd pointed out. "All right." He wondered why she was being so cautious. Maybe she had a grandfather like Ben.

As they stood, she held the painting tightly to herself. "Thank you for this, Alex. You can't possibly know what this means to me. This is one of my favorite places. I go there because it's beautiful."

He bowed his head at her kind words. "I painted it because it's beautiful. That you like it is a greater reward for me than you could know."

He still wanted to know how he could have painted a place she knew, a place she knew so well, but he sensed the tension in her posture and decided to go easy. She'd said that she wanted to explain things, so he thought it best if he didn't intimidate her out of wanting to do so.

Alex picked up the rolled canvases and then tucked them under an arm as they started down the hall.

"How did you come by the name Jax?"

She brightened, almost laughed, at the question. "It's a game. You toss jax on the ground, throw a ball up in the air, and then try to pick up the jax and catch the ball in the same hand after it bounces once. It's a simple child's game but as you try for ever more jax it requires a sharp eye and quick hands. Certain people were amazed at how quick I am with my hands, so my parents named me Jax."

Alex frowned as he tried to reconcile the story. "But when you were born you couldn't have played anything yet. A kid has to be, what, five to ten years old before they can play that kind of game? How could your parents know you were going to be quick with your hands when you were just born?"

She stared straight ahead as she walked. "Prophecy."

Alex blinked. "What?"

"A prophet told them about me before I was born, told them how everyone would be amazed at how quick I would be with my hands, how it would first be noticed because I would be a natural at the game of jax. That's why they named me Jax."

Alex wondered what kind of weird religion her parents belonged to that put that much stock in the words of prophets. He thought that if her parents expected her to be quick with her hands then they would encourage her to practice and as a result she would end up quick. He wanted to say so, to say a lot of things, ask a lot of questions, but a growing sense of caution reminded him to take it easy and let her tell her own story. So he kept his questions on the light side.

"But Jack, like in jacks, is a boy's name."

"The boy's name Jack is spelled with a *k*. My name is spelled with an *x*. J-A-X comes from the game of jax, not the boy's name."

"But the game is called jacks, J-A-C-K-S."

"Not where I come from," she said.

"Where's that?"

"You wouldn't know it," she said after a moment. "It's a long way from here."

For some reason she had avoided answering his question, but he let it go.

As they strolled down the hall he watched her out of the corner of his eye. He often watched people, studied their posture, their natural way of moving, their attitude expressed through the way they carried themselves, to help him accurately paint the human form.

Most people when in public conveyed either a casual or a businesslike attitude. People were often focused on the place they were headed, never really aware of anything along the way. That tunnel vision affected the way they moved. Those projecting a businesslike attitude held their bodies tight. Others, being self-absorbed and out of touch with their surroundings, moved in a looser fashion. Most people were self-absorbed, unaware of who was around them or of any potential threat, and their body language betrayed that fact. In some cases that casual attitude drew dangerous attention. It was what predators looked for.

Most people never consciously considered the reality that bad things happened, that there were those who would harm them. They simply had never encountered such situations and didn't believe it could happen to them. They were willfully oblivious.

Jax moved in a different way. Her form, unlike the tight businesslike posture, carried tension, like a spring that was always kept tight, yet she moved with grace. She carried herself with confidence, aware of everything around her. In some ways it reminded him of the way a predator moved. Through small clues in her posture she projected an aura of cool composure that bordered on intimidating. This was not a woman whom most men would approach lightly.

In fact, that awareness was what he found the most riveting. She watched the people moving through the halls—every one of them—without always looking directly at them. She kept track of them out of the corner of her eye, measuring each, checking each one as if for distance and potential threat.

"Are you looking for anyone in particular?" he asked.

Absorbed in thoughts of her own, she said, "Yes."

"Who?"

"A different kind of human."

In an instant Alex yanked her around a corner and slammed her up against the wall. He hadn't intended to be so rough about it, but the shock of hearing those words tripped something within him and he acted.

"What did you say?" he asked through gritted teeth.

He held her left arm with his right hand. The painting was pressed between them. His left forearm lay across her throat, his hand gripping her dress at her opposite shoulder. If he were to push, he could crush her windpipe.

She stared unflinching into his eyes. "I said I was looking for a different kind of human. Now, I suggest that you think better of what you're doing and carefully let go of me. Don't move too fast or you'll get your throat cut and I'd hate to have to do that. I'm on your side, Alex."

Alex frowned and then, when she pushed just a little, realized that she was indeed holding the point of a knife to the underside of his chin. He didn't know where the knife had come from. He didn't know how she had gotten it there so fast. But he did know that she wasn't kidding.

He also didn't know which of them would beat the other if it came down to it. He was fast, too. But it was not, and had not been, his intent to hurt her—merely to restrain her.

He slowly started to release his hold on her. "My mother said the same thing to me a few days ago."

"So?"

"She's confined to a mental institution. When I visited her she told me that I must run and hide before they get me. When I asked her who it was that was trying to get me, she said 'a different kind of human.' Then the report came on about those two officers being murdered. It said they were found with their necks broken. My mother said, 'They break people's necks.' Then she retreated into that faraway world of hers. She hasn't spoken since. She won't speak again for weeks."

Jax squeezed his arm sympathetically. "I'm sorry about your mother, Alex."

He glanced around to see if anyone was paying attention to

them. No one was. People probably assumed that they were two lovers whispering sweet nothings to each other.

His blood was up and, despite her calming voice and her gentle touch, he was having trouble coming back down. He made himself unclench his jaw.

Something between them had just changed, changed in a deadly serious way. He was sure that she felt it as well.

"I want to know how it is that you said the very same thing my crazy mother said. I want you to tell me that."

From mere inches away she gazed into his eyes. "That's why I'm here, Alex."

10.

THE DOOR TO THE REGENT GRILL, covered in tufted black leather, closed silently behind them. There were no windows in the murky inner sanctum of the restaurant. The hostess, a pixie of a woman with an airy scarf flowing out behind, led them to a quiet niche that Alex requested. With the exception of two older women out in the center of the room, under a broad but dimly lit cylindrical chandelier, the restaurant was empty of patrons.

Empty or not, Alex didn't want his back to the room. He got the distinct feeling that Jax didn't, either.

They both slid into the booth, sitting side by side, with their backs to the wall.

The padded, upholstered walls covered with gold fabric, the plush chairs, the mottled blue carpets, and the ivory tablecloths made the restaurant a quiet, intimate retreat. The location in back felt safe in its seclusion.

After the hostess set the menus down and left and the busboy had filled their water glasses, Jax again glanced around before speaking.

"Look, Alex, this isn't going to be easy to explain. It's complex and I don't have enough time right now to make it all clear for you. You need to trust me."

Alex wasn't exactly in an indulgent mood. "Why should I trust you?"

She smiled a little. "Because I may very well be the only one who can keep you from getting your neck broken."

"By who?"

She nodded toward the rolled-up canvases on the bench on the far side of him. "By the people who did that to your paintings."

His brow twitched. "How would you know about that?"

Her gaze turned down to her folded hands. "We caught a glimpse of him doing it."

"'We'? What do you mean, *we* caught a glimpse of him doing it?"

"We were trying to look through the mirror in Mr. Martin's gallery. We were trying to find you."

"Where were you when you were 'looking' through the mirror?"

"Please, Alex, would you just listen? I don't have the time to explain a hundred different complicated details. Please?"

Alex let out a deep breath and relented. "All right."

"I know that the things I'm telling you might sound impossible, but I swear that I'm telling you the truth. Don't close your mind to what is beyond your present understanding. People sometimes invent or discover things that expand their knowledge so that they accept as possible what only the day before they had thought was impossible. This is something like that."

"You mean like how people used to think that no one would ever be able to carry around a tiny little phone without it having to be connected to wires."

She looked a little confused by the analogy. "I suppose so." She turned back to the subject at hand. "One day I hope I can help you better grasp the reality of the situation. For now, please try to keep an open mind."

Alex slowly twirled the stem of the water glass between his thumb and first finger, watching the ice remain still in place as the glass spun. "So, you were saying how you were looking for me."

Jax nodded. "I knew that you had a connection to the gallery. It's how I knew where you were today. I had to hurry if I was to catch you. Because we had to hurry we couldn't prepare properly and as a consequence I don't have much time here."

Alex wiped a hand across his face. He was starting to feel like maybe he was being played for a fool. "You need a room with my mother."

"You think this is some kind of joke?" She looked up at him with fiery intensity. "You have no idea how hard this is for me. You have no idea the things I've been through—the chances I've had to take to come here."

She clenched her jaw and swallowed, trying to keep her voice under control. "This isn't a joke, Alex. You have no idea how afraid I am, how lost I feel here, how alone, how terrified."

"I'm sorry, Jax." Alex looked away from the pain in her brown eyes and took a sip of water. "But you're not alone. Tell me what's going on?"

She let out a calming breath. "I'll do my best, but you have to understand that for now I simply can't tell you everything. It isn't just that I don't have the time to explain it all right now, it's also that you aren't yet ready to hear it all. Worse, we're in the dark about a lot of it ourselves."

"Who is this 'we' you keep mentioning?"

She turned cautious. "Friends of mine."

"Friends."

She nodded. "We've been working for years, trying for years to figure some of it out. They helped get me here."

"Get here from where?"

She looked away and said simply, "From where I live."

Alex didn't like her evasive answer, but he decided that there was no harm in just letting it play out for the moment.

"Go on."

"We finally came to a point where we thought it would work, so despite the risk we attempted it, but we don't yet know how to make it work reliably. Not like the others do."

"You mean work to get here, to where I live, from where you live?"

"That's right."

"What would have happened if you hadn't gotten it right, if it didn't 'work'?"

She stared into his eyes for a long moment. "Then I would have been lost for all eternity in a very bad place."

Alex could tell by the tension in her expression how real the peril was—to her, at least—and how much the thought of failure frightened her. Considering that this woman was not easily intimidated, that in and of itself gave him pause.

He was about to again ask who the others on her team were when a waitress came up to the table and smiled warmly. "Can I get you two something to drink? Maybe a glass of wine?"

"I could really use some hot tea," Jax said.

The tone of that simple request revealed how weary she was, and how close she was to her wits' end.

"I'm fine with water. The lady doesn't have a lot of time, though.

Maybe we could order?" He turned to Jax as he picked up a menu. "What would you like? Chicken? Beef? A salad?"

"I doesn't matter. Whatever you're having is fine."

It was clear that she didn't care about food, so Alex ordered two chicken salads.

As the waitress left, Alex's phone rang. He reflexively asked Jax to excuse him a moment as he pulled the phone out of his pocket.

"Hello, this is Alex."

He'd thought that maybe it was Mr. Martin calling to say that he'd changed his mind. Instead, Alex was greeted with garbled noises. He heard a strained, disembodied voice torn by howling that sounded like it said, "She's there. She's there." Otherworldly whispers and strange, soft moans underlay the crackling static.

And then Alex made out his name in the background whispers.

Jax leaned in. "What's wrong?"

He was going to flip the cover closed and tell her that it was nothing, but for some reason he decided that maybe she should hear it. He held the phone up to her ear.

She leaned in closer, listening.

And then the blood drained from her face.

"Dear spirits," she whispered to herself, "they know I'm here."

"What?" Alex asked. "Do you recognize it?"

Stricken with alarm, she stared wide-eyed at him as she listened to the sounds. "Make it stop."

Alex took the phone back and closed it.

"They're tracking you with that thing."

"Tracking me?"

Her face still ashen, she said, "From the other side."

Alex frowned. "The other side of what?"

When she only stared with a haunted look, Alex turned the

phone off. Before putting it in a pocket, just to be safe, he popped out the battery and put it in a different pocket.

The waitress swooped in and set down a cup for Jax and a pot of hot water along with a small basket of tea bags.

After the waitress left, Jax poured herself some hot water. Her hands were trembling.

For a moment she sat staring at the cup of hot water, as if she expected it to do something. She finally picked up the cup, brought it close, and peered down into the water. She set the cup back down.

Jax nested her hands in her lap. Her brow wrinkled as she fought back tears.

"What's wrong?" he asked.

For a woman who had the presence of mind to put a knife to his throat when he had unexpectedly shoved her up against the wall, she seemed pretty shaken.

"How do you make the tea work?" she asked in a broken voice on the ragged edge of control.

Alex was baffled. "Make the tea work? What do you mean?"

"I never imagined how hard this would be," she said, more to herself than him.

"The tea?"

She crumpled her napkin in a tight fist as she fought back tears.

"Everything." She swallowed and then with great effort summoned her voice. "Please, Alex. I want some tea, but I don't know how to work it."

Seeing her genuine distress made his heart hurt. He wouldn't ever have imagined that this woman would let herself be seen as helpless. Something was bringing her to the edge.

Alex gently touched his fingers to the back of her hand. "It's all right, Jax. Don't let it get to you. We all have days when we're overwhelmed. It's no big deal. I'll help you."

He pulled a package of tea from the basket, opened the paper flap, and pulled out the tea bag. He held it up by the square paper at the end of the string.

"See? The tea is in here, in the tea bag." Her gaze tracked the tea bag the whole way as he lowered it into the cup and draped the string over the edge. "Just let it steep for a little bit and you'll have tea."

She leaned in and looked down into the cup. As she watched, the water started darkening.

Jax's sudden smile banished her tears. Her face took on the look of a child who had just seen a magic trick for the first time.

"That's how it works? That's all you have to do?"

Alex nodded. "That's it. You obviously don't have tea bags where you come from."

She shook her head. "It's very different here."

"You like it better where you live, don't you?"

She considered the question only briefly. "Yes. It's home. Despite the trouble, it's home. I think you would like it there, too."

"What makes you think that?"

She reached over and trailed her fingers tenderly across the painting. "You paint such places. You paint beauty." She looked back up at him. "This will help me convince the others."

"Convince them of what?"

"Convince them to trust my choices."

"Who are these others, Jax?"

"Others something like me."

"They live in this other place? Where you live?"

"Yes. Do you remember the two men when you first saw me?" she asked, seemingly changing the subject. "The two that the authorities stopped?"

Alex nodded. "The pirates. Do you know who they were?"

"Yes. They were a different kind of human. Different from you. Different from your mother. Among other things, they will break the necks of anyone who gets in their way. Those are the people your mother feared."

"What do you mean they—"

The waitress appeared with two plates. "I had them put a rush on it, since you haven't much time."

"Thank you," Jax said with a sincere smile.

After the waitress had hurried off to her work, Alex went back to his questions. "What do you mean—"

"Do I have to do anything to this so that I can eat it?" Jax looked up from the salad. "Is there anything I need to do first?"

Alex held up a fork. "No. Just dig in." He stabbed a piece of chicken with the fork. "The chicken is cut up so you don't even have to use a knife." He realized that if a knife was needed she would have that knack down pat.

He ate the bite to demonstrate.

She smiled. "Thank you, Alex, for being patient. For understanding that patience is needed in this."

If she only knew how impatient he was, but he didn't want to spook her.

"Why?"

"Because if I were to tell you everything right now you wouldn't believe me, and you need to believe me. But, on the other hand, time is slipping through my fingers, so I have to tell you at least some of it."

Alex almost smiled at the curious dance they were doing, both trying not to spook the other.

"Jax, how did my mother know those things—know about a different kind of human, about men who break people's necks?"

"I think in part because we tried to warn her."

"About what?"

"That people were hunting her. But we couldn't get here, yet. The others could. They've been coming here for some time now. We tried to warn her through mirrors, but they apparently got to her. We tried to warn you, too."

The hair on the backs of Alex's arms stood up on end.

"My grandfather showed me some papers about an inheritance. Does that have anything to do with these other people you tried to warn my mother about?"

She stared down at her plate for a time before answering. "All we know at the moment is that there are some very dangerous people who are up to something. We haven't yet managed to fit the pieces together."

Alex wanted a better answer. "My grandfather said that the inheritance was supposed to go to my father on his twenty-seventh birthday, but since he died before then it was reassigned to my mother. She had to be put in an asylum before the inheritance could go to her on her twenty-seventh birthday. It seems logical that this inheritance might be connected with what happened to her."

"I don't know, but it's possible. I'm sorry we weren't able to help her, Alex. I'm sorry your family has had such trouble."

Alex ate silently for a moment. "My grandfather, Ben, says that he thinks that the whole troublesome matter has something to do with the seven—the seven in twenty-seven."

"The seven?" She looked incredulous. "That's just crazy."

"That's what I thought."

She shook her head to herself. "The seven. How could he ever come up with something like that? It's the nine."

Alex's forkful of chicken paused on the way to his mouth.

"What?"

"It's the nine. It's not the seven in twenty-seven—it's the nine. Two plus seven. Nine. Nines are triggers."

"That doesn't make sense. I was nine, once. My father was. My mother was. We were all eighteen. The one plus the eight in eighteen equals nine, just like the two plus the seven in twenty-seven equals nine."

Alex couldn't believe he was arguing such a point.

Jax was shaking her head. "Yes, but the nine and the eighteen are the first and second occurrence of a nine. Twenty-seven is the third nine. It's the third that's important."

Alex stared at her. "The third nine."

She nodded. "That's right. Threes are pivotal numbers—spells of threes and such."

Alex blinked in disbelief. "Spells of—"

"Three is a base component of nine. The multiplying element." Jax gestured with her fork, as if to imply that it was self-evident. "That's why twenty-seven is key: it's the third nine. It's called the Law of Nines."

"The Law of Nines," Alex repeated as he stared. "You've got to be kidding."

"It's easier than tea."

"Somehow, I don't think so," Alex said.

The woman believed in numerology. Alex thought that Ben should be the one sitting there having such a conversation.

Alex couldn't believe that a number could have any kind of real meaning. A thought came to mind. He almost hated to mention it.

"I was born on September ninth. Ninth month, ninth day, at nine in the evening."

"To be precise, you were born at nine minutes after nine."

A chill tickled up between his shoulder blades to the nape of his neck. "How do you know that?"

"We checked." She took a sip of tea as she watched him over the rim of her cup.

"What else do you know about me?"

"Well, you don't remember your dreams."

Alex's frown deepened. "How in the world would you know that?"

"You're a Rahl." She shrugged. "Rahl men don't remember their dreams."

"How do you know about Rahl men? Are there Rahls where you come from?"

"No," she said with a suddenly wistful look. "Where I come from the House of Rahl has long since died out."

"Look, Jax, I'm only getting more confused." He refrained from using a stronger word than "confused." "You're making me think all kinds of things about you that I'd really rather not think." He was starting to think that she was crazy—or maybe that he was. "Why don't you clear it up for me."

"I'm not from your world," she said in quiet finality as she looked into his eyes. "I'm a different kind of human than you."

11.

A LEX STARED FOR A MOMENT. "You mean you're an alien. From Mars, or something."

Her expression darkened. "I may not know what Mars is, but your tone is all too clear. This isn't a joke. I risked my life to come here."

"Risked your life how?"

"That isn't your concern."

"What is my concern?"

"That there are people from my world, dangerous people, who are likely to come after you for reasons we don't yet fully understand. I wouldn't like you to be unprepared."

He wondered how one prepared for people from some other dimension or time or twilight zone or something—he couldn't imagine what—who were liable to come looking for one.

Alex tapped his fork on a piece of chicken in his salad as he considered her words. If there was ever a look that meant business, she was giving it to him.

Still, he just couldn't bring himself to take seriously such talk of people coming from a different world. He wondered yet again if his lifelong worry was coming to pass: he wondered if he could be going crazy like his mother had. He knew that she believed things that weren't real.

He pushed the thoughts aside. He wasn't crazy. Jax was real enough. It actually made more sense for him to believe that she was crazy. Yet, despite how absurd her story was, she simply didn't strike him as crazy.

Even if he couldn't believe that this woman was from some other world, something seemed to be going on, and it was serious. Deadly serious, if he was to believe her.

He wanted to ask her exactly how she had traveled from this other world, but he instead checked his tone and started over. "I'm listening."

She took a sip of tea. "Someone is meddling."

"With my family?"

"Yes."

"Why?"

"Most likely because you're a Rahl. We believe that unless you have children you will be the last in the Rahl bloodline."

"And you think someone is interested in the Rahls?"

"If I had to guess I'd say that they may have killed your father to prevent him from getting to his twenty-seventh birthday."

"My father died in a car accident. He wasn't murdered."

"Maybe not." Jax arched an eyebrow. "But if you had been run down the other day don't you suppose it would have looked like an accident?"

"Are you saying that was intentional? That those men were trying to kill me? Why?"

She leaned back and sighed as she dismissed the suggestion with a flick of her hand. "I'm only saying that if they had been trying to kill you it would have looked like an accident, don't you think?"

He stabbed a piece of chicken as he recalled the murderous look the bearded man had given him. He looked up at her. She was watching him again.

"Why are these people so interested in the Rahl bloodline?"

"We're not entirely sure, yet. Like I said, we don't fully understand their reasons or what is going on."

She seemed not to be sure about a lot of things. Alex didn't know if he believed that she was as in the dark as she claimed, but he decided that since she chose not to tell him yet she must have her reasons, so he let it go.

Jax sat back a little as she went on. "When I was but a child, a few people started to get an inkling that something was going on, something nefarious. They dug into things, followed people, spied on them, and eventually, along the way, as one thing led to another, they found out that your mother was in danger. They tried to help her. In the end they weren't able to do so. They didn't yet know enough."

"If twenty-seven is so important, what with the Law of Nines and all," he asked, "then why didn't these dangerous people do anything to my grandfather, Ben? He's a Rahl." There were just too many holes in her story. He gestured with his fork to make his point. "Or, for that matter, why not come after any of the previous generations?"

"Some of my friends believe that these other people simply weren't able to get here yet."

"But you think differently?"

Reluctantly, she nodded. "I think that important elements of the prophecy weren't yet in place. It was too soon. Up until now it had been the wrong time, the wrong Rahl, for the prophecy."

"I don't believe in fortune-telling."

She shrugged. "It could be that you're right, that it's nothing more than some kind of baseless lunatic idea they came up with. They would hardly be the first group of people who acted on a completely deluded idea."

He hadn't expected her answer. "That's true enough."

"Whatever their reasons, some time ago they found a way to come here. These are people who, in my world, kill for the things they believe in."

Alex again thought about the plumbing truck that had nearly run him down. He thought about the two dead officers, their necks broken. He remembered his mother saying "They break people's necks." He didn't want to ask the question for fear of lending credibility to a subject he didn't think deserved it, but he couldn't help himself.

"What is this prophecy?"

She glanced around the empty room, checking that no one was near. The two women had already paid their check and left. The waitress was at a distant wait station, her back to them, folding a stack of black napkins for the dinner setting.

Jax leaned in and lowered her voice. "The gist of the prophecy is that only someone from this world has a chance to save our world."

He bit back a sarcastic remark and asked instead, "Save it from what?"

"Maybe save it from these people who are coming here to make sure that the prophecy can't come to pass."

"Sounds like a dog chasing its own tail," he said.

She opened her hands in an empathetic gesture. "For all we know, it could be that they don't believe you're a part of this prophecy. Maybe they want something else from you."

"But you think I'm involved in this in some way."

She laid her fingers on the sunlit place in the painting beside her before looking up at him. "You may live in this world, be a part of this world, but you have links, no matter how insubstantial, to our world. You proved it by painting a place in my world."

Or so she said. "It could just be a place that resembles it."

She remained mute, but the look she gave him was answer enough.

Alex ran his fingers back through his hair. "Your world, my world. Jax, I hope you can understand that when all is said and done I can't really believe what you're telling me."

"I know. I couldn't believe it when I first came here and saw what looked like huge metal things floating in the air, or carriages moving without horses, or any of a dozen other things that to me are impossible. It's not easy for me to reconcile it all in my own head. This will not be easy for you, either, Alex, but I know of no other way if there is to be a chance to save our world."

He felt as if he had just seen a sliver of light through the door she had opened a crack. This was a mission of desperation as far as she was concerned. She meant for him to help her save her world.

He wasn't sure if she had intended for him to see that brief glimpse of her purpose. Rather than try to pry at that door and have her slam it shut in his face, he asked something else, hoping to put her at ease.

"How is your world different from mine? Is it that they don't have advances like airplanes, cars, and the technology we have?" Were he not sitting with a woman who seemed deadly serious, he doubted that he could have asked such questions with a straight face. "What makes the people there, what makes you, a different kind of human?"

"This is a world without magic," she said without a trace of humor.

"So . . . you mean to imply that there is magic in your world? Real magic?"

"Yes."

"And you've seen it? Seen real magic."

She studied his eyes for a moment before a slight but intimidating smile grew at the corners of her mouth.

"Among other abilities, I am a sorceress."

"A sorceress who can't make tea."

"A sorceress who in my world can do a great deal more than make tea."

"But not in this world?"

"No," she finally admitted, her daunting smile fading. "Not in this world. This is a world without magic. I have no power here."

He found that to be rather convenient.

"So, we come from very different worlds, then."

"Not so different," Jax said in a way that sounded like it was somehow meant to be comforting.

Alex studied her placid expression. "We don't have magic. You say your world does. How much different could our worlds be?"

"Not so different," she repeated. "We have magic, but so do you, after a fashion. It's just that it manifests itself in a different way. You do the very same things we do, if with different methods."

"Like what?"

"Well, that thing in your pocket."

"The phone?"

She nodded as she leaned back and pulled something out of a pocket near her waist. She held up a small black book.

"This is a journey book. It works much like that phone you get messages on. Like your phone, we use this to get messages from people and to convey information to others. I write in my journey book and through magic the words appear at the same time in its twin. You say words on your phone device and words come out somewhere else. I am accustomed to writing messages, not speaking them. But you can also make your phone device function as a journey book, make words appear in it, am I right?"

Bethany's text messages sprang to mind. "Yes, but that's all done through technology."

She shrugged. "We do the same things you do. You do it by means of technology, we use magic. The words may be different but they do basically the same thing. They both implement intent and that's all that really matters. They both accomplish the same tasks."

"Technology is nothing at all like magic," Alex insisted.

"Technology itself is not what's important, is it?"

"What do you mean?"

"Do you really know any better than I do how a phone device works? Can you explain to me how the message gets from one place to another"—she waggled her fingers across in front of them—"how the words come invisibly through the air and end up here, in the device in your pocket, in a way that you can understand them? Do you really know what makes all that technology work? Can you explain all the unseeable things that happen, the things that you take for granted?"

"I guess not," he admitted.

"Nor can I explain how a journey book works. What's important is that the people here used their minds to create this technology in order to accomplish their ends, much like those where I come from think up ways to create things using magic to accomplish what we need to accomplish. It's as simple as that. It's second nature to both of us. We both use what has been created. For all you know, your phone really could work through magic and you would never know the difference."

"But there are people here who understand the technology and can describe exactly how all of the parts work, how the phone works, how the words appear."

"I know people who can describe exactly how a journey book works. I've even sat through long lectures on the subject, but while I get the general nature of it I still can't tell you exactly how to align the fibers within the paper with Additive and Subtractive elements to give them the sympathetic harmony needed to make words appear. It's not my area of expertise. What matters most to me is that someone somehow did create it and I can use it to help me accomplish the things I need to do.

"We simply say that it works by magic and leave it at that. How it works isn't so important to me. That it does work is what matters.

"If you wish to describe what we do in our world as merely a different form of technology rather than use the word 'magic,' if that makes it easier for you to accept, then call it by that name. The name makes no difference.

"Magic and technology are merely tools of mankind. If you called that phone a magic talking box, would you use it any differently?"

"I concede the point." Alex gestured. "So, do something. Show me."

She leaned back and slipped the little black book back where she kept it. "I told you, this is a world without magic. I can't use magic here. Magic doesn't work here. Believe me, I wish it did, because it would make this a lot easier."

"I hope you realize how convenient that excuse sounds."

She leaned in again with that deadly serious look she had. "I'm not here to prove anything to you, Alex. I'm here to find out what's going on so I can try to stop it. You just happen to be in the middle of it and I'd not like to see you get hurt."

That reminded him of what he'd said when he had pulled her back from getting run over by pirate plumbers—that he'd not like to see her get hurt.

"A little difficult, isn't it, if you can't use your sorceress powers, considering that you don't know how this world works. I mean, no offense, but you didn't even know how to make tea."

"I didn't come here thinking it would be easy. I came out of desperation. There is a saying in our world that sometimes there is magic in acts of desperation. We were desperate."

Alex scratched his temple, unable to contain his sarcasm. "Don't tell me, the people who sent you are sorcerers. A whole coven of sorcerers."

She stared into his eyes for a moment. Tears welled up.

"I didn't risk eternity in the black depths of the underworld to come here for this."

She set down her napkin, picked up the painting, and stood. "Thank you for the beautiful painting. I hope you heed my warnings, Alex. Since you don't seem to need my help, I'll attend to other concerns."

She stopped and turned back. "By the way, covens have to do with witches—thirteen of them—not sorcerers. I'd not like to even contemplate thirteen witch women all together in one place at once. They're known for their rather rash temperament. Be glad they can't get here; they'd simply gut you and be done with it."

She marched away without a further word.

Alex knew that he'd blown it. He'd crossed a line he hadn't known was there. Or maybe he crossed a line that he should have known was there. She had wanted him to listen, to try to understand, to trust her. But how could he be expected to believe such a preposterous story?

The waitress had seen Jax leaving and headed for the table. Alex pulled out a hundred-dollar bill—the only kind of cash he had—threw it on the table, and told the waitress to keep the change. It was the biggest tip he'd ever left in his life. He rushed across the quiet room, weaving among the tables.

"Jax, wait. Please?"

Without slowing she glided through the door and out into the halls, her black dress flowing out behind like dark fire.

"Jax, I'm sorry. Look, I don't know anything about it. I admit it. I'm sorry. I shouldn't be so flippant—it's one of my faults—but how would you react if the situation were reversed, if before today I told you how we make tea?"

She ignored his words.

"Jax, please, don't go."

He broke into a trot trying to catch up with her. Without looking back she turned down a small, dimly lit hall toward a side exit. Long skeins of wavy blond hair trailed out behind her like flags of fury. An exit sign cast the hall in hazy red, otherworldly light.

Jax reached the door before he could catch up with her. She stopped abruptly and turned to him in a way that made him stop dead in his tracks. He was almost close enough to reach out and touch her. Something warned him to stay where he was.

"Do you know the meaning of the name Alexander?"

Alex wanted to say something to her, to apologize, to talk her into staying, but he knew without a doubt that he had better answer her question and no more or he would cross a line . . . forever.

"It means 'defender of man, warrior.'"

She smiled to herself just a little. "That's right. And do you value your name, its meaning?"

"Why do you think I sign my work, my passion, 'Alexander'?"

She gazed at him a long moment, her features softening just a bit. "Maybe there is hope for you. Maybe there is yet hope for all of us."

She abruptly turned and threw open the door. Without looking back she said over her shoulder, "Heed my words, Alexander, defender of man: Trouble will find you."

Harsh afternoon light flared into the hall, turning her figure into nothing more than a harsh fragment of silhouette twisting the shafts of light.

Alex reached the door just as it slammed shut. He threw it open again and ran out into an empty side parking lot. Trees grew in a green band close to the building. Beyond grassy hillocks waited parked cars that in the flat gray light of the overcast afternoon no longer looked nearly so lustrous.

Jax was nowhere to be seen.

Alex stood staring around at the quiet, empty surroundings.

She'd been out of his sight for only a few seconds. She couldn't have been more than a half-dozen steps ahead of him. It seemed crazy, but she had vanished. The woman had just vanished into thin air.

Just like she had vanished the last time.

He wondered if this was how it had been for his mother.

12.

A LEX REALIZED THAT it was dark and that he had been driving around in a daze for hours. He found it unnerving that he hadn't even noticed that it had gotten dark.

Jax's final words, her warning, kept echoing in his thoughts. He didn't know if she had meant them literally, or in the way his grandfather always meant them. He was beginning to wonder if his grandfather had always meant more than Alex had thought. While Ben had the seven wrong—according to Jax—he had been on to something, or close to it, anyway.

But that was only if the things she had been saying were true. If not, then it made Ben just the eccentric old man most people believed him to be. But Alex knew him to be a strong and wise man, a man in many ways shaped, perhaps haunted, by his years in special forces, doing only god knew what back before Alex had been born.

Alex had learned only obliquely, from his parents' conversations, the shadowy shape of Ben's history. Alex had on occasion seen medals usually kept out of sight. Twice he had heard phone calls from men Ben only addressed as "sir." Ben would smile in that distant way he had and thank the caller for letting him know. Ben never talked about the things he had done, dismissing them as his past, as his time away.

But he did pass on lessons from those times. Ben thought it was important for Alex to know certain things that few others could teach him. Those lessons spoke volumes about the teacher.

Alex again wondered about Jax's warning, and about Ben's.

Alex didn't know what to do. He didn't know how to handle such a strange situation. It just didn't fit any template he knew of. No one, not even Ben, had ever told him how to handle a person who said they were from a different world.

He felt foolish taking such a story seriously, but at the same time he wanted to believe her. She had needed him to believe her. He felt trapped in a situation where if he believed her he might end up being a fool, a dupe, but if he didn't believe her, and what she was telling him actually was true, then he might end up being responsible for some undefined but terrible consequences.

But how could such a story be true? How could he even consider believing such a story about visitors from other worlds? It simply wasn't possible.

Yet his mother had warned him of some of the very same things Jax had tried to warn him about. He couldn't make that add up. How could he not take such a thing seriously?

Jax was the key to finding the truth. More than that, even, it felt to him like she was somehow the key to his life.

He felt drawn to her in a way he'd never been drawn to anyone else. She was a mesmerizing woman. For Alex, her insight and intelligence amplified her beauty. Despite all of her mystery and the strange things she had to say, he felt comfortable with her, more comfortable than he had ever felt with anyone. She had the same inner spark—some way of looking at the world—that he had. He could see it in her eyes. He almost felt as if he could look into her eyes and see her soul laid bare to him.

Gloom crushed him for having driven her away.

In his mind, he again ran through a speech he would like to make. He would like to ask her to imagine how she would feel if he were to abruptly show up in her world and tell her that he talked into a metal device and people anywhere in the world could hear him. How would she have taken the news if he told her that people in his world flew in metal tubes tens of thousands of feet in the air? He couldn't stop his racing mind from coming up with examples of technology that she would surely find impossible to believe. If he had come to her in the way she had come to him, would she have believed him?

It troubled him somewhat that even thinking of what he might say to her might be taking her story too seriously and falling into some kind of con game.

He wanted to tell her so much, to find out so much. Some of the things she'd said were just flat too eerily correct to discount, but at the same time her story was beyond hard to swallow. Other worlds. Who was she trying to fool? There were no other worlds.

Did she expect him to believe that some sorcerers had boiled up a magic brew and somehow beamed her to the Regent Center? And that yet others had placed a call to his phone from a different universe, or planet, or dimension, or something?

He wondered why, if her story was so hard to swallow, he had smashed his cell phone.

He realized that he needed to talk to her more than any other person in the world. Or in both worlds, if it really was true.

But if it wasn't true, then what had he seen? What about the things she knew, the things she could tell him that she shouldn't be able to know. How in the world could she know that he didn't remember his dreams? That was just plain creepy. Was she simply taking a wild stab in the dark? Guessing? After all, a lot of people probably didn't remember their dreams.

Or did she really know?

Yet again he worried that the whole thing could be some kind of elaborate trick. There were stage magicians, after all, who could make a woman, an elephant, or even a plane disappear. Even though they made it look completely convincing he knew that such things weren't real, knew it was all a trick.

Alex didn't like being tricked by magicians. It always struck him as a form of dishonesty about the nature of reality. Maybe that was why he didn't like magic tricks—and magic, real magic, simply didn't exist. He'd always felt that reality was better than magical; it was wondrous. That was part of the reason he never tired of painting the beauty of the world.

But why would Jax try to trick him? What reason would she have for doing such a thing? What was there for her to gain?

The fifty thousand acres came to mind.

He couldn't stop wondering if it could be some kind of trick to con him out of the inheritance. That much land was worth a fortune.

She claimed to have watched through a mirror as someone had gone into the gallery and defaced his paintings, but wouldn't it make more sense that it had been done by someone working with her? It seemed like a lot of money for a con, but if she was really after the land, the cost of the paintings would be a pittance in comparison to what they stood to gain if they could somehow trick him out of a fortune likely to be worth millions.

Such a motive easily made more sense than that she had come from some distant world, that she was a different kind of human, a sorceress with magical abilities. Who was she kidding? A sorceress. What kind of fool did she take him for? Did she really expect him to believe her?

But he did.

Against everything, he did. He couldn't explain why, but he believed her. There was something about her that struck him as not only sincere but desperate.

Either she had to be the best con artist ever born, or she really was a different kind of human from a different world. He couldn't imagine how it could be anything other than a trick or the truth. It came down to one of those two choices, and that was what was driving him crazy.

If she really was telling him the truth, then maybe his father, who had died in a car accident, had really been murdered and his mother's brain damage wasn't anything natural, like a stroke, as the doctors had thought. If Jax really was telling the truth, that meant that there really was something going on, something deadly serious.

But instead of telling her that he believed her, or at least listening respectfully, he'd chased her away. He desperately wished he hadn't done that, but he hadn't been able to help himself.

Maybe he'd just been afraid of being a sucker, of being the dupe of a beautiful woman. Wasn't that how con artists worked? Use a beautiful woman to lull a guy into believing anything, doing anything?

But he did believe her.

Right then, more than anything, lacking Jax, Alex decided that he needed to talk to Ben. His grandfather, strange as he could sometimes be, seemed like the right person to help unravel what had become a tight knot of doubts.

Alex smiled at the thought of explaining that it wasn't the seven in twenty-seven, but the nine, a number powered by threes, that was really what was important. His grandfather would be astounded. His grandfather would take such talk seriously. His grandfather might even be able to put it all into some kind of context that made sense.

As Alex turned onto Atlantic Street, headed home, he saw a red glow in the sky. Within a few blocks it became clear that it was a fire. A house in the distance was burning. A red glow lit billowing black smoke.

He soon realized that the blaze was in the direction of his house. Alex gripped the steering wheel tighter and tighter the closer he got to home. Could someone from this other world already be trying to cause him trouble, maybe even kill him? He sped up, suddenly eager to get home, hoping that it wasn't his house that was burning—there were valuable paintings there. Valuable to him, anyway.

When he spotted flashing lights in the rearview mirror he pulled over. An ambulance raced past. He suddenly felt guilty worrying about mere paintings and hoped no one was hurt in a fire. He couldn't imagine the horror of being burned.

His heart in his throat, Alex pulled around the corner, accelerating up the street, past houses with lights all on and people standing out in their yards looking toward the blaze.

With a jolt, he realized that it was his grandfather's house that was burning.

Alex slammed on the brakes as he pulled to the side of the street and parked crookedly at the curb. Cars with onlookers had parked to watch.

Fire trucks crowded the street, all parked at cockeyed angles. Amber lights on the fire trucks strobed the night. A police car, blue lights flashing, was parked crossways, blocking traffic.

Alex set the brake and leaped out. He ran with all his strength toward his grandfather's house. His vision narrowed down until all he saw was the familiar home engulfed in a terrifying glow of yellow and orange flames. He didn't even see all the firefighters in heavy yellow coats and helmets striped with reflective tape. Panic powered his legs as he ran.

An arm suddenly hooked him around the middle, spinning him around, stopping him cold. He pushed at the arms that came around and encircled him.

"Let me go! It's my grandfather's house! Let me go!"

"Hold on there," a big cop said. "You can't get any closer."

"I have to! We have to get him out!"

Two firemen stepped in around him.

"He's already out, son," the older man said.

Alex stared at him. "He is?" He looked around as the cop finally released him. "Where is he?"

The senior fireman put an arm around Alex's shoulders and walked him toward one of the two ambulances. All the flashing lights up and down the street made the scene seem surreal, other-worldly. One red-and-white ambulance was parked, all its doors closed. The back doors of the other were spread wide. Paramedics stood around, not looking at all in a hurry.

Even at a distance the heat was so intense that it hurt the side of Alex's face. Acrid smoke burned his throat. Hoses snaked all over the street. Streamers of water arced off into the furnace of flame. It was easy to see that there was shortly going to be nothing left of his grandfather's house.

As they got closer, Alex saw a gurney with the slight form of what might have been a body entirely covered in a gray blanket. Two paramedics stood over it on the far side.

"I'm sorry," the man holding Alex's shoulders said as they approached. "He was long gone when we got in there."

Alex stood staring at the gurney. He ran the words through his mind again, and then again. They didn't seem real.

"He's dead? Ben is dead?"

"I'm afraid so. From the looks of it, the fire started downstairs in a workshop. That's where we found the gentleman. One of my men looked in the basement door and spotted him reflected in a mirror. He was on the floor not far to the side. There wasn't much left of him by then but we were at least able to use the hoses to cool the doorway enough to manage to recover his remains. I'm sorry, son."

"I'm his only family," Alex said in a distant voice, somehow feeling that it all couldn't be real. "The only family left. I always told him to be careful with torches and soldering irons down there."

"It very well may be that he passed on from a heart attack or stroke and then something hot left unattended started the fire. I've seen it happen that way with older people."

"But he was burned?"

"I'm afraid so, but it's very possible that it was after he was already gone. We don't know yet."

"Ben," Alex said in a tearful voice as he knelt beside the remains covered in a gray blanket, "please don't leave me like this. I need you so much right now."

It felt like the world was falling in on him.

Some of the rafters gave way and the entire roof came crashing down. Huge flames roared up into the air. Columns of sparks and billowing smoke lifted into the night sky.

Alex laid an arm over his grandfather and broke down in tears.

13.

THE CORONER'S OFFICE HAD BEEN unable to determine the actual cause of death. They said that the remains were too badly burned to make that determination, but that since he had been found on the floor down in his workshop, rather than in bed, it was improbable that Alex's grandfather had been overcome by smoke in his sleep. The fire extinguisher, hanging nearby on the foundation wall, was charged and in working order, but it hadn't been used. There was an exit door not far away.

Considering those factors and the lack of any evidence to the contrary, the coroner's finding was that Benjamin Rahl had most likely lost consciousness or died of natural causes before the fire started, and the fire had been the result of something hot left unattended at his workbench while he was either unconscious or already deceased.

Alex had his grandfather's remains cremated. Ben had always said that he didn't want his corpse rotting in the ground, that he'd rather have the clean purification of fire consume his worldly self.

Still, considering what had happened, having Ben cremated seemed insensitive. Alex knew, though, that it was what his grandfather had wanted.

But more than that, Ben, who Ben was, was gone. The remains were not Ben, not to Alex, anyway. Those remains had been released by the fire to return to the elements of the universe.

The house was gone as well. Even much of the foundation had collapsed and what hadn't was unstable, leaving a hazardous sight. After the fire marshal and the insurance company adjuster finished their investigation, they had turned the property over to Alex. At the city's insistence Alex had hired a company to haul away the debris and fill in the hole.

Since then, whenever he walked up the street to his grandfather's place, the journey felt dreamlike. Even standing there staring at the open gap in the neighborhood, at the smoothed-over lot, he couldn't believe it. His mind filled in the empty hole with a ghostlike memory of the home. It seemed impossible that it was all gone—both his grandfather and the house where Alex had been raised for the last half of his childhood.

In the weeks that followed, that wasn't all that felt dreamlike. Alex at times wondered if it was possible that he had imagined Jax.

In the beginning, under the choking weight of grief, he hadn't thought a lot about her. He lost himself in the routine of his daily workouts. All he could really think about was Ben. He had real issues to deal with and there was no one else to handle things, no one else to help him.

But over time, nagging thoughts of Jax returned. With his mother in a mental institution it was only too easy to imagine that he was falling prey to the same sort of delusional madness that had overcome her. It sometimes felt like that madness was lurking just out of sight, ready to smother him, too.

He tried hard to keep such fears in perspective, tried hard not to give them any power over him, tried hard not to let his imagination get the best of him. Yes, his mother was sick, but that didn't mean that the same thing would happen to him.

His mother hadn't spoken since his birthday, when she had told him to run and hide, when she had warned him about a different kind of human who broke people's necks. He worried at times that he'd somehow built upon his mother's strange words to come up with Jax and her story—created a delusion of his own.

On one hand he knew that it wasn't possible that he could have imagined Jax, but on the other hand it often seemed easier to believe that he had dreamed her up, much the way he did the scenes he loved painting. He knew, though, that such thoughts were most likely born of his dejection that she had never tried to contact him again. He was just beating himself up over having driven her away, just feeling sorry for himself.

For a time his desire to believe Jax's story had been bolstered when he had spotted a popular science magazine in the store. On the cover had been a star field strewn with galaxies. The headline read "Our universe and multiplicity theory; maybe we're not alone."

That night Alex sat in his quiet house and carefully read the series of articles revolving around the possibility of other universes beyond what was called the "Light Horizon," the term used in Big Bang cosmology to describe the edge of the observable universe, the farthest distance astronomers could see. Since the light beyond the Light Horizon had not yet arrived to be seen, it was not known how large the universe actually was or what, if anything, might be beyond it.

Astrophysicists speculated how the universe, made up of space, time, and matter, might be able to bend back on itself through wormholes so that the most distant parts of the universe would be but a step away. They went further to talk about how the universe itself might not be singular, not everything there was, and that there might be others out beyond. Through theories that touched on black holes, white holes, dark matter, dark energy, the nonlinear oddities of the space-time continuum, string theory and superstring theory which suggested as many as ten dimensions, it was hoped that physicists would eventually be able to come to understand if and how other universes existed beyond our own.

Some astrophysicists postulated that the universe was like a bubble, and the events that created the bubble of the universe created others, a whole mass of them, each bubble a separate universe sparking into existence, growing, and expanding in a larger mass of universe bubbles. Other scientists believed that the universe was in fact like a sheet of time, space, and matter—four dimensions—floating in a greater void of a fifth dimension along with other universes, other four-dimensional sheets of time, matter, and space.

These physicists believed that there were dimensions beyond the four familiar dimensions, and that these additional dimensions were membranes that when they touched threw matter into the four dimensions we know. In other words, created universes that floated in this fifth dimension.

They even proposed that these other dimensions might be gateways between the universes.

Alex couldn't help wonder if Jax had come from one of those places. Perhaps she wasn't so much from another world as she was from another universe and had traveled through a gateway of other dimensions. While it gave him chills to ponder the possibilities, he felt in his heart that it was nothing more than daydreaming, a mere hook upon which to hang his hope that she was real and that she had been telling him the truth.

He needed her to be telling him the truth, or his entire impression of her, what he thought of her—her intelligence, her passion for life, her presence—would crumble. He didn't want to believe she was from another world. How could he believe such a story?

But if she was lying to him that would be worse.

Alex felt trapped in that dilemma, not wanting to believe her story, yet not wanting her to end up being nothing more than a scheming con artist, a liar.

But Jax was gone. He didn't really have any reason to hope that she would return. Alex knew that he'd missed his chance to ever find out more, to ever solve the riddle.

By the time he'd finished reading, it was dark in the house beyond the single lamp beside his chair. He felt not only alone but lonely in that enveloping darkness. The information in the articles hadn't convinced him of anything, as he had hoped. In fact, in an odd way it only left him feeling more convinced of the impossibility of it all. It seemed to him that the physicists were seducing themselves into ever more grand, fantastical theories. The science, if it really was science and not the projection of wishes, was beyond him.

As the rhythm of life demanded his attention he increasingly lost interest in the magazine articles. He had real life to deal with.

A week after finally cremating his grandfather, Alex had gone back to painting. At first it had seemed like it was only something to do to try to fill the emptiness. The world felt so quiet, so dead, so sad. It had never seemed that way before. He had talked to Ben almost every day. In many ways it was Ben who had made the world all the more alive for him.

As time wore on, Alex found that painting at least took his mind to other places, other worlds, and helped him forget his grief. He was alone most of the time, gone into those worlds that came to life on his canvases, and that suited him.

He supposed that he could at least find some solace in the fact that Ben had led a full life. He had relished every day he'd had. That was more than most people ever did. A lot of people merely marked time until a holiday, until they could go on vacation, until they could retire, always waiting for their life to begin. Ben never waited. He had lived each day.

After a few weeks, when Alex thought that maybe enough time had passed, he had called Mr. Martin to see if he would consider taking some paintings for the gallery. Mr. Martin was apologetic but said that he didn't feel comfortable doing so. The man was insistent. Alex saw no point in pushing. It was the way it was.

Rather than dwelling on the problem, Alex decided that he needed to find a solution, so he made the rounds of galleries where he thought he would feel comfortable showing his work. He finally managed to find one down in the old market district that agreed to take on a few smaller pieces. The shops were less expensive there, but they drew a variety of people and within a week the gallery had managed to sell a small painting for nine hundred dollars. The gallery had been pleased and asked Alex to bring in a few more paintings, one or two a little larger, so they could try to sell some of his more expensive work.

Before the month was out Alex had also contacted Lancaster, Buckman, Fenton, the law firm in Boston, and asked if they could see to transferring the title to the land to his name. They assured him that they could handle it and in fact, according to the stipulations in

the will, they were the only law firm legally allowed to handle anything to do with the land.

It also turned out that there were hefty legal fees involved if he
wanted to take title to the land, but considering the money he had
from the six paintings that had been defaced at Mr. Martin's gallery
and the settlement check for his grandfather's house due from the
insurance company, Alex would have no problem handling the legal
fees. The land would be his and the matter would be settled.

He hadn't yet decided if he wanted to sell the land, but he figured
that he had the rest of his life to decide. Mr. Fenton from the law
firm assured Alex that he could sell the land to the Daggett Trust
at any point should he decide to do so. Alex asked if Mr. Fenton
thought they could afford to pay fair market value for so much land.
The man went out of his way to assure Alex that the Daggett Trust
was well funded and would be able to handle such a purchase without any difficulty.

If Alex died without ever deciding to sell, and if he had no heir,
the land would revert to the conservation group without them having to pay a penny, so in a way it made sense to sell the land, because
then the money would be his no matter what happened. But, on the
other hand, if he died he wouldn't be able to spend money from the
grave.

Mr. Fenton told him that the Daggett Trust had made inquiries,
hoping for Alex's decision on selling sooner rather than later. Something about it riled Alex and made him come to a decision. He asked
Mr. Fenton to tell the people at the trust that he was taking title and
had every intention of keeping the land. The lawyer had then gone
to great lengths to make certain that Alex understood the restric-
tions to the deed, and that any violation would result in him losing

the land, even after he had title. Alex had assured the man that he understood.

Alex was looking forward to the transfer of title being completed. He wanted to spend some time alone in the woods painting. He was warming to the idea of such a vast place being his, of having a world to explore and call his own.

As he sat in his studio listening to the rain beat against the window, he realized that after nearly a month he was finally starting to feel better, to get beyond his grief, to again find satisfaction in his work and at least a little quiet pleasure in life. He had a new gallery that wanted his work, and he was starting to think about a trip to Maine to begin to explore the wilderness and fill his mind with impressions to paint.

It felt like things were getting back to normal. Things were moving forward. In a sense, it felt like a new beginning, like his life could at last really begin.

Jax, as well, was becoming a distant—if haunting—memory. Whatever the real story with her was, she hadn't made any attempt to contact him again. The more time that passed the more his hopes faded. If she was real, if her story was for real, she surely would have done something by now. She would have contacted him, sent a message . . . something.

He couldn't be sure that she hadn't been involved in some scheme with people trying to con him. He didn't think that was true, but the possibility existed and it troubled him.

He'd seen no evidence of otherworldly people. In fact, he didn't like to dwell on her revelations because the whole idea was seeming more absurd with each passing day and he didn't like to think of Jax in such an unflattering light. He didn't like to think of her as playing a part in a con game, but neither did he like to think of her being a wacko who imagined she was from a different planet. Having a mentally ill mother was more than enough craziness for Alex.

In the end he didn't know what to think, so he tried to put thoughts of Jax aside and devote himself to his painting.

Outside, in the blackness, lightning ignited in staccato flashes, giving ghostly form to the glistening trees. When the wind blew and the lightning strobed and flickered, it made the branches seem to move in abrupt fits, almost as if the trees were staggering through the inky blackness. At times the rain pattering against the window became heavy, turning the soft sound to a low roar. As the night wore on, the rain at times came down in curtains that swept over the house as if trying to beat it down and wash it away.

The storm suited Alex as he painted mountains with clouds stealing in among the towering peaks. The thunder brought nature in to him in a visceral way as he worked on the gloom in the forest beneath towering clouds.

Near midnight the doorbell rang.

14.

A LEX FROZE FOR A MOMENT, brush in hand, as the echo of the bell slowly died out. His first thought was to wonder if it was possible that it could be Jax.

He quickly discounted the notion. It was foolish to think it was her. But then he realized that if by any chance it was her it would be even more foolish to keep her standing out in the rain.

He stuck the brush in the jar of water on the table to the side of his easel and wiped his hands on a towel while rolling back his chair. As he stood a reflection caught his eye. He glanced briefly in the mirror across the room to rake back his disorderly hair. He didn't take the time to do any more to clean up, fearing that if it was Jax she might leave before he got to the door.

The only lights on in the house were the ones in his studio. As he ran down the dark hall, his way was lit sufficiently by the flickering flashes of lightning, so he didn't pause to fumble for switches and instead rounded the turn into the dark living room without slowing. Thunder following each crackling bolt of lightning rumbled through the structure of the house. The rain outside rattled against the windows. In the living room the flashes of lightning coming in the tall window threw a glaring slash of light across the hardwood floor.

Alex stopped before the door. His heart didn't. Hope kept it racing.

When he took a quick look through the peephole he saw what he hadn't at all expected.

Bethany stood near the porch light, just in under the overhang and out of the rain. She was alone.

Standing in the dark living room, Alex's heart sank. It wasn't Jax after all. He let out a heavy sigh.

He hadn't talked to Bethany in weeks. After Jax had warned him that a different kind of human was tracking him through his phone, he'd smashed it and thrown it in a dumpster at a convenience store. At the time it had made sense.

He bought a generic phone from a rack inside the store. It had a different telephone number, of course, so he left the new number with his new gallery and a couple of other places that might need to get ahold of him, like Lancaster, Buckman, Fenton. The simple phone was enough to serve his needs. Not one for long phone conversations, he hadn't yet even had to buy more minutes.

In the case of Bethany, having a new number had been an advantage; she couldn't call him or send him text messages. He had thought that if she couldn't contact him she would soon forget about him and move on with her life. Apparently, he had been wrong about that.

He could see through the peephole that she was wearing a slinky silver dress cut rather low. The dress was designed to make clear what lay beneath. In Bethany's case that was near perfection. She was a gorgeous woman, but that was all and it just wasn't enough for Alex. There was no substance to support the looks. There was nothing about her that inspired Alex to desire her. She seemed to be a living example of the saying that looks weren't everything.

The only lights on in the house were those in his back studio. The rest of the place was dark. The thought occurred to him that he could simply not answer the door and pretend he wasn't home.

But that would be cowardly, and worse, dishonest.

Since he really didn't want to start up another conversation with her—or worse, get in an argument—he decided he would state his feelings briefly, but clearly. Tell her the truth but keep it short and to the point.

Alex pulled open the door to face her.

As soon as he did, before he could open his mouth to say a word, Bethany lifted her arm, pointed a gun at his chest, and pulled the trigger.

15.

BEFORE ALEX WAS ABLE TO DODGE more than a few inches to the side, the gun went off.

At the same time that he heard the bang, it felt like a bolt of lightning slammed into him. Instant, overwhelming pain drove out a scream.

Every muscle in his body abruptly went rigid. It was all so sudden that he couldn't make sense of what was happening. He knew he'd been hit, but he couldn't tell where. Paralyzed by a shock of enormous force clamping down on him, his body wouldn't respond to his wishes.

Alex toppled backward. Try as he might, he couldn't even lift an arm to break his fall. Somehow, it didn't seem to matter.

As he fell back he saw twin coils of fine wire unspool from the gun.

It wasn't a regular gun, he realized, but a Taser. As he shuddered under the grip of the pain, it seemed that it might as well have been a regular gun. He was surprised that, despite the agony that made his body unresponsive, his mind worked.

Bethany stepped into the room to stand over him.

Alex could hear himself screaming in unendurable agony, but he could do nothing other than endure it.

He'd had time to move only inches before she'd pulled the trigger. One of the steel darts had stuck in his left pectoral muscle. At the same time the other dart, going lower by design in order to spread the electrical charge through the largest muscle mass, had firmly lodged in his lower abdomen. All his muscles had cramped iron stiff with all-consuming pain. It felt like a mountain was crushing him.

Regular stun guns caused pain. Because he had no control of his body, he knew that it wasn't one of those older models, but one of the newer Shaped Pulse generators. The way they interrupted muscle control in addition to causing pain was enough to take down an angry bull. He could hear the snapping, clicking sound of the electrical discharges.

There was nothing he wanted more than for the torment to stop.

After a five-second eternity, it finally did.

When the voltage abruptly cut off, the pain also vanished. When it did, Alex lay on his back, panting, trying to recover not just from the physical ordeal but the sudden shock of it. Mere moments ago he had been absorbed in painting the quiet beauty of a forest scene. Now he was flat on his back, disoriented, trying to catch his breath, and scared out of his wits.

He knew that a Taser could deliver countless hits. He moved his arms a little just to make sure he could, but not enough to look threatening. At that point, he didn't know what Bethany was capable of. He saw that she still had her finger on the trigger. With the darts already stuck in him, she had but to pull the trigger to deliver another charge. Until he decided what to do, he thought it best to do nothing and let her think he wasn't going to put up a fight.

Glaring flashes of lightning illuminated her figure standing over him. When the bright flashes flickered out and the rumble of thunder died away, only the faint light of the streetlamp off through the rain beyond the open door softly lit the curving edge of her figure.

"Hello, Alex," she said in a silky voice.

Alex thought that she looked remarkably calm. She looked like she had complete control and knew it.

"Bethany, what do you think . . ."

Two big men stepped out of the dark night and through the open doorway into his living room. A few cracks of lightning backlit wisps of vapor, like mist rising into the humid night air off the heat of their hulking forms.

Alex didn't recognize the men, but they certainly looked like a nightmare come out of such a night. He noticed that, despite the rain, none of the three was wet.

"Now, Alex," Bethany said, "if you know what's good for you, you'll be a good boy and not cause me any trouble—you've already caused me enough. If you're good, I think you will find this far more pleasurable than you ever imagined." She flashed him a self-satisfied smile. "And I bet you have imagined it often enough."

Alex couldn't make sense of what she was talking about. He wondered if a Taser could scramble a person's mind. He didn't think so. Everything else seemed ordered and logical. Up was up, down was down. He recognized her. It was only what she said that didn't fit into any context.

Bethany glanced briefly at the men. "Get him into a bedroom."

Alex couldn't imagine what in the world Bethany and the two men intended to do with him. But whatever they intended, he had no illusions that it was going to be anything other than bad. He wondered if Bethany, in her anger over his rejection of her, had hired a couple of thugs to beat him senseless.

He wondered if it could be something worse than a beating. He wondered if she intended for them to murder him.

Such a vendetta carried to the point of violence would be absurd, but people did absurd things all the time.

Ben had taught him that you had to consider any attacker as having deadly intent, because once you were dead it was too late to wish you had defended yourself. Alex knew that if he was to survive he was going to have to use his head. He knew that he couldn't afford to wait and hope for an opening.

He was going to have to make his own opening before things got any worse. He could not afford to be restrained.

The men stooped over him at a steep angle to lift him up. Alex feigned limp, groggy compliance. When Bethany glanced briefly toward the back bedroom, he acted.

In a sudden and violent burst of motion Alex whipped an arm around one man's head and used their off-balance weight to pull them both the rest of the way over. In the same instant that he clamped his forearm around the man's neck he grabbed his own wrist to lock his arms tight together and flexed his fist back, bulging the muscle in his forearm against the side of the man's neck, making the muscle hard in order to help shock the carotid artery.

He knew, though, that he wouldn't have the several seconds needed to bring the move to a lethal conclusion, so instead, as they plunged backward toward the floor, he planted his foot to break his fall. As the three of them came crashing down Alex added all his muscle to the man's falling weight, bringing the man's head down over his knee as if it were an anvil.

The man's neck snapped over with a loud pop. His muscular bulk immediately went limp, sprawling atop Alex's legs as they both hit the floor. The second man rolled and sprang to his feet.

Bethany spun back and pulled the trigger.

Alex instantly went rigid again as the voltage from the Taser hit him. He screamed under the agony of overpowering pain as his muscles shuddered uncontrollably. The man's dead weight lay sprawled over his legs, but even without the weight it would have been impossible for Alex to move his arms or legs the way he wanted, impossible to do anything. Despite monumental effort, his muscles would not respond. The electrical charge was in control of his body.

Bethany stepped close. He expected her to launch into an enraged lecture at the least. Instead, she appeared calm, as if she were accustomed to administering agony.

When the timed voltage from the gun abruptly halted, Alex sagged with a moaning sigh of relief.

Bethany gestured to the man with her. He understood and lifted the dead weight of the other man to get him off the coils of wire. Once clear, he let go of the man, allowing him to slump to the side. It wasn't hard to tell that the man was dead. From the corner of his eye, Alex watched, gauging the distance to the one still alive.

Alex had thought that the steel darts would pull out in the brief but violent battle. He was wrong. They were stuck fast.

When the dead man had been moved out of the way and safely off the wires, Bethany squatted down beside Alex. Her blond hair, lit by lightning, slipped forward over her shoulders.

"If you want to cause me trouble, Alex, I can keep pulling this trigger all night long. Is that what you'd like?"

Focused on trying to find even a fraction-of-a-second opening in which to act, he wasn't paying close attention to what she'd said. Fast as he could, he reached up to snatch the wire connected to the barb stuck in the left side of his chest in order to yank it out.

He wasn't even close to quick enough before she pulled the trigger.

Another lightning shock of pain crashed through him. She jammed the Taser down into his thigh, adding a third electrical contact to make the charge going through him all that much stronger. Despite how desperately he tried to move, to skitter away, it proved impossible. He cried out as tears of pain rolled down his face. He wanted to draw up into the fetal position. His arms and legs flailed, but not in response to his conscious direction. In that moment, Alex thought that he would do anything to make it stop. When it finally did, his screams again trailed off to a groan.

"If you want to keep trying to pull out the wires, go ahead, but I guarantee you that I can pull the trigger faster and I can keep pulling it all night. Is that what you want? I've already asked you once, Alex. Do you want me to keep pulling the trigger?"

Alex immediately shook his head. He desperately didn't want that. The ordeal already had him at the edge of exhaustion. His muscles were aching from the repeated strain. From what he knew of Taser guns sold to law enforcement, they advised that several hits were often needed to gain compliance from combative individuals.

He knew that as long as her attention was on him he wouldn't be able to move fast enough. Her finger on the trigger would beat any move he could make.

She smiled in satisfaction as she patted his cheek. "You look good, Alex. As good as I remember. I couldn't stop thinking of how hot you get me."

At first he thought she couldn't have said what he'd thought she said, but the suggestive smile she was giving him told him that he'd heard her right. Alex couldn't imagine what crazy scheme she was up to, but he thought he'd better keep his mouth shut.

"Now, Alex, I want you to be a good boy. If you are, this will all be over soon enough." She kissed the end of a finger and pressed the finger to his lips. "Don't worry, I'll make it good for you. Really, really good. You're going to enjoy it. I promise."

Alex couldn't keep from asking. "What are you talking about?"

She rested her forearm on her knee as she leaned closer in darkness punctuated occasionally with the harsh illumination of lightning. She arched an eyebrow. "Why, your birthday present, Alex. Don't you remember what I promised you for your birthday? Pretty little Beth always keeps her promises."

16.

THERE WAS A DEAD MAN lying next to him, there was another big man glaring murderously down at him, and there were two barbed steel Taser probes stuck in the flesh of his chest and abdomen. Alex couldn't imagine anything less conducive to romance.

"Bethany, you can't possibly be serious."

"Oh, but I am," she said with a wicked little grin. "Now, as I said, if you'd like I can keep pulling this trigger until you wish you were dead, even if it won't actually kill you. Sooner or later, though, the agony will be too much and you'll give in. Your other choice is to forgo the drama, accept what is going to happen one way or another, and just lay back and enjoy yourself."

She arched an eyebrow again. "What's it going to be, lover boy?"

Alex didn't want to agree, but he was sure that he didn't want her to pull that trigger again. When she lifted the stun gun, making a display of waggling it in front of him as she cocked her head in a questioning manner, he reluctantly nodded.

"Good boy." She rose up. "Get him in the bedroom," she told the man.

He reached down with a big hand, seized Alex's arm, and hauled him to his feet. The man spun Alex around, careful not to get tangled in the wires, and shoved him in the direction of the bedroom. Bethany warned Alex to keep his hands up and well away from the wires. He didn't try to stall or protest as they made their way down the dark hall. He was sure that any pleas would fall on deaf ears. She'd already proven that she could pull the trigger faster than he could snatch the wires.

Brief but bright lightning flashes made his two captives seem to be nothing more than a procession of garishly lit statues. Whenever the lightning died out they turned into unseen ghosts pursuing him.

As Bethany followed Alex through the bedroom doorway, lightning flickered again. Rain beat against the two windows like a thing alive wanting in.

"Nice," she said, glancing around in the sporadic fits of illumination. "Not what I'm used to, but nice."

More distant flashes of lightning lit her again, but less harshly. She reached out and ran a finger along the metal bedpost as she smiled. "I especially like the iron bed."

She gestured to the man. He shoved Alex to topple him backward onto the bed. The wicked steel barbs, still solidly lodged in the meat of his muscles and connected to the Taser by fine wires, were starting to hurt in earnest.

The man pounced on him, straddling his hips, using his weight to hold Alex down. He pulled out some beefy nylon zip ties, pressed one against Alex's wrist, and then looped it around a stout piece of the iron headboard. He stuck the loose end through the little ratchet block and pulled it tight enough to cut painfully into the flesh. Alex had used such ties before. He knew they could be cut without a great deal of difficulty, but pulling on them to try to break them would accomplish nothing except to cut his wrists down to the bone.

The man zip-tied Alex's other hand to the headboard, then bound both ankles together and fastened them to the footboard.

"Double them up," Bethany said to the man as she watched Alex's eyes, "just to be sure."

Alex fought back rising panic as the man added more ties to both wrists and his ankles. One tie would be impossible to break; more than one was meant to reinforce the message that not only did he have no chance to get away, but that Bethany was the one who dictated his fate.

Alex imagined that Bethany intended to torture him in some fashion before killing him. He fought back gnawing dread.

He could hardly believe that he had just killed a man. He wished he could kill the other one as well. He wished he could get his hands around Bethany's throat.

"That should do it," the man said. "There's no way he can break those."

Bethany again waggled her Taser as Alex watched. "Well, just in case he gives me any trouble, I'll leave the barbs in him. If he doesn't cooperate . . ." She shrugged as she flashed him a meaningful smile.

The man stood at ease behind her and folded his arms.

Bethany tilted her head, indicating the door. "Why don't you go wait outside. This is rather private business. I don't think having you as an audience will help him get it up."

Alex wasn't sure that he'd heard her correctly.

"All right," the man grumbled. "Just don't be long."

Bethany turned a glare on him in a way that seemed to cause him to shrink an inch. "Who do you think you're talking to?" she growled through gritted teeth. "How long have I planned, have I worked, have I waited? How dare you presume to tell me to rush through it? It takes as long as it takes.

"It only matters that I get what I came for. To that end I intend on staying here the whole night to be sure that when I leave I leave pregnant."

She planted her fists on her hips and leaned toward the man. "Got it?"

"Got it," the man answered in a contrite tone.

"Now, get out. I'll let you know when I'm done, then you can have your fun with him. You just wait outside until then."

The man nodded and then pulled a knife from a sheath behind his back. After he licked the blade he gave Alex a grim grin.

"When she's finished with you, then I settle the score for what you did out there in the other room."

As he left he turned once to glare back over his shoulder at Alex. Bethany watched through the doorway until the front door slammed behind the man.

She turned back, her tone becoming airy again. "Better, lover?"

"Why is it better? I still have to look forward to having my throat cut."

"Well," she said with a shrug, "at least you get me first. You should be thankful that it's me who found you and not Jax."

Alex's breath caught with the shock of that name. His mind reeled. Regaining his senses, he hoped that the flickers of lightning had hidden his reaction. He thought he ought to help cover his surprise by sending her off topic.

"Who's Jack?"

"Not Jack, Jax. Lucky for you I'm the one who found you first—I'll at least make sure you die with a smile. Jax would simply have bled you out."

"Why? Who is she?"

Bethany's smile ghosted away. "Jax is a diplomatic assassin."

Alex's brow tightened. "Diplomats are the opposite of assassins."

"No, no, dear boy, she's an assassin." Her gaze focused a million miles off. "A very special assassin, for very special targets."

Alex didn't want to believe her. But he remembered all too well the way Jax had pulled a knife on him, remembered how fast she had gotten it to his throat, though she'd had just cause at the time. He had, after all, just slammed her up against the wall and had his arm against her throat. He couldn't really fault her reaction. Still, Bethany's words gave him pause.

"Special targets. What do you mean?" he asked. "What kind of special targets?"

"Jax kills those who seek peace."

He finally grasped her meaning. "Like diplomats."

"Among others. She's a specialist. She is sent after only the most exceptional individuals, individuals, like diplomats, who are seeking unity, order, and prefer peaceful resolution to conflict."

In the softer flickers of lightning, Alex could see the distant look in Bethany's eyes, as if she were looking into another world. Dark animus colored her expression. "She'd love nothing more than to get her blade into me."

Alex said nothing.

Bethany's gaze, along with her smile, returned, almost as if to reassure him. "But she never will. I'm too well protected, even for Jax."

"Why would this very special assassin want to kill you?"

What he really wanted to know was what made her think she was so special, but considering his circumstances he thought better of phrasing it that way.

All the things Jax had told him about being from another world raced around in his mind, trying to find a proper fit with what Bethany was saying.

Bethany ran her fingers through his hair. It almost seemed a deliberate attempt to distract herself from what were obviously troubling thoughts of Jax. "Let's not worry about such unpleasantness. Let's just worry about you and me. This is a special night for both of us."

She leaned even closer, trailing a finger along his cheek. Her seductive tone returned. "Time for what Bethany promised you."

Alex couldn't see that he had any choice in the matter. He tried to think of a way he could get a hand free, but there wasn't anything within reach of his fingers. He knew that twisting his hands would accomplish nothing. Even if he tried she would use the Taser to take the fight out of him.

A thought he'd had before returned. If she was touching the steel darts when she pulled the trigger, the Taser would do the same to her as it did to him. He wondered if she knew that. He wondered how he could manage such a thing. He wondered what it would accomplish even if he could. Nothing, probably.

She had it all planned out. She was in control of the situation. When she was finished, the man with the knife would have his turn.

Bethany unbuckled his belt, then unzipped his pants and started tugging them down. When she had them down to his knees she smiled wickedly and slunk on all fours up the length of him.

Straddling him, she reached around with one hand and unzipped the back of her dress before pulling it off over her head. She wasn't wearing anything underneath. Everything the dress had advertised about what lay beneath the silver sheath was true.

"You spoiled this on your birthday, Alex, and caused me a great deal of trouble. I had to wait another whole moon until the correct time in my cycle came around again."

Things were starting to make sense to him. Crazy sense, but sense.

She leaned down to kiss him on the mouth. When he turned his face away she lightly kissed his cheek instead. "But now I'm told that I'm as ready as ready can be. I've had experts confirm that tonight's the night, lucky boy.

"Time to make an heir."

17.

ETHANY PRESSED HER NAKED THIGHS tight to either side of him as she leaned forward. She tenderly kissed his neck as he stared up into the darkness. He found her tender advances revolting.

He was enraged at being bound up and helpless. He was angry with himself for allowing it to get this far. He didn't know what else he could have done, but he should have done something. Worse, he didn't delude himself about what was in store for him when she had finished getting what she wanted. The mental image of the big man licking the blade before delivering his threat was not something Alex could easily put from his mind.

"Are you ready to take our relationship to the next level?" Her intimate whisper in his ear sounded as if she was ready. "Or are you going to need Bethany to help get you in the mood?"

The situation was so absurd that he couldn't find words. The only thing he was in the mood for was breaking her neck.

His sense of panic had already melted away under the heat of anger.

She leaned forward, pressing herself against him. Her firm breast pushed the steel barb harpooned into the left side of his chest deeper into the muscle. It felt like it was bottoming on rib bone. He gritted his teeth against the sting of pain.

As she nibbled his ear, caught up in what she was doing, Alex tried to pull away, tried to stall. "Bethany, why in the world are you doing this?"

"Why in the world." She laughed softly in his ear. "That's funny, Alex. Which world do you mean?"

The magnitude of her words shook him to his core. He wished he had believed Jax. He had thought her story was crazy. Now he wished he had listened to her. He remembered the last thing she had told him: "Trouble will find you."

It was the last thing his grandfather had told him as well.

Alex struggled to focus. "What I mean is, I don't know why you are doing this, since you can't seriously think that you're worthy of bearing my child."

That shocked her into sitting up—not what he had wanted.

Her brow tightened. "What?"

"You're hardly suitable. Let's face it, considering all of your un-desirable traits you're not really fit to bear a Rahl."

When the illumination of lightning flared in through the window he could see her indignant glower.

"Is that right?"

"If you weren't so stupid you'd know it is. My offspring deserves better than the likes of you for a mother."

"You arrogant bastard," she hissed. "You're wrong. You will give me a child—your heir—and I will be the one to guide him, not you. After you do this much of it there will be no further need of you. That child will be devoted to me. Your only part in his life is that you are going to father him."

He looked up into her eyes. "I'll see you dead, first. You have my promise on that."

"How dare you!" When the lightning cracked again he could see that her face had gone scarlet. "How dare you talk to me that way, you little bastard."

She lifted the Taser in her fist and pulled the trigger.

The shock of the high-voltage arc slammed into him. He couldn't believe how much it hurt. He flailed helplessly. The zip ties holding his arms ripped into the flesh of his wrists.

With Bethany sitting up, her skin wasn't touching the probes, so she felt none of it. She glared down at him as he screamed incoherent curses. She wasn't bothered in the least by his agony. She seemed incapable of empathy.

When it finished and he sagged back on the bed, she gave him a moment to recover before leaning over again to whisper in his ear. "We have all night, Alex. Would you like me to pull the trigger a few more times just to get it through that thick head of yours that I'm going to have my way? I would rather you just give in without all the drama. It really is getting quite tedious, you know."

In the darkness he could feel her belly pushing against the lower probe and her breast pressed firmly onto the other. When he didn't argue she writhed a little, rubbing herself against him seductively, as if to show him the benefits of her better side. His sweat from the ordeal made her skin slick. She started nibbling on his ear as she got down to business.

"You've got to be pretty stupid, Bethany, if you think that that fat ass of yours is ever going to get a guy hot for you. You're really making a fool of yourself trying to be sexy, if you want to know the truth of it."

That had the desired effect. She growled in rage and without bothering to sit up pulled the trigger.

She didn't realize that with her flesh touching the steel probes the Taser would give her the same paralyzing shock it gave him.

Through his helpless grunts of pain he could hear her cries of terrified torment. He'd known what to expect, at least. He'd known it was coming. The shock of it was far worse for her because she hadn't been expecting it.

Bethany didn't know what was happening to her. She screamed not just in pain, but in panic.

Alex didn't think she was all that familiar with technology.

In the throes of agony, her arms flailed. Alex heard the Taser hit the floor and bounce a few times. When the five seconds passed and the pain ended, she sagged limp atop him.

He decided that whatever her long-range plan was, he wasn't going to go along willingly. She would just have to pick up the Taser gun and pull the trigger all night long if that was what she wanted to do, but he wasn't going to cooperate.

As she regained her wits, she pressed a hand against his chest to push herself upright. With her other hand she swept her hair back off her sweaty face.

She looked down into his eyes. "Where I come from, that's nothing."

"It's nothing here, either," he lied.

A smile stole its way back onto her face. She lay back down against him, her warm breath in his ear again.

"I know what you're doing, Alex," she whispered, "but it isn't going to work. I'm not falling for your little ploy. I'm not going to let you get me angry enough to cut your throat. I came here to accomplish what needs accomplishing and I intend to see it through.

"Be as stubborn as you want, but it won't do you any good. You're going to get me pregnant tonight. There isn't anything you can do about it—it's just the way men are made.

"Afterwards, I'm going to use a knife on you myself and make sure that you regret every word you said."

In the darkness of the room lit only occasionally by flashes of lightning filtered through the sheets of rain, Alex felt the gloom of his situation settle back in on him. He had been momentarily euphoric that he had been able to trick her into getting a jolt from the Taser, but what good did it really do him? He wasn't going to be able to trick her into it again and he wasn't going to be able to free himself from his bonds.

It might have been satisfying to see her take such a jolt for a change, but it didn't stop her. He knew she was going to get even and then some.

He turned his gaze off into the darkness as he gave in to despair.

18.

ALEX THOUGHT OF BEN, and the lessons his grandfather had taught him. Ben had been in terrible, desperate situations. He had faced death. Those were the kinds of situations Alex's grandfather had wanted to prepare him for. Ben had wanted him to be prepared to face death with resolve, should he ever find himself in such a situation, in order to survive.

Ben had framed it in the mantra "Trouble will find you." It was a way of reminding him to always be ready, that trouble of any sort could come at any time. His grandfather had often said that trouble usually came when you were alone. Ben had been right.

Alex reminded himself not to give up. Ben had taught him better than that.

He decided that if all he could do was to make Bethany angry enough to kill him rather than follow through with her plan, if that was the only success he could have, then he was going to take that option. He didn't have only the choices she had given him. He didn't have to abide by her rules.

He knew that above all else he could not let her have what she wanted or in the end more people would die. He didn't know how that would come about, but he was certain of the eventuality.

This was not an absurd battle with a headstrong woman. This wasn't simply a matter of her wanting his child. This was something much bigger, something she and the people with her were willing to kill to get. This was something that he knew he couldn't allow her to win—even if it meant that he had to die to prevent it.

Jax had come to this world because there was something terribly wrong. She had said that to get here she'd risked being lost in eternal darkness. No one would take such a risk without a powerful reason. This was in some way connected with the trouble that had so concerned Jax.

She had been telling him the truth. If only he had believed her at the time.

Bethany impatiently reached down between her legs to grab hold of him. He held his breath.

"You might as well relax, lover boy. I'm going to have my way and you know it."

He didn't answer. He focused on how angry it made him that she thought she could have her way by trying to get him to give in to lust.

To divert his mind from Bethany, from the soft warmth of her, from her insistent attempt to engender that lust, he thought about the night Ben had died.

His mind drifted to thoughts about his mother locked away for the rest of her life in that awful place. She knew something about this, he was sure of it now.

Dread of what was going to happen to him when Bethany used a knife on him to make him regret his words also lurked in the back of his mind. He could imagine lying there with his arms and legs securely restrained as she started cutting him. He would be helpless. He knew that Bethany had no empathy for pain.

In light of such things, it wasn't hard to ignore her insincere cooing.

"I think I'm actually going to enjoy this," she whispered in his ear. "Make me enjoy it, Alex."

It wasn't at all hard to wish her dead.

In a distant flickering of lightning he saw her back abruptly arch. The movement caught his attention because there was something very odd, very unnatural, even alarming, about the swift, upward curving movement of her naked body and the sudden breath she sucked in.

He was about to hurl an insult at her in an effort to take her off track when another bolt of lightning crashed to ground not far away. As the harsh light coming in through the window fell across Bethany's face, Alex saw her blue eyes go wide. Thunder shook the house.

Before the light died out he thought he caught the glint of a blade.

For an instant he wondered if she had finally had enough of his resistance, if she had become enraged enough that she had decided to slaughter him right then and there in his own bed and be done with it. Visions of her stabbing him as he lay restrained and help-less ran in a sudden panic through his mind. Even though there was nothing he could do to stop her, he reflexively tensed for the expected thrust of a knife slamming down into him.

Instead, Bethany's chin lifted even farther as her neck curved back in line with her arched spine.

As the lightning flashed again Alex was stunned to catch just a glimpse of a fist holding Bethany's hair, pulling her head back. The odd, unnatural arch of Bethany's back and neck suddenly made sense. His immediate thought was that the man had come back in and had decided to take matters into his own hands.

A bloody blade swept around in front of Bethany's throat. It sank in deep as it was pulled from ear to ear.

Gouts of blood from severed arteries pumped out through the horrific gash. The fist held Bethany's head back. Her arms flailed weakly as her chest heaved, her breath bubbling out of the gaping wound with a scream unable to be delivered.

Lightning again flared and thunder rumbled. Founts of thick blood running from the yawning cut funneled down between Bethany's breasts. Her hands flexed, clutching weakly at the air to her sides. Her mouth worked as she tried to gasp for a breath. Bloody froth from her severed windpipe sprayed everywhere.

Alex was paralyzed by the sight of this woman in her death throes. The killing was so grisly it didn't seem real.

When light from the storm ignited in a long fit of flashes he could see Bethany blinking in confused desperation as she convulsed.

Her whole body went limp as her last breath of life gurgled from her failing lungs.

The fist holding her by the hair tossed her off the side of the bed. She hit the floor with a bony thud.

In another flash of lightning Alex saw Jax standing before him holding the blood-slicked knife.

She was gazing into his eyes as if there was nothing else in the room, nothing else in existence.

19.

YOU JUST WOULDN'T BELIEVE how long I've wanted to do that," Jax said in a voice that sounded better than he remembered, and he remembered it as mesmerizing.

Alex wondered if she could have hunted Bethany from another world and followed her to his bedroom in order to catch her without all of her protection.

"She mentioned something about that."

In a flicker of lightning he saw a hint of satisfaction curve her mouth.

Alex had wanted Bethany dead, and he grasped that she was involved in something that would result in harm to a great many people. She had promised the thug with her that he could cut Alex up, and then changed her mind and decided to do it herself just because he had insulted her. Still, he had never seen anything as gruesome as her death.

Jax must have read the look on his face because she addressed his unspoken thought. "Alex, it was quick. What she would have done to you with her knife would have lasted hours. In the storm no one would have heard you screaming and crying. She would have enjoyed your suffering."

Alex swallowed and nodded. He was relieved that she had put it in perspective.

"Jax—" He glanced to the rain lashing at the window. He turned a puzzled frown on her. "How come you aren't wet?"

"It wasn't raining where I came from."

He saw wisps of vapor, silhouetted by the flashes of light coming in the window, curling up from her arms and shoulders just as they vanished.

The last time he'd seen her she had basically told him that he was on his own and that she was going to go tend to her own business. She had warned him that trouble would find him.

He wondered why she'd had a change of heart. "What are you doing here?"

Her gaze was still locked on his. "We happened across some of what they had planned. I got here as fast as I could."

"I'm really glad to see you. I mean, really, really glad."

"Well, since you're finished with your sick little part in this coupling, pull up your pants and let's go. We need to get out of here."

"I didn't take any part in it, and don't you think that if I could pull my pants up I would?" When she didn't answer he signaled with his eyes toward his wrists. "Cut me free. Please?"

The thought of what Bethany had told him about Jax crossed his mind. Watching Bethany die in such a brutal fashion left him shaky and sick to his stomach. In his whole life he'd never seen anything so horrific. He was covered with splatters of her blood. Only moments before, her living, breathing body had been pressed up against him. Now she lay on the floor dead and he was covered only in her blood.

With the way Jax was staring at him, he wondered if he might be next.

At last withdrawing her gaze from his, she glanced up at his wrists. In flashes of lightning she could see that he was tied to the bed and finally grasped the reality of the situation. She looked back at him and at last smiled just a little.

"Sure."

As she bent close to him to cut the zip ties, distant flickers of lightning lit her growing smile. By the nature of it he thought that it revealed how happy she was about his helpless condition—not because he was helpless, but because it told her that he was telling her the truth that he hadn't been a willing part of it.

As she leaned across him to cut the tie on the far side, he caught a hint of her fragrance. It complemented everything else about her.

Alex would have given just about anything not to have been this close to Bethany. He would have given just about anything to stay this close to Jax.

"Thanks for coming, Jax," he said softly. "I guess I owe you one—in addition to an apology."

She paused to look down into his eyes from only inches away. She was pressed lightly against his chest. He could feel her steady heartbeat.

"I'm sorry I couldn't have gotten here sooner, Alex. I really am."

"You got here in time."

She slowly shook her head. "Not in time to save your grandfather."

Her words hit him like a blow. "You mean that Bethany had something to do with that?"

Jax stretched farther to finish cutting his wrist free, then straightened. "I wasn't there, but I was able to catch a glimpse through the mirror in his workshop. I saw Queen Bethany and I saw fire."

Alex sank back against the bed. He'd buried his grief, but hearing that Ben had likely been murdered not only resurrected the anguish, it also awakened a smoldering fury.

Ben hadn't died from natural causes. He would still be alive if not for Bethany. Maybe Ben would still be alive were Alex not somehow involved. But how could he have avoided being born a Rahl?

As Jax cut his ankles free, Alex yanked out the barbs and pulled up his pants. It was a great relief. She had the grace not to make a point of his embarrassing situation.

"Queen Bethany? What do you mean, 'Queen'?"

"In our world she was a queen. A very troublesome queen. She hurt anyone she didn't like, and she didn't like a lot of people. I had to come to this world to get close to her."

Her words caught him by surprise and reignited his sense of caution. He wondered if he had been part of some grand scheme after all—a scheme to assassinate a troublesome queen. He wondered if he had been nothing more than human bait.

"What's a queen from your world doing in my world?"

Jax considered him for a moment. "She apparently had some use for the House of Rahl."

"What use?"

Jax arched an eyebrow. "Don't tell me you didn't understand what she was intent on doing here tonight in this bed."

"I get that much of it."

Alex reminded himself to cool the heat in his voice. It wasn't her fault that Bethany had tied him to the bed and intended to kill him after she finished getting what she wanted. It wasn't Jax's fault that Bethany had murdered Ben.

He buckled his belt as he collected his thoughts. This woman had, after all, just saved his life. She could have just as easily let him spend the last few hours of his life being cut up by Bethany.

Somehow Alex couldn't think of Bethany as a queen. He could barely think of her as an adult.

"What I mean is that I don't know why she had a use for the 'House of Rahl,' as you put it. I don't know what's going on."

"We have that in common," Jax said under her breath as she glanced down at Bethany's corpse lying in a spreading pool of blood.

20.

ALEX PULLED THE PHONE out of his pocket. "I'd better call the police."

With his thumb he flipped it open. Jax snatched his wrist before he could dial. She used the tip of the bloody knife in her other hand to flip the phone closed.

"You're not going to alert anyone. The last thing we need is the authorities giving us trouble. We already have enough trouble. We need to get out of here, and we need to get out now."

He tried not to take too deep a breath, because the smell of blood was gagging him. "But the body is going to be found sooner or later. When it is, the police are going to think that I murdered her. I've got her blood all over me."

With a finger and thumb, as if to prove his point, he lifted his blood-soaked shirt away from his body for her to see. He wanted the sodden shirt off of him. He needed to change it. He needed a shower.

"If I run it will only make me look guilty. Attractive women who end up dead are usually killed by their husband or some other man in their life. The police will naturally think that I murdered her."

Jax glanced down at the body. "Did you really think she was attractive?"

"Yes—no—" Alex raked his fingers back through his hair. "Yes, she was obviously attractive, but no, I wasn't attracted to her."

"Calm down, Alex."

As he gathered his thoughts he realized that she was right. Calling the police would be a problem. What was he going to tell them? How could he possibly explain it?

"How in the world are we going to get rid of her body—and not be found out?"

"I'll take care of it," Jax said.

"There's blood everywhere!" He swung his arm around at the room. "You can't possibly clean up all this mess. The police have ways of finding even the tiniest speck of blood. They have technology that makes blood glow in the dark so that they'll still find the tiniest specks of blood that you miss no matter how well you clean it up."

"They're not going to find any blood, even with their technology."

Alex didn't think that she grasped how good technology could be or the way it was going to look to the police. He had dated Bethany. People had seen them together. She had been killed in his bedroom. She was naked. What else were the police going to think? He certainly couldn't tell them the truth, and lying would only get him in deeper trouble.

"Jax, they will find traces of blood, and then what am I going to tell them? That she was from another world? That she wanted to have sex with me so that I would get her pregnant with my Rahl heir and then she was going to kill me? They'll never believe me. I'd be lucky if they thought I was crazy, but they won't. They'll think I murdered her."

Jax gripped his arm. "Calm down, Alex. Let me handle it. I know what I'm doing."

"Let you handle it? In five minutes you're liable to vanish again." How could he tell her how much he feared being locked up? "You'll be gone again and I'll be left here alone to handle it."

"Not this time," she said in a somewhat haunted voice.

Alex looked up. "What do you mean?"

She gazed into his eyes for a long moment. "If I hadn't gotten here in time you would have been lost."

"Lost? You mean I would have been killed when she was finished?"

"Yes. I had to get here as fast as possible. I wasn't able to take certain . . . precautions."

"Precautions?"

"I had to forgo the procedures I used before."

"What procedures?"

"I didn't have time to establish a lifeline this time."

"A lifeline . . ." Alex paused a moment. "Do you mean that you can't get back to your world?"

Her gaze broke away. "Not for now."

He suddenly realized the magnitude of what she had done in order to save his life. His worry about everything else evaporated in his sudden concern for her. "When will you be able to get back to your home?"

"You let me worry about that. For now I'm stuck here."

"For how long?"

"Maybe a day or two."

"But maybe longer?"

She swallowed. "Maybe forever."

The lightning died out again, plunging the room into gloom lit only by the faint glow of streetlights, but it was enough to see the worry in her eyes.

"It's all right, Jax. You won't be alone. I'll help you."

She gestured with her knife to the still body on the floor. When lightning crackled again a flickering rectangle of light coming in the window fell across the curve of Bethany's naked hip. "Yes, I can see that you have everything well in hand."

Despite everything, Alex was able to smile just a little.

"Do you think your friends will send anyone to help you?"

She shook her head.

"Why not?"

"Because right now I'm the only one able to undertake such a journey. We're on our own."

He let out a deep breath. "Jax, I need you to know how sorry I am for the way I treated you the last time." He discarded the speech, the excuses, that he'd rehearsed in his mind a few hundred times. "You came to help me and I didn't listen. I didn't mean to belittle what you and others have done. I just didn't understand. It was so hard to—"

She lifted a hand to keep him from going on. "When I went back the last time I told people about some of the things I saw here, some of the technology I saw. They reacted much the same way as you. They didn't believe me, didn't believe that I had succeeded in coming to this world. Many of them thought I was making it up to cover failure.

"It made me realize just how hard it had to be for you. I suspect that were the situation reversed and were it you who had come to my world instead, I wouldn't have believed you, either.

"For now let's both try to be a little more understanding of the gulf between us. We need to help each other if we're to survive what is coming."

Alex didn't know what was coming, but he nodded. It felt as if a weight had been lifted from his shoulders, a weight that he'd been carrying since she'd left the last time.

Still, it was profoundly difficult to get his mind around the idea that this woman had actually come from another world.

"Where is this world of yours? Your home? Is it across the universe? In another universe? Through some wormhole in space that allows you to step out of your world and into mine?"

"I can only tell you that the place I come from is on the other side of darkness, on the other side of nothing."

"I don't understand."

"We don't either." She lifted a hand in a helpless gesture and then let it drop to her side. "There's a lot I can't explain. All I know for sure is that they are very different places, but at the same time they are very much the same. Right now, though, that's not our problem. Right now, our problem is that if we're going to find answers we first of all need to stay alive and to do that we need to get out of here."

Alex nodded. "What are we going to do with Bethany's body?"

"Send her back to my world," Jax said as she squatted down beside the dead woman.

When next the lightning flashed Alex was shocked to see Jax using the tip of her knife to cut strange symbols in Bethany's forehead. "What are you doing?"

"I'm sending her back to my world."

"But before you said this is a world without magic. How do you expect to do such a thing if there's no magic here?"

"She came here with a lifeline, the same as I did the two previous times. I'm merely activating it."

He gestured to the bed. "Jax, there's blood everywhere—it's all over me. Even if you get rid of Bethany's body, her blood is still going to be everywhere just waiting to be discovered."

Working at the grisly task, Jax spoke without looking up. "The blood is hers and not from this world. It will return with her." She looked up and grinned. "I wish I could be there to see their faces when I send their queen back to them like this."

As lightning flashed, the room lit for a moment in its harsh glare only to plunge back into shadows as a cracking boom of thunder shook the house. Outside, branches clattered together in the wind. Rain beat steadily against the windows.

Jax swiftly cut two more mysterious symbols. Despite Bethany being dead, blood oozed from the strange network of lines. Alex couldn't help taking in the design with an artistic eye, seeing the sense of movement in the lines' composition.

"There," Jax said to herself as she stood.

"There what?" In the harsh illumination of another flash of lightning he peered down at the dead woman. "What's supposed to happen?"

Bethany might have been beautiful in life, but in death, with the way the wound across her neck gaped open, she was grotesque. The sight turned his stomach. In the next flash of lightning he noticed a stab wound in her lower back. Jax's blade had been bloody when he'd first seen it. It dawned on him that she must have stabbed Bethany first to disable her.

As Jax stood, the flickers of lightning died out and the room again went dark. Rain thrumming against the window made the darkness feel altogether creepy.

When the lightning crackled again, there was nothing at their feet. No body, no blood.

Alex blinked in surprise and disbelief. Bethany was gone.

Just . . . gone.

"There," Jax said. "Feel better?"

"How did you do that?" he asked in shock, pointing at the empty place on the floor.

"I told you. I activated her lifeline to pull her back."

Unable to believe his own eyes, Alex backed up until he bumped into the bed. "No, I mean, really. How did you do that?"

He turned and in the next flash of lightning saw that the sheets were pristine white. There was no blood. Not a speck. He looked down at himself, then ran his hand over his clean shirt. There was no blood on it.

It was as if Bethany had never been there.

Jax leaned in. "Are you all right?"

Alex nodded dumbly. "It's impossible, but I saw it."

"I've told you every word true, Alexander."

He could only nod.

She let out a sigh. "This must all be hard for you, Alex. Later on maybe I can help you understand it better, but right now we have to get out of here." She cast him a suspicious look. "By the way, what happened to that fellow out in the other room, out near the door?"

"What—" Alex remembered then. "Oh, him. I broke his neck."

"Really?" Jax arched an eyebrow. "Well done, Alex. Well done."

"There were two. After I broke his neck the other one tied me to the bed. Then Bethany sent him out to wait until she was finished with me. He'll be out there in the rain somewhere, waiting."

Jax looked unconcerned. "I already took him out and sent him back. I need to send back the one you killed; then we can get out of here."

"Well, if the threat has been removed, maybe we don't—"

She gripped his arm. "Alex, we need to get out of here."

"You think Bethany's people might send others after us?"

"That, too."

He wondered what she meant. "How long will we have to be gone?"

She gave him a heated look, then relented a little, her expression softening. "Alex, you need to listen to me.

"Dangerous people have been coming here, to this world, for some time now. While I know some of what's going on, I'm in the dark about much of it. I don't think, though, that they're coming here for a holiday.

"Many innocent people have already died. This is a matter of survival for us. A matter of life and death.

"But that's my world, not yours. You enjoy peace here in your world. You have your own life. We believe that it's each person's right to choose to live their own life as they see fit. You have no obligation to help us.

"But if that's your choice then please tell me now. I don't have any time to waste.

"Someone from my world killed your grandfather and tried to kill you tonight. Your family has probably long been involved, possibly even been a target, though they've been unaware of it. Prophecy from my world suggests that you're involved in this. The Law of Nines confirms it.

"You can choose to ignore my warning. You can choose not to believe that prophecy from my world applies to you. You can choose to do nothing and see what will happen, to stay out of it and just worry about keeping yourself safe.

"You are free to run and hide, if you so wish.

"But when they come after you, and I believe they will, you will have to face it alone. I can't wait for you. I won't.

"You have to make a choice, not because I say so, but because of the things that are happening. No matter what you choose to do, nothing is ever going to be the same—not for you, not for me.

"I will respect whatever choice you make, Alexander, but I will not come back for you again. You will be on your own.

"If you choose to come with me, then you must understand that we're fighting people who don't belong in this world, and those people are killers. Make no mistake, if you choose to come with me, then you are choosing to fight them. The man you killed tonight will likely not be the last."

"But maybe we could get help, get the authorities to understand and to help us—"

"No. Their involvement would only end up costing more lives. Remember the two officers who detained those men when I first came here? Those officers ended up with their necks broken. If we call authorities to help us, those two will hardly be the last. I don't know who is here from my world, or even if some from your world might be involved."

He hadn't even considered that. "You think people in this world might be cooperating with those who have come here?"

"We can't ignore the possibility. Evil people, and those willing to help them, exist everywhere. We can't risk being betrayed. Our only safety lies in no one knowing about us.

"The authorities in this world wouldn't believe that there are people from another world among them. I don't have the time to try to convince them, and besides, I don't have any way to do so. I can't do magic here. I've already used precious time convincing you."

"But maybe I could help convince people—"

"No one will believe you. You have insanity in your family. They will assume you're crazy, too."

Alex knew that she was right. How many times had he questioned his own sanity since first meeting Jax?

"Your grandfather was one who knew that sometimes the best way to fight is a small covert force, not a big battle involving a lot of men."

"How do you know that?"

"We learned a little about him, that long ago he served with such shadow forces. Did he tell you some of it?"

Alex nodded. He stood in the darkness for a time listening to the storm rage all around, thinking about Ben's lessons.

"And if I choose to come with you, what then?" he asked.

"If you come with me you might have to face dangers I can't begin to guess. In my world I would know what to expect, but in this world I don't. We will have no help. Whatever comes we will be facing it alone. We very well might die."

"You make it sound pretty hopeless."

"I can promise you only one thing," she said with grim intensity. "If you come with me I will protect you with my life."

Alex blinked in surprise. "Why would you do that?"

"This is not the time to get into it, but know that I will lay down my life before yours is lost."

She had already saved his life. Her solemn oath seemed like a portent of some grim future lurking in the darkness waiting to envelop him.

"I could really use your help to try to figure this out," she finally said, "but I have to know that if you come with me you won't be a liability. A lot of people, a lot of lives, are depending on me. I won't risk my life lugging along dead weight. I need to know that if you come with me I can count on you."

He had protected her life the first time he'd seen her. He couldn't imagine ever allowing harm to visit her.

"This may not be a choice you want to make, Alex, but it is the choice you face. We have spent too long here already. Are you coming with me or not?"

She leaned closer in the darkness. "Decide."

Alex gazed into her eyes, feeling as if he could see into her soul. He had always had the vague feeling that he never really knew who he was. It had always seemed like he had been waiting for something. It seemed now like he had been waiting his whole life for this moment.

"I knew from the first instant I saw you tonight—when I saw that you had come back—that I'm in this with you. Something is going on, something I don't understand, but something deadly. This involves me. Somehow we've been thrown together from worlds apart. I can't turn away. I won't. I'm in this."

A small smile softened her expression. She reached out and gently grasped his arm, giving it a squeeze as if in sympathy for all the trouble that had found him, trouble she couldn't shelter him from.

Her voice turned intimate and gentle. "Let's go, then."

"Wait a second," he said as he hurriedly knelt down and threw the bedcovers back out of the way.

He reached under the bed, letting his fingers settle into the four tabs of the gun safe bolted to the floor. He pressed the proper sequence and the door popped open.

He reached in and pulled out the gun and all six spare magazines.

"What's that?" she asked.

"A Glock 17."

Jax frowned. "A weapon made with technology?"

"Yes, technology that will help protect us."

In the dark, he ran his index finger over the tab behind the ejection port, making sure that it was raised, indicating that a round was chambered. He always kept the gun loaded, but this was no time to find out otherwise.

"What makes the three dots glow?"

"Tritium. The sights are made with it so you can aim better in low light."

"In my world I can make a substance that glows much like that."

He noticed that she paid close attention to the weapon. He recalled how well she handled a knife. This was a woman who knew the value of weapons in staying alive. He retrieved the molded polymer paddle holster and pushed it down over his waistband. When he holstered the gun, the retention lock clicked into place. He threw on a light jacket to hide the gun, then took several boxes of hollow-point ammunition from a drawer and put them in the jacket pockets along with the loaded magazines.

He retrieved all the cash he had in the safe and stuffed most of it in his pockets. He handed some to Jax. She looked at it as if she were seeing some otherworldly secret.

"It's money," he told her. "We'll need money. You should have some on you just in case."

Without questioning, she folded the cash and slipped it into a pocket at her waist.

"We're going to need to get you some clothes."

"I'm wearing clothes," she said.

"Yes, but you kind of stand out in that black dress and cloak. If we're trying not to be found, then I think it would be best for you not to stand out. We need to blend in, be invisible among people."

She smiled. "Good thinking. Hurry, now. It would be bad if we were trapped here."

The whole idea of people from another world chasing them seemed like some crazy waking nightmare to him. At the same time, it felt more real than anything in his life had ever felt.

"Do you know who is after us?" Alex asked.

"Yes," she said. "Pirates."

21.

WAIT HERE UNTIL I MAKE sure it's clear and I start the truck," Alex said, gesturing out at his faded red Cherokee sitting in the drive.

Jax glanced back into the dark house from the kitchen doorway. "All right, but hurry."

She was clearly more focused on what might be behind them in the darkness. The intruders had come through the front door the last time. He wondered if she expected more of them to arrive and come up behind them through the house.

Alex carefully ducked his head out, took a quick look, then pulled back in. The rain wasn't letting up. He looked out a second time, checking the other direction. The Jeep was parked right outside in the driveway that ran along the side of the house.

"I don't see anyone," he told her.

She turned back from her survey of the darkness within. "That doesn't mean a lot. It's dark and hard to see in the rain. They could be hiding anywhere. But more than that, just because you don't see anyone right now doesn't mean they couldn't show up at any moment."

That was a disturbing thought. "Can they do that anywhere they want?"

"Theoretically, yes, but as a practical matter, no. Queen Bethany and her thugs knew this location. They came to this world right here, in this place. It only makes sense that others might have this point plotted as well."

"You mean that to come here you have to know specifically where you want to go?"

"Not exactly. It's not so much that it's a problem having to do with coming here as it is knowing specifically where you want to be when you get here. The worlds—yours and mine—are big places. Imagine if you were to go to my world, not knowing anything about it. How would you find me, one person, in that whole world, among millions of people? Coming here is one thing, knowing where you want to be when you get here is quite another."

"I see what you mean. Sounds like it must be difficult."

"When I was trying to find you the second time I watched the area of the art gallery because it was a place I knew you went. It was where we first located you and at the time the only known place I had for you. That's why we need to get away from your known locations."

"That complicates things."

"I didn't promise you it would be easy."

"I guess not."

With his index finger he absently pressed the release lever on the side of holster and lifted the gun just enough to make sure that it was clear. He let the weapon drop back and click into place.

"Best if we stick to the plan, then. You stay hidden in the shadows and keep a lookout until I start the truck. And pull the door shut behind you when you leave the house," he added. "I'd like to have a home to come back to one of these days."

Jax smiled sympathetically. "I know how you feel."

Alex slipped out the doorway and into the rain. It felt to him like stepping out of his old life and into a new one.

Everything felt new to him, different, as if he were seeing the world with new eyes.

It seemed he could feel each individual muscle in his body as he moved. He thought that he could have counted every cold drop of rain that fell on him. He was aware of the different sensations of the rain on his face, of it matting his hair, of it wetting his pant legs, and of it spattering on the backs of his hands. He could smell the wet dirt, the concrete, and the trees. He could hear the rain beating against the roof of the house, gurgling down the gutters, splashing in puddles, whispering against the leaves of the big maple tree at the rear corner of his house, and drumming on the metal panels of the Jeep. Clouds lit from within by lightning revealed their greenish, roiling shapes before going dark again. He could feel the thunder in the distance rumbling through the ground. Lightning flickered closer in the west, illuminating the glistening, wet scene in stark, colorless contrast.

All of his senses were firing. The world was not just new to him, but an alien place.

He swiftly unlocked the driver's door and popped it open only enough to turn on the interior dome light. He looked in the windows, checking that no one was hiding in the back. Once he knew the truck was empty he hopped in and hit the unlock button so that Jax would be able to get in on the passenger side.

When he turned the key in the ignition he heard only a click. His pounding heart seemed to skip a beat. He tried again, and again it only clicked. The starter was resting in a dead spot. He knew from experience that he could turn the key all night and it wouldn't start the engine.

Alex was furious at himself. He could hardly believe that he hadn't replaced the starter when he'd had the time. With everything surrounding Ben's death he had ignored the matter of the starter. The excuse was pointless. An excuse wouldn't undo the mistake.

Jax ran from the house to stand in the open door of the truck. "What's wrong? Does it always take this long?"

"It won't start."

"Magic is a lot more dependable than technology," she said as she leaned in a little under the shelter of the roof.

"Really? How's your magic working for you right now?"

She sighed when she realized she had no argument.

"I just need to roll it down the driveway to get it to start."

He always backed the truck up the sloping drive for just such an eventuality.

"I'll push it to get it going. I do it often enough. It will be fine. Run around and get in the—"

Alex looked up just as a dark form slammed full force into Jax from behind. The breath left her lungs in a grunt. The violence of the impact drove her onto Alex, knocking him back over the center console. The armrest jammed painfully into his kidneys. His shoulders were pressed down against the passenger seat, his neck bent at a torturous angle. In such an awkward position, the full weight of both Jax and the huge man atop her prevented him from drawing a full breath.

Time seemed to stop.

The growling man had a meaty arm around Jax's neck. Lethal

rage lit his dark eyes. He was only an instant away from twisting her neck and snapping it like a twig.

Alex held his breath against the strain of monumental effort.

His gun had already cleared the holster.

He drove his fist past Jax's head and rammed the end of the barrel into the man's left eye socket.

Without an instant's hesitation, before the man could react, before he could jerk back away from the gun, before he could snap her neck, Alex pressed the trigger.

The hot glare of the muzzle flash lit the inside of the truck. The sound of the gun going off was deafening. In the darkness Alex could also see the flash of the muzzle blast coming out the back of the man's head, lighting a cloud of blood, bone, and brain as the hollow-point round blew through. The recoil snapped Alex's hand back.

Most of the debris went out the open door, but some of it splattered against the inside of the windshield and side window in the back seat. The ejected brass shell casing ricocheted off the headliner, then pinged off the passenger window.

The instant the bullet tore through his brain, the hulk of a man went as limp as mud. He wasn't thrown back like in the movies; he simply dropped dead in place. The man, who an instant before had been a blur of ferocity, was suddenly stone still.

Jax gripped the bottom of the steering wheel for leverage and with a growl of effort arched her back. Alex helped push her up. The dead man slid off her back and down into a heap at the side of the driveway. One arm splayed over his head, as if trying to hide the ghastly wound.

Alex at last drew a needed breath. His ears rang from the sound of the gunshot. The gun had been right beside Jax's head when it had gone off. He hoped it hadn't deafened her.

He hoped, too, that the gunshot hadn't roused the neighborhood. On any regular, quiet night it would have awakened everyone within a couple of blocks, but with the thunder booming enough to shake the ground, a single gunshot was lost in nature's mayhem.

It had all happened so fast. The night was suddenly back to normal. The rain droned on. In a blink the killing was over and done with, a man's life ended.

Jax rubbed her neck with both hands as she twisted her head around experimentally. Blood dripped from sodden strands of her blond hair.

"Are you all right?" he asked, checking the darkness. "I was afraid that he might have broken your neck."

"He would have," she said, still catching her breath. "I guess that answers the question of whether or not I can count on you. Your Glock technology works pretty good."

"That's a Glock for you. Pull trigger go boom."

"Thank you, Alexander. That was quick thinking."

He nodded. "Just returning the favor."

He holstered his gun as Jax bent down to the dead man and swiftly began cutting symbols that Alex recognized as the same design she had cut into Bethany. Ordinarily a gory sight like the aftermath of such a shooting might have made him sick, but he was too angry to be anything but angry.

Jax stood as soon as she had finished. She was getting faster at it. It had taken mere moments this time. He supposed that practice at magic that invoked travel to another world was just like any other practice that helped make one faster, like drawing a gun and firing at a threat.

Somewhere between the sporadic flashes of lightning the man wasn't there anymore. It still seemed impossible the way he simply vanished. Alex glanced into the truck. The blood that had been splattered all over and running down the side of the dashboard was gone as well. It looked as if it had never been there, as if nothing had happened.

"Alex, we need to go. Men like that usually travel in pairs. The second will be here any—"

There was a soft thud to the air that Alex felt as a thump deep in his chest. For an instant it seemed like there was a dark smudge swirling in the air right beside Jax. As soon as he saw it, the indistinct, dark stain in the night changed into a vortex of vapor in the humid air.

The vapor almost instantly condensed into a shape.

Alex was already starting to draw the gun even as he could still feel the thump deep in his chest. The shape came into being before his weapon had cleared the holster. Jax was already spinning toward the threat.

There was no question in Alex's mind; he had just seen a man step out of another world and hit the ground running, charging at them out of the downpour. The vapor rising from his beefy arms evaporated into the rain as he came at them.

Before Alex could get the gun up and on target to fire, Jax spun, slashing open the man's abdomen.

As the man stumbled to a stop to stare down in shock at his insides erupting out of the long gash just as he had appeared in a new world, Jax rammed her knife up through his eye. The blade went in hilt-deep. It was as effective as the hollow-point round had been.

The man went down before he'd known what happened.

In the quiet whisper of rain, Jax looked up at Alex. "Like I said, usually in pairs."

Ben had always said that in close-quarters combat, a knife was often faster than a gun. Alex was a believer.

As she hurriedly squatted down to repeat her task of activating the man's lifeline, Alex holstered his Glock. "Let's get away from here before we find out they travel in quads."

Jax glanced up, giving him the oddest look. She then gestured. "You said that you had to push the, the . . . what did you call that thing?"

"Truck. I have to push it down the drive to get it to start," he said as he ducked in and released the parking brake. He leaned his weight into the windshield pillar to get the truck rolling. "Hurry with him while I get the truck started. When I do, jump in."

The truck rolled down the drive, picking up speed. Alex ran beside it, pushing, then when it was going at a good clip he hopped in and put it in gear. As he turned to the right out into the street, in the downhill direction, he lifted his foot off the clutch. The engine caught. He pumped the gas a few times to make sure it wouldn't stall, then put it in reverse, spinning the wheels on the wet pavement as he backed to the drive. Jax ran down the driveway to meet him. The second man was gone.

Alex rolled his hand, urging her to hurry.

Jax pressed up against the door. She slapped the palms of her hands against the passenger window as the truck started rolling forward.

"Alex! Wait! How do I get in?"

Rather than try to explain where the handle was and how to push the button, he leaned across and popped open the door. The woman had opened a doorway between dimensions or worlds or something, and yet she couldn't open a truck door.

Jax jumped in. "Sometime you will have to teach me how to do that on my own."

As he shifted into second, leaving his house in the distance behind, he noticed that she had a death grip on the console and the door's armrest.

"Do we have to go so fast?" she asked in a breathless voice.

Alex glanced down at the speedometer. "We're only doing thirty."

"Can you make it go slower, please?"

For someone who had just gutted a man three times her size and given him a lobotomy for good measure, she suddenly seemed pretty squeamish. He guessed that he was starting to feel pretty squeamish himself. He slowed down a little to let her get used to the sensation.

With her blond hair plastered against her head she looked half drowned. He noticed, too, that her hair was no longer stained with blood. Her wet dress was a shambles from the brief battle. Seeing her alive, though, he doubted that she could have looked any better to him. At least she also looked like she was starting to relax, if only a little.

"I'm sorry, Alex."

"About what?"

She waited until he looked over at her. "That you had to kill that man."

"I'm just thankful that he wasn't able to hurt you."

As they raced away slowly down the street, he noticed her hands fisted in her lap. She looked like she wanted to pound rocks.

"What's wrong?"

She stared off through the passenger window. "I should have been paying more attention. It's not like me to be so careless. I almost got us both killed."

Alex was angry as well, but for a different reason. He was still in the grip of rage—rage at a man who had tried to hurt her and had come so close to doing so.

"Don't be so hard on yourself. We're both alive and they're both dead. That's what matters."

"Not to me," she said under her breath as she looked away. "I didn't come here to be stupid." He could detect a catch in her voice when she said, "People are depending on me."

"Jax, look at me." Reluctantly, she did. "We survived. I don't think those people depending on you would give you points for style. They'd only care that we survived so that we can find out how to stop this."

She smiled a bit at last. "You're right. We survived. I would lecture you for being so sloppy, Alexander Rahl, but I was no better. Let's hope that we both are more careful so that the next time it isn't nearly so close."

He returned the smile. "Deal."

22.

ALEX SLOWED AS HE TURNED the truck into the well-lit parking lot. Even in the middle of the night it was half full.

"What is this place?" Jax asked.

Alex pointed off to the right. "That's a gambling casino over there. Gambling isn't legal on land, but it's allowed on boats, so they build the whole place on big barges and tie them to docks at the edge of the river."

"Do you spend time at this place?"

Alex knew what she was getting at. He remembered her admonition about places he was known to frequent. He had been afraid, though, that if he simply parked in a strange neighborhood or an empty lot they would draw unwanted attention.

"I know of it, but I've never been here before."

She pulled a strand of hair back off her face. "Good."

"This place is always busy, so we won't look suspicious parked here. We can pull the cargo cover over the back and sleep under it.

It will be cramped, but it will keep us out of sight for the rest of the night."

"I'm not so tired. I'll stay up and stand watch."

Alex shot her a look. "Stand watch? Anyone sitting in a parked car might attract attention. You, in that dress, with that long blond hair, this time of night, are bound to draw a crowd. That's the last thing we need."

"I look a mess," she said as she glanced down at her dress. "Besides, I wore this dress so that I wouldn't draw attention."

"Trust me," he said. "A crowd."

Out of the corner of his eye he saw her start combing her fingers through waves of her damp hair, trying to coax it back into place. Alex thought that her disheveled condition somehow made her look all the more alluring. He had always thought that if he saw a beautiful woman with her clothes and hair in disarray and he still thought she was beautiful, then she truly was beautiful. Jax was more than that. She was gorgeous.

A thought he definitely didn't like crossed his mind. He wondered if her looks helped her get close to men she intended to kill.

He forced his thoughts off of how attractive she was and pulled into a parking place between a couple of minivans. They would make the Jeep harder to spot for anyone looking for it. Centered between towering light poles, it was as dark a place as he could manage in the casino lot.

He knew that casinos had cameras that watched their parking lots, but as long as no one approached his Cherokee he doubted there would be any reason for security to notice them. People darted through the rainy night, hurrying to get to their cars or into the casinos. He hoped that none of those figures hidden by shadows and rain were looking for him and Jax.

Once he had turned off the wipers, with the way the rain was coming down, it was hard to see much in the blur of water flowing down the windows. Alex gestured off to the left.

"Over there are some outlet stores. We can get some more clothes there, but they don't open until morning."

She gazed into the distance where he pointed. "Morning is still hours away."

"So we'd better get what rest we can."

"But I—"

"Didn't you say that you weren't paying good enough attention and you almost got us killed? You need sleep to stay alert."

Jax sighed. "I suppose you're right. Maybe we should try to get some rest while we can."

Rather than go out in the rain and get wet going in through the tailgate—and risk being watched by security—they both climbed over the seats into the rear cargo area. With the way the rain was coming down he was pretty sure that any security camera that happened to be pointed in their direction wouldn't be able to see anything inside the Jeep.

Alex kept a blanket and a small duffel bag filled with emergency gear in the back. He spread the blanket over the floor, then pulled the cargo shade over them and hooked it in place. Once it was secure he turned on a small LED light from the bag. It wasn't bright, but in the confined space it was more than ample. Jax watched him as he squirmed out of his jacket.

"Lie down," he told her.

She didn't object. He put the duffel bag under her head for a pillow, then draped his jacket over her, covering her as best he could. She had to pull her knees up to fit in the small area.

"Thanks," she said as she watched him.

Alex nodded as he leaned back against the wheel arch. It wasn't very comfortable, but he found it far preferable to being someplace where guys from another world could suddenly pop up and break his neck.

Once they were settled he turned off the light. Yellowish lamplight from the tall poles leaked in around the edges of the cargo shade. The rain running down the windows made the light waver softly on her face. She was still watching him.

"We need to figure out our next move."

Alex shrugged. "Maybe not. Maybe it's over."

Her face was a picture of incredulity. "Over?"

"Maybe we've finished it, tonight. Bethany is dead. Once they all realize that they've lost their leader, isn't it likely they'll quit? Maybe you've already accomplished what you came here to do."

Jax twisted a thread sticking out from the edge of the blanket for a moment as if trying to find words, or maybe trying to decide how much she wanted to tell him.

"I can see why it would seem that way to you, Alex—I really can—but it's more complicated than that. Queen Bethany wasn't the real problem."

She certainly had seemed like a problem to Alex. "What are you talking about? She came here from your world. You said that they have probably been interfering with my family for a long time. She killed Ben—you said so yourself. She wanted a Rahl heir for herself, and then she planned to kill me." Alex folded his arms. "She even had some guy buy my paintings and ruin them."

"The man who did that had no connection with her."

Alex frowned. "How do you know that?"

"Because when I was looking for you through the mirror in the gallery I saw the man who ruined your paintings. His name is Sedrick Vendis. He had nothing to do with Queen Bethany."

"Sedrick Vendis? Who the hell is he? And what do you mean he had nothing to do with Bethany? What's this all about?"

Jax lifted a hand, urging him to calm down. "Queen Bethany was on the same side as these people, but lately she's been operating outside of areas where she belonged."

"You lost me."

Jax sighed. "Bethany was a petty queen, but she was ambitious, so she aligned herself with powerful people. In the course of helping them she apparently learned about you and saw an opportunity for herself. Somewhere along the line she hatched a scheme to gain more power. She snuck here behind their backs.

"The people who have been coming here, who have caused your family trouble, the people who are endangering both our worlds, weren't aware of what she has been up to. If Sedrick Vendis had known that Queen Bethany had taken to meddling—especially if he had known what she was trying to do with you—he would have killed her himself."

"So who is this Vendis character?"

"He's the right-hand man to Radell Cain, the real power behind all the trouble. I could hardly believe it when I saw Vendis here that day. It's a bad sign that Vendis himself would come here, and that he was that close to you. Vendis is the one Cain sends to do his dirty work."

"What do you mean about them endangering your world? What's Cain after?"

Jax sighed. "Power. In the end it's nothing more complicated than that. Just like other people throughout history, he lusts for power. He doesn't care what or who is destroyed in the process, as long as he gets what he wants. It's hard to believe, but deaths in the millions mean nothing to men like that. They only care about power for themselves.

"For the longest time we had peace and prosperity. People valued hard work and achievement. Most of us had a sense of the goodness of life. Over time, though, those kinds of things came to be seen as outmoded by more and more people who felt entitled to prosperity without effort. They resented being told that their desires were a recipe for ruin."

"You mean they blamed the messenger."

Jax nodded. "There are always people like Radell Cain who are ready to take advantage of public resentment. He played on people's emotions by blaming everything on those who were still productive and prosperous, saying that they were uncaring and insensitive. People swooned at Cain's simplistic, populist notions. He made what was really nothing more than simple greed sound somehow morally righteous. He made taking what others had worked to earn sound like justice. People ate it up.

"In the middle of unrest and difficult times, Cain won people over with promises of change—a new vision, a new direction. He made change sound like a miracle solution to all our problems. People mindlessly embraced the notion of change."

"I guess people love hearing that nothing is their fault," Alex said, "that other people are to blame for their troubles."

Jax nodded. "For a lot of people it beats hard work and personal responsibility."

"So, what was the great change that Radell Cain wanted?"

"He made magic into a scapegoat. He said that it tainted everything it touched because it was unfair. So, to solve all our problems, he called for bold change: a world without magic."

Alex shrugged. "I live in a world without magic. What's wrong with that?"

"But you live in a world with technology. In many ways technology and magic are interchangeable. You could almost make the case that for all practical purposes they're really the same thing. Most of us don't really understand the complexities of magic, like with my journey book, we simply use it. In your world there must be people who understand the complex technology of phones, but I bet that most people using phones don't really know how they work.

"Technology, like magic, helps everyone live better. It doesn't merely help you to survive, it helps you to be prosperous and healthy, to live longer, to live better. But because magic is used by everyone, and actually understood by so few, that knowledge has become distrusted and viewed as somehow sinister. Radell Cain plays on those common fears."

"How is it that you know so much about the technology we have and yet you didn't know how to make tea?"

"We've studied things here as best we could, learned what we could, but it's only a dim overview captured in small snatches. We partially grasp the great sweep of how technology applies to life here, but we never understood all the details.

"We know, for example, that you somehow use cars and trucks to help you get places, deliver food and goods, but we don't understand how those machines work. We know they're important only because we see them all the time. We've seen people talk on phones, and while we never understood exactly what they were, we got the general idea. We once saw a red vehicle arrive to help an injured person, saw hoses and boxes and strange technology used to save their life. While we don't know what was being done or how it worked, we grasped that it was something like a healer in my world would do.

"What little we know is mostly a result of trying to learn about the Rahls in your world as we tried to figure out what Radell Cain is after, here. During that search we saw things, learned a little about the technology you use. Our view, however, is profoundly limited. It's like a deaf blind man trying to recount a visit to a new place.

"While our tools are limited, we did the best we could. It took decades just to isolate the Rahl line here. That's why I know a little about your grandfather's history and how technology is woven into your lives. We know a few random, isolated things. Making tea just wasn't one of them."

"So you're saying that what Radell Cain wants to do in your world is the equivalent of stopping us from using technology?"

Jax nodded. "It's not the same, exactly, but it's a good enough comparison. And he doesn't merely want to stop people from using it—he wants to entirely strip the world of it, take it entirely out of existence. He paints it as a utopian world."

"Do you think it would be as bad as you fear?"

"Some of us understand exactly what it would mean for us, and we're terrified."

"Why?"

"Well, imagine life here without technology. Imagine life without the technology that heats your buildings, helps grow food in abundance, makes your lights glow. What would your lives be like without your phones, your trucks, your medicines and cures, without the means to supply the people in your cities with goods and services?

"Imagine all the people in cities deprived of every kind of technology, technology that they use every day to survive. Imagine everyone suddenly having to find a way to grow their own food, to preserve it, to store it safely."

"People are pretty ingenious," Alex said with a shrug. "I'm sure it would be hard but I think they would cope."

"Cope? Think of the reality of your world, tomorrow, suddenly stripped of your technology—no phones, no computer devices, no way to find out anything. Think it through, Alex.

"Without your technology the fabric of civilization itself would come apart within days—if not hours. Everyone would be on their own. One city wouldn't know what the next was doing, or if they were even alive. There'd be no planes or cars or anything else. You couldn't travel to other places unless you walked. Do you have any idea how long it takes to walk just a few dozen miles? A distance that in your cars takes a brief time would be days of hard travel on foot.

"There would be no way for people to know what had happened to their far-flung loved ones. No one would know what had happened to their government. No word would come about anything. Everyone—everyone—would be in the dark, literally and figuratively. You would all be sitting there with no phones, no electrical devices, no heat, no way to get anything or summon help. Your world would fall silent.

"It wouldn't be long until supplies of food started to rot and run out. How long would it be until roving gangs started to loot what they wanted? Who would stop them? How would the police know when and where crimes were being committed? How would they hear anyone cry for help? How would they get there? Law and order would quickly become a thing of the past.

"When it turns cold, then what? Millions of people will rush to cut wood to try to keep warm, that's what. Makeshift fires used to keep warm will inevitably get out of hand. Your technology to fight the fires would be gone. Once fires catch hold, they will rampage

176

unchecked, growing to firestorms that will gut cities and leave tens of thousands homeless.

"Disease will spread like a plague with no means to stop it. Life will be not merely cheap but short.

"When all the food is gone you will begin dying by the millions. Those still alive will not have the strength or the will to bury all the dead. In the end, in the grip of starvation, the living will eat the dead.

"The only law will be survival.

"Those who once held idyllic notions of how simple and clean life would be without the demon of technology—like those in my world who believe the same thing about life without magic—will die filthy, terrified, and confused. Their idealistic notions will crumble in the cold face of reality. Like those in my world, they will be unprepared for the consequences of their pompous beliefs.

"What before had been simple will become tremendously difficult or impossible. The ignorant, the frightened, the weak, the criminal, will defecate in runoff areas, in streams, and in rivers, wanting their waste to be washed away. They won't care about anyone downstream. Finding water will be a monumental chore. Finding clean, disease-free water will be impossible.

"Sewage and garbage will lie in the open. Vermin will multiply into a nightmare of filth. The stench of human habitation will be unbearable, but you will live in it, sleep in it, have sex in it, bear children you cannot care for in it. Without technology, the product of your minds, mankind will be marked by the stench of sickness and death.

"Schools, of course, will be a thing of the past. Learning will be stopped in its tracks; knowledge will wither daily. Survival itself will be an all-consuming struggle. As people die in droves the aptitude for technology, the skills, the expertise that was so common and taken for granted, will be lost. Without it your world will plunge headlong into the depths of a bottomless dark age of filth and misery. Millions upon millions of lives will be cut short as they are born into profound ignorance, abject poverty, backward superstition, and the rule of the most brutal.

"That is the reality of a world without technology—brief lives of unimaginable misery, filth, and savagery."

Only the rain droning on filled the sudden silence. Jax sat quietly for a moment, letting it all sink in, letting the horror of understanding settle over him.

Alex knew that the Dark Ages had been a time much like she described. The knowledge built up by past civilizations had been lost as mankind plummeted into a black abyss. Survival was such a struggle that there were stretches of centuries about which next to nothing was known. That mankind emerged in the Renaissance was a testament to the nobility of the human spirit. It was only when mankind rose up and began to develop technology to shape the world that light came into their dark existence.

But it had taken a thousand years for that light to return.

"That is what Radell Cain's ideas mean to our world, Alex," she said softly. "That will be our fate. We will be stripped of everything we've made of our world and our lives."

Alex sat sobered by such a description. He'd never really considered the far-reaching ramifications of such a thing. He now realized that Jax had. If anything, she was painting a kinder picture than what would be the horrifying reality.

If technology were suddenly taken away, the suffering and dying would be beyond imagining. Without all the factories and common technologies that people whined about, they'd be lucky to be able to grub enough worms to keep them alive.

Alex gestured vaguely. "You could use technology instead—build things, make things, create the things you need—just like we did. Mankind here developed what we have from nothing."

She cast him a reproachful look. "And how many millennia did you live in a world of darkness lit only by fire?"

He knew she was right.

"It took the people here centuries to create, invent, and discover things to improve your lives. We, too, have spent countless eons developing parallel abilities that enable us to live without suffering the most common afflictions and wants. We use those abilities to tell us the best time to plant, the best time to harvest. Without those methods, thousands would starve. There are endless examples of how abilities developed over a long history help us live—help us live in an unnatural and evil way, according to Radell Cain.

"Because he wants to rule, because he needs something to blame simply so that he can gain power, everything we have will be forever lost, and once lost, it can't be recovered."

"But why would Cain want to do that? He would rule a wasteland."

Jax arched an eyebrow. "You just said it. He would rule. He is willing to lay waste to civilization just to gain immense power for himself.

"If he really cared what became of people under his rule he wouldn't incite such hatred for values, hold the victims responsible for the crimes against them, and shift blame to the innocent when-ever anything goes wrong. He would work to solve problems instead of using them to seize complete power for himself.

"After Cain gets what he wants, no one will be able to challenge him. He will rule the world—a cold, dead, starving world—but he will rule it nonetheless, living in lavish excess with all the trappings his heart desires. What little of everything there is, he will control. That's all that really matters to him. He is a man completely without empathy for others. It only matters to him that he gets what he wants. If a few million die he doesn't really care—the dead don't eat."

Alex stared off as he listened. "It seems impossible to believe that people would go along with such a thing."

Jax sighed. "I know. It's hard for us to believe, too, but every day people willingly undergo a process called 'the Cleansing' to remove any gifted ability—that means magic. Afterwards, after this rebirth, the magic they were born with and learned to master is forever gone. They tell other people that they feel free for the first time in their lives and pressure them to give up their 'tainted' abilities as well. Crowds wait in lines to have it done, to go along with everyone else, to prove their virtue."

Jax looked away, her eyes filling with tears. "That's the worst part, that so many would not value their own unique abilities, not value themselves, much less respect those who have fought and died so that they could live free to make the choice to surrender that precious right of choice—along with their gift and their individuality."

She gripped the blanket in a fist. "I often think that they deserve everything they're going to get. I only regret that those of us who value what we have will suffer the same fate. They're the ones I fight for. The rest of them be damned."

Alex swallowed at the pain so clearly evident in her voice. "We have people like that in our world, too. People who say that freedom is no longer practical, that we must surrender it for a greater common good."

"Fear them," she whispered. "They are the heart of evil. They tolerate tyranny, excuse it, compromise with it. In so doing they always bring savagery and death upon the rest of us."

Alex listened to the rain drumming on the roof for a time. There was something about the power in her voice, the fierce intensity, the conviction, the passion of purpose, that added to his impression that this was no ordinary woman. This was a woman who knew what she was talking about.

This woman was not a follower of anyone. She was a leader.

"If Sedrick Vendis is Cain's right-hand man, and important in his own right, then why would he travel to this world and buy my paintings just to deface them?"

Jax glowered with dark thoughts for a moment. "I don't know," she said at last. "At the time I thought it seemed rather strange, to say the least."

"So," he finally asked, "you really think that Radell Cain wants something from me?"

Her eyes turned back up to lock onto his gaze. "The Law of Nines says that you are central in this."

He didn't budge from her steady gaze. "Bethany told me that you're an assassin, and that you would kill me."

23.

JAX DIDN'T SHY FROM THE QUESTION. "If I came to kill you, then why aren't you dead?"

Alex didn't like her evasive answer. He chose his words carefully, but kept it simple and sincere. "Back at the house you said that if I came with you, you had to be able to depend on me. I deserve no less, Jax. I think you owe me the truth."

"Now you sound like a Rahl," she said.

His voice took on an edge. "I am a Rahl."

She let out a long, deep breath and looked away from his eyes again.

"Well, the truth is I did come here expecting that I might end up having to kill you."

Somehow, that didn't surprise him, but it did surprise him that she so freely admitted it.

"But you said that I'm the one named in this prophecy of yours—"

"It's not my prophecy. It's an ancient core prophecy, well known in certain circles."

"Well, if I'm the one the prophecy pertains to, then why in the world would you want to kill me, and why am I not dead?"

"You are not dead because I chose not to kill you."

Alex decided to wait for her to explain. She picked at a loose thread on the blanket for a time before doing so.

"The prophecy says, 'Someday, someone born not of this world will have to save it.' That's all that it says.

"Short prophecy, such as this, is often the most troublesome and the most dangerous. While it may sound simple, you can't assume it is.

"Since it's so obviously important, the prophecy has been studied extensively, but it still remains one of those great unsolved questions that frustrate the experts. From the beginning it's been a prophecy associated with the House of Rahl.

"In certain circles it has been known for just as long that there are members of the House of Rahl in this world who—"

"How could there be members of the House of Rahl in your world and in my world? They're separate worlds, separate places, maybe not even the same universe or dimension. How can there be the same line of people in both worlds?"

Her eyes had a timeless look of authority, or perhaps wisdom, about them. "Because your ancestors and the ancestors of a great many other people here once lived in my world."

Alex stared at her. He wasn't even sure that he had heard her correctly.

"That's impossible."

Her serious expression was unwavering.

"The ancestors of people here at one time lived in my world. This world was born from mine, or at least some of the people were."

He had seen things that proved she was telling the truth that she had somehow traveled here from some other place, or time, or dimension. But this? This was just plain crazy.

Alex realized then that maybe he was taking her too literally.

"You mean that ancient stories say this. That it's a legend, a myth, some kind of Dark Ages fairy tale."

"It's the reason that there are Rahls in both worlds—or, at least there used to be. There are no longer any Rahls in my world. At one time they were only in my world. Long ago some came here, to this world, to start new lives."

He thought then that he could see how the whole thing had started and how it might have come to be misunderstood. "All right, I get it. All you're really saying is that long ago some people named Rahl came to this world, much like you came to this world, and started lives here living among the people here. That's why there are Rahls here. The Rahls here are descendants of a few people who once traveled here—sort of like you did."

"No, it's more than that. History says that long ago our world was engulfed in war. There were many people who didn't want magic in their lives—didn't want it to exist. They believed it was evil. They were adamant that they wanted to live in a world free of it. They were willing to die for that cause. They were unwilling to allow anyone with magic to live free. They were unwilling to allow anyone with magic to live at all.

"Because there could be no peace with them, because they refused to coexist peacefully with the gifted, because they were fanatically committed to killing any gifted and wiping magic from existence, they were granted their foolish wish to live in a world without magic. But they weren't allowed to undo our world. They were all banished here, to a world where magic didn't exist."

"You mean, they didn't want magic back then, either? The same as now? The same problem all over again?"

She paused for a moment, thinking. "No, it's not the same. Before, it was a movement, a fundamental religious belief that was larger in its scope. It was a fanaticism that would not tolerate any other point of view. They believed that this was the will of the Creator and that they would be rewarded in the afterlife for killing the gifted.

"Now it's nothing more than a cynical ploy Radell Cain is using to cover a grab for power. Tyrants don't want their subjects to possess weapons. Eliminating magic takes a weapon away from anyone who might resist. That's what Cain is really after—taking away the ability of people to resist his rule.

"Those who didn't want magic back then got their wish; they were sent here. Some of the Rahl line who weren't born with the gift chose to also come here to start new lives."

"So we're aliens? Our ancestors traveled here from your world?"

Her nose wrinkled as she thought it over. "They didn't exactly 'travel' the way you're thinking, the way I did or the way Cain and his people do. The worlds were said to have been joined together—at least for an instant they were at the same place at the same time—then they split apart, with the people who wanted to live without magic left in this world. I don't know how many were banished, but vast numbers, well over half the people in our world, were gone after the parting."

He thought the whole idea was too far-fetched to take seriously, but he decided not to debate it for the moment. Instead he asked something else.

"How long ago is this supposed to have happened?"

"Our scale of time might be different from yours, so I can't be certain, and we have only the bones of history left, but that history suggests that in our world it was long ago.

"There would be virtually no record of the event here in this world. The memories of the people who came here degraded. The breakdown of memory was part of the process. The loss of magic would have been for the most part instantaneous, though some of it might have lingered for a short time. After a while it would have faded, along with any memories of its origin.

"It would have been a very dark and terrible time for those who came here. Even starting a fire, which with our ability is simple, would have been a struggle.

"As a result, generation upon countless generation would have lived in savagery and ignorance that would have been ruled by superstition and hardship. Recording events would have been a luxury beyond the scope of people struggling just to survive another day. There would likely be no real record of it here.

"The era would now seem a black hole in your history."

"So that's why we don't have magic and you do?"

"Yes. Your ancestors—like mine—were people who lived lives with magic as a routine part of everyday life. The difference is that the people in our world still have their magic; the people who came to your world don't."

Alex wiped a weary hand across his face. He tried his best to keep the impatience out of his voice. "I guess that I can imagine that there is magic in your world, Jax. It's a different place. For all I know, the laws of nature could be different there. But here things don't work that way. It isn't just that magic doesn't exist here—it can't exist here. The laws of nature don't permit such a thing."

He had almost said "such a silly thing" but restrained himself.

"So?"

"So, I can't believe that it was ever part of reality for the people of my world."

"It wasn't, once they were here." Seeing that the answer didn't satisfy him, she looked up, thinking for a moment before asking a question. "You don't have have wizards, witches, sorceresses, dragons, or magic here in this world?"

"No, not real ones."

"Then why are those things part of all cultures, all peoples, throughout your history? Why do different people in different places in different times speak of them? Why do they even have the words for things that can't possibly exist?"

"It's just ancient legend, myth."

Jax arched an eyebrow. "Why has this myth always been basically the same in every culture, in every corner of your world? Why do they all have the same words for the same imaginary things—myths—that can't exist? Where do you suppose such common myth was born?"

Alex didn't have an answer.

She leaned closer. "It was born in my world. The reality was left behind in my world. Why is magic such a universal part of your language, your culture, even though it does not exist here, cannot exist here? Why?

"Those who came here could bring with them only the fading memories of those things. As you say, magic is not part of the reality of nature here. It can't exist here. I'm sure that those who resettled here soon came to deeply regret ever having wished for a life without magic. There could have been nothing worse for them than getting exactly what they had wanted.

"Those things lost lived on in this world but only as a ghost of what once was, of what is now gone.

"That myth, that legend, is all the history that's left from those who came here from my world.

"They left magic behind, yet it still haunts you."

24.

ALEX COULDN'T BRING HIMSELF to accept her story as true—it just seemed too far-fetched and there were too many things that didn't seem to fit with what he knew of the history of the world. Yet at the same time it had a haunting quality to it, some kind of lingering whisper that he couldn't entirely banish. There had been vast dark stretches in human history about which virtually nothing was known.

"I don't have an answer for you, Jax, but just because I don't know the answer doesn't mean that there isn't one. For all I know, it could be that your history is really the one based on legend and myth."

"Have it your way, Alex," she said with a sigh. "If it's too much for you right now, then let it be. Besides, that isn't what matters at the moment. What matters now is that the Law of Nines indicates you are the one named in the prophecy from my world, where prophecy is magic and magic is real."

He knew that she was right about at least some of it. He knew that what was going on now was real. His muscles ached from the shocks Bethany had given him with the Taser. He'd seen bodies vanish. He'd seen a man appear out of thin air.

He didn't know the truth about the past or if he could ever believe the whole far-fetched notion, but he did know that something was going on now, and it most definitely involved him.

"All right, I'm listening," he said. "What matters now?"

"We believe that Cain's people have been coming to this world to find something that will help them tip the balance to their side once and for all. We don't know what it is they're after, but they're expending a lot of resources on it, so we fear that if they find what they're after, we're finished."

Alex lifted his hands in exasperation. "But if your people believe in prophecy and that I'm the one who can save your world, then why would they want me dead? I die, you all die."

She regarded him with the kind of expression that made him a little uncomfortable. "Prophecy can mean something very different from what you think it does. What if you were to cooperate with Cain's people? What if you were tortured into helping them? What if you helped them without realizing what you were doing? Any of those would result in the same end. You would be directly responsible for the deaths of millions.

"If any of those things turned out to be true, then the only way you could be our salvation would be if you died before you could help Radell Cain.

"The prophecy, you see, does not say that you must be alive to save our world. It could mean that you must die if our world is to be saved."

Alex ran his fingers back into his hair and held his head. He wanted the whole nightmare to be over. He hated the deliberately vague nature of prophecy. Prophecy always tried to make any outcome look like a prediction or else it spoke of war, floods, and droughts because there would always be war, floods, and droughts. As far as Alex was concerned, prophecy, like magic, was childish nonsense that depended on the gullible.

"Why then," he finally asked, "didn't you kill me?"

"If I believed that version of the prophecy you would already be dead."

"So you believe this prophecy, but the other way around?"

"We have a saying: 'The House of Rahl is not ruled by prophecy; the House of Rahl reigns over prophecy.'

"The first time you saw me, you pulled me back to save me. It was a test. My test. You passed that test. Had I judged you to be the kind of man to help the enemy I would have killed you on the spot and have been gone before you hit the ground."

"So, because I pulled you back from getting run over by pirate plumbers, you decided not to kill me?"

"In part. I subscribe to the Rahl view of prophecy, that it needs the balance of free will in order to exist. Free will in the House of Rahl meant that they did not abide by prophecy."

That bit of common sense made him feel better. "So the Rahl line in your world didn't believe in prophecy, either."

She laid a hand on his forearm. "I came because of prophecy—not because I believe it, but because Cain does. I believe that you, Alexander Rahl, are the key to solving what's going on. Radell Cain believes it as well."

"If he needs me, then why hasn't he acted? You said they've been coming to this world for some time. Why haven't they done what they came to do? Why haven't they snatched me?"

"I asked myself that same question," she said. "What I finally decided is that he must not know enough about what he's looking for. I'm sure that he knows in general, but I don't think he knows nearly enough, yet, to act."

"How could he be here looking for something and not know what he's looking for?"

"Well, let's say, for the sake of argument, that when the worlds were parted, besides sending people here, an important book was also sent here. Things like that have been done before to keep dangerous information out of the wrong hands."

"You think he's looking for a book?"

"I'm just using that as an example. How would he find it here? He couldn't use magic here to help him—magic doesn't work here, remember? Where would he look?"

"So for some reason he'd try to find it through a Rahl?"

"Do you know where to find such a book that came from my world and didn't belong here? How would you know where it was, or even what it was? You couldn't. Maybe he's already killed members of your family trying to make them tell him and he found out that that didn't work. So, what's he to do, now?"

"I'd like to know the answer to that question," Alex said.

"He knows that you're involved in all this—that's why he has been watching you through mirrors, tracking you with your phone. He's trying to find answers. But since you're his last lead, he has to be careful."

For the first time since they had fled his house Alex felt a bit of optimism. "So if Cain needs me, then those men who tried to run us down when I first saw you must have been Bethany's men."

"No, they were Cain's men."

Alex lifted his hands in frustration. "That doesn't make sense. If he needs something from me, if he's been watching me, then why would he suddenly have his men try to run me down?"

"They weren't trying to run you down. They were watching you. When they saw me, they recognized me. They were trying to run me down. You prevented them from doing so."

Alex paused a moment. "You recognize them? You know them?"

"I know the big one, the one who was on the side closest to us. His name is Yuri. I killed his brother."

Alex sighed. This was one determined woman.

"That was my first, brief visit here. I wasn't able to stay long. When I returned home we immediately began making preparations so I could come back again, but it takes time. It was while I was watching the gallery through the mirrors, looking for you, that those preparations were finally completed. That was when I saw Vendis. When I returned to this world you gave me that painting.

"You have no idea what it meant to me."

"I think I do," he said softly.

She smiled a little but shook her head. "When I saw that painting I knew that you are central to solving what is going on. So, I thought that if I told you some of the nature of the trouble, you might be motivated to help me. But . . ."

"But I made you angry instead."

Jax smiled as she nodded. "When I went back I told people how you so faithfully painted the Shineestay, the place I told you about. People understood, then."

"Just because I painted a forest that looked similar?"

"No. Because I told them how you painted the exact place, down to the placement of every tree—except the one tree I mentioned that was missing from the scene."

Alex remembered. He had painted over that particular tree because it didn't fit the composition. He didn't say so, though, as he listened to her go on with her story.

"You see, it's said that long ago the Rahl leader at the time—the one who is said to have separated the worlds—believed that magic involved art, that the creation of new magic in some ways involved the application of artistic principles at the least and maybe even artistic ability."

"Oh come on. Now you're telling me that art is magic?"

"No, not at all, but Lord Rahl believed—"

"Who?"

"The man who was the leader at the time of the separation event was a Rahl, the last Rahl we know anything about before the House of Rahl vanished somewhere in history. Back then he was called simply 'Lord Rahl.' He fought and won much the same battle of survival that we find ourselves fighting now. The title of Lord Rahl has since come to represent the preservation of magic and individual liberty, to represent for us the very concept of freedom.

"We don't know a great deal about the time back then, but it is known that Lord Rahl's victory against all odds ushered in a period of peace and prosperity known as the Golden Age that lasted hundreds of years. This man was its architect. His victory over tyranny and the banishment of those who wanted to eliminate the gift made it all possible.

"For this reason the very concept of the Lord Rahl is hated by Radell Cain and his ilk.

"Anyway, Lord Rahl believed that new forms of magic are acts of creation that necessarily involve elements of artistic visualization. Art—good art—involves principles of balance, flow, placement, and composition, among other things. These elements must be in harmony, each element working with all the others, in order for art to have deep meaning to us, for it to truly touch our souls. So magic and art, he believed, were inescapably linked. When you painted a picture of my world, you were somehow tapping into that elemental concept that he used to bridge worlds, time, and space."

"Does this mean that you're not going to try to kill me?" he asked with a smile.

She returned a sleepy smile. "I'm here to protect you, Alex. I need your help if we're to solve this. Other than finding you and trying to keep both of us alive, I don't know what to do next. That part is up to you."

Alex blinked in surprise. "Me? How should I know? These people came here from your world. I'm in the dark about the whole thing. Why would you expect me to know what to do?"

She stared at him as if it should be self-evident. "You're Alexander Rahl."

"Jax," he said at last, looking away from her eyes as he considered how to put his thoughts into words, "I don't know if you really have the right person."

"The Law of Nines says you are the right person."

"That's not what I mean." He lifted a hand in a weak gesture. "I think that maybe you're putting too much faith in me. This Law of Nines business is just superstition. I fell into the prophecy by chance, that's all. None of it says anything about me as an individual. I'm just a guy who paints pictures for a living. I don't know about any of this. I don't know how to fight people from another world."

"You've done all right so far."

He shrugged off the notion. "I was just trying to stay alive. That doesn't mean you should put your faith in me. Even if people from the House of Rahl really did come here, exactly as you say, that was an awfully long time ago. I can't live up to what they could do in your world." He ran his fingers back through his hair in frustration. "I just don't think you—"

"Alex, listen to me." She waited until he looked at her. "There is a mirror in the room where you paint. When I was waiting for the preparations to be made for me to make a longer visit here, I sat for hours at a time watching you paint, wishing I could find a way to warn you through that mirror of all the forces homing in on you."

Alex had remembered well her advice when he'd first met her that people could watch him through mirrors. He had been careful with mirrors even before that warning. And he had purposely placed that one in his studio, hoping he would be watched—hoping that Jax would see him through that mirror and decide to return. He had placed it there specifically for her.

"I learned a lot watching you through that mirror."

He smiled a little. "A lot about how to paint, maybe."

"No. A lot about you. When you watch a person for a long time you come to understand their dedication, their focus, their moods, their emotions—the way they think, or don't bother to think. You come to learn what's important to them.

"One day, as you turned to wipe your brush, I saw a picture catch your eye. It was the picture of your grandfather that you kept on the desk beside you. You laid down your brush and picked up that picture and sat staring at it for a time until tears ran down your face."

"It's human to grieve," Alex said. "There's nothing meaningful about that, nothing special."

She nodded. "I know. It's natural to grieve, to be sad, to pine for one lost, to have a broken heart. But as you wept, your other hand fisted. Your jaw clenched. Your face turned red with rage. You pounded your fist on the desk as you wept."

Alex swallowed at the memory of the heat of that emotion. "What of it? I was angry."

"You were angry at death for taking him. You were raging against death itself. You raged against death because life means that much to you. You're the right man, Alexander Rahl. You're the man I came here to find."

Alex listened to the rain as he thought about her words.

"Then that bell rang," she said. "I saw Bethany's reflection in a window.

"In that instant I saw all that was about to be lost.

"We're still struggling to learn to come here. It's very difficult and takes us quite some time to craft a lifeline. Passing into the great void is daunting beyond imagining."

Alex couldn't picture such a thing. "In what way?"

Jax stared off into the memories for a moment. Flashes of lightning cast her face in an otherworldly bluish light.

"It's like leaping off a cliff into eternal night . . . falling without end. Every second you expect to hit the bottom. Your muscles and nerves ache in expectation of a sudden, bone-shattering impact. An eternity of fear is compressed into every one of those moments that you exist in a place without anything but that fear.

"At first you may feel like you have leaped into endless night, but a point comes when you realize that there is no up, no down, no hot, no cold, no light, no sensation of any kind, not even breathing, not even your own heart beating. You are without anything that makes you feel alive.

"In that moment comes panic."

When lightning hit nearby, giving off a loud crack of thunder that shook the Jeep, Alex jumped. Jax didn't. It was as if she was in another place beyond the reach of the real world.

"How long does it take?" Alex finally asked after she had been silent for a time. "How long must you endure such a thing?"

Her haunted eyes stared unblinking into memories. "You feel

as if you have somehow plummeted into eternity. You feel alone beyond anything I could explain.

"There comes a time when you begin to believe that you've died. You can't see anything, you can't hear anything. You feel as if you must be dead."

Jax seemed to force herself to abandon the memory, as if staying there any longer might cause the place to snatch her back. She took a purging breath and looked over at him.

"When I start for this world I have a reference point found with the aid of magic, so from here there is no way for me to find a reference point in my world, no way to know where to return to. That's why I need a lifeline to pull me back through that eternal void to my world. Without a lifeline there is no way to return.

"When I went back the last time I took the painting you gave me, but I lost it in the void. I loved that painting and wanted more than anything to take it back with me for others to see. I held it as tightly as I could, but I lost it. I don't remember where or how it was gone, it just was. That experience proved what we had thought—things can't be brought back from this world to ours.

"I'm sorry, Alex, that I lost your beautiful gift."

He offered her a smile of comfort. "I'll paint you another."

She nodded her thanks for his understanding.

"When I saw Bethany and her thugs at your door I knew that I didn't have a moment to lose. I had to come immediately, even though I had no lifeline ready.

"I had to come because you are the right man, Alex."

Alex listened to the rain drumming steadily against the roof of the Jeep and the distant rumble of thunder. He remembered the day in his studio that she had described. He had forgotten all about the mirror by then; he thought that he would never see her again. That hadn't been the only day he had raged against death for taking Ben. If she had been watching him, she would know that, too.

Ben wouldn't be dead were it not for these people coming to his world, coming for his family, coming for him.

If he didn't stop them, who would? How many more would die?

Jax laid a hand on his arm. "Are you all right, Alex?"

He nodded. He wondered how she could be all right, knowing that she had no way to get home.

"We need to stop them," he said with quiet resolve. "I don't know if I'm the right man, but I'm the only Rahl you've got. If I can do anything to help, I will. If we can figure this out and stop them, then maybe other people won't needlessly lose their loved ones."

"Thank you, Alex," she whispered. She again gently rested her hand on his arm, as if to say she understood all that his words conveyed, and was sorry to have to ask so much of him.

He knew that, for her, there was no turning back. There wasn't any turning back for him, either. No matter what happened, they were now committed.

Her face brightened with a small smile. "So, any ideas?"

"Well," he said, "Bethany knew something about what these other people were after. She wanted to bear my successor. That could only gain one thing: the inheritance that came to be mine when I turned twenty-seven. I think we need to find out about this land that I'm inheriting."

"I suppose that it makes sense for us to look into it. But I can't see how it would have anything to do with what they're after. What do they need with land?"

"I don't know, but Bethany sure seemed intent on having it."

"Not necessarily. It makes more sense to me that what she was really after was your child, a Rahl child."

"What good would a Rahl child do her?"

"A Rahl in my world would be currency of immense value. A Rahl heir would have made her far more important than she otherwise was."

"You think she intended to get pregnant and return to your world? You just said that you can't take anything back."

"But if she got pregnant, the child would have been hers as well. It would have been a part of her. That, I'd be willing to bet, she could have taken back through the void to my world."

"I was sure it had to be something to do with the land," Alex muttered.

"It may be," Jax said. "I'm only saying there are other important reasons she would have wanted you to get her pregnant. I can see why she would want a Rahl child, but I can't imagine what she would want with land. She has land—a lot of it."

"So you're convinced it's not the land they're after?"

Jax shrugged. "I'm only pointing out that there are other reasons people from my world might be interested in you."

Alex let out a sigh. "Well, as far as I know my mother is the only other living Rahl. I've heard her say that people always want to know things from her.

"The land is far away, but my mother is close. Before we consider the land angle I think we should go ask my mother what these people want to know from her. I'm not sure if she'll be able to talk, but we can try."

"You said she was crazy."

"Maybe she isn't as crazy as I thought. Maybe they've driven her crazy. Anyway, it's a place to start."

Jax watched his eyes for a moment. "That makes sense. Tomorrow, then, we go see your mother." She lay back and yawned. "You were right, we'd better get some sleep."

Alex nodded as he yawned in turn. He watched as she rearranged her duffel-bag pillow. Her eyes closed.

"Jax, you're someone important where you come from, aren't you?"

"I'm just a woman, Alex. A woman who has no powers here. A woman who is afraid that she will never see her home again. A woman who is afraid for the lives of those she loves."

"Those you love. Like a man you love?"

"No," she whispered, her eyes still closed. "Not that kind of love. I have no one like that."

He watched her breathing slow for a time. She looked bone-tired. Traveling from a distant world through that void had sounded like more than merely an exhausting experience.

"Jax," he asked softly, "are you like a queen or something?"

She smiled sadly without opening her eyes, "In my world, queens once bowed to those like me, but not anymore. Now they bow to Cain." Her voice seemed halfway into the world of sleep. "Now I'm just a frightened, desperate woman a long way from home. A woman who often fears she is foolish to think she can win against these people."

He watched her for a time. "I don't think you're foolish in the least," he whispered as he tucked the jacket around her, "I think you're the bravest person I've ever met."

She was already asleep and didn't hear him.

25.

T HAT'S FINE," MR. FENTON SAID. "I shouldn't have any trouble having the final title documents ready for you in a few days."

"Thank you," Alex said into the phone. "That should work out. I'm not sure of my travel plans yet, but I imagine that it will take me at least a few days to get there."

"I'll give you a call, Mr. Rahl, and let you know when the documents are ready."

"Uh, no . . . don't bother," Alex said, his mind racing for an excuse. "I'm having trouble receiving calls on my phone. There's something wrong with it. When I get time I'm going to have to see about getting it fixed or replaced. I'll let you know when I do. In the meantime I'd hate to miss your calls and I wouldn't be aware that you were trying to reach me. Tell you what, I'll call you in a few days and let you know when I'll be in Boston."

"I look forward to seeing you. Thank you for calling. Oh, and the people at the Daggett Trust were quite pleased with your decision and are eager to meet you."

Alex wondered why.

"All right, then, I'll call you as soon as I know something about my travel plans."

"Thank you, Mr. Rahl. I'll talk to you soon."

Alex flipped the phone closed and then dropped it in his large cup of water. Bubbles rose from the phone as Alex carefully folded over the top of the paper cup several times to seal it. He placed the cup upright in a trash container so that the water wouldn't spill out, at least for a time.

He clearly remembered Jax saying that people on the other side had been using his phone to track him. He didn't have any sure way to know if the same people had somehow locked on to his new phone or not. For all he knew, placing a call to the lawyer's office could somehow enable Cain's people to find him through the phone.

Possible or not, he wasn't going to take any chances. It was a cheap generic phone. He would buy another. The number would be different, but he'd told the lawyer not to try to call him. There was no one else he needed to talk to, at least not enough to risk his life.

His new gallery might want to get in touch with him, especially if they sold one of his paintings, but in light of all that had happened that wasn't important for the time being. He had new concerns. He had a new life, it seemed. He wondered how short that life might be.

Alex glanced down the hall, toward the restrooms. He had already finished washing up. Jax was still in the ladies' room. An outlet mall was not the best place to clean up, but it was better than nothing.

They'd already had a breakfast of sausage and egg sandwiches in the food court. Jax had devoured three.

Remembering that she hadn't been able to open the door of the Jeep on her own, he had carefully explained the faucets and toilets to her, just in case she didn't know how to use them. She'd listened with interest, like a student paying attention to a lecture in a course she needed to pass.

The morning had dawned with bright blue skies, but it was windy, a remnant of the violent storms that had passed through the night before. At least the rain had moved on. Seeing the bright blue skies as they had emerged from the cargo area of the Cherokee had made the night before—the lightning and thunder, the desperate fights, the killing, the blood—seem like a distant nightmare.

The next time he glanced down the hall, he saw Jax coming. She smiled when she saw him. It was a smile that sparkled in her warm brown eyes and lifted his heart. After the night before they both knew that they only had each other to depend on. They had a bond of purpose.

Surprisingly enough, she looked for the most part to be back to her normal self. He didn't know how she had accomplished such a feat after how soaked they had been, and after sleeping in the cramped quarters of the Jeep, but she had. He smiled to himself when the thought crossed his mind that it seemed like she had to have used magic to restore her lush fall of blond hair to full glory.

The only problem with the way Jax looked was that she looked too good. In Regent Center she fit in. In an outlet mall near the casinos, where fancy dress was too-short skirts or muffin-top jeans, a tank top, and flip-flops, she stood out.

With most of the men in the mall looking her over from top to bottom, he didn't know how to tell if Jax was being watched by someone from another world or not. Alex was eager to get her something else to wear so that she wouldn't draw quite so much attention.

"You look very nice," he said as she joined him.

"Yes, I know what you mean. Let's get me some other clothes so that I don't look so very nice."

Alex wondered if such a thing was even possible. He was sure, though, that different clothes would at least draw less attention. Jax was apparently well aware of how different her attire looked from that of other people in the mall. Being a target as she was, she had to worry about standing out.

"Did you have any trouble using the faucets or anything?"

"No, but a thin girl in the washing room was a little too curious about me."

"Why? What did she say?"

"She said, 'So, like, are you a supermodel or something?'" Jax quoted, mimicking the adolescent voice. "I wasn't entirely sure what she meant, but I think I got the idea. When I told her no, she said, 'So, like, what do you do, then? Like, for a living.'"

Alex smiled at the story, and the predicament Jax had found herself in.

"What did you tell her?"

"I told her that I killed people for a living."

Alex lost a step. "You told her what?"

"That I kill people. I'm not familiar enough with your world to come up with a credible lie, so I told her the truth." Jax flicked her hand, dismissing the alarm on his face. "People usually don't believe the truth. They'd rather hear a good lie."

"What did the girl say when you told her that you kill people?"

"She said, 'Like for real? That's so cool.'"

"Good. I thought for a moment you might have scared her."

"No, she seemed rather preoccupied with death. Her fingernails and lips were painted black. What's the purpose of trying to resemble a corpse?"

"I think it's a phase some girls go through," Alex said. "Didn't you ever, I don't know . . . rebel against adults when you were young? Want to be different?"

Jax frowned up at him. "No. Why would I do such a thing?"

Alex sighed. "I guess you really are from another world. What did you do, then, when you were her age?"

"I studied and practiced."

Alex frowned over at her as they walked among the scattering of people all looking at them on the way by. "What did you study and practice?"

A little smile curved one side of her mouth. "How to kill people."

He watched her for a moment. "Is that one of those truth tricks of yours, or a lie you think I might believe?"

"Both," she said.

"What does that mean?"

She smiled to herself. "I studied languages. I speak a lot of the languages in my world. Feel better?"

He decided not to press her and changed the subject. "Considering that other people are likely to ask questions, too, and we might find ourselves questioned when we're not together, I think we'd better come up with a believable story, something we can use if need be."

"Don't tell me," she said, fanning her face as if feeling faint, "we're madly in love, I am betrothed to you, and we're to be married."

Alex winced a little. "Well, as a matter of fact, that is what I came up with—the engaged part. I thought it would be a useful story. I mean, if I'm to take you into the hospital where my mother is locked up I should have some kind of plausible story. They don't let just anyone in. You need to be someone close, like a relative, a spouse, something like that."

"Why is your face red?"

"Look, I just figured that if we said that you were my fiancée it would satisfy people and avoid a problem. I didn't realize that you'd object."

"Relax," she said with a smile. "I thought of that same story myself."

"Oh. You did?"

"Of course. What else could we say to people where your mother is held? That I'm a woman who dropped in from another world and I would like to speak with the crazy lady?"

"Is my face really red?"

She glanced up at him. "A little."

"So, you're my fiancée? You're all right with that story?"

She arched an eyebrow at him. "Unless you're planning on us going through with the marriage."

He slowed and gestured to a window filled with female mannequins dressed in casual clothes, glad to have a change of subject. "We should be able to get you something in here."

He held the big glass door open for her. She looked back over her shoulder. "Your face is still red, Alex."

"Well, actually," he said, "I was thinking that maybe it would be best if we did actually go through with it and get married. If it was legal it would solve a lot of problems. When we get to the lawyer's office, already being married would help the transfer of the title to the land go smoothly. . . ."

He was pleased to see her freeze and stare at him. "Just kidding," he said. "Your face is red."

She shook her head to herself. "I imagine it is."

Round racks with pants, tops, and skirts crowded the floor of the store. Alex directed Jax toward a rack with jeans. As they made their way through the islands of clothes, he leaned close.

"Jax, is there any way to tell if someone is from your world? A way to tell if they're a different kind of human?"

"No. They're the same as you, except that in my world they have magic. Here they don't. I only know they're from my world if I recognize them."

"Or if they try to kill you."

"Well, in my world we would call that a clue."

"My world too," he said, disconcerted to realize that there was no way to tell friend from foe.

When they reached the rack with the jeans he found the size-8 section and pulled out a pair.

"This looks like it might fit you," he said.

Jax glanced around at the circular racks stuffed with clothes. "To think, there are so many things already made that you have a good chance to happen across some that will fit."

"They're sized," he said. "They come in standard sizes."

She shook her head in wonder as she took the jeans from him. Her brows drew together. "These are worn out. Are they a donation for the poor? Is that what this place is?"

Alex laughed softly. "No, no, they're new. They're made to look used. Believe me, they're not for the poor."

Jax appraised him suspiciously.

"It's the fashion," he assured her.

She looked like she suspected that he might be putting her on again. "The fashion is to look destitute, with holes in your clothes? Why would anyone choose to look that way?"

"I don't know." He scratched his temple. "I guess the fashion is to look as if you're wearing comfortable old clothes. It's meant to look casual."

"Like making yourself look like a freshly dead corpse?" She sighed as she laid the jeans over the rack. The saleswomen were all acutely interested in Jax. In such a shop her graceful black dress and blond hair made her look like a queen visiting a dump.

"Please, Alex, can we get clothes that don't have holes in them? I want to fit in, but . . ."

"Sure." He pulled out another pair that he thought might be more to her liking. "These aren't even as expensive as the ones with the holes already worn in them."

"Now you're joking at my expense."

"I'm telling you the truth, the ones with holes cost more. Would you like me to tell you a lie that you'd rather believe?"

When she still looked skeptical he pulled out another pair and showed her the price tags.

She took the jeans from him. "I like these better."

"You won't be as fashionable."

"Will I fit in?"

"Yes."

"Then may I have these instead? Please?"

Alex smiled. "Of course you can. We'll get you whatever you feel comfortable wearing. You pick." He gestured with his chin. "Over there is a fitting room where you can try them on to see if they fit and how they look."

"I can try anything I want?"

"Sure."

She looked relieved and started searching through the rack herself. With a critical eye she appraised the different styles and picked out several pair that didn't have holes and cuts already put in them for the convenience of the busy, fashion-conscious woman. As she searched, she handed him jeans to hold.

Along the way to the fitting room they stopped at several more racks with slacks and several with tops. She wasn't interested in skirts; she thought they would show too much of her legs and draw attention. From what Alex had seen of her long, muscular legs, he had to agree. In the end, though, she changed her mind and decided to try one.

She was picking up the knack for shopping pretty quickly. Alex didn't think that the saleswomen would find anything at all odd about the way she shopped. They would think that she was a woman who knew exactly what she wanted.

As Jax went in to try on her armload of clothes, Alex found a chair and casually pulled it out to the side so that he could have a view of the fitting-room door and also the entrance to the shop. He wanted a clear view if anyone unwelcome came in.

He hoped that no one like that showed up. Firing his gun at night in the middle of a thunder-and-lightning storm was one thing; having to fire the weapon in the middle of a shopping mall was quite another. If the bad guys didn't get him, the good guys were sure to.

Jax soon emerged from the fitting room wearing a pair of low-rise jeans and a black top. "How does this look?"

"Hot."

She frowned. "Not really. I think I would need my cape over this to keep me warm if it gets at all chilly."

"No, I mean it looks hot—attractive, beautiful. Hot."

She got the picture. "Well, I'm glad you think I look hot, but is it good enough to serve the purpose of fitting in?"

"Yes. It's perfect. Try on some more. You'll need a few outfits. Try on the black pants, the ones that look tailored."

When she came out in a simple white blouse and the black pants, he nodded. "Good. That's the right look."

The lawyer said that the transfer of title would be ready in a couple of days, but Alex would have to sign the papers in person. As meticulous as the lawyer sounded, Alex didn't want Jax to raise eyebrows. He was hoping the lawyer might be able to give them some information, or at least a clue, that could help them. If they were to put a man of such orderly nature at ease, Alex thought, he and Jax needed to appear respectable.

They picked out a few more outfits, mostly jeans, that would look normal in most situations and be good for traveling. After they paid for the clothes they sat at a table in the food court so he could cut off the tags. He used his pocketknife for the task, warning Jax not to pull her knife out in public. After he was finished with a pair of jeans and the black top that she liked, she went to the bathroom to change while Alex removed the rest of the tags and labels.

He noticed that when she came out she still attracted attention, but it was a little different. It was admiring glances rather than frowning curiosity.

She came to a halt before him as he picked up the bags with their purchases. She handed him a bag with her black dress. He felt a little guilty about asking her to wear clothes she wasn't accustomed to.

"Well, what do you think?" he asked.

She gave him a crooked smile. "I think I look hot."

Alex heaved a sigh of relief, glad that she was taking it well. "You'll get no argument from me. Better yet, you look like you belong in this world. Hopefully, Cain's people won't recognize you now."

"That may be too much to hope." She took his arm as they started back to the truck. "Thank you, Alex, for helping me fit in better here. It will make it easier to find answers."

On the way through the mall back toward the parking lot, Jax abruptly pulled him to a halt. He looked over to see her staring into a store window.

The shop was called Pandora's Treasure Box. The place sold an extensive variety of figurines and such. They had a lot of wizards and dragons from what Alex could see.

Jax shot him a meaningful look. "What is this?"

Alex shrugged. "Some people are interested in that kind of thing."

Without further word, she marched in the door of the shop.

26.

ANDORA'S TREASURE BOX SPECIALIZED in items that, for the most part, looked to be related to some aspect of magic. They had everything from board games with flying creatures, to amulets, to fairies, to gnomes, to dragons of every sort, to wizards and witches, to crystals, to intricate handmade magic wands that cost hundreds of dollars. Glass shelves in the center of the shop held more elaborate collectible figurines. Books on the shelves against the far wall had titles about spells, wizards, and magic.

Alex had seen places like Pandora's Treasure Box before. As a boy he had visited such shops a time or two. He'd outgrown them in his early teens.

A smiling, overweight woman in a baggy maroon sweatshirt came out from behind the counter. A small dragon comb adorned her short, curly brown hair. Reading glasses hung around her neck on a chain festooned with delicate winged fairies. She looked to be in her fifties.

"I'm Mary, welcome to Pandora's Treasures. May I help you two find anything special?" she asked in a warm, friendly voice.

"We're just looking," Alex said before Jax could say anything. It didn't help.

"Why do you have these things?"

The woman's face creased with a perplexed smile as she glanced around. "They're treasures. People love to collect them. There's nothing like a wizard sitting on your desk to brighten your day."

"Depends on the wizard," Jax said.

The woman chuckled. "You're right, my dear. Some of them can be quite mischievous."

"What makes you think so?"

Mary held a hand out to a display in the center of the shop. "Well, just look at them. We have all sorts. Some wizards are very serious, but there are some—like this fellow here—who love a bit of mischief." The wizard was levitating a dog.

The woman was right about the variety. There were jolly-looking wizards in peaked hats, wizards with long pointed beards pondering books or crystal balls, and wizards in black robes with glowering, hooded eyes that looked like they really could cast spells. Some were plain pewter while others had been painted in elaborate detail.

Alex thought they had better things to do and wanted to leave.

The woman gazed lovingly at her display. "These figures are reminders to people that magic is in the world all around us."

"No, it's not," Jax said.

She did not look at all pleased. Alex was beginning to worry.

"Why, of course it is," the woman said with a jovial chuckle. "We may not be able to see it, but magic is very real. You just have to be attuned to it." She heaved a sigh. "It would be a sad world if we didn't have magic."

"Yes," Alex said before Jax could say anything, "I can see why people would want to collect these, but magic isn't real."

Mary winked at him. "Oh, don't let the magic go out of your life. That would be a sad thing, wouldn't it, to become so cynical? We all have the capacity to tune in to magic if only we pay attention. We have but to open ourselves to it."

She lifted a delicate chain off a stand. "We have these crystals on necklaces you might like for your lovely lady. They would be beautiful on her, don't you think? People say that the crystals help them feel the waves of magic emanating up all around us."

Jax wasn't listening. "These things are dead wrong," she said to herself under her breath. Mary, showing Alex the necklace, didn't seem to notice.

Jax leaned in a little to peer intently at the items displayed on the second shelf down. A card read "exclusive pieces." When the woman saw Jax's area of interest, she put the necklace back and turned her attention to the center display.

Jax carefully pulled a figure out from the back.

The woman looked pleased at the selection. "Ah, you have good taste."

Jax lifted the figure, an acrylic casting of a nicely sculpted woman with long flowing hair and a simple white dress cut square at the neck.

"Woman of mystery," Mary said softly.

Jax looked up. "What?"

"They call her the Woman of Mystery."

"Is that right?" Alex put in, trying his best to sound cheery. He wanted out of the shop. He could see how quietly upset Jax was getting. "Well, we—"

"She's an ancient figure." The woman leaned a little closer. "I've owned this shop for twenty-seven years and I rarely come across examples of this particular personage."

"Twenty-seven years," Alex said. "Isn't that something." He saw Jax cast him a sidelong glance.

"Yes, that's right. In that time I've seen the Woman of Mystery offered for sale in a few different forms. Always fine pieces, though, like this one. I like to keep one in the shop. That distinctive dress is a hallmark of the Woman of Mystery. It's how you can identify her."

"Really," Alex said, paying more attention to Jax.

"Yes." Mary sighed. "Not a lot of people seem to be interested in collecting her. I usually end up having each figure for quite some time before they sell, but I still can't resist always getting another so that I always have one in stock."

"Why don't people usually collect this piece?" he asked.

"Maybe because so little is known about her. I know a great deal about all of my better pieces, but even I am not sure of her powers."

"Her powers?" Jax asked, looking up sharply.

"Yes," Mary said. "It's not known if she's a sorceress, a white witch, or some other figure of mysterious magic. For that reason she's always called the Woman of Mystery. I know her when I see her—I recognize her by that dress and her long hair. I've never seen her called by any other name, except by people who don't know her."

"What do you mean, 'know her'?" Jax asked, heat evident in her tone. "How could anyone possibly know her?"

The woman reverently lifted the small statue from Jax's hands. "The figure was originally found in a few very old books. Very old— and they were from different places. Though she looked somewhat different in each of the books, the plates in those books always depicted her in this dress." Mary ran a finger along the neckline of the dress. "Always white, always cut square at the neck. That's how I know her as the Woman of Mystery when I see her. She's very special."

"Why?" Alex asked, caught up in the story.

The woman's smile broadened at having interested customers. "Well, she's mysterious. No one knows her origin or who she is. And, like I said, no one knows her powers. But she has them, that much is sure."

"How do you know that she's even supposed to have powers?" Alex asked. "Maybe those pictures were of a queen, or a famous woman from the time—a saint, a patron of the arts, something like that."

"Alex," Jax whispered, "can we go, please?"

Mary was talking and didn't hear Jax. "What little is known from those ancient books is sketchy, however they do say that she had great power, though they never say what those powers were. Some translations hold her in reverence, while others indicate that she was greatly feared." Mary sighed. "She's a woman of mystery." Her smile turned sly. "But she has magic."

"I don't see how you can say that," Alex said.

The woman peered into his eyes for a time. "I know, because people are afraid of her. I have customers who collect figures of every sort—even some of the most frightening wizards. Not a lot of those people, though, will have her in their collection."

"Superstitious nonsense," Alex said. "If they don't know anything about her, why would they be afraid?"

The woman shrugged. "I don't know. To tell you the truth, she's my favorite." She gazed proudly down at the statue as she turned it in her hands. "For as long as I've owned the shop, the Woman of Mystery has always been my favorite."

She at last remembered herself and lifted the statue out to them. "Are you interested in having a Woman of Mystery in your life?"

Jax, looking a little ashen, deliberately turned away.

Alex already had a woman of mystery in his life, but he didn't say so. "Possibly another time."

The woman smiled sadly. "I understand. A lot of people are afraid of her."

"I'm not afraid," Alex said, defensively.

"Good." The shop owner set the figure back on the shelf, where a little spotlight shone on it. "The Woman of Mystery needs friends in this world today."

"Alex, I want to go," Jax whispered again, more insistently this time.

Alex put a hand on her back, reassuring her, letting her know that he'd heard her.

"Well, thanks for your time, but we have to be on our way."

Alex had to hurry to catch up with Jax.

"What's wrong?" he asked as he leaned toward her. She didn't answer as she marched on through the halls.

"I don't want to talk about it."

"Jax, what's the matter? Are you all right?"

"No, I'm not all right. That was an awful place."

"What do you mean it was awful?"

"They have everything all wrong, yet in some of it I can see the specter of its origin."

"All right, but why are you letting that get you so upset?"

"Because they have the trappings but not the humanity behind it all. It's a fixation on the wrong things. Those things don't care about the life behind the magic. They have a wizard waving a stupid wand to lift a dog, while the real man, the real wizard, would touch some-one who is suffering and lift a burden from their heart. Instead, they show people like game trophies on display."

"But they mean no harm, Jax. They're just knickknacks."

"It's more than that."

"Like what?"

She halted abruptly and turned to gaze up at him as if pleading not merely for understanding, but for her very life.

"Don't you get it, Alex? Don't you see what was lost? Can you begin to imagine the wonder of what it must have been? People here can't remember it, yet they can't forget it. After all this time this whole world still longs for it, still mourns what they lost. It was such a remarkable, magnificent, glorious part of life that they ache to have it back, even though they don't remember what it was."

"But that's past. If it really was lost, as you say, what difference does it make now? We are who we are."

She tapped a finger against her chest. "The difference it makes is that it's going to be my world, too. That's going to happen to us. We're going to lose it all, just as the people here lost it all. The wonder this world misses we have, but we're going to lose it just so a few people can seize power for themselves. Everything we have is going to be taken from us. It's all going to be destroyed at the cost of millions of lives just so a few people can grab power."

It was heartbreaking to hear the anguish in her voice and to see the torment in her eyes.

Alex put a hand on the side of her neck and with a thumb wiped away a tear as it ran down her cheek.

When another tear followed, and then another, he leaned back against the inside corner of a projecting wall of a shoe store and pulled Jax into his sheltering arms.

Once in his protective embrace she dissolved into tears. He tightened his arms around her as she wept softly.

Alex glanced down the hall at the shoppers going about their day. Most didn't notice Jax and Alex. Those who did thought that they were simply a couple hugging in a nook—not all that uncommon in a mall. The passersby were polite enough not to stare.

"Jax, listen to me," he said in a quiet but firm tone. "The people you're fighting are coming here because they need something. We're not going to let them get what they need. We'll stop them, then the people in your world will have a chance."

"You don't know these people, Alex," she said as she wept. "I couldn't begin to describe their brutality. If we don't find out what they're after, then the people in my world will lose everything. I'm only one person with no power here."

He ran a hand down the back of her head. "Jax, we'll stop them. That's why you came here. That's why you found me. We'll stop them. I'm not going to give up or let you face it alone. I'll help you. We'll stop them."

"But I feel so alone, so homesick. . . . And I can't ever get home."

"I know," he whispered as he held her.

Her fingers finally tightened on his jacket, gathering it into her fists. "I'm sorry," she said through tears, "forgive me."

"You don't have anything to be sorry for."

"Yes, I do. So many people are counting on me. So many people need me to be strong. Sometimes, though, I'm afraid that I'm not strong enough for them. I'm terrified that I'll fail them."

Alex smiled despite how much it hurt his heart to see her miserable. "Jax, if I had to pick one word to describe you, it would never be 'weak.'" He rubbed her back as she quieted a little. "We'll figure it out. We'll stop them. Whatever they came here to do, we'll stop them. I promise."

She nodded against his chest, content to be there for the moment, content to be in the shelter of his arms, relieved for the moment not to have to face a world that was alien to her.

Something about the way she clung to him told him that she wasn't used to ever getting that kind of protective comfort, of ever having the shoulder of a friend, or anyone who would simply put an arm around her.

Something told him that she also wasn't used to ever showing weakness of any sort. He couldn't imagine the strength it took to be in an alien world, to know that you couldn't get home, and be able to remain as composed as she usually was. Alex didn't know how long he would be able to maintain his cool under that kind of stress.

"Thank you, Alex, for being strong, for reminding me to be strong."

"That's what friends are for—to be strong for you when you need a moment to find your own strength."

"I guess I never had a real friend before."

"You haven't?" When she shook her head against him, he said, "Well, you have one now. Sometimes, one is all you really need."

"Tell you what," he said after a time. "How about if I take you to meet your future mother-in-law."

That made her laugh. It was a good sound, as beautiful as everything else about her.

"All right," she said, sniffling. "Let's go meet Mom."

27.

I T WAS EARLY AFTERNOON when they arrived at Mother of Roses in the older section of Orden. As was his custom, Alex found a parking place on a hill and at the end of a block so that if he had to he could let the car roll to get it started. The spot was only a few blocks from the hospital.

He cocked the wheels against the curb, set the brake, and then turned to Jax. "We can't take weapons into this place."

"They won't see my knife."

"They don't have to see it. They have technology that detects metal. The machine will set off an alarm if we have any weapons on us."

Jax sighed. "We have ways of detecting weapons, too."

"I have to leave my gun here. You have to leave your knife."

"Knives," she said.

"How many do you have on you?"

"Three."

"Well, you have to leave them all here."

She didn't appear to like the idea one bit. "Without my knives I can't defend us as well."

"I understand, but we have to go through the detector in order to be allowed in to see my mother. If we set off an alarm they won't let us go in, period. Worse, if they find the kind of knife on you that I saw the last time, then we're going to have problems we don't need."

When she hesitated he asked, "Do you want to wait here? I can go alone and see if my mother can tell me anything. You could wait here until I—"

"No," she said emphatically. "Your grandfather's place is gone, you don't go to that gallery anymore, and you've left your house. Not being able to find you at places they know—the patterns of your life abruptly changing—may spook them into changing their plans. You come here regularly. They could be watching the place to find out where you are. I have to be there to protect you."

"All right, but since we have to go unarmed let's try to make it as quick as possible. If my mother is out of it, then there's no need to stay anyway; she won't answer anything when she's in that state.

"I'm hoping, though, that if she sees you with me that might draw her out. I'm hoping that you might have a positive influence."

Jax frowned. "Why would that make any difference?"

"She's my mother. You're going to marry her baby boy. She'll want to wring your neck."

Jax smiled as she hooked a stray lock of wavy blond hair behind an ear. "Maybe you're right that a new face will get her attention. Maybe I can help get her to talk."

"I sure hope so, since we're pretty much in the dark and we need some kind of answers. I really don't want to have to come back every day until she's aware enough to talk to me. Sometimes that can take months."

"We don't have months. With the things that have been happening, I'm not even sure that we have days."

Alex let out a sigh. "Let's hope she can tell us something, then."

He wrapped his gun, safely in its holster, in one of the old T-shirts he kept in the truck. He used them as rags for cleaning brushes when he went on painting excursions to the countryside. He reached down and stuffed the bundle under the driver's seat where it would at least be out of sight.

He had also stashed nearly all of his money farther back under the seat. He didn't like walking around with large quantities of cash, so he had placed it beneath the carpet in a depression in the floor.

When he looked up, Jax handed him three knives. He wondered where she'd been keeping them.

Two of the knives, with leather-wrapped handles, were in simple but well-made brown leather sheaths. The third sheath was a fine-grained black leather, trimmed in silver that matched the knife's silver handle. Elaborate, beautifully engraved scrollwork decorated the silver handle. Not wanting to take the time to admire it, Alex hurriedly rolled the three knives up together in another old T-shirt from the bag on the floor behind him and stuffed the bundle under the passenger seat.

"What about your pocketknife?" she asked.

"It's more of a common tool. It doesn't look scary like those knives you carry—especially that silver one. They don't want anything that could be used as a weapon going into the hospital, so I have to give them my pocketknife and keys for safekeeping when I visit.

"I've been coming to visit my mother for years. I know most everyone who works here. This isn't a place like when we went shopping for clothes where there were strangers coming and going all the time. I know most everyone here."

Jax looked at him out of the corner of her eye. "That's all the more reason to be careful."

"You said that Cain's people don't know enough yet and they're just watching me."

"These people are killers, Alex. I'm only making guesses about what they're doing and what they may be thinking. We can't count on that assumption. I could have it all wrong."

"All right, I get it. We still have to worry about getting our necks broken."

"We should be so lucky if they catch us."

Alex cast her a suspicious look. "What do you mean?"

"They only break people's necks when they don't have the luxury of time and the person isn't important enough to warrant closer attention."

"What do they do if they have time?"

"Any number of things," she said. "They're pretty inventive."

Alex wondered why she was being evasive. "What do you mean?"

Jax looked away, staring out the window for a time. She finally turned a serious look on him.

"One of the things Sedrick Vendis likes to do to get people to talk is to hang them up by their wrists, stretched up high enough so that they can just barely touch the ground with their tiptoes. Suspended by your wrists like that, you have to stretch on your toes to take some of the weight off your arms in order to breathe. It's an agonizing effort to pull air into your lungs. After a short while, if you don't use your toes for support, it's impossible to breathe.

"I'm told that it feels rather like you're drowning. You struggle for every breath as you slowly suffocate. It takes all your strength and effort to help keep enough weight off your arms so that you can get each breath. As you become exhausted, panic sets in, heightening the terror of it.

"After a night like that, alone, unable to sleep, having great difficulty breathing, exhausted from the effort of taking enough weight off their arms so they can get each breath, people are only too eager to tell everything they know, eager to believe that if they cooperate they will be let down.

"Talking, though, doesn't do them any good. Once the person has confessed all they know, they are of no further use. Strips of skin are peeled down their back and left hanging to attract animals. Birds, ravens especially, will clean the meat right off the exposed ribs. Maggots start growing in the exposed flesh while the person is still alive.

"Dehydration, shock, blood loss—it's not a pretty way to die, nor is it fast. Unless, of course, they grant you mercy and break your legs so that you can't support your weight. Then you suffocate and death comes quickly."

Alex didn't know what he had been expecting, but it was nothing like this. He couldn't have imagined such a thing.

He had to remind himself to breathe. "I can't imagine anyone being that inhuman, that barbaric."

"Then I won't tax your imagination by telling you the things they do that are worse." Her brown eyes turned to focus on him. "You think about that before you let yourself get caught."

Alex hadn't been thinking about not getting caught. He'd been thinking only about not letting them catch her. That was the thought that truly terrified him.

He finally took a full breath. "Jax, I'm sorry. . . . I shouldn't have asked such a question."

He wiped a hand back across his face. He felt hot and a little sick to his stomach.

"I didn't mean to sound angry at you for asking," she said. "I'm angry at the people who do these things. You were right to ask—after all, it's you they're interested in. You need to know what these people are really like. You need to understand the consequences of hesitation."

Alex clenched his jaw as his revulsion began to melt into smoldering rage.

Her expression softened into regret. "I'm sorry I have to bring such things into your life, Alex. I'm sorry that I—"

"You didn't bring them into my life," he said as he held up a hand to stop her. "The truth is the truth. Only a real friend would warn me about the kind of people who are after me."

She smiled sympathetically, relieved that he understood.

"Now," he said, "let's get in there and see if we can find out what these bastards want from my world."

28.

WITH A CASUAL BUT CAREFUL LOOK, Jax scanned the entire area before opening her door. He saw her appraise the same older couple walking up from behind them that he'd noticed in the rearview mirror. Jax returned a smile when the couple smiled as they passed by. He noted that she trusted no one, not even an old couple shuffling along the sidewalk.

He wondered how she could summon a smile. He couldn't.

Alex tossed his jacket in the back seat and then locked the Cherokee. He checked the back hatch to make sure that it was locked as well. He didn't like leaving a gun in the truck that a thief could discover and steal, but he had no choice. Even though he was licensed to carry a concealed weapon, they still couldn't be taken into a mental institution.

He wondered what he was going to do if they ended up having to leave the state. While he was licensed to carry in Nebraska, that license wasn't valid in other places, especially Boston, where the law took a dim view of people protecting themselves.

Alex had a very clear-cut belief about his fundamental right to his own life. He didn't think that he should have to die just because a criminal wanted to take his life. He had only one life and he believed that he had the right to defend it, simple as that. Ben had taught him how.

In light of the kind of people they were up against, the kind of animals Jax had just told him about, he knew that he would rather risk facing a gun charge than be without a means of protecting himself, and more than that, protecting Jax. He wasn't willing to die because of the dogmatic principles of imperious public officials. It was his life, not theirs.

From bits and pieces Jax had revealed, he knew that Cain would love nothing more than to have her in his clutches. Alex knew that if they ever got their hands on her they would do those things that she'd said he couldn't even imagine. Whatever those things were, he didn't want to know. He was already angry enough.

The limbs of the maple and oak trees lining the residential streets whipped back and forth in the gusty wind, filling the bright day with a rush of noise. Jax had to use one hand to hold her hair back off her face as they made their way quickly along the sidewalk. She used the other to hold on to his arm, playing the part of his fiancée.

The storms had left the ground littered with leaves so that it looked a little like autumn, except that the leaves were green instead of bright colors. Here and there limbs that had been torn off during the storms lay on lawns and at the sides of the street. The air had an odd, dry feel to it, as if hinting at the looming change of season.

Jax silently eyed the imposing front façade of Mother of Roses as they walked down Thirteenth Street. Many of the people climbing the broad bank of steps on their way to visit patients carried flowers or small boxes wrapped in bright paper and decorated with ribbons.

As they continued past the front entrance, without turning up the steps, Jax frowned questioningly up at him. "Family visiting the ninth floor can go in the back," he told her. "It's easier."

"The ninth floor," she repeated in a flat tone.

He knew what she was thinking. "I'm afraid so."

Around the side, the usual collection of service vans were crowded into the small lot that was really nothing more than an irregular blacktopped area off the alley. The back of the building was virtually deserted compared with the activity in front. That had always added to Alex's feeling of alienation; he wasn't visiting a normal patient, someone who would eventually get better and go home, he was visiting someone who was imprisoned because she was a danger to society and would never be released.

He guessed that in the back of his mind he had always felt a sense of shame over that, not to mention anxiety that he might end up the same as his mother. Now he felt a sense of anger, because it was seeming more and more likely that her condition was the fault of strangers meddling in their lives, strangers who wanted something and didn't care who they had to hurt to get it.

Out of habit, as they took a shortcut across the grass and patches of bare dirt beneath the shade of the huge oaks, Alex glanced up at the windows on the ninth floor. He saw nothing more than shadows through the nearly opaque glass.

"Are all the windows covered with wire?" Jax asked as she noticed him looking up at the top floor.

"All the ones where we're going."

When he pulled open the steel door at the back entrance, Jax paused and wrinkled her nose at the unfamiliar hospital smell. She stole a quick glance to each side before stepping through the doorway.

Inside, the smell of food mixed unappetizingly with the hospital smell. The kitchens were back off the entrance area. Oftentimes smaller supplies were taken to the kitchen through the back entrance.

As he did at every other visit, Alex tossed his keys, change, and pocketknife in a blue plastic tub on a table to the side of the metal detector. His phone was taking a bath in the outlet mall. As he had coached, Jax walked slowly through the metal detector. With her hands hooked in her back pockets, she looked completely natural, as if she did it every day. Wearing jeans and the black top she looked completely normal, as if she belonged with him. Except that he had never been with any woman as breathtaking as Jax.

The older security guard, Dwayne, who never smiled at Alex, smiled at Jax. She returned the smile. As well as Alex was beginning to know her, though, he recognized that her smile wasn't sincere.

After Alex had gone through the metal detector, Dwayne reached in the tub as he usually did to hand back the phone.

He looked up. "You don't have your phone."

Alex snapped his fingers. "Must have left it in the truck."

The guard, with no phone to give back, simply placed the tub on a table against the wall that he used as a desk. He would return the keys, change, and pocketknife when they were on their way out. There were no other blue tubs on the table against the wall. The rest of the empty tubs were stacked together beside the metal detector. As was often the case during the day, Alex was the only visitor to the ninth floor.

At the steel desk beyond the metal detector he picked up the registry clipboard and blue plastic pen attached to the clipboard by its dirty string. He signed his name, paused, and then wrote "Jax, fiancée" in the guest column.

Doreen, who had been paying close attention to Jax, took the clipboard from him and turned it around to see how he'd filled in the "guest" portion. Alex had never brought a guest with him when he went to see his mother.

Doreen looked up with a grin. "Fiancée! Alex, I never knew. I'm so happy for you."

Alex returned the smile and introduced Jax. They shook hands. Doreen seemed unable to look away from Jax's mesmerizing eyes. Alex knew the feeling.

"How long have you two been together?" the beaming Doreen asked.

"It all happened pretty fast," Alex said. "She just dropped into my life out of the blue. Surprised the hell out of me, to tell you the truth."

"Oh, that's so exciting, Alex. When's the big date?" she asked Jax.

"As soon as we work out the details," Jax said.

Alex was relieved that Jax had handled the question with such simple grace.

On their way to the elevator, Alex leaned close. "That telling-the-truth trick of yours works pretty well."

She gave him a smile at their inside joke. He noticed that she smiled differently at him than she did at anyone else. There was something special about it, something he liked very much.

When the green metal door of the elevator opened, Alex took a step in. Jax balked, her hand on his arm dragging him to a halt.

"What is this?" she asked.

Before anyone noticed them stopping, he put an arm around her waist and ushered her inside. "It's an elevator. It takes us up to the ninth floor, where my mother is held."

She turned around the way he did and faced the front as the door glided closed. "I don't like being locked in a metal box."

"I can't really blame you, but it's fine, honest. It's just a device that goes up and down, nothing else."

"Aren't there stairs?"

"There's a fire escape on the outside of the building, but you can't use it except in an emergency. The regular stairway is kept locked to control access to the ninth floor."

Jax tensed at every clunk and clatter of the elevator's ascent through the building. She only seemed to relax when it wobbled to a stop and the doors opened.

As she stepped out, her gaze swept the nurses' station, taking in everything, noting the position of everyone working behind the counter. There were four nurses, three female and one male, plus a woman at the computer. Back down the hall Alex could see an orderly getting a mop and bucket out of a utility room. He was sure that Jax was also checking to make sure that she didn't recognize anyone.

Standing at the high counter at the nurses' station, Alex signed his name and wrote in the time. Not a lot of people visited the ninth floor. He saw his signature from previous visits several places higher up on the sheet. He slid the clipboard over and motioned Jax to step up to the counter.

"You need to sign your name and write down the time," he said under his breath. "Sign your name on the line below mine and copy the time I put in."

Alex watched her sign her name. He hadn't known her last name before. When she had finished he slid it back across the counter to one of the nurses on duty. The big, hunched orderly spotted the two of them through the large window in the pharmacy and came out to greet them.

"Alex, what have we here?" Henry broke into a rare grin as he stared at Jax.

"Henry, this is Jax, my fiancée. Jax, this is Henry."

She didn't blanch at the size of the man the way most people did. "Nice to meet you, Henry."

Henry smiled at the sound of his name coming from her lips. "I had begun to worry about Alex, but I can see now that he was just waiting for the right woman to come along."

"You have that right," Alex said. Eager not to be pulled into a "How'd you two meet?" conversation, he changed the subject. "How is my mother doing?"

Henry shrugged. "Same. You know the way she is. At least she hasn't been causing a ruckus lately."

"That's good," Alex said as he followed Henry to the solid oak door leading to the women's wing.

In her sweep of the area, Jax noted a man—a patient—staring at them through the little window in the door to the men's wing. She turned back and watched as the orderly pulled his keys out on the cable extending from the reel attached to his belt and then unlocked the door. He ducked and glanced through the window before tugging open the heavy door.

"Your mother was in the sunroom last time I did rounds. You two have a nice visit." Henry handed Alex the plastic key for the buzzer. "Ring when you're finished, Alex."

Alex had probably heard the man say "Ring when you're finished" a few hundred times. It seemed he should realize that Alex would know the routine.

Jax glanced at the varnished oak doors to each side as they made their way down the long corridor toward the sunroom. He knew that she was calculating every threat, watching for any source of trouble. Of all the places that concerned him, Alex didn't really think this was a place they had to worry about. Still, Jax's attitude was making him jumpy.

"We're locked in here?" she asked. "There is no way for us to get out on our own if we have to?"

"That's right. If we could get out, then so could the patients, and they don't want that. We have to go back out the way we came in. There's a fire escape that goes downstairs on the side of the build-ing," he said as he gestured surreptitiously ahead to the fire exit, "but the door is locked. A nurse or an orderly would have to unlock it. There's a stairway in the back of the nurses' station. It's kept locked along with the elevator."

When they reached the sunroom, Alex spotted his mother alone on a couch against the far wall.

She saw Alex coming. He could tell by the look in her eyes that she recognized him.

29.

HI, MOM," ALEX SAID in a sunny voice as he came to a stop before her.

She was wearing powder-blue pajama pants and a flowered hospital gown tied in the back. He sometimes brought her nice things to wear but she rarely wore them. She was seldom connected to reality enough to be aware of what clothes she had put on, or to care. On the occasions when she had been aware, she had told him that she was saving her good clothes for when she got out.

Some of her lack of interest in what she wore, he knew, was her mental condition, but a large part of it was the result of the drugs. It was the Thorazine syrup they gave her that left her so heavily sedated, largely indifferent to what was going on around her, and made her shuffle when she walked. It weighed her mind down and made her seem twice her age.

Fortunately, they had arrived not long before she was due for another regular dose of medication. Alex had learned over the years that he had the best chance of seeing her a little more aware when the drugs had started to wear off a little before it was time for her next dose of medication. He often wondered what she would be like, how much better she might be able to communicate, if she were not on such powerful drugs. It was frustrating in the extreme not to be able to have a normal conversation with her.

Alex had often asked the doctors if she couldn't be taken off the Thorazine, or at least put on something less powerful. Dr. Hoffmann, the head psychiatrist at Mother of Roses, insisted that in her case there was no other antipsychotic drug that was as effective. He claimed that it was the only thing powerful enough to suppress her violent psychosis. He said that it was all that was keeping her somewhat human, keeping her from being a raving lunatic.

Dr. Hoffmann had said that he was sure Alex wouldn't want that for his mother, nor would he want to see her physically restrained twenty-four hours a day. He'd said that he was sure Alex would want her to have as much human dignity as possible. The drugs, he said, were what made that possible.

Alex had never been able to argue against that.

His mother rose from the worn-out brown leather couch. She didn't smile. She almost never smiled.

She took in Jax with a quick glance and then frowned up at him. "Alex, what are you doing here?"

Alex was gratified that she not only remembered his name, but used it. She almost never did that. He wondered if maybe Jax was having a positive influence. He hoped so.

"I came to visit you. I wanted you to meet—"

"I told you to run and hide. Why are you here? You should be hiding."

"I know, Mom. You're right. But I had to come here first."

"You should be hiding from them."

Alex gently grasped Jax's elbow and guided her forward. He realized he had butterflies. He wanted his mother to like Jax.

"Mom, listen to me. I want you to meet my friend. This is Jax. Jax, this is Helen Rahl."

Jax extended her hand. "I'm so very pleased to meet you, Mrs. Rahl," she said with a warm smile. "Now I know where Alex got those penetrating gray eyes of his."

His mother looked down at the hand for a moment, then took it. She put her other hand over the top in a less formal manner.

"You are Alex's friend?" she asked without releasing Jax's hand.

"I am. We're good friends."

"How good?"

Jax smiled. It was a broad, genuine smile. "I care for Alex a great deal, Mrs. Rahl. That's the truth of it."

"Jax is about as good a friend as anyone could have," Alex put in.

His mother stared at him a moment. "You should be hiding." She pulled Jax closer by her hand. "You should be hiding, too."

"I think that's pretty good advice," Jax said. "As soon as we have a visit with you I'm going to help Alex hide."

His mother nodded. "Good. You both need to hide."

Alex checked the other women in the sunroom. Most were watching the visitors rather than the TV.

"Mom," Alex said, taking her arm, "we really need to talk to you. How about if we go to your room?"

Without protest she let Alex and Jax hold her hands and lead her out of the bright sunroom into the darker corridor. Most of the women on the other side of the room watched them leave. A few were engaged in conversations with no one in particular. One woman waved her arms in a loud argument with someone who wasn't there.

Alex was relieved to see that his mother's older roommate, Agnes, was watching the soap opera on the TV and didn't follow them. While she never spoke, she did often sit in the room and stare at him when he visited his mother.

As they went through the doorway into his mother's room, Jax first casually glanced in both directions down the hallway to see who might be watching them go in. A nurse, with an orderly to assist her, was at the far end of the hall, taking a tray of medications into the sunroom. Two orderlies coming down the hall in the other direction smiled as they went by.

Alex guided his mother to a leather chair against the wall beneath the window. The nearly opaque glass let in only a frost of light. He and Jax sat on the side of the bed, facing her.

Before they could ask her anything, his mother rose from the chair and shuffled over to a small wardrobe. After a brief search she pulled a shawl from the shelf. When his mother draped the shawl over the polished metal square screwed to the wall that served as a mirror, Jax glanced over at him out of the corner of her eye. He knew what she was thinking.

"They look at me," his mother muttered on her way back to them.

"We know," Jax said. "I'm glad that you know to cover your mirror."

His mother paused to stare at Jax. "You know?"

Jax nodded. "They've been watching Alex the same way. That's why we're here. We want to stop them from looking at you, and from looking at Alex."

There wasn't a lot of room between the bed and the chair against the wall. As she shuffled by, she rested a hand on Jax's knee for support.

She paused, then reached out and ran her thin hand down Jax's wavy blond hair. "You have such long, beautiful hair."

"Thank you," Jax said. "So do you."

As she sat, Alex's mother reached up and ran a hand down over her own hair. "I brush it to keep it nice. I won't let them cut it."

"I never let anyone cut mine, either," Jax said.

Satisfaction at Jax's words brought a small smile to her thin lips. "Good." She turned her gaze to Alex, as if she had forgotten he was there. "Alex, why aren't you hiding, like I told you?"

"Mom, we need to know about these people who are looking at you."

"They ask me things, too."

Alex nodded. "I remember you saying that. That's why we're here. We need to know what they want."

"What they want?"

His mother, when she was lucid, or lucid after a fashion, became easily confused. Alex also knew that she wasn't likely to remain aware of the real world around her for long. If they didn't get answers soon her mind would very likely turn inward. On the other hand, he knew that they needed to be gentle in their questioning or she would simply switch off. In years of trying, he was rarely successful at walking the razor's edge with her.

There was also the problem that when they brought in her medication she would quickly get groggy. Her speech would begin to slur. Soon after, nothing she said would make sense. But that was the drugs, not her mind switching off. As far as Alex was concerned they simply needed to get answers before she couldn't answer, no matter what the cause. .

"That's right, Mom. The people who watch you want something. You told me about it before. You said that they want something from you. We need to know about that."

She touched a slender finger to her lower lip. "They ask about,

about . . . the way they talk, it's not easy to remember. I don't under-stand what they want from me. Always asking things, such confus-ing things. I don't understand."

"I know. It's confusing for us, too. But we need to know what they want from you. Please, Mom, just try to remember what it is they want to know."

When his mother only frowned, as if she didn't understand what he was asking her, Jax leaned in, resting her forearms on her knees.

"Mrs. Rahl, they probably say something like 'Tell us about . . .' and then they say something. Remember? When they say, 'Tell us about,' what's the rest of what they say?"

His mother smoothed down her hair for a moment as she con-sidered. She looked up suddenly.

"They say, 'Tell us about the gate,' I think. Is that right?"

Jax didn't so much as blink.

"That can't be it," she whispered to herself as she slowly stood. "That can't be what they mean."

"What?" Alex stood up next to her. As her gaze cast about dis-tantly, he could almost see her mind racing. "What does that mean?"

Jax didn't seem to hear him. She abruptly looked back down at his mother, her voice becoming insistent, almost demanding.

"Is that what they say? 'Gate'? Is that the exact word?"

His mother shrank back into her chair a little. "The exact word?"

Alex could tell that she was getting confused by the pressure to come up with an answer. Seeing the grave look on Jax's face, though, he decided not to interfere.

"Maybe you're thinking that's the word they meant," Jax said, "but maybe that's not the word they used. Could it be a longer word that made you think of the word 'gate'?"

She puzzled up at Jax. "Longer word? Maybe . . ."

"Maybe what?" Jax pressed.

Alex thought that Jax looked like she was about to grab his mother by the collar and haul her to her feet.

His mother's eyes brightened a little as she suddenly seemed to remember.

"Not 'gate.' 'Gateway.' That's the word." She held up a finger. "They say, 'Tell us about the gateway.'"

Jax went ashen.

"Dear spirits, have mercy on us."

Alex put a hand on the small of her back to steady her. "What's wrong?"

"I know what it is they want," she whispered. Her fingers trembled as she pushed her hair back from her face. "Alex, we're in a lot of trouble."

Just then the door opened. "Time for your afternoon medications, Helen."

It was a nurse. Alex was so rattled he couldn't recall her name. She was middle-aged, big-boned, and wore white from head to toe. Her white nurse's hat had a small red stripe around the edge, but her crisp dress was pure white. It went to midcalf, where it covered opaque white hose. Her thick white shoes were spotless.

"I don't want them!" Alex's mother shouted.

"Now, now, Helen," the woman said as she came closer, "you know that Dr. Hoffmann wants you to take your medications so that you'll feel better."

"No! Leave me be!"

The door opened again as Henry pushed his way in. He saw Alex's mother waving her arms, trying to keep the nurse at bay.

"Helen, you be nice, now," Henry said. "You don't want to be making a ruckus in front of your nice visitors."

Alex's mother sometimes tackled the nurses when she got the chance. The orderly was there to make sure that that didn't happen. Alex considered taking the medication from the nurse and giving it to his mother himself so that maybe she wouldn't become so agitated that Henry would have to intervene.

"We won't be a minute, Alex," the nurse whispered to him.

Alice. That was her name. "Thanks, Alice. I understand."

He watched Jax out of the corner of his eye as she moved out of the way so that Alice could squeeze in between the bed and the chair. He was worried about Jax.

Alex wanted Alice and Henry out of the room so that he could find out why Jax had become so upset at hearing the word "gateway."

Henry looked embarrassed to have to intrude and cause a scene. "I'm sorry, Alex," he said as he came closer. "We'll be out of your way as soon as we make sure she takes her meds."

Alex nodded, moving farther down the bed, trying to give the nurse room. As she stepped closer she held the tray up out of the way, in case his mother took a swing at it.

Jax, deep in thought, turned away. Upon hearing the word "gateway" she'd said that she knew what they wanted. Alex wanted to know what she'd figured out, what this was all about. He wanted to find out what had her so upset and distracted.

Whatever it was, it appeared that they had found the answer they'd come for.

"Leave me be!" his mother yelled, snatching for the tray.

"Come on now, Helen," Alice said, holding it out of reach, "settle down."

The next time Alex glanced over, he saw Henry with a syringe held partially out of sight. He knew that the orderlies sometimes brought a syringe along when they thought there was the possibility of trouble. They'd told him in the past that they would rather give his mother a shot when she became violent than try to restrain her physically and risk hurting her.

"I told you before, Alice," his mother yelled, "I don't know anything about a gateway!"

Jax looked over sharply.

As she did, Henry snatched her by the hair. At the same time he stabbed the syringe into her rump. Before she knew what had happened or could react, he jammed the plunger home.

Alex was already diving over the corner of the bed toward the man. Henry turned and swung a meaty fist at him but Alex blocked the blow with his forearm as he dove inside the man's defenses.

Behind him, as he crashed into Henry, the nurse swept another syringe off the tray she had been holding up out of sight and rammed it into Alex's behind. Alex felt the hot stab of the drug cocktail being injected into his backside as Alice shoved the plunger all the way into the syringe. Having his hands full with Henry, he hadn't been able to turn in time to stop the woman.

Jax landed a full-force side kick in the woman's ribs, sending her flying. Alice knocked his mother back into the chair before crashing headlong into the wall by the headboard. The tray clattered against the floor. The lamp attached to the wall broke off as she snatched it for support on her way down. The bulb shattered with a pop, sending glass everywhere.

As he struggled with the big man, Alex saw Jax reach for a knife at her waist. There was no knife there. She faltered, stumbled, and then started to go down even as she tried to swing at Henry. She missed by a mile.

Alex was lost in rage. Grappling with the powerful orderly, he growled in fury as he swept a leg around behind the man's legs to take him off his feet. It upended Henry and they both went down, Alex on top of him. They hit hard, Henry on his back. Alex followed up immediately with a blow from his elbow that crushed Henry's nose.

Henry cried out in pain. Out of the corner of his eye Alex saw another orderly charging into the room.

Alex tried to swing his fist as the second man jumped him and swept an arm around his neck, but his own arms were tingling and going numb. They wouldn't respond to his wishes. He tried harder. When Henry punched him in the middle Alex reflexively rammed his knee up into the man's groin. Henry cringed in pain. Alex struggled to get up, but the second man at his back had him securely by the neck.

Out of the corner of his eye Alex saw Jax trying to crawl toward him to help. Alice planted a white shoe on Jax's neck, pinning her to the floor. Jax moved as if she were mired in mud. She cried out his name, but it came out as a slurred murmur.

The world began to blur. Everything looked small, as if it were at the distant end of a dark tunnel. Alex yelled Jax's name, but only a whisper made its way out.

His fingers found hers, then. Both of them held on for dear life as the room dimmed.

Alex felt himself being engulfed by thick, tingling blackness. It was all happening too fast.

His last thought, before thought ceased to exist, was of Jax, of the terror in her eyes.

30.

ALEX DIDN'T REMEMBER OPENING HIS EYES. He didn't remember waking. He merely became gradually aware that he was awake. After a fashion.

Everything looked soft and fuzzy, unreal, distant, dim. He could hear snatches of sounds but he didn't know what they were. Figuring out what the sounds were didn't strike him as at all important.

He was aware of the world all around him, but it seemed far away, not something he was a part of. He was alone . . . somewhere else.

His whole body tingled in a thick, numb, twilight way.

With the way that everything seemed less than real, it occurred to him that he might actually be asleep and only dreaming that he was awake. He couldn't decide which was true. He didn't know how to find the solution to such a puzzle.

Try as he might, Alex could not, simply could not, form a complete, coherent thought.

Fragments of ideas, bits of things that seemed as if they might be important, floated beyond his mental reach. He couldn't pull them in, couldn't make those fragments come together into a complete thought. He knew that he should be able to, knew what he wanted to do, but his mind wouldn't make it happen. He could not exert enough willpower to bring himself to think.

It felt like his brain was shut off. He struggled to form a complete sentence in his mind, but his mind could not pull anything together. He would start a thought, but it would trail off into nothing as his brain simply failed to complete the task. He could not coax it to stay on track, to work, to think. Monumental effort didn't help.

Somewhere in the back of his mind his inability to form complete thoughts, to think deliberately, was giving rise to a vague, distant, claustrophobic panic. Those feelings, even as they began to surface, sank back down into the black depths of indifference, never to fully surface, leaving only fuzzy emptiness.

The panic somewhere inside him could not manifest itself into something solid enough to concern him.

Alex wanted to be angry, but there was nothing there to form anger.

Every time he struggled to feel emotion, he only fell back into feeling nothing.

He turned his dim perception away from the futile effort and realized that he was sitting in a chair. He tried to get up, but his body didn't respond. With great effort he looked down to see his hand resting on the arm of the chair. He tried to lift it, but it only levitated a few inches. He couldn't make himself care enough to accomplish the simple task.

He squinted, trying to make out the fuzzy white shape not far away, trying to understand what it was doing.

"You awake, Alex?"

He thought it was a woman's voice.

Answering was too unimportant to even try.

"I'll have your bed made in a jiff. Then I'll let you be so you can get your rest."

That was what she was doing: making up a bed. She was tucking in sheets. Just grasping that much of the mystery around him felt like a profound accomplishment, but the accomplishment failed to be satisfying.

He didn't know if he knew the woman in white. He couldn't make himself concentrate on her face long enough to tell. His gaze kept sinking to the floor. The gray swirls in the linoleum echoed his thoughts.

He wanted to break down in tearful despair at not understanding any of it, but there was nothing in him that knew how to cry, so he could only sit and stare.

"I'll let the doctor know you're awake. I'm sure that when he makes his rounds he'll want to stop in and see you. Okay, hon?"

The woman came closer. She pulled a tissue from the box on the windowsill, then leaned toward him and wiped the side of his mouth and chin.

"That better?" she asked as she threw the tissue in the wastebasket beside the chair.

Alex wanted to say something, but nothing came to mind.

She touched his shoulder sympathetically before moving away. The square of light darkened. He wondered distantly if maybe she had gone out and shut the door.

Snippets of things echoed through his head, fragments of conversations, flashes of sights. He sat unmoving as the obscure turmoil tumbled inside him.

He wondered where he was and how he had come to be there. He couldn't think it through, couldn't come up from the depths toward the distant surface. He wanted to get up out of the chair, but it seemed too monumental a task.

The world kept going dark. Each time he again became aware, he realized that he must be nodding off.

As he sat staring, going in and out of consciousness, the daylight behind him gradually went dark.

"Alex?"

It was a man's voice. Alex lifted his head a little and realized that he must have been asleep again. He blinked slowly, trying to clear his vision. It took great effort to blink, but it didn't help.

The man leaned down toward him. "Alex, hi, how are you doing?"

The man had a clipboard in one hand. A stethoscope hung around his neck. He had on a white coat and a blue tie. Alex couldn't muster the will to look up enough to see the face.

The man picked up Alex's hand and shook it. Alex was too limp to participate.

"I'm Dr. Hoffmann, Alex. I've met you before. Remember? In the past we've discussed your mother."

Alex didn't remember much of anything. He remembered that he had a mother, but he couldn't remember what she looked like. The effort to remember details about her was simply beyond his ability. He could do little more than stare at nothing.

"Well, I can see that you're still pretty out of it. It's the Thorazine. After a while, when you get a little more acclimated to your medication, you'll be able to function better. You won't sleep so much, either."

As Alex finally managed to turn his eyes up, the man smiled. He looked nice. Alex hated him. At least, he guessed that maybe he hated him. Somewhere inside he wanted to hate him, but he couldn't feel any hate. He couldn't feel anything.

"Best thing to do is just take it easy for now, maybe get up in bed and take a nap. You've been through quite an ordeal, from what I've heard."

With all his strength Alex managed to say, "What?"

Dr. Hoffmann looked down to search through his papers. He lifted a page on his clipboard, then another.

"Well, from what I've been told and from this report, you became violent, apparently convinced that the staff was trying to harm your mother. Seems you hurt one of the orderlies, Henry, pretty badly. Alice was shaken up as well."

Alex remembered only foggy flickers of a fight. He thought that he remembered being afraid—not afraid for himself, but afraid for someone else.

"The staff here would never hurt your mother, Alex, or any patient, for that matter. They're dedicated to helping people who are ill."

The man looked through the papers on his clipboard again. "With your mother's history, I'm afraid that your violent outburst is not entirely surprising." He let out a sigh. "Sometimes this sort of psychosis runs in families. In the case of your family, it seems to lead to violent aggression."

Alex managed to lift his back away from the chair a few inches. "What about . . ."

The old bed squeaked as Dr. Hoffmann leaned back against it. He clasped his hands together as he held the clipboard in them and stared down at Alex.

"I'm sorry, Alex, but I don't understand what you're asking."

"Someone . . ."

"Someone? Who are you asking about?"

Alex didn't know.

"Your mother? Is that who you're asking about? Helen is doing fine. She was understandably frightened by the whole episode, but she's fine. I saw her earlier. She's resting comfortably. I don't think she even remembers the incident."

Alex wanted to talk, but he couldn't. He could feel drool running down his chin again.

"Here, let's have your arm before I go, make sure you're doing okay."

The doctor pulled Alex's arm out and wrapped a black blood-pressure cuff around it. He put the stethoscope to the crook of Alex's arm as he pumped the bulb in his other hand. He concentrated, remaining still for a moment as he watched the dial, then turned the knob to release the rest of the air.

"It's pretty low," he said as he wrote on the chart, "but that's to be expected with Thorazine. We'll need to keep an eye on it. As I said, you'll acclimate to the medication over time."

"Over time?"

The man looked up from the chart. "Alex, I'm afraid that you've had a full-blown psychotic episode that requires aggressive intervention. Considering what happened, along with your family history . . ." He peered down at his chart, reading for a moment. "As a matter of fact, your mother was the same age, twenty-seven, when her psychopathic symptoms first manifested themselves."

Alex was dimly aware of his nearly lifelong fear of ending up like his mother.

"Well," Dr. Hoffmann finally said with a sigh, "let's hope for the best. Often, with the right balance of medications, people like you don't have to live with the delusions and mania of such an illness.

"But I'm afraid that you're going to have to be here for a while."

"While?" Alex mumbled.

"With the violence of the assault there is the possibility that charges will be brought."

The doctor patted the side of Alex's knee. "But I don't want you to worry about that at the moment." He smiled. "If it comes to that we'll ask the court to have you confined here, under our care. Jail wouldn't be the proper setting for a person with a serious mental condition. I'm afraid that it might be necessary to have you placed here indefinitely—for your own safety, of course."

Alex was not able to form a response, but somewhere deep inside he felt a distant sense of alarm.

With a thumb the doctor clicked the cap on the end of his ball-point pen and slipped it into his coat pocket, all the while watching Alex.

"Once you get used to your medication, once it settles you down, we'll talk more about all of this. I'm going to want to know about the thoughts you have that seem to control you and make you do the things you do."

There was a soft knock at the door. Someone with a tray poked her head in. "Am I interrupting, Doctor? It's time for his medications."

"No, no, come in. We're done for today."

A woman in white came close. She held the tray out as if she expected Alex to do something. He could do little more than focus his vision on it.

"I think he's going to need some help until he's more used to the medication," the doctor said.

The woman nodded and set the tray on the bed. She held a small paper cup up to his lips. Alex didn't know what to do. It seemed so unimportant. With her other hand on his forehead she tipped his head back and poured syrupy liquid into his mouth. She pushed his chin up with a finger, closing his mouth.

"Swallow. That's it. There you go."

When she removed her hand Alex's jaw hung from the effort of drinking.

"I've got rounds, Alex," Dr. Hoffmann said. "I'll check up on you in a day or two. For now try to take it easy and let the medication do its work, all right?"

Alex sat unable to form a response as the man patted the side of Alex's knee again before leaving. The room darkened a little when the door closed.

The woman in white tipped another cup up. This time pills rolled into his mouth. She poured water from a third cup into his mouth. He swallowed to keep from drowning.

"Good," she said in a soothing voice as she swabbed his chin with a tissue. "Soon you'll be doing it on your own."

Alex just wanted to go to sleep.

"Soon," she said, "we'll have you talking up a storm."

31.

ALEX SAT ON THE EDGE of the bed, exhausted from the effort of getting dressed. Every day they told him to get dressed. He wasn't sure why he had to get dressed, but they had told him to, so he did.

Whatever they told him to do, he did.

He didn't want to comply with their orders, but he didn't have the will to fight them and couldn't think of a reason why he should. He knew that he had no choice, no way out. He was at their mercy.

At the same time, his imprisonment seemed unimportant. What difference did it make? Confinement seemed trivial.

The thing that concerned him the most, in fact the only thing that concerned him, was his inability to think, to form complete, coherent thoughts. That was the most exasperating thing of all to him. He would sit for hours staring blankly at nothing, the whole time trying his best to form a sentence in his head, but nothing would form. It left him feeling hollow, empty, and distantly frustrated.

He knew that it was the drugs that were causing him to be unable to focus. More than anything he wanted out from under the mountainous weight of what those drugs were doing to him. He couldn't envision a way to bring that about.

One time when he had turned his face away, saying that he didn't want them anymore, they had warned him that if he refused, if he became difficult, they would strap him down to his bed and give him injections.

Alex knew he didn't want that. He knew that it was hopeless to fight them. After they threatened to strap him down to his bed, he took his medication without further complaint.

But more than anything, he wanted out from under the dark weight of the drug-induced stupor.

He had the sense that he had been confined for a couple of days. He couldn't figure out how many, but he didn't believe it had been long. He vaguely recalled the doctor coming again to talk briefly with him.

The doctor had wanted to know about the things that Alex thought about. Alex wasn't able to identify any thoughts. The doctor had then asked if Alex was guided by voices. Alex asked what kind of voices. The doctor said that perhaps he heard the voice of the devil, or maybe even people from another world who haunted him, wanted things, told him things. Alex had felt a vague sense of alarm at the question, but he didn't know what the doctor was talking about.

The doctor had left, then, saying that he would return another day and they would talk more about it then, adding that Alex was not going to be going home anytime soon.

Home. This was his home now.

A fleeting thought flashed somewhere deep in his mind. It was about his mother. He felt that he needed to know if she was all right.

Although the drugs suppressed any emotion, every waking moment Alex felt unsafe in the place, even if it was only a vague concern, and so he felt that his mother was in some kind of trouble as well. He was completely helpless to do anything about his fears.

When the door opened, he saw a big man lumber in.

Alex looked up and saw white bandages over the middle of the face.

"How you doing, Alex?"

"Fine," Alex answered by rote before he stared off at the floor again.

"They put my nose back together for me. Said it's going to be fine."

Alex nodded. He didn't like the man standing as close as he was, but he couldn't imagine what he could do about it.

"I wanted to come back to work as soon as possible and see how my patients are getting along. Everyone here knows how much I love my work and how concerned I am for the patients."

Alex nodded. In the back of his mind he felt a sense of danger in the pleasant voice, the casual conversation.

"The doctor said that you need to start going out and sitting in the sunroom. He wants you to get accustomed to being around other people without becoming violent—get used to fitting into society, I guess you could say. The only society you're ever going to see again, anyway.

"But before I walk you down to the sunroom, I want you to tell me about the gateway."

Alex blinked slowly as he stared up at the man with the bandaged face. "What?"

"The gateway. Tell me what you know about it."

"I want to see my mother."

"Your mother?"

"I want to see her safe."

Henry, that was his name, Alex remembered.

The big man sighed. Then he chuckled softly to himself. "All right, Alex, let's go for a walk and see your mother. Might do you some good to see for yourself that she's fine—as fine as she'll ever be, anyway. Then, after you see that she's fine, I guess you'd better think real hard about telling us what we want to know—if you want your mother to stay healthy."

"Please." Alex managed to look up. "Don't hurt her."

Henry leaned down toward him and smiled. "I guess that's pretty much up to you, now, isn't it?"

Alex saw to each side of the bandage that both the man's eyes were blackened. A few of the pieces came together. Alex thought that he had done that to Henry, that he had hurt him, broken his nose. Try as he might, he couldn't remember why he'd done it.

Henry plucked a tissue from the box and wiped Alex's chin. "Okay, let's go see your mother."

Alex began slowly levering himself to his feet. He immediately got light-headed. Henry stuck a big hand under Alex's arm to keep him upright.

"The doctor said that your blood pressure is pretty low, so you have to be careful or you're liable to pass out. Got to take it easy, he said, or else you could get hurt."

Holding him up with one hand under his arm, Henry suddenly punched Alex in the abdomen.

Alex doubled over from the shock of the blow and fell back into the chair. He covered the cramping pain with one arm, even though the ache seemed remote. With his other hand he gripped the arm of the chair. He looked up to see Henry grinning.

The big man reached down and pulled Alex to his feet again, then punched him twice, both blows harder than the first.

Alex crashed back into the chair, moaning.

"Do you want to fight back, Alex? Take another swing at me?" He chuckled again. "Guess not. Thorazine takes the fight right out of you, doesn't it? Makes it impossible to work up any aggression at all. That's what it's for, you know. It's to keep dangerous psychopaths like you from hurting anyone."

Alex was aware of the pain, but it was only a distant awareness. It seemed inconsequential. Even though he knew he should, he simply didn't care. He couldn't imagine how to care.

"Thorazine represses aggression so well that you can't even work up a little anger when you need to. But I guess you know that."

Henry pulled him up, held on to him, and in rapid succession pounded his fist into Alex's middle. The blows staggered him back, but Henry was big and strong enough to keep Alex from falling.

Alex couldn't get his breath. He knew that he was struggling to breathe, gasping, but the drugs were preventing him from being able to react. It felt like they were preventing him from being able to breathe as fast as he needed to.

Henry released his hold on Alex's arm and gave him another mighty punch. Alex crashed back down into the chair, holding his middle. He couldn't pull in a breath. He thought he might throw up. He sensed desperation in the way he gasped, but he felt like he was no more than a distant observer.

With his nose all bandaged up, Henry was looking a little winded, too.

"All right, let's go for a walk and see your mother. Get it over with."

Alex couldn't get up. He was having great difficulty drawing each breath. Henry pulled him to his feet and rammed a knee into his groin. Alex collapsed to the floor, curled up, moaning.

Henry watched a moment, pleased by the sight, then yanked Alex to his feet again. He had great difficulty straightening up. Henry spun him around and shoved him, getting him moving toward the door. Alex tried to walk, but his legs wouldn't move fast enough to walk. He could only shuffle in a hunched posture.

Henry followed close behind. "Don't you think that this is over, Alex, or that we're even. I haven't even begun to get even."

32.

AT THE HEAVY DOOR Henry pulled his keys out on the reel attached to his belt and used one of them to turn the lock. A few people looked up when Henry led Alex into the central nurses' station, but after satisfying their curiosity they went back to what they were doing.

Alex could see several women in the back, down the aisle between the tall shelves, either pulling file folders or putting them away. Beyond the wide window in the pharmacy room a lone nurse worked at taking inventory. A couple of other nurses behind the front counter were drinking coffee and discussing their home life, their conversation animated from time to time with laughter. None of them gave Alex and Henry any more than a passing glance.

Alex felt invisible.

He shuffled along, unable to move any faster, not caring if he did or didn't. He wanted to care, somewhere deep inside he desperately wanted to care, but he could not bring forth concern. His mind was mostly occupied with the single, simple task of following Henry.

He noticed the elevator, remembering that he used to use it when he left the hospital. He couldn't entirely recall how he had come to be locked in the place, to be a patient with his own room. He couldn't focus his mind enough to put the sequence of events together, to grasp it all. It was frustrating to be so in the dark about what had happened and how he had come to be there. Even that frustration, though, failed to rouse emotion.

At the next locked door, Alex waited for it to be unlocked in order to go into the women's wing and see his mother, to see if she was all right. He followed the burly orderly through the door and waited as he locked it behind them.

He watched the light from the room up ahead reflect off the ripples in the polished gray linoleum floor as he shuffled down the endlessly long corridor. Henry stopped to poke his head in one of the doors to the side.

"She isn't in her room," he said before continuing on toward the sunroom at the end of the hall.

When they finally entered the big, bright room at the end of the corridor, several of the woman clustered near the television looked up, but then went back to their show. There were a few other woman scattered around the room but Alex didn't pay any attention to them as he followed Henry.

"Helen, you have a visitor," Henry said.

She was sitting in a plastic chair at a table, her hands nested in her lap. She stared straight ahead, not seeming to hear the orderly.

"Helen, your son is here to see you."

She looked up at the orderly, blinking slowly. When Henry pointed at Alex she looked over. There was no recognition in her eyes. She didn't know who she was looking at.

Alex knew that she, too, was on heavy medications to suppress her aggression. He knew just how she felt in that regard. But he knew, too, deep down inside, that with her it was more than just the medication. There was something fundamentally broken in her.

Alex had wanted to know that his mother was all right, but once seeing that she didn't look hurt, his mind began sinking back into the meaningless static that served for mental activity.

It occurred to him that maybe he should say something.

"Mom, how are you?" His own words rang hollow in his mind. He knew they were the right words, but they contained no meaning for him. He could summon no emotion to pair with the words.

She stared. "Fine."

Alex nodded. He didn't know what else to say.

"Satisfied?" Henry asked.

Alex looked up at the man. "Yes. I want her to be well."

A smile broke out beneath the white bandages. "Good. You remember that. You remember that you want your mother to be well."

Alex knew that Henry was threatening him but he felt no emotional reaction to that threat. It was frustrating that he couldn't find a shred of anger within himself.

"Well," Henry said, "now that we all know that Mom is fine, let's get you back to your room. It won't be long until it's time for your medication."

Alex nodded.

As he turned, he saw someone sitting not far away on a couch against the wall. She was wearing jeans and a black top, but it was her long blond hair that had caught Alex's attention.

It was Jax.

Alex froze. He felt a rush of emotion welling up within him, coming close to breaking the surface of awareness, but the too-distant feeling remained mired in a wilderness of nothing.

Jax was sitting alone on the couch. Her hands rested limp at her sides. Her brown eyes stared straight ahead. She didn't seem to be aware of anything. Alex distantly thought that she was achingly beautiful.

Henry, who had noticed Alex stop and stare, grinned.

"Good-looking woman, eh, Alex?"

For the first time that he could remember, Alex felt the presence of the dark shadow of anger somewhere within.

"Do you want to say hello?" Henry asked. "Go ahead. Might as well as long as we're here."

Alex shuffled closer and came to a stop before her.

"Jax?"

She looked up. She blinked slowly.

Alex saw within those beautiful eyes a spark of recognition.

That spark was layered over with the same numbing weight of drugs that he knew so well, the same drugs he hated, but he still saw it there.

If Jax recognized him, and he was sure she did, she didn't act like it, showing no more sign of recognition than had his mother.

Alex realized that it had to be deliberate. She didn't want to betray that she recognized him. As drugged as she was, she was trying to protect him by not acknowledging that she knew him.

"Well," Henry said, "looks like she isn't interested in a date." He nudged Alex with an elbow as he leaned a little closer. "Maybe she'd like a date with me later tonight after lights-out. What do you think, Alex? Think she might like that?"

Through the unfeeling haze, Alex knew that Jax was in great peril. He again felt the shadowy presence of anger, but this time it was closer, darker, stronger, even if he couldn't reach it, couldn't connect with it.

He managed to muster deception. "Maybe."

Henry chuckled. "Maybe she'd like you to tell us all about the gateway. Think so, Alex? Think she would be relieved if you did what we want?"

"I suppose," Alex said in a flat, distant tone, deliberately playing dumb. It wasn't at all difficult.

Henry turned him and shoved him, getting him moving. As he shuffled away, Alex glanced back over his shoulder. Jax's head didn't move. Her hands stayed limp at her sides.

But her eyes followed him.

He knew the private, lonely hell she was in. He knew because he felt the same way.

If Alex was in a daze before, he was even more dazed as they made their way back across the ninth floor to the men's wing, to his room. He was beginning to remember pieces.

He recognized, if distantly, that he had to do something.

He knew that no one was going to show up to save him.

He knew that he had to help himself or things were only going to get worse. Henry had made that clear enough. His mother was going to suffer, but the worst of it would be reserved for Jax.

If Alex wanted to prevent that, he had to do something.

"Here we go," Henry said as they finally made their way across to the men's sunroom. "You should sit here and enjoy the sunshine while you think things over."

"All right," Alex said.

The orderly guided him over to the couches against the wall. Alex sat without protest. On the other side of the room men stared at the television. Alex stared at the floor.

When he heard squeaking he looked over and saw that the squeak was coming from shiny black shoes. "Snack time, folks," the overweight orderly said as he pushed the cart into the room.

"You should have yourself a sandwich, Alex," Henry said.

Alex merely nodded.

"And in the meantime, you think about things. You think real hard on the answers we want because we're running out of patience. Do you understand?"

Alex nodded again without looking up.

Henry handed him a paper plate with a whole-wheat sandwich on it and a plastic glass of orange drink from the cart. "We'll talk later."

Alex nodded again without looking up. As he watched Henry walking away, he took a sip of orange juice, holding the cool liquid in his mouth under his tongue as his mind frantically tried to summon action. It was like trying to push the dead weight of a mountain.

He ate a few bites of the tasteless sandwich to the sounds of contestants in a game show giving answers to questions. Frequently the television audience broke out in laughter. The men watching didn't react.

Alex needed answers.

Not at all hungry, he set down the plate with the sandwich. He sat for a time staring at nothing, his mind hopelessly blank, feeling overwhelmed with frustration at his inability to think.

The only thing that he seemed able to keep in focus was the image of Jax. The emotion connected to that image was buried somewhere deep within him.

He finally got up and began making his way back toward his room, the whole way struggling to reason out what he could do. But under the dampening fog of Thorazine, his thoughts would not crystallize. Shuffling his way down the hall, he knew that the drugs were preventing him from thinking of a way to fight back.

From somewhere, realization suddenly seemed to be there. Being able to think was not the immediate solution, it was the problem. He'd been focusing on the problem, rather than the solution. The real solution was to eliminate what was preventing him from thinking: the drugs.

In his room, he sat in the chair. Light coming in the frosted window behind slowly faded away to blackness. After a time he smelled food and heard the dinner cart being wheeled down the hall to the sunroom, where they fed the patients. When one of the women from the cafeteria stuck her head in to remind him that it was dinnertime, Alex only nodded. He wasn't hungry.

As he sat listening to the buzz of the overhead lights, he held tight to the core of the real solution: getting off the drugs so that he *could* think. He worked at that notion like a mental worry stone. He grasped that if he was to solve anything, he first had to find a way not to take the drugs they gave him. After that, his mind would work.

He didn't know how he could manage such a thing. They made him take his medication. They waited and made sure he took it. If he didn't, they would force him. He couldn't fight them off.

And then, the answer was simply there.

He had to somehow make them think that he had taken his medication. He had to trick them. But how in the world could he do such a thing?

He sat for hours as the evening wore on, struggling mightily to come up with a way to do it. If he didn't somehow accomplish what he needed to do, Jax was going to suffer.

He wasn't aware of the idea coming to him. But he realized that it had. Some part of him, some inner will, held on to that solution for dear life so that it couldn't slip away from him.

He knew that if he could pull it off, then without the drugs his mind would begin to work and then maybe he would be able to come to his own rescue.

He got up and turned on the smaller reading light over the bed, then shut off the main ceiling lights. The smaller light gave off a muted illumination, but it was plenty of light to see by, and it made the room dimmer than the hall. The partial darkness would help cover what he intended to do.

Exhausted from the effort of plotting and adjusting the lights, he flopped back into his chair to wait for the nurse to arrive with his evening medications.

He nodded off twice before she arrived.

He woke with a start when she knocked and announced "Medication time" in a musical voice. She was one of the nicer nurses, a top-heavy woman with at least a dozen moles on her face and more on her plump arms. She always had a ready smile.

"I have your medications for you, Alex."

Alex nodded and reached up for the cup of Thorazine on the tray before she had a chance to wonder if he might need help.

He tipped his head back as he poured the syrupy medication into his mouth, then brought his head back down, making a face as he swallowed. He crushed the paper cup in one hand and tossed it in the wastebasket beside his chair.

He hadn't swallowed the medication, though. He held the Thorazine syrup in the hollow under his tongue.

She held the tray out for him. He dumped the second cup with the pills into his mouth and immediately captured them under his tongue as well as he tossed the cup in the trash.

The nurse yawned while she waited for him to wash down the pills. Alex had to repress his urge to yawn in sympathy with her as he immediately took the third cup with the water. He drank it down as he tipped his head back, pretending that he was swallowing the pills with the water, and then as his head was coming back down after swallowing the water, he used his tongue to push the syrup and pills out and into the cup.

Alex immediately crumpled the paper cup with the Thorazine and pills in it as he had done with the previous two and tossed it in the wastebasket.

"Have a good night, Alex," the nurse said as she hurried away.

Alex sat in the dimly lit room, unable to summon joy, exhilaration, or triumph.

But he knew that when the drugs in his system began to wear off, he would feel all of those delicious things and much more.

33.

B Y THE NEXT MORNING, Alex was noticeably more alert. While not
entirely out from under the numbing influence of the drugs, he
did feel as if he was coming out of a long, dark sleep. He knew
it would take more time for the drugs to get out of his system. Also,
even though he had spit out the last dose of Thorazine, it wasn't possible to spit out one hundred percent of it. At least he'd been able to
completely eliminate the pills.

The first thing he did when he woke was to take the cup from the
night before, the one with the medications in it, and crumple it up
inside a paper napkin just to make sure that there was no chance the
people who collected the trash would see any syrup or pills and alert
the staff.

If anyone found out that he wasn't being controlled by the drugs,
they would put him in physical restraints. These people were only
posing as medical professionals, after all. They were hardly interested in his well-being. He didn't know how many of the staff were

involved in the scheme, so he dared not trust any of them. For all he knew, the whole place could be in on it.

When a nurse came in with his morning dose of medications, Alex acted the same as he had been acting for days—lethargic, uninterested, sleepy—and repeated his trick of spitting the Thorazine and the pills into the water cup and throwing it away.

Almost immediately after the nurse left, Dr. Hoffmann strolled briskly into the room. Alex concentrated on sitting still and staring. He finally looked up, blinking slowly as he met the doctor's gaze.

"How are we doing this morning, Alex?"

"Fine."

"That's good to hear," he said as he pulled the blood-pressure cuff from a pocket.

He wrapped the cuff around Alex's arm and pumped up the bulb, then read the dial as he let air out. When finished, he pulled the stethoscope from his ears.

"Just as I promised, you're getting acclimated to the medication." He wrote on his chart as he talked. "Your blood pressure is coming back up. It's a little surprising, but everyone reacts differently. You're young and strong, so your body is handling it well."

Alex stared without answering.

"Feeling any more alert?"

"A little," Alex said, trying to sound distant.

The doctor's face took on a serious set. "Good, because it's about time for you to start answering questions. Some people are going to be arriving soon for a visit, and they're going to want to talk to you."

"All right," Alex said as if he didn't care.

"These people think it's time for answers. They aren't going to be as indulgent as we've been in the past."

Alex let his gaze wander to the floor. "All right."

"You had better be prepared to give them those answers or things are going to became rather unpleasant. Especially for other people. You don't want that, now, do you?"

"Please," Alex mumbled, "don't hurt my mother."

Dr. Hoffmann stood, sliding his pen into his breast pocket. "That's going to be up to you, Alex. If you don't want people hurt, then the easiest thing to do is to simply answer their questions. Understand?"

Alex nodded.

"Good." He started away, then turned back. He stood near the door frowning as he studied Alex's face. Alex stared off without blinking, without moving.

"I'll see you soon," he said at last.

Alex nodded. The doctor tapped his palm against the doorframe for a moment as he watched Alex, and then he was gone.

Once alone, with the door closed, Alex paced. It felt good to pace, to move his muscles. He also hoped pacing would help to work more of the drugs out of his system.

Until he could figure out what to do he needed to avoid raising suspicions, so when it was time for lunch he shuffled down to the sunroom with the other patients. He ate about half of the beef-and-noodle casserole even though he was too excited at being able to think to be hungry. Afterward, he stayed in the sunroom for a couple of hours, sitting and staring and keeping up appearances as he kept an eye on the staff, the whole while trying to come up with a plan.

As he sat pretending to be in a stupor, he let anger course through him. It felt good to be able to feel angry at the people doing this, to embrace that rage and focus it.

He was worried about his mother, but he was far more worried about Jax. She was the one from another world, so she was the one in the greatest danger. She had said that she recognized people from her world, like Sedrick Vendis, and Yuri, the passenger in the plumbing truck that had almost run them down. It was likely that some of these people would recognize her. Icy dread washed through him at the thought of what they might do to her.

Alex returned to his room, where he paced some more as he ached with worry for Jax. He missed her. He missed being with her, talking to her, seeing her smile. He wanted her safe. He felt responsible because she wasn't. He'd brought her to the hospital and right into a trap.

He returned to the sunroom when a woman from the cafeteria told him it was time for dinner, and after dinner waited in his room for the nurse to bring his evening medication. As before, he sat with only the reading light on and when she came in he repeated his trick of disposing of the medication.

Not more than an hour later, when he was thinking that maybe he should go to bed so that no one would be suspicious, Henry showed up.

"How you doing, Alex? Doc says that he told you about meeting some new people."

Alex only nodded.

"Well, don't just sit there staring, let's go."

Alex hadn't been expecting it to be this soon. He hadn't come up with a plan yet. He blinked slowly up at Henry. "What?"

Henry huffed in irritation and marched over to haul Alex up out of his chair. "Come on. People are waiting."

Alex followed behind the orderly, shuffling along in imitation of the way he had walked when under the influence of the drugs. He had to force himself to go slow. Henry whistled to himself as he led Alex down the hall and through the nurses' station.

It was late, long after visiting hours, so there were fewer people on duty. Several of them talked about charts and changes to medication orders, paying little attention to Henry and his charge. They were cooking something on a hot plate sitting on a small counter at the head of the aisles with the charts. It smelled good, like chicken soup.

Alex was puzzled as to where Henry was taking him. He did his best to make it a slow journey. Rather than go into any of the patient rooms, or to the sunroom, Henry surprised him by turning him in to the women's bathroom.

Alex couldn't imagine what was going on, but he had to play along, not ask questions, and act uninterested. His only safety was in everyone thinking he was drugged. The bathroom looked almost identical to the one on the men's side, only reversed. They passed the row of sinks and empty stalls. The place was deserted. At the back of the room Henry pulled out his keys and unlocked the door leading to the showers.

Alex could see that inside the entrance area it looked just like the men's side, with benches bolted to the wall. The entire entrance was done in white tiles. The grout was old and discolored. Pipes, covered in what looked like dozens of layers of white paint, filled one corner from floor to ceiling. The showers were around a corner and Alex couldn't see them.

Henry shoved him through the doorway. Dr. Hoffmann was waiting in the entrance area. There were a couple of other men there as well, orderlies, and Alice, the nurse.

A man came out from around the corner. He was bigger than the doctor, about Alex's size. He wore tan slacks and a beige shirt with a vertical blue stripe down the left side.

He had the eyes of a predator. He moved like one as well.

The hair on the back of Alex's neck stiffened. He knew who the man was from the description Mr. Martin, the gallery owner, had given. It was the man who had bought six of Alex's paintings and then defaced them. Jax had also told him about this man.

He was Sedrick Vendis, right-hand man to Radell Cain.

"This him?" Vendis asked.

Henry nodded. "Alexander Rahl."

Sedrick Vendis glided close, until he stood almost toe-to-toe with Alex. He studied Alex's face before gazing into his eyes. Alex didn't like how close the man was standing. It was a violation of physical space intended to challenge and intimidate. He forced himself to stay still and act numb.

Alex knew that, being this close, he could probably kill the man before anyone would be able to react. He gave serious consideration to doing so. The rage within wanted him to act.

But if he did, it wouldn't help Jax. It was the wrong time and place. It would gain him nothing in the bigger picture. He had to use his head. At least now his mind was working.

He blinked slowly, keeping his eyes out of focus as he stared at nothing, trying to look completely passive.

"Tell me about the gateway," Vendis said in a quiet tone of undiluted threat.

Alex shrugged, but didn't answer.

Vendis smiled. It was as wicked a smile as Alex had ever seen.

"I'm not here to play games, as you will soon learn," Vendis said, just as quietly, just as menacingly. "Come with me. I have something to show you."

"All right," Alex said in a slur.

He shuffled along behind Vendis, the rest of the people following behind Alex.

As he rounded the corner, the long row of showerheads sticking from the white tile wall came into view. Just like the men's shower, there were no partitions. The showers were in one long, open room with a drain beneath each showerhead.

Alex went numb with dread.

About in the middle of the row, Jax, blindfolded, her hands bound together, was hanging by her wrists from one of the shower pipes projecting from the wall. She had to stretch in order for her tiptoes to reach the floor.

She was naked.

34.

STANDING NEXT TO JAX was a man Alex instantly recognized. He was the burly passenger from the Jolly Roger Plumbing truck that had almost run over Jax the first time Alex had seen her. He was still wearing the same dark, dirty work clothes.

Jax's clothes, the clothes she and Alex had bought together, lay where they had been carelessly tossed to the side as they'd stripped her.

The bearded man's grin displayed crooked, yellow teeth. His dark eyes remained fixed on Alex, giving him a meaningful look while putting an arm around Jax's waist in a familiar manner. She flinched slightly at his touch. In her drugged state she probably wouldn't be able to understand it all, or to care a great deal.

"Glad you finally made it for the show," the pirate said as he reached over with his other grimy hand and rubbed Jax's bare belly. "We didn't want to start in on this fine bitch until you was here."

Alex could see Jax's muscles tense at the man's rough touch. She held her breath.

Alex put all his effort into keeping the rage off his face. It was a monumental task. More than anything, he wanted to kill everyone in the room and get Jax free. Most of all, though, he wanted to get his hands on the man who had his on Jax.

He knew, though, that if he did the wrong thing Jax was going to pay the price. He had stopped taking the drugs so that he would be able to think. That was what he had to do. As Ben had always said, it was his mind that was the real weapon.

"Now," Vendis said, "I want you to tell me all about the gateway."

Alex didn't reply. He simply blinked dumbly, as if he wasn't sure what they wanted him to say.

"Oh, I'm sorry," Vendis said in mock apology, gesturing to the filthy man with his arm tightly around Jax's waist. "I forgot to introduce you. This fellow here is Yuri. As it so happens, Yuri knows this young lady. In fact, she killed his brother. Isn't that right, Yuri?"

The look on Yuri's face darkened. "Sure is. But I'm about to settle the score."

"As you can see," Vendis said, "Yuri has a rather unsympathetic attitude toward the young lady's predicament. That's why I invited him to come along. Men with grudges tend to be much more focused on getting revenge."

Alex judged that he and Jax would have little chance to get away as long as she was so heavily drugged. She wouldn't be able to help him and she wouldn't be able to run. Trying to carry her and fight off pursuers at the same time would never work. He needed her at least partially alert in order to change the odds enough that they would have any real chance.

"All right," Alex said in a slur. "Can I go now?"

"I didn't come here to have you play games," Vendis snapped.

"Don't act stupid with me. We're finished with all this nonsense of gentle pretense to coax answers forth. I've put up with games and the promises of results for long enough!

"You are going to tell me what I want to know, or else Yuri here is going to start cutting on her. Nothing fatal, you understand, but definitely disfiguring and, more importantly, agonizing. If you don't want to cooperate and tell me about the gateway, I can tell you from experience that she is going to quickly become a rather gruesome, bloody sight."

Alex shrugged. "All right."

Vendis glowered. "What do you mean, 'All right'?"

"Go ahead. Cut her up."

A curious smile came to Vendis's face. "You want me to start cutting her up?"

"If you want to," Alex said.

When the man's frown returned, Alex went on, slurring his words slightly. "She's drugged. She won't feel it. I know. I'm drugged the same way and I don't really feel much of anything or care. If you kill her, you will be doing us a favor."

"A favor?" The man looked truly puzzled. "What favor?"

Alex shrugged. "She will die without really suffering. She won't feel it much or care. It will all be over."

Vendis stepped closer. His voice became louder. "You're making no sense."

"I only know part of what you want. She knows the other part. Without the half she knows about the gateway, my half is of no use. If you kill her you will be doing us both a favor because you will fail to get what you want from this world and I won't even have to feel sad about her death because, with the drugs, I can't feel sad.

"The way she's drugged, she won't really feel it when you cut her,

278

so go ahead. Cut her, let her bleed out and die. Then it will all be over and done with and you won't get any of what you want."

"You both will die, though. Die an agonizing death."

Alex blinked slowly. He wavered a little on his feet for effect. "If we are to die a horrible death, what better way? This drugged up, neither of us will really feel it or care. That will be the end of it. Finished."

Vendis turned to the doctor. "Do these potions you gave them do as he says?"

The doctor spread his hands. "The drugs are how we control them. It keeps them in a stupor."

"And she won't feel it if we cut her? He won't care?"

"Well, not exactly. She'll feel it." The man cleared his throat. "But perhaps . . . not as much as you would like. It would be only a distant pain. She may cry out a little, but it's as he says. She really won't be that aware of the pain, or care. Being on the same drugs, he can't feel any anger or sadness about it. The drugs' actual purpose, after all, is to prevent patients from feeling either hostility or emotional distress."

Vendis ground his teeth before turning away from the doctor. He stalked to Jax. Yuri backed away.

Vendis lifted the blindfold to peer into Jax's eyes. They were half closed. She didn't look like she was much aware of anything. Alex knew only too well how out of touch she was with what was going on.

The thought crossed his mind that if what he was doing didn't work, then it probably was just as well that she was drugged. He ached for her and what she was going through. He wanted nothing more than to break the necks of these people, but he had to mask his anger if he was to have a chance to save her.

Vendis reached out then, and viciously twisted her left nipple.

She should have cried out. She didn't flinch or try to pull away. She only hunched her back a little in a dull response to the pain. No more than a whisper of a moan came from her lips. Her glassy eyes showed virtually no reaction.

Vendis pulled the blindfold back down. He turned to see Alex staring off, his eyes out of focus, not reacting. He let out an angry breath.

"You are being paid for results," Vendis growled at the doctor. "This is hardly producing results."

The doctor shrugged apologetically. "Well, I don't think that this kind of approach can be expected to be compatible with—"

"If you stop these potions you're giving her," Vendis cut in, "how long until she will be fully awake?"

"Within twenty-four hours she would be largely back to herself," Dr. Hoffmann said. "But I would respectfully advise that we not do that. Need I remind you how dangerous she is?"

"I don't need reminders of anything from the likes of you."

The doctor swallowed at the look in Vendis's eyes. "Of course not. I only meant to point out . . ." When he saw that his attempt at an explanation was only darkening the glower on Vendis's face, he changed his approach. "With your approval, I could cut the dose enough so that she will be aware, yet still be controllable. I think we can strike a balance that will work to our advantage."

"Will she be awake enough to scream her lungs out when Yuri starts cutting her?"

"Absolutely. If we reduce the dose enough, absolutely." The doctor fiddled with a button on his white coat. "I can adjust the dose to still take some of the fight out of her, but leave her awake and aware enough to feel the pain and scream when you cut her."

The smile returned to Vendis's face. "Good. How long?"

The doctor looked relieved to have been able to redeem himself. "She should be the way you want her by tomorrow night at this time." He gestured to Alex. "What about him?"

Vendis turned to study Alex's face a moment. "If he is left like this, are you sure that he won't care when she screams?"

The doctor scratched his temple, then answered reluctantly. "He's not bluffing. With as much Thorazine as we're giving him he can't bluff. With as much as we're giving him he doesn't have the ability to care about anything. I believe he really would rather we kill them both right now while he's drugged. He knows it would be an easy way to go compared to what's in store for them. Maybe it would be best if I also cut back on his Thorazine. Maybe that would be a good idea."

Vendis's glare slid from Alex to the doctor. "Maybe it would."

"The drugs will be worn off for your purposes by tomorrow night," the doctor assured him. "We'll wait for your return, then."

"I have matters I must attend to." Vendis's gaze shifted to the others. "See to this. Any of you knows how to cause agony and make it last until you get what you want. I don't need to waste my time standing around while a couple of troublesome people bleed and scream and cry for mercy. I only need the information once they give it up."

Everyone except Alex bowed.

Vendis gestured to the doctor. "Show me out."

After they had gone, everyone let out a sigh of relief.

"Well," Alice said, "I guess we'll have to wait and do this tomorrow night."

Henry gestured to her and the two orderlies. "You three get him back to his room." He grinned as he glanced back at Jax hanging naked from the showerhead. "Yuri and I will take good care of her tonight."

Alex's knees went weak.

One of the orderlies seized Alex's arm, turning him around. "Let's go."

Alex's mind raced. He had to do something to buy Jax time. He dug in his heels and looked back over his shoulder.

"I know that tomorrow, once you reduce our drugs, you'll be able to get us both to talk. I also know that after you get what you want you'll kill me. When I'm dead I won't be able to know or care about anything anymore.

"But if either of you touches her tonight, before I'm dead, then once I'm off the drugs I will care and I will have plenty of reason not to talk. If you touch her, I swear on my life you will be trying to explain to Vendis why you failed to get anything from me."

"Well, well," Alice said. "I think we just found out how much he really cares for her. He's going to make this easy for us."

Yuri's eyes glinted with menace. "And if he cares for her so much, once off the drugs we won't have to disfigure her too much before he's eager to tell us everything he knows." He glanced over at Henry. "Then we can have her, and we won't have to be concerned about what damage we might do. Besides, the way she is right now it wouldn't be much better than screwing a corpse. It would be a lot more satisfying if she was awake and kicking."

At first displeased, Henry considered a moment. "I guess you may be right. Alice, I don't trust our patient, here. And I don't trust a nervous doctor to adjust the dose correctly. He's worried about his own neck but it's our necks on the line. We take orders from His Excellency, not a doctor from this world. You make sure that Alex gets enough so that he can't fight, but not so much that he won't care about her screams."

Alice coldly appraised Alex. "I would have to agree with you about the doctor." She smiled crookedly. "I'll make sure that my patient is able to be terrified, but not able to fight back. In the meantime, if you two do anything to ruin her so that she can't talk, or he won't, I'll have you both hanging there in her place when Vendis returns. Got it?"

Henry made a sour face. "Got it."

Yuri folded his arms and finally nodded.

She shoved Alex. "Let's go."

35.

THE NEXT MORNING, after an endlessly long, sleepless night of staring up at the ceiling in the dark, Alex got dressed and sat on the edge of his bed to wait. All he could think about was Jax hanging there, alone, no one caring how much agony she was in. Alex was the only one who cared, and he couldn't do anything about it. Not yet, anyway.

Not long after he'd gotten dressed, Henry showed up. The big man looked to be in a foul mood. It became obvious just how bad his mood was when he pulled Alex to his feet and began punching him in the abdomen. Henry apparently didn't want marks that would be obvious. Maybe the others had told him not to damage their prize.

Alex could do nothing but take it. He knew that such a beating to the abdomen could cause dangerous injuries. He also knew that he couldn't fight back if he was to keep Henry believing that he was drugged. They had to believe that, if he was to have a chance to help Jax.

This time, though, as Henry slugged him, Alex didn't have the benefit of drugs to dull the pain. This time it hurt in earnest and left him gasping on the floor. He fought back the urge to vomit. For a time as he lay on the floor convulsing in agony, Alex was hating life.

"You know, Alex," Henry said as he stood with his fists at his sides, towering over Alex, catching his breath, "you would think that we would be even by now. But I have to tell you, when I woke up this morning and my nose was bleeding again, I realized that we're not even close to being even."

The big man unexpectedly kicked Alex in the side of the head. It caused Alex to bite the inside of his cheek. He swallowed the coppery taste of blood. He struggled to stay conscious, and to stay quiet, to act thoroughly sedated.

"Since I have to wait to screw the bitch, I figure you owe me even more. One way or another you two are going to end up talking up a storm for me."

Henry squatted down to be close when he delivered the rest of the threat. "Tell you what else. Your day is going to end badly. I'm going to tie a tourniquet here, and here." Henry used a finger to mark a place on each of Alex's upper arms. "Then I'm going to cut off your arms, right here. Then I'm going to do the same things to your legs. The tourniquets will keep you from losing so much blood that you miss the show.

"You're going to tell us everything you know or we'll be doing even worse things to your lady. And let me tell you, when it comes to using a knife, Yuri is a real artist. Once he gets started he gets inspired and you just can't stop the man. I think he's kind of sick in the ways he enjoys hurting women, but maybe that's just me. You're going to be eager to tell me everything you know to keep Yuri from getting started on her."

Alex lay curled up on the floor gripped by pain and rage. He pretended to be gripped by neither.

Henry stood. "Alice will be in with your morning medication any time now. Last night's dose will be wearing off by tonight, and this morning's dose is being reduced. You'll be clearheaded enough to hear Jax screaming and begging you to tell us what we want to know."

Even if he wanted to, Alex couldn't tell them what they wanted to know. He didn't know what a gateway was or anything about it. He didn't think, though, that they were going to believe that.

"You understand?" Henry demanded.

Alex, curled up on the floor holding his arms across the cramping pain in his middle, could only nod.

Henry seized Alex's shirt and hauled him to his feet, then heaved him into the chair. "You sit there and have a nice rest. Alice will be in with your medication in a bit. Got that?"

Alex nodded as if he didn't care.

Henry paused at the door to look back and smile. "You just got to love a world that comes up with Thorazine. Just think, I can pound the crap out of you and the Thorazine keeps you helpless to lift a finger to defend yourself. What a great world."

After Henry left, Alex put his throbbing head in his hands, recovering, trying to clear his vision from the brutal kick. His neck muscles hurt so much that he could hardly move his head.

He let the anger rage through him. He held his hand out to see his fingers trembling. He knew that he needed to get them under control or someone might get suspicious.

He wanted the day to be over. He wanted to see Jax. She would still be drugged, but not nearly as much. He needed her to be more alert if he was to have a chance of helping her.

He hated to see her doped up with Thorazine and whatever else was in the pills. He didn't know if they would stop the pills. Since his mother was on Thorazine he'd long ago asked questions about them. Thorazine, he had learned, greatly amplified the effect of whatever pills were taken with it.

Alex leaned back in the chair and drew deep, even breaths, trying to calm himself as he waited for his morning medications to arrive.

One more dose of drugs to dodge.

He was pretty sure that they wouldn't bother with the evening dose, since the morning dose wouldn't be worn off that soon and they surely intended to kill him that night after they got the information they wanted.

Except Alex didn't have any information to give them. He didn't know anything except that Jax had figured out what they were after. She hadn't had time to tell him what that was.

Still, even that much information was dangerous to them both. That information in and of itself might be all they needed. If Alex couldn't find a way to stop them, they would be able to get him to reveal that Jax knew what they were looking for, and then torture her to get her to tell them everything she knew. Alex's grandfather had told him once that everyone had a breaking point and everyone would eventually talk under torture.

These people were obviously experienced at torture. They knew what they were doing. He couldn't expect either Jax or himself to be able to hold out forever.

Alex knew that he couldn't let it go that far. He had no option but to try to do something before it got to that point. He'd been awake most of the night trying to come up with something, but it was next to impossible to plan when he didn't know exactly what it was that they were going to do. If they came to get him and first bound his hands or put him in a straitjacket before taking him to Jax, it would be all over. He needed them to believe he was drugged enough that he couldn't fight them. He needed to keep up the act and put them at ease.

If they tried to restrain him, though, he would have no choice but to act.

If he had to fight them in his room first, he didn't know how in the world he was going to get all the way across the ninth floor of Mother of Roses. He couldn't break down the heavy doors. They were designed to keep mental patients from breaking them down.

If he could get keys he could unlock the doors, but not all the staff carried keys. Even if he managed to get his hands on a set of keys, he couldn't simply stroll through so many locked doors, or through the nurses' station, without being seen and an alarm being raised.

His head spun as he tried to think through the different scenarios. His thinking was beginning to become mired in panic.

Just then the door swung open. It was his morning medications. Except that this time it was Alice who marched in with a med tray. Alex sat limp, staring off at nothing.

Alice glared down at him a moment, then lowered the tray with the three cups. "Time for your medications. Don't give me any grief. I have things to do, other patients waiting for my caring touch, so hurry it up."

Alex nodded and took the cup with the Thorazine. He trapped the syrupy liquid in his mouth under his tongue as before, then added the pills to it. He spit the whole thing into the water cup after drinking down the water. He crushed the cup and threw it in the wastebasket with the first two.

Alice had watched him the whole time. Her gaze moved to the wastebasket. She stood for a moment, then tossed the tray on the bed and bent to retrieve the larger of the three cups, the one that had held the water and now contained the discarded drugs.

She looked in the cup and then angrily threw it in his lap.

"Nice try. You have ten seconds to drink it all down or I'm going to go get a couple of orderlies and we're going to put you in a straitjacket."

Alex blinked as he had when he'd been heavily drugged. "But I'll need water to swallow this."

"Clock's ticking, Alex."

He caught a glimpse of her other hand behind her back. She had a syringe.

Alex exploded out of the chair.

A brief, clipped cry of surprise was all that made it out before he broke her jaw.

He immediately grabbed her throat with both hands. He saw her hand with the syringe come up. He kept hold of her throat with one hand and with the other seized her hand and bent it downward until her wrist snapped. The syringe dropped to the floor, bouncing several times.

Alice couldn't cry for help, not only because he was crushing her windpipe, but because her jaw was broken and hanging crookedly. Blood ran in strings from the side of her mouth, leaving a bright red stain that spread across the shoulder of her stark white dress.

Her back arched as she tried to get away, but Alex had her throat in a death grip. She beat her good fist against him to no effect as he took her to her knees. All the while she tried to lean back away from him.

Alex was lost in a life-or-death rage. He could see as well as feel his thumbs crushing her throat closed. He put every fiber of his strength into squeezing harder yet. He gritted his teeth, letting out a low growl with the effort.

Alice's eyes bulged. She frantically swung her arm, trying to beat him back. Alex was immune to her impotent blows. She began turning blue. Her tongue swelled from her mouth as she desperately tried to gasp a breath, but it was impossible.

Alex followed her to the ground, straddling her as he choked the life out of her. He held her head against the floor, using his weight to help crush her throat. Her arms flailed weakly. Her mouth moved as if she was trying to say something, but her distended tongue prevented her from even mouthing words for which there was no air.

Alex let his anger rage at this woman who intended to be a party to torturing Jax. He wanted this woman dead. He wanted them all dead.

Alex had for so long been holding back his rage, his need to strike out and fight back, that it felt exhilarating to finally be able to let that fury loose.

He didn't know how long she had been dead before he even realized it.

He finally sat back on his heels, catching his breath. With the back of his wrist he wiped sweat from his brow.

She was purple. Her eyes were wide open, staring at nothing. Her tongue bulged from her mouth, lying over to the side. Saliva and blood trickled out.

Alex raked his fingers back though his hair. He thought he might be sick.

He finally got up off the corpse. He saw the syringe and picked it up. The cap was missing. He realized that she must have popped it off with a thumb. He cast about and finally found the cap under the bed. He replaced it and put the syringe in his pocket.

In the eerie silence, the bed squeaked as Alex leaned back against it. He stared at the dead woman sprawled in the middle of the floor.

He'd had no choice, of course, but this complicated things. He had to figure out what he was going to do with her now. He considered stuffing her in the wardrobe, but when he opened the door to check its size, he realized that there was no way she would fit. He could push her under the bed, but the bedcovers didn't hang down far enough to hide anything under such a high hospital bed.

He paced, trying to think. Soon, someone was going to come in and they would see her. If nothing else they would come that night to get him and take him over to their private torture session in the women's shower.

He considered putting Alice against the wall, behind where the door opened, cleaning up the mess, and then going down to the sunroom to wait. It would probably be Henry who came looking for him. If Alex only left on the reading lamp over the bed, Henry might pop his head in, not see Alex, and go to the sunroom.

He realized that that was a lousy plan. Any number of things were likely to go wrong. People were soon going to wonder where Alice was and start searching for her. The orderlies were quick to pick up on such things. Some of the patients could be dangerous and they didn't allow staff to go unaccounted for. They knew that she was doing med rounds. It was probably only a matter of minutes before they came looking for her to make sure she was all right.

Alex paced, frantically trying to think of what he could do, glancing over at the corpse every time he turned to pace in the other direction. He needed to somehow make Alice disappear.

He stopped suddenly and stared down at the woman. She was a mess. Blood from when he had struck her and broken her jaw lay in a long string halfway across the floor. Alice had lost control of herself as he had strangled her. There was a spreading puddle of urine under her sprawled legs.

He needed her to disappear.

Alex wondered if it was possible.

He could try. At this point he had no other ideas and nothing to lose.

He ran to the bed. It was old and squeaked whenever someone leaned against it. When things squeaked like that it usually meant that screws had worked loose. He ran his fingers along the metal bars and quickly found a self-tapping metal screw sticking up at the end of the side rail. He used his thumb and the side of his first finger to loosen it. He gritted his teeth with the effort. Had he not been so frantic he might not have been able to unscrew it with his bare hands.

The screw wasn't long—certainly not long enough to be an effective weapon—but it had a relatively sharp point and was long enough for his purpose. He hurried over to Alice and squatted down beside her purple face.

He held the screw over the dead woman's forehead as he thought. He closed his eyes as he worked to remember. He had seen Jax activate a lifeline several times. The first time it had been shocking to see her carving in Bethany's forehead. Such surprise helped indelibly fix the picture in his mind.

More than that, though, he was an artist. Designs stuck in his head. He remembered forms, spatial relationships. He clearly recalled that every time Jax had drawn the design it looked the same. He was pretty sure that he remembered the way Jax had cut that design into foreheads. He let himself see it in his mind.

He could hear orderlies talking as they walked along the hallway outside his room. He had no choice but to try.

With the point of the screw Alex started carving the lines into Alice's forehead. He made the arc that Jax had done first, then added two angled lines on the right and one on the left. He cut each line in turn, concentrating on the mental picture he had of the lines in Bethany's forehead, making them precisely the same angles he remembered.

Alex lost himself in the task, just as he lost himself in painting. He made each stroke with confidence, the way Jax had. The point of the screw dragged against bone as he pulled it across the skin of Alice's forehead. He finished with the pattern that overlaid the beginning arc, just as Jax had done.

Alex sat back on his heels, holding the screw in his fingers, looking at the thing he had drawn. Blood covered his fingers and ran down his wrist.

Unexpectedly, Alice ceased to be there. She didn't become transparent and slowly fade away like in a ghost movie. It didn't look like some spooky special effect. There was no drama to it. She was there one moment, and the next instant she simply wasn't.

Alex blinked in astonishment. He looked around. The blood across the floor was gone. The puddle of urine was gone. He looked at his bloody fingers holding the screw. There was no blood. He sat still for a moment, taking it in.

He had just drawn a spell and made someone disappear before his very eyes. He had done it. It was so astonishing, and such a huge relief, that Alex laughed.

He heard orderlies coming down the hall. By their brief, muffled words, he could tell that they were putting their head into each room along the way, asking if anyone had seen Alice.

Alex scrambled to his chair and sat, working up a dazed look. He stared ahead, waiting for the door to open.

That was when he saw the med tray on the bed.

Alex jumped up and snatched the tray. He shoved it under the mattress. He wiped his sweaty hands on his thighs as he looked around the room. Everything looked normal. Nothing looked out of place.

He plopped down in the chair, letting his hands lie limp at his sides.

The door opened partway as an orderly leaned halfway in and glanced around the room. "Have you seen Nurse Alice?"

Alex gave the man a stuporous look. "She gave me my medicine and left."

The orderly nodded and hurried away. When the door shut, Alex let out a sigh of relief.

Now he had to wait for night, when they would come to get him. They would expect him to be more awake but they would also believe he would still be sufficiently sedated that they could torture answers out of him and he wouldn't fight back.

Alex allowed himself a smile of triumph for this much of it. The next part would be vastly more difficult, and he didn't know if he would succeed, but he had finally taken back control of his life.

As he sat waiting, he worried about Jax, hoping she could hold out. He couldn't fail. The price of failure was unacceptable.

He had promised her that as long as he could help it, he wasn't going to allow them to hurt her. He meant it.

36.

ONG AFTER DARK ALEX WAS STILL WAITING. He worried that they might have hatched some new plan. A thousand different terrors ran through his mind as he waited. As the night wore on, there was nothing he could do but wait. He had no way to get to Jax on his own.

Henry and Dr. Hoffmann finally showed up long after lights-out. The doctor was without his usual stethoscope, although he was wearing his white coat. Henry, looking smug—as smug as he could look with bandages covering his nose—waited back near the door.

Before the door had closed, Alex had seen two more orderlies fold their arms and take up posts just outside. They apparently were going to be ready if his reduced medication had rendered him more alert than they expected. They expected him to be at least aware enough to care what happened to him and Jax, but rather slow and submissive. Alex wanted them to see what they expected to see, so that was the part he played.

He rose from his chair as the doctor approached, trying to do it in a way that would look dull and a little awkward.

"Alice gave you your medication this morning?" the doctor asked as he smoothed thin strands of hair over his bald patch.

"Yes." Alex gestured to the wastebasket. "I threw the cups away after I took the medication."

The doctor glanced toward the trash. Alex didn't think that the man would actually go through the trash and inspect the discarded paper cups, and fortunately he didn't. He instead looked back at Alex's eyes.

"Throughout this entire thing I've tried to do this without people having to get hurt. I believe that such methods are the best way of actually getting the truth. Torture is a poor way to get good information. It isn't reliable. People being tortured will say anything they think the questioner wants to hear. People being tortured will confess to witchcraft if that's what is expected. But whether I like it or not, the time for trying to find answers my way is past."

He pressed his lips tight for a moment. "Take my advice, Alex. Answer their questions."

"Did they touch her?"

The doctor glanced back over his shoulder at the big orderly waiting by the door. "No. But she's been hanging there since last night. The drugs are wearing off and she's coming around, but that may only be making it worse for her. Hanging by your arms like that is dangerous in and of itself. She's having trouble breathing."

Alex's insides roiled. He remembered Jax telling him about how Sedrick Vendis liked to hang people up by their arms and how it slowly and painfully suffocated them. He was so angry that it was making him dizzy. Rage strained to be let loose.

Instead, he kept quiet as he waited. He knew that the doctor was working up to something.

"I have a deal to offer you, Alex."

Alex frowned a little. "What kind of deal?"

"If you cooperate and tell us everything we want to know, right now, right up front, I'll see if I can't get them to let me give you both an overdose."

"An overdose? You mean to kill us?"

Dr. Hoffmann nodded as he looked into Alex's eyes. "One way or another, after you both give up what you know, you're both going to die. They're pretty adamant about wanting you dead and being rid of the Rahl line—after they get what they need from you, of course—but they're especially eager to waste Jax."

"Do they know you're making such an offer?"

"No," he admitted. "But if you cooperate and tell me everything, I'll see if I can't talk them into letting me give you each an injection. They want the information, and they want you both dead. Give me the information without having to resort to torture and I can make it a peaceful death for both of you. You'll just go to sleep and never wake up."

Alex knew that Vendis, Yuri, and Henry would never go for such a deal. They were looking forward to what was coming and they had well-founded confidence that they would get all the information they wanted in their own way.

"You're in the wrong line of medicine, Dr. Hoffmann. You should have become a veterinarian."

The doctor frowned. "Why do you say that?"

"Because veterinarians get paid for performing euthanasia. When you do that to people it's called murder. Murder is punishable by death."

A small, cruel smile touched the corners of his mouth. "But if you don't let me help you, I won't be committing murder—they will."

Alex tried to act a little slow in his response, as if he had to work to talk. "The nurses' station is filled with records. You've no doubt been billing the state for care while trying to extract information from people. After all, you have to justify the patient count and all the drugs you've been using. I'm sure that you've been going through large quantities of controlled substances.

"Sooner or later when the state authorities audit the hospital's drug records they're going to discover that something strange has been going on here, that the numbers don't match. They're going to want to talk to your patients, but your patients, listed in those records, will be dead.

"By the way, what do you plan to do with the bodies? Are you experienced at disposing of dead people? How many deaths have you been party to, Doctor? What are you going to do if corpses of your patients are found? The authorities will certainly have a lot of questions for you." Alex let him wonder how he would explain it, let him worry about all the evidence sitting there in those records that would tie him to murder.

The doctor glanced briefly in the direction of the nurses' station, where the files were kept on shelves.

"They aren't going to learn anything," he finally said.

He didn't sound confident. He sounded concerned.

"How much are they paying you to be a party to murder, Doctor? Or were you a killer before they ever came along? Did you become a psychiatrist to hide your need to kill? To hide your urges? Did you think that being a doctor to psychopaths would be the perfect cover for your own perverted needs?"

Dr. Hoffmann's expression soured. "Have it your way. You can't say I didn't offer to help you out. Maybe if you give up the information quickly enough you'll get lucky and they'll cut your throat before they start in on Jax. I would have thought you would have taken the offer for her sake if not your own."

Alex almost grabbed the man by the throat the way he had Alice. With the greatest of effort he restrained himself. He had to get to Jax. After what he had just heard about her condition, that was more important than ever.

"Let what they do to her be on your conscience, since that's the choice you made for her." The doctor gestured toward the door. "Let's go."

"Any ideas?" Henry asked as they approached.

"Alice must have gotten cold feet and taken off," Dr. Hoffmann said.

He sounded annoyed and short-tempered. Alex knew that he had gotten to the man. He wanted him distracted and preoccupied.

"Just as well." Henry's face betrayed anything but worry for the woman. "She was too uppity for my taste. I often suspected that she was planted here to watch us. Maybe now that it's being wrapped up she was recalled. We have more important things to worry about. Let's go."

Alex fell in behind Henry as they turned down the hall. The lights were mostly off, leaving the corridor to gloomy shadows. Two more orderlies that Alex hadn't known were part of the scheme shadowed the doctor. He wondered if the whole place could be a front for their activities.

The nurses' station was staffed by three nurses, all engaged in a light conversation with an orderly sitting at a desk to the side. Charts and a jumbled stack of files sat on the desk. When they saw the somber group enter their station on the way through, they made themselves busy.

The women's ward on the ninth floor was just as dark as the men's wing had been. The small group paused when Alex's mother unexpectedly shuffled out of the bathroom. She was wearing pajamas and a pink robe that Alex had given her. She only briefly glanced in their direction before yawning and turning back toward her room. She had looked at Alex, along with the rest of the party, but he didn't think she had recognized him.

When she had shuffled down the hall and turned in to her room without looking back, Henry shoved Alex into the women's bathroom. It was better lit than the hall so that patients could use the bathroom in the night if they needed to. A sign saying "Out of Order" was taped to the shower door.

A nurse leaning against the wall unfolded her arms and looked down at her watch. "You're early."

"What difference does it make?" the doctor snapped.

She shrugged. "Just that Yuri isn't here yet. I had Dwayne stay late to let Yuri in when he gets here."

Dwayne was the security guard inside the back door Alex always used. As he waited, Alex stood slump-shouldered, trying to act passive. With the way the orderlies stood at ease, it seemed to be working. If only he could slow down his galloping heart.

Henry came forward, pulling out the keys attached to the reel on his belt. "We don't need Yuri to get started."

"What was Helen Rahl doing in here?" the doctor asked as Henry worked the lock.

"Taking a pee," the nurse said.

As the doorway leading into the shower opened, Alex could see that only one light was on. The cavelike room beyond had a ghostly cast to it. He thought that it looked like a place where death itself waited.

His heart felt like it came up in his throat when he saw Jax still hanging there. In addition to the blindfold, she was now gagged with a cloth through her mouth and tied behind her head. She trembled slightly. It was clear that she was having a lot of trouble breathing. She had to push up on her toes as best she could to draw each ragged breath. Her arms shook with each effort.

Alex was so enraged that it was hard for him to focus on where everyone was around him. He reminded himself that he had to keep track of where everyone was or he could be blindsided. Surprises could be deadly. He had to take a measure of the situation and not make a reckless mistake. He couldn't afford a mistake.

Jax couldn't afford a mistake.

The nurse dragged a straight-backed wooden chair from the side. The chair's feet stuttered across the tile floor, the sound echoing around in the shower. She set the chair in the center of the room, not far in front of Jax. Alex remembered seeing Jax's clothes thrown to the side, but he didn't remember seeing the chair before.

Henry, grinning with anticipation, pulled off the blindfold. Jax squinted and blinked at the sudden light, even though the light wasn't bright. She took appraisal of everyone in the room. When she met Alex's gaze there was a world of meaning, a shared understanding, in that silent connection.

Henry slid his hand down her belly and between her legs. "Getting eager for me, aren't you?"

Alex thought the deadly glare Jax gave him should have backed him up a few steps, but it didn't.

Henry, obviously enjoying his control over her, probed further as he used his other hand to pull the gag from her mouth. He let it hang around her neck. "Oh, sorry." He chuckled. "I couldn't hear you."

"You're already dead," she told him. "You just don't know it yet."

Henry removed his hand from between her legs and put it over his heart in mock alarm. "Really? Don't tell me, you intend to kill me?"

By the look in her eyes Alex could see that her rage easily matched his. She let that lethal look be her only answer.

"Did you find Alice?" the nurse asked, tiring of the game Henry was playing.

The doctor gestured irritably. "No one has seen her."

"We looked everywhere," Henry said as he turned his attention away from Jax, "and like the doc says, there's no sign of her. She's vanished."

Jax's gaze immediately sought Alex. He smiled the smallest bit in answer to the question in her eyes. A hint of a smile came to the corners of her mouth. In that smile he could see that she grasped that he'd had something to do with Alice's disappearance.

But then she had to close her eyes with the effort of pulling herself up with her arms as she stretched on her tiptoes to get a breath. Alex could see how mightily she was struggling to fight back panic at not being able to breathe.

"Maybe she went back for some reason," Henry suggested.

The others started speculating as to why Nurse Alice would have left without saying anything. It seemed to be common consensus that the woman typically did things without telling others what she was up to, so, as far as they were all concerned, it wasn't entirely out of character.

No one was looking at Alex as he stood submissively. He wanted Jax to be ready. When her eyes turned to look at him again, he gave her a small wink. The smile grew and stayed on her lips as she returned the wink. He didn't know if she grasped his full meaning or if she was merely heartened by the wink.

Losing interest in the talk about Alice, Henry pulled a folding knife from his pocket, letting everyone know that it was time to get on with it. Pressing on the thumb stud, he flicked his wrist and snapped open the blade. One of the other two orderlies did the same. Alex saw that the nurse had a syringe.

Henry used the point of his knife to back Alex up a few steps. "Have a seat."

The nurse shoved the chair against the back of his legs. Alex flopped down in the chair. In his peripheral vision he tried to keep track of the syringe.

His level of alarm rose suddenly when the other orderly stepped up close behind, pressing against the chair to hold it in place. The orderly in front of him with the knife pulled a handful of zip ties from his pocket.

Alex realized what they intended to do.

37.

URRY UP AND SECURE HIM to the chair," Henry said. "Thorazine or no Thorazine, I don't want to have to worry about either of them being loose and getting difficult to handle when we start cutting."

It appeared that they weren't going to wait for Yuri to show up. While that was one less man to worry about, Alex knew that he had to remain aware that Yuri could show up at any moment. The nurse had said that they were early, though. Maybe Henry had decided to grab the glory, and Jax, for himself.

Alex kept an eye on the knife hand of the orderly in front of him. He knew that it was the hands that were the killers.

"Put your arms behind your back," the big orderly growled as he seized Alex by the hair.

Alex knew that if they restrained him he would have no chance at all. Jax would have no chance.

He had run out of time and options.

He remembered lessons Ben had taught him from a young age,

warnings that you couldn't always choose the fight. The best thing to do was to avoid a fight, if you could. But the way that it all too often happened, his grandfather had told him, was that you would find yourself in a fight you didn't want, outnumbered, and outmatched in weapons. That was because people would generally only attack if they felt confident enough in their superiority to feel sure of the outcome.

Alex recalled, as a boy just entering adulthood, being troubled by the warning. It didn't seem fair. He asked Ben what he should do if he ever found himself in that situation. That question was the gateway to a whole new level of training.

Ben had told him that in such a case there wasn't any such thing as fair. His only chance was speed, surprise, and violence of action.

Henry stepped up beside the orderly facing Alex. "Come on, let's get this over with so we can get to her."

As the man with the zip ties took a step forward, Alex pushed his shoulders back against the man behind him, as if trying to back away from the two knives in front of him. The man behind leaned in to keep Alex from sliding the chair back. That was exactly what Alex had wanted him to do.

There was no choice now. He had only one chance.

Alex pressed his shoulders against the man behind him. The man pushed back.

In an instant of exquisite, unrestrained rage, Alex put all his force into screaming a battle cry as he uncoiled, throwing a mighty kick squarely into Henry's chest.

The blow was powerful enough to break ribs. It drove a grunt from the big man as it knocked him back.

The orderly in front of him was so surprised by the sudden burst of movement that he stood motionless for just an instant. An instant was all Alex needed. With Henry clear, in that instant when everyone else was frozen in shock, before the man behind could get a better hold on him, Alex bounded out of the chair and seized the wrist of the hand holding the knife.

With an iron grip on the man's wrist, Alex dove under the arm and came up behind. As he sprang up he used all his momentum and strength to violently twist the arm up in a way it wasn't meant to go. The shoulder popped out of its joint. Sinew separated with a sickening rip. Alex spun around, taking the arm with him. In less than a heartbeat the man's shoulder was torn apart enough that the arm was useless.

Jax was the only one who had been ready for the sudden attack. At the same time as Alex was taking out the orderly with the knife, before Henry could recover, Jax threw her legs around him, pinning his arms to his side. She locked her ankles.

The man with the ruined arm let out a shriek of pain that echoed through the shower. Alex wrenched the knife from his dangling hand. The shock and pain—the violence of action—had immobilized the orderly. Without giving him any time to recover his wits, Alex immediately rammed the captured knife three times in rapid succession into the small of the man's back, aiming for the kidney.

By the way the orderly's mouth opened with a scream that couldn't make its way out, the blade had found its mark. He twisted toward the floor, the torn arm hanging, the other reaching blindly back toward the fatal wound. On his way down, Alex ripped the knife across the man's neck, severing arteries, to be sure of the kill.

At the same time the second orderly dove in toward Alex before the first had smacked face-first onto the floor. Alex dodged to the side. As the man missed, slipped on blood, and crashed headlong into the wall, Alex wheeled around, stretched up, and slashed the ties holding Jax to the shower pipe. Her hands sprang free.

She kept her legs tightly locked around Henry as she gripped his hair with both fists to keep from being thrown off his back. As exhausted as she had to be, Alex knew that she couldn't last long. Fortunately, the violent kick, besides breaking ribs, had taken enough of the fight out of Henry that she was able to keep him immobilized—at least for the moment.

Alex knew, though, that the big man would recover his senses and wind all too soon and become a raging bull turning on her. Even so, Alex could do no more than free her before he had to turn to the man bounding back off the wall and coming at him, slashing with his knife.

Out of the corner of his eye, Alex spotted the doctor scrambling away toward the door.

Alex ducked under a wild swing, the knife missing his face by a good foot. As he sprang up, Alex punched a quick thrust of the blade in under the man's armpit, hoping to hit the space between ribs. He felt the blade slide over bone on the way in. The orderly cried out and jerked back. Alex had wanted to puncture a lung, but as heavily muscled as the man was, he wasn't sure the relatively short blade had gone deep enough.

It slowed the man for only a second. He came back at Alex, swinging with a vengeance. Alex had to dance back to avoid a half-dozen savage thrusts. He waited and picked his spot, and when the man thrust again, Alex stepped inside the attack and slashed down across the wrist. His blade cut cleanly through tendons drawn tight. Once parted, they snapped back up into the man's forearm. His fingers instantly lost their ability to grasp. The severed veins gushed blood at a prodigious rate.

The knife clattered to the tile floor. As Alex went for it, the nurse swung the chair. Alex ducked. The chair shattered across his back. In the grip of rage as he was, the pain seemed distant.

The orderly used the opening to roll under Alex, knocking his feet out from under him. The nurse dove in with the syringe. Before she could stab it into him, Alex threw an arm around the orderly's neck, getting him in a headlock that also served as an anchor point. He used the man's weight to brace himself as he kicked the nurse's hand before she could stick him. The blow broke her fingers. She let out a cry. The syringe went flying.

Alex had his hands full with the big orderly. It was like trying to hold on to a big, powerful, twisting, thrashing alligator. The injuries weren't enough to put him out of commission; if anything they made him fight all the harder.

Alex seized his own wrist to lock his arm tight around the bull neck, applying pressure to the carotid arteries. At the same time he leaned back, pulling the man back over the top of a hip, arching his back to keep him off balance and under control, and to use the man's weight to add pressure on his neck.

Above him, it was obvious that Henry was recovering. He twisted away from the grip of Jax's legs. She landed on her back not far from Alex. Henry went for her. Jax kicked up into his groin. The blow staggered the angry orderly.

As Henry reflexively bent over from the pain, Jax snatched the keys on his belt. Alex couldn't figure out what she intended to do with his keys, but he hoped she did something fast, or despite his obvious pain Henry would have her and start breaking her bones. He was big enough to break her neck with one meaty hand if he ever got it around her throat.

Jax scrambled away, staying just out of his reach. He called her every vile name in his vocabulary as he took swings, trying to grab her.

Jax pulled the keys out, gathering up the wire hand over hand as it unspooled, turning Henry, keeping him off balance. When it reached the end she scooped up a couple of broken chair legs. In a flash she twisted the legs into the wire, wrapping several loops of it around each stick of wood.

When Henry lunged at her, she dodged to the side and, with a good grip on her improvised wooden handles, gave the wire attached to his belt a mighty yank. It jerked him around. He stumbled a few steps. In a blink she circled around behind him.

Jax whipped a loop of wire over Henry's head as she bounded up onto his back, compressing her body as she planted a foot between his shoulder blades. She let out a mighty cry of rage and effort as she used all her strength to straighten her coiled body while at the same time pulling on her improvised wooden handles.

For an instant, as he realized the danger, Henry's meaty hands clawed at the wire around his throat. It was too late. As Jax screamed with effort the wire sliced cleanly down through his throat. Henry's eyes bulged.

As Jax, her foot on his back, pulled the wooden handles she'd made, the wire knifed down through the carotid arteries as well as the esophagus and windpipe. It sliced all the way through everything but a bundle of the tougher tendons.

With most of the supporting neck muscles severed, his head flopped to the side. Alex could see that the wire had to have hit perfectly between two vertebrae, rupturing the disc.

The nurse screamed at the sight of Henry toppling over. Jax, a foot against his back and her hands holding the wooden handles as if she were holding the reins to a monster, rode the towering orderly all the way down. He hit the tile floor hard. His head smacked the hardest, making a sickening crack on impact. A thick red pool spread across the white tiles.

The instant Henry landed, Jax snatched the knife from his hand and sprang catlike up off the man, using him as a launching pad to make a dive for the nurse.

Just as the woman turned to run, Jax landed on her back. They both sprawled forward. Before they hit the floor Jax sliced the woman's throat just as efficiently as she had once sliced Bethany's throat in Alex's bed.

Alex had been holding the orderly in a headlock for only a moment, yet already the man's arms moved slowly, blindly, as he tried to fight for his life. When his arms swung, the hand with the severed tendons flopped without control. As he lost consciousness the fight was going out of him.

Alex used the opening to swiftly reverse his hold and throw a leg over the man. He used the leverage to give power to a quick twist that snapped the big man's neck.

As the orderly went limp, Alex untangled himself and scrambled across the floor to Jax. She was just pushing herself up off the back of the dead nurse.

When she saw Alex her look of lethal rage instantly switched to tears of deliverance. She threw her arms around his neck. He felt a lump in his own throat. With the strength of her hold on him she wordlessly conveyed her profound sense of relief.

In the sudden silence, their breathing echoed softly in the shower room.

"Are you all right?" Alex asked as he held her head to his shoulder.

"I'm not sure. I felt like I'd become lost in some dark nightmare.

I couldn't understand it. I'm better, but I still feel strange, like I've lost my mind, lost myself."

"You're going to be fine. It's the drugs they gave us. The rest of them will wear off in another day or so. Just stay with me. It will get better, I promise."

She nodded against his shoulder. Now that the desperate fight had abruptly come to an end, the adrenaline rush was fading. Her arms loosened around his neck as her strength ebbed. Her voice, too, was weak.

"I thought it was over. I thought I was going to die hanging there. But when I saw you I knew it would be all right."

He smiled as he held her shoulders and lifted her away from him. "We're not out of this yet. I need you to stay strong a little longer. Get dressed. Hurry."

Alex found the keys at the end of the wire cable that had nearly decapitated Henry. He hurriedly worked to disconnect the keys from the fitting at the end of the cable.

"I guess now I know how you felt," Jax said as she pulled the jeans up her muscular legs, trying to cover herself as swiftly as possible.

"How I felt? What do you mean?"

"When I came to save you at your house and caught you with your pants down."

Against all odds, despite the blood everywhere, despite the way his heart still pounded from the terror and rage, Alex laughed.

38.

URRY," ALEX SAID, avoiding looking at Jax in her half-naked condition. "Hoffmann is probably raising an alarm, getting together help. The last thing we need is to get trapped in here."

"Yuri is due to show up, too," Jax reminded him as she pulled her boots on. "Yuri is not someone to mess with. He's not like these two in here were, or even Henry. He's better than good with a knife."

"Let's see if we can get out of here before we have to worry about him."

Jax was already moving before she finished pulling the black top over her head. Alex put a hand to the small of her back not only to guide her as she was frantically trying to finish dressing while they headed for the door, but to be ready if she faltered from exhaustion. He couldn't imagine how she could even stand after having to strain up on her tiptoes all night just to get each breath. She had to be running on fumes.

"What happened to the nurse they were saying disappeared?" Jax asked as they both carefully peeked around the corner.

"I strangled her."

"I expected something like that," she said, still struggling to get her breath. "What I want to know is why they couldn't find her body? How were you able to hide it in this place?"

Alex squatted beside the door that had been left open when the doctor had run out. He looked out into the well-lit bathroom and then under the row of stalls. It seemed to be clear. He turned back to Jax as she pulled her long blond hair out of the neck of the black top.

"I activated her lifeline."

Jax froze. "You what?"

"I cut those symbols in her forehead, like I saw you do. When I finished, she vanished."

Jax stared at him. "Alex, that was a complicated spell form. It has to be done precisely right."

"Well, I guess I was precise enough. It worked. Why are you looking at me like that?"

"I practiced for months before I was able to do it properly. Not only does it have to be drawn exactly right, but each part of it has to be added in the correct order, at the proper time. How could you remember it?"

Alex shrugged. "I remember visual things." He winced a little as he leaned closer. "I didn't do magic, did I?"

"No," she said with a bit of a smile that put him at ease. "You merely activated a lifeline that was already there within her. It doesn't take magic to do it, just the precise form to activate it."

She looked back into the shower room at the four dead people sprawled on the tile floor. Blood was running toward the shower drains. "I think that maybe I ought to activate the lifelines of these people. I don't think that we want the bodies left lying there to be

discovered. It would be better for us if people wondered what happened, wondered where they were. Until word is sent here about
their return we'd have the advantage of the others here in this world
being in the dark about what happened."

When she pulled her hair back from her face he saw that her
hands were shaking. He didn't know how much strength she
had left.

Alex agreed with her but he feared they couldn't spare the time.
"I think it would be worse if we were to get trapped in here and have
it start all over again."

"Yes, but what if—" She paused and frowned. "Do you smell
smoke?"

Alex realized that he did. "Yes. That can't be good."

He put an arm around her waist to help her as he started through
the bathroom. At the outer door they squatted down again, pressing
up tight against the wall to the side in case anyone burst through the
door. With a finger, Alex slowly eased the door open a few inches.
He carefully checked out into the hallway but could effectively look
in only one direction: back toward the nurses' station.

The partially opened door allowed a stronger smell of smoke into
the bathroom.

"We'd better find out what's going on. Are you ready?"

Jax nodded. "Which way are we going?"

Alex looked out again. He pointed with a thumb.

"Toward the nurses' station. I want to know what's burning.
There are a lot of people locked in this place. Fire in here could end
up being a disaster.

"Let's stay to the side of the hall and stay low. If there's anyone
waiting in ambush, I don't want to give them an opportunity to surround us."

When Jax nodded, Alex took her hand to keep her close as he slipped out the door. Staying low, they moved quickly along the edge of the dimly lit corridor. He didn't see anyone in either direction. The lights were on in the nurses' station. He could see a gray haze of smoke beyond the glass windows. He wondered why the smoke alarm wasn't going off.

Jax pulled him to a stop. She was breathing heavily. "I'm sorry. I need to rest a moment. I can hardly move my legs."

Alex helped her sit and lean back against the wall. "I can't believe that you can move at all, after what you've been through."

She closed her eyes and worked at getting her breath. Besides the physical ordeal, she was still on a partial dose of the Thorazine meant to take the fight out of her. He had stopped taking his, but she was still far from clearheaded.

Alex pressed a hand to her shoulder. "Rest here a moment. I'm going to go take a peek into the nurses' station. I want to know what's going on."

"No." She seized his arm, holding on as if her life depended on it. "We need to stay together. I'm better now. Let's go."

She looked exhausted but he realized that in her drugged condition, in a strange place, in a strange world, she had to be terrified to be left alone, especially as weak as she was. He wanted nothing more than to take her in his arms and hold her tight, protect her, and keep her safe. But they weren't safe, not yet, anyway.

He realized that she was probably right, they should stay together. If anything happened, he didn't know if she had enough strength left to defend herself. Although she never failed to amaze him.

"If you need to stop to get your breath just say so. All right?"

Jax nodded as she rose up into a crouch. They stayed low enough as they approached the nurses' station to be under the bottom of the window. He could hear flames crackling on the other side of the door.

When he carefully rose up to get a glimpse, he didn't see anyone at the counter inside. He tried different keys until he found the one that fit the lock. He turned the lock slowly, trying to be as quiet as possible.

Once he had the door unlocked, he again snuck a quick glimpse in the window. He still didn't see anyone, so he opened the door and slipped inside. The smoke stung his eyes. He had to resist the urge to cough. They stayed low as they went in.

Alex peeked over the top of the counter and saw that way in the back the doctor was frantically throwing liquid on the fire already raging in the aisles between the files. An orderly pulled files off the shelves and threw them on the burning pile as the doctor doused them with yet more liquid.

Alex went back to the wall beside the door, out of sight of the two working to torch the place, and pulled the lever of the fire alarm. Nothing happened. He looked up at the sprinklers. They remained off. He snatched up the phone to dial 911. The line was dead.

Jax slipped in the door. Alex squatted down beside her.

"What's going on?" she whispered. "What's burning?"

"They've started a fire to destroy the files." He kept his voice low even though the noise of the fire covered it. "The fire alarm doesn't work and the phone is dead. They were obviously prepared to destroy the whole place to cover their tracks if anything ever went wrong. The doctor panicked and is implementing those procedures."

They both rose up just enough to take a look over the counter. Alex could see that the fire was already burning strongly and spreading fast. It would be hard to put out.

He looked around and spotted a fire extinguisher on the wall, but he doubted it would be big enough. He was sure that the hospital had to have fire hoses. He didn't know where they were, but assumed that they were in the back of the nurses' station.

Alex knew that he had to put out the fire or the whole building would go up in flames. He tried to think of where there would be more extinguishers. There weren't any out in the wards, because they couldn't trust the patients. The extinguishers were heavy and could be used as weapons.

The doctor threw more of the flammable liquid on the burning mound of files on the floor until the bottle was empty. It appeared to be a bottle from the pharmacy, probably alcohol. The doctor pulled another from his pocket and threw it against the shelves. The bottle shattered against the steel shelving, spilling the liquid all down the files. Fire erupted up the side of the shelves, the flames roaring and crackling, lapping at the ceiling.

As he started to turn, Alex saw Jax on the floor. His first thought was that she had passed out from exhaustion. She tried to push herself up on her arms. It looked to be a struggle.

Realizing that something was wrong, Alex started to bend down to help her. Just then, out of the corner of his eye, he caught sight of a nurse behind him.

Almost at the same time as he saw the nurse, Alex felt a sharp stab in his left hip. With an icy flood of dread and alarm he instantly knew what she had done.

Almost at the same time, before he could react, a heavy office chair arced through the air, crashing into the nurse, sending her sprawling.

As Alex yanked the syringe from his backside he was shocked to see that it was his mother who had thrown the chair. She had thrown it just in the nick of time. The nurse had only started to push the plunger in before the chair had clobbered her. Alex had gotten some of the drug, but not nearly all of it.

His mother had just saved his life.

"The nurse hit her," his mother said, pointing at Jax on the floor. "Mom—"

An orderly loomed up out of the darkness behind her and threw an arm around her neck. As she screamed, Alex dove for the man. Even as he was still in midair he saw that it was too late.

His mother collapsed dead to the floor as he sailed over her, crashing into the orderly who had just broken her neck.

The man made the mistake of trying to catch Alex. He expected a fight. He wasn't expecting a knife.

His eyes widened with surprise as the blade plunged deep into his lower abdomen. Alex gave it a mighty pull, slicing up until the blade hit ribs.

Alex shoved the suddenly stiff, gravely wounded man to the side and fell to his knees beside his mother. He stared in shock at her lifeless form for a moment, unable to think what to do. His mind went blank.

Jax appeared beside him. Her hand urged his face away. "There's nothing you can do."

39.

ALEX KNELT BESIDE HIS MOTHER'S BODY, in shock that she was dead. As Jax turned his face away from the terrible sight, he looked up into her sad eyes, eyes that seemed to understand all he was feeling, to sympathize with the long, dark journey that had started when she first showed up in his life.

Seeing bright red blood matting the right side of her blond hair brought Alex abruptly to his senses.

He reached out, putting a finger to the side of her chin, turning her head a little so that he could take a look.

"I'm sure that it looks worse than it is," she said. "It stunned me for a moment, that's all."

It wasn't bleeding heavily, and her eyes weren't dilated. She didn't look disoriented or confused. He wasn't an expert, but it looked to him that she wasn't badly hurt. The ordeal of hanging in the shower was much more of a continuing worry.

Alex knew that he couldn't sit there mourning his mother or

they would die, too. His mother had just saved his life. He couldn't let that sacrifice be for nothing.

He had to fight against the dulling effect of the drugs that he'd gotten from the syringe. It was only a portion of the dose that had been in the vial, but it was enough that he could feel it slowing his thinking. He had to force himself to focus, to move, to act.

The immediate problem returned with clarity. It was night. Patients were asleep. He had to alert all the people in the hospital or they would likely end up trapped in a burning building.

The man on the floor not far away lay on his side, both arms across his abdomen, holding the grievous wound closed.

"Please," the man moaned, "help me."

Alex ignored him, stood up, and snatched the fire extinguisher off the wall. As he did, Jax straddled the nurse who had blindsided her and tried to inject Alex with whatever was in the syringe. Before the woman came to, Jax sliced the artery on each side of her neck so she would quickly bleed to death.

Jax flipped the woman over and swiftly cut symbols in her forehead. When the woman vanished, Jax looked up at him.

"I guess that answers that. There seem to be a lot of people from my world working here."

He wondered how deeply the tentacles from another world reached into his. There was no time to consider the problem, though. Fire extinguisher in hand, he headed for the blaze.

Alex yanked the pin out of the extinguisher as he rounded the corner and raced toward the shelves. He knew that if he was to have a chance to knock down the fire he would have to act quickly. He doubted that one extinguisher would be enough, but one was all he had at the moment.

He pointed the nozzle and squeezed the lever. Nothing happened.

The extinguisher was dead. It was a sickening, helpless feeling to be facing leaping flames with a dead extinguisher.

When he looked up he came face-to-face with Dr. Hoffmann.

The doctor held his hands out, urging Alex to stop and listen. "Alex . . . you don't understand."

Alex gritted his teeth and rammed the bottom of the extinguisher squarely into the man's face. Grunting in shock, the doctor put his hands over his face as he staggered back. Blood in his eyes blinded him and ran out between his fingers. One arm waved blindly, trying to find something for support. He stumbled and fell backward into the pile of burning files.

An alcohol bottle in his pocket broke when he hit the side of the shelving. His pants, soaked with the alcohol, burst into flames. As he scrambled to his feet, fire ascended his white coat with a whoosh. The roaring orange flames engulfed his face. His screams went up an octave.

The orderly who had been working at pulling down the files heard the screams and came running from behind the next row of shelves, where he had been working to burn files. Alex swung the extinguisher. Even over the sound of the fire, he could hear the clear ring of steel on bone as the heavy extinguisher caved in the side of the orderly's skull.

Jax seized his arm and pulled him back. "Alex! Hurry! We have to get the people out of here or they'll all burn to death."

"Wait. Maybe there's a fire hose and I can put it out."

Without waiting for her to answer, he ran around the outside of the shelves, making his way toward the back. The growing flames leaped and lapped at the ceiling. He found the hose on the wall near the stairway.

He yanked the hose off the wall and spun the wheel to turn on the water. No water came out. He spun the wheel until it came to the stop at the limit of its travel. No water. They had shut down the fire hoses along with the sprinklers.

Growling in anger, Alex ran back to find Jax kneeling beside his mother, closing her eyes. She looked up at him.

"I'm sorry, Alex. I wish we didn't have to leave her."

He nodded as he took her by the hand. "I know. Come on, we need to open the fire-escape doors and get people out of here or they'll be trapped."

Alex left the door leading to the men's side closed for the moment in the hope that it would keep the fire from spreading. Together, they ran into the darkened corridor of the women's wing.

"Wake the people in every room. Tell them there's a fire and they have to get out. I'll go unlock the fire-escape door. Send them down there."

Jax nodded and turned in to the first room as he continued on. He screamed "Fire!" at the top of his lungs, hoping that it would wake at least some of the women. It did. By the time he got to the door he could see women in nightgowns emerging from their rooms to see what the shouting was about.

Alex worked frantically at the door, finally found the right key, and got the door unlocked. He threw it open and waved his arms, signaling to the women farther back up the hall.

"Come on! Fire! Everyone out!"

A few of the women started down the hall, but more simply stood staring. Jax came out of a room, pushing two women. She gathered up others along the way, shoving them, urging them to hurry.

Alex started going into rooms on the opposite side of the corridor from Jax, pulling women out of bed and herding them toward the fire escape. In short order they had most of the women moving out of the fire-escape door.

Alex took Jax by the arm. "Come on, we need to get the men's wing opened."

"I don't think we have all the women out. Some ran from me and hid."

Alex could see the flames leaping out toward the counter in the nurses' station. "There are nine floors in this building. We don't have time to do more than what we've done. We need to keep moving and get as many people out as we can. I'm hoping that as we go down to the other floors, where the people aren't as mentally ill or as heavily sedated, we can get some of them to help us. But we're running out of time."

Alex unlocked the fire-escape door at the end of the corridor on the men's side as Jax started rousing the male patients. All the while he screamed, "Fire!"

When the two of them had ushered the men out onto the fire escape, telling them to go down to the ground where they would be safe, Alex and Jax turned back in to the heart of the building. The fire, already racing through the ceiling, had jumped over the walls of the nurses' station into the wards on both sides.

Gritty black smoke billowed along the ceiling. As they ran toward the center of the building, Alex could see bright yellow and orange tongues of flame licking out through the greasy black smoke. Paint on the walls bubbled and crackled and curled.

Alex couldn't believe how fast the fire had gotten out of control, or how hot it was. Just since they got the men out the fire escape, the smoke rolling along the ceiling had lowered to half the height of the hall. He worried about being caught by the flames, but he knew that smoke was deadly, too. It could render a person unconscious.

Pulling Jax by the hand he headed for the nurses' station. He could tell by how much effort he had to put into urging her along that she was well beyond exhausted. She stumbled several times. The drugs were making it difficult for him to hurry. He hoped Jax didn't simply pass out. If that happened he didn't know what he would do.

Beyond the front of the counter, on the other side of the nurses' station, he could see the body of his mother. There was nothing he could do for her now. There were people still alive who would die if he didn't leave her and try to get people to safety. He knew it was the logical thing to do, but he hated how cruel it felt.

"Help me," the orderly lying near her pleaded. "Please . . . don't leave me."

He was lying on his side, holding his guts in with both arms. He lay stiff and still, fearing to move.

This was the man who had killed his mother. He had no trouble killing a helpless woman. Now, fearing for his own life, he was reduced to begging for mercy. Alex only briefly met his beseeching gaze and then hurried on. He was in anything but a merciful mood.

They had to skirt the far side of the utility room to get past the flames to make it to the internal stairway in the back. Alex stopped Jax as he reconsidered the plan to go down to each floor alerting patients to the fire. Jax leaned back against the wall, closing her eyes as she caught her breath.

Alex realized that he had no way of knowing how many of the staff were involved in Dr. Hoffmann's plot. For all he knew, everyone could be involved.

They could be rushing down into an ambush.

For all he knew, Hoffmann had alerted the staff before starting to set fire to the files. They might be torching the place on the floors below.

"Do you think that all the people working here could be from your world?" he asked Jax.

She opened her eyes, struggling to focus. "I don't know, Alex. I suppose it's possible. We know they've been coming here for a long time. It's possible that over that time they've infiltrated the whole place. But why would they do such a thing?"

"Dr. Hoffmann was taking orders from Sedrick Vendis. Maybe they weren't just trying to get information from my mother. Maybe they used this place to get information out of other people when they needed to. After all, they kept you and me here in an attempt to find out what we knew."

"That's possible," she said, running her fingers back into her hair as she tried to think. "We know they've been working on things here in this world for a long time, but we don't know the extent of their meddling. They would have had plenty of time to set up this hospital as a place for questioning people. From what I've seen it would certainly have given them the seclusion, anonymity, and cover they would have wanted."

"So then there's no telling how many of staff could be involved," Alex said, thinking out loud. "For all we know, they could all be involved."

Jax wiped a weary hard across her face. "I can't answer that."

"From what I can tell, it seems most of the people working up here on this floor were from your world. Others, like Hoffmann, were cooperating with them. This is a large facility. The top two floors are relatively small, but below that the hospital extends along the whole block. It has a lot of different mental-health services. It could be that they confined their activities to this floor and maybe the unit below. Being locked down as they are they could control everything easier. Dr. Hoffmann could have seen to that control."

Jax gave him a look. "But we'd better not take that for granted."

"I think you're right."

If there were other people involved, they could be looking for him and Jax. Going down to the next nurses' station could get the two of them captured. But without an alarm to warn them, a lot of innocent people could die in the fire. He tried to think of what to do.

Struck with an idea, Alex went into the utility room and snatched a couple of the longer white coats off the rack. They looked like lab coats that went to mid-thigh. He handed one to Jax. "This might help fool them."

They buttoned up the coats on the way to the stairs. It took Alex a frustratingly long time to find the right key out of the dozens on the fat key ring. He was finally able to unlock the stairway door. Once in the stairway, he shut the door tight, hoping it would slow the spread of the fire.

Jax followed close behind as they raced down the stairs to whatever waited.

40.

ALEX UNLOCKED THE DOOR on the eighth floor and raced past the utility room and the shelving area with the files. He didn't see any fire. That much of it was a good sign.

Several nurses turned when they heard Alex and Jax coming.

One of them, frowning, stepped toward them to block their way. "Who the hell are—"

"Fire!" Alex screamed. "The top floor is on fire! It's already spread through the ceiling. The whole upper floor is involved. We opened the fire-escape doors and got everyone we could out of the place."

"I'd better go check it out," one of the other nurses said.

"You need to evacuate your whole floor! Do it now!"

"There's been no alarm," the first nurse said. "We can't evacuate a secure facility without an alarm—especially when we don't know who you are."

Alex, gritting his teeth in frustration, ran to the wall and yanked down the lever on the fire alarm. Nothing happened.

"See? The alarm doesn't work. Hurry! The fire is spreading out of control. You need to get everyone out, now!"

One of the nurses at the counter picked up the phone. She pressed the line of buttons one at a time.

"The phone lines are dead." She sounded stunned.

Alex snatched the fire extinguisher off the wall. He pulled the pin and squeezed the handle.

"Dead." He held it up, squeezing the lever, demonstrating. "See? The extinguisher upstairs was dead, too. The sprinklers don't work. There's no way to fight the fire or even slow it down. The people in here have only one chance—they have to get out and they have to get out now!"

The first nurse frowned at him. "What department do you work in? Who are you?"

"Get moving or you're all going to burn to death!" Alex yelled.

His tone of voice changed their attitude and sent them scrambling into action, rushing to the locked doors to each side. One of the nurses ran for the stairway Alex and Jax had come down. As two of the other nurses pulled keys from their pockets and unlocked the doors, Alex spotted a purse on the lower working counter behind the higher public counter.

He grabbed the purse and dumped the contents out onto the desk. A cell phone slid across the counter. Alex snatched it up. As soon as he had the power on, he punched the buttons.

"Nine one one. What's the nature of your emergency?"

"Mother of Roses Psychiatric Hospital is on fire."

"What address?"

"It's the old hospital on Thirteenth Street." Alex pressed his fingertips to his forehead, trying to think. "I don't know the exact address."

"Can you see flames, or smoke?"

"I'm inside the building. The fire is on the top floor."

"How extensive is the fire?"

"The entire top floor is ablaze. The fire alarms don't work. The sprinklers and the fire hoses don't work. Get the fire department here now!"

"They're on their way, sir. Please stay on the line. What is your name?"

Alex ignored the question. "I have to help the staff get people out of here! Hurry—get the fire trucks here!"

He tossed the phone on the counter without hanging up. He saw the nurses out in the wards rousing the patients. He headed for the stairs in the back to go down to the next floor. Jax was right behind him. At the doorway into the stairwell he met one of the nurses coming back down. Her face was nearly as white as her dress.

"It's a solid wall of flame up there!"

"A building this old is going to go up in a hurry," he told her. "Help get everyone out. There's not much time. I'm going to warn the floors below."

She nodded. "All right."

Alex pointed toward the front counter. "Nine one one is on the cell phone. Tell them your name and that you work here. Confirm what I told them about the fire being out of control. Keep the phone with you, keep them on the line, but help everyone get out the fire escape and then follow them out and help the people from the ninth floor already down there."

The woman scooped up the phone and with barely contained panic in her voice started telling the operator about the fire and how many hundreds of people were in danger. She told the operator to send ambulances as there were bound to be casualties. Alex didn't wait to hear the rest of it. He raced for the stairs, pulling Jax along behind.

As they burst through the stairway door, a red-faced orderly, nearly out of breath, was just arriving at the top step. Alex skidded to a halt and drew back as the man slashed wildly with a knife.

Alex seized the knife hand and twisted the man's arm at the same time as he spun him around, then shoved him face-first down the stairs. The tumbling man stopped at the middle landing between floors, smacking into the far wall. Jax bounded down the steps after him and rammed her knife into his back half a dozen times before he had a chance to get up. As soon as she had dispatched the orderly, the two of them raced down the last half of the stairs to the next floor.

On the seventh floor the nurses were equally surprised, but perhaps because people in their ward weren't locked down, they were more easily convinced. At seeing that the alarm, phones, and extinguisher didn't work, they wasted no time springing into action. One of the nurses started calling 911 on her cell phone as the others enlisted a staff of orderlies and aides to help them clear the wards.

Unlike the top two floors, the doors weren't locked. The wards on the seventh floor were also much larger, extending out past the footprint of the eighth and ninth floors into the rest of the old hospital complex. The staff was also larger.

"The fire department is on its way," the nurse on the phone reported.

"Do you know people in other parts of the hospital?" Alex asked. She nodded that she did. "Call them. Get anyone with a cell phone to call people as well. With the alarm not working people in the rest of the hospital need to be alerted. Call everyone you can and tell them to get the patients out."

Before she had a chance to ask any questions, Alex headed back to the stairs. He and Jax slid to a halt at the top step. He could hear, just out of sight around the turn of the landing, what sounded like a lot of men racing up the stairs. By the things they were saying Alex instantly recognized that the men were looking for him and Jax. One of the men called them "Vendis's prisoners."

Without pause Alex spun Jax around and pushed her out ahead of him, back the way they had come. Once out of the nurses' station, he took her hand and ran with her down the dimly lit corridor. She was having trouble keeping up. Her legs weren't working in a coordinated manner. He knew that her muscles were so spent that they were failing.

"Hold on, not much longer," he said, trying to encourage her and keep her moving.

As they raced down the corridor, he glanced back over his shoulder and saw men spilling out into the hallway, but they were too far away and it was too dark to make out their faces. Alex knew by their numbers, though, that they had to be orderlies he hadn't met before. That confirmed his suspicion that there were more people involved than just those he had seen working on the ninth floor.

Alex slowed a little to try to make it look like they were urgently helping people and less like they were running. He was counting on the white coats they were wearing to help throw the people hunting them off track.

He and Jax helped the nurses by rushing into rooms and pulling people out of their beds, then guiding them to the fire escape. Jax was swift and decisive in getting people moving, while managing to also be compassionate and supportive. It was all the more impressive to him because he could see by the look in her eyes that she was fighting the effect of the drugs in her system. He knew all too well what that was like; he was having to work past them as well.

The people followed directions as Alex calmly but forcefully urged them to hurry. These patients were far more alert and coherent than the people up on the ninth floor had been. He guided the growing throng to the fire escape, letting himself and Jax become lost in the mass of frightened people. He saw the men coming down the hall, searching in each room along the way.

Out on the fire escape they were greeted by cool night air. Fresh air had never felt so good. Alex was a little surprised to find himself giddy with relief to be out of the place. For a long time he had feared that he would never again be free. He wished that his mother could have tasted freedom with him.

Jax leaned closer to him so she could whisper as they made their way down the metal steps along with what seemed like hundreds of other people. "When we get to the ground we need to run before those men can find us. I don't think that I have enough strength left to fight them."

They slowed at a landing, inching ahead, waiting for the congested line of people to start moving more quickly again. "I need the keys to the truck," he reminded her.

"But the keys are inside." She knew what he was thinking and clearly didn't like the idea. "We'd have to go back in. Now that we're out, when we get to the ground, let's just run."

"You can hardly stand anymore. How far do you think you can run? Where will we go on foot? How can we get away? We can't hide—they'll be looking everywhere for us. We need the truck to get away—as far away as possible."

As the line started shuffling ahead a little faster, Alex heard glass breaking. He glanced up and saw flames roar out of the windows on the top floor. Thick smoke swirled out into the darkness.

He also saw two men dressed in white pushing past people to get down the stairs faster.

"We need to get down, now," he whispered to Jax.

She glanced up and, seeing the men coming for them, stayed close behind him as he started gently nudging people aside so that the two of them could get by. He needed to keep distance between them and the men coming after them, but at the same time he didn't want to make it too obvious lest the men spot him and Jax running.

Alex excused himself to the people on the stairs, repeating along the way that he needed to help patients on the ground.

The descent of the seven flights of metal stairs, even pushing past people, seemed like it was taking forever. Alex kept track of the distance back to the men hunting them. The men were getting closer all the time, because they were far rougher about pushing people out of the way. At least most people, when they saw the white coats he and Jax were wearing and heard his repeated explanation, did their best to let them by.

A lot of the patients were petrified to be up on the rickety metal fire-escape stairs at night. They held on to the railing for dear life, inching along at a snail's pace. They bottlenecked the people above them trying to get down. Jax gently but firmly lifted the hands of more than one person from the railing and with encouragement and reassurance got them moving.

From his vantage point up on the stairs among the confused people making what they considered to be a terrifying descent, he gazed out over throngs of people screaming, crying, running, wandering aimlessly, even sitting down, in the middle of a near-stampede. The thought occurred to him that he couldn't imagine a scene any more chaotic than mental patients trying to escape a fire.

Irrational people in the hundreds were unable to cope with the necessary but simple task of getting away from a burning building. Half of them, it seemed, were crying for help and waiting for it to show up rather than escape the area.

Pushing past the frightened people on the stairs, Alex and Jax finally made it to the ground. They found themselves in the rear of the hospital among hundreds of people all rushing about in confusion. In the distance people were also pouring down emergency stairs from other areas of the institution.

There were a few orderlies and nurses trying to organize the patients and tell them where they needed to go. There were patients who were staying at the hospital for less serious conditions and some of them, too, were trying to help their fellow patients away from the burning building. There were a few people, driven by insanity, who, like salmon trying to swim upstream, were trying to push their way up the stairs against the flow of people coming down.

The lights suddenly went out as the electricity failed. The emergency generators should have kicked in. They didn't. Two battery-backup security lights did come on, but they were far from adequate to light the whole back area of the hospital.

In the near darkness the fire looming above them seemed all the more frightening. The eighth floor was now also fully involved. Alex could see flames making their way across the roof from there to the main part of the hospital. He also saw fire on the fifth floor. He suspected that it had been set, just like the fire on the top floor had been.

Panicked people cried out and rushed faster to get away from the building as glass blown out of windows by the fire rained down on them. People on the ground were speared by shards of falling glass. Bloody people cried out for help. Some people stumbled and fell in the darkness. Alex and Jax helped a number of them to their feet so that they could get away.

All the while, they steadily and silently made their way across the flowing current of people coming off the fire escapes and running away from the building. Alex had walked over the uneven ground that rose and fell over the roots of the big old trees often enough that he could probably have done it with his eyes closed, so the near darkness wasn't a hindrance.

Over the bobbing heads of people, he spotted a couple of the orderlies coming through the back parking lot. They pawed through the escaping people, searching, looking at everyone.

Alex rose up on his tiptoes and waved an arm to get their attention. He figured that they wouldn't be able to recognize him in the flickering light of the flames, and they would only key in on his white coat. When they saw him, he pointed urgently away from the hospital.

"They're over there!" he yelled. "They went that way!"

The bluff worked. The two men turned away and took off in the direction he had pointed to.

Jax arched an eyebrow at him. "That was risky."

"Not as risky as them catching up to us."

At the metal entrance door, he gently pulled, testing it. It was locked. He searched through the keys, trying each in turn, not knowing if Henry would have had a key to unlock an exterior door. The fourth key worked.

Alex paused to glance back over his shoulder at Jax.

She gave him a look. "I'm not waiting here," she said before he could suggest it. "Hurry up. Let's get what you need and get out of here before those men find us."

Alex opened the door just enough for them both to slip inside.

There was one emergency, battery-powered light some distance down a hall to the side. The exit sign above them over the door was lit up, casting the room in an eerie red glow that gave them at least a little light to see by. The sudden silence inside the place was unnerving.

Alex smelled gas.

He looked down the dark corridor toward where he knew the kitchens were, but he couldn't see anything.

"They must have opened a gas line," he whispered to Jax.

"What does that do?"

He looked at her, realizing then that she wouldn't know, and realizing, too, how much the drugs were affecting him. He explained as he made his way through the dimly lit room toward the metal detector. "Natural gas is used in the kitchens, in the ovens and stoves, to make fire. It's highly flammable. If it isn't controlled, and enough of it escapes out into the air, it can easily explode."

"Then we should get out of here, now."

"You're right. I just need to get the keys first."

Jax skirted the metal detector and stood at the desk where Doreen usually sat, waiting as Alex groped around in the dark and finally located the table against the wall. He felt along the back of the tabletop and found a lone tub. He reached inside and to his relief his keys were still there along with his pocketknife.

"Got it."

"Alex!"

He spun around to see Dwayne silhouetted against the red exit light. He came out of the dark swinging a nightstick. As Alex ducked, Jax snatched the blue pen attached to the clipboard and yanked it off, breaking the string.

Before Alex had finished ducking the swing of the nightstick, she used the pen to stab the side of the guard's neck three times in rapid succession. He cried out. His hands flew to the puncture wounds in his throat. At the same time he turned to attack her. That was a mistake. As he lifted his nightstick Jax stabbed his eyes out with two lightning-quick jabs.

Before he could let out much of a scream, Alex had him from behind. He gripped the man's jaw and twisted with all his might until he heard a sickening crunch of sinew and bone. He let the limp Dwayne slip to the floor.

"Why didn't you use the knife?" he asked as she dropped the bloody pen.

She looked on the verge of frustrated tears. "My fingers are numb. They're not working very well." She gestured vaguely. "I must have dropped the knife out there somewhere."

Alex put an arm around her waist when he saw her start to sink. "It's all right. You'll be able to rest as soon as we get to the truck. You'll be all right after the drugs wear off and you get some sleep."

"I'm not sure I can make it, Alex."

"Sure you can. I'll help you." He tried to sound more confident than he was.

She glanced back toward the door. "I remember them saying that Dwayne was waiting to let Yuri in when he came back."

Alex nodded. "I remember. I've got my keys. Let's get out of here before Yuri gets here or the place blows up. We've done everything we can."

41.

SIRENS WAILED IN THE NIGHT as Alex hurried Jax along the sidewalk. It seemed like dozens of emergency vehicles were converging on Mother of Roses. Reddish orange light from the blaze reflected off the low overcast. Through the trees Alex could see crackling streamers of hot yellow sparks ascending through billowing black smoke. From time to time great gouts of flame lashed up toward the clouds.

The noise of all the sirens had sleepy people emerging from their houses to see what was going on. Leaves were lit by red, blue, and yellow strobes of emergency vehicles racing toward Mother of Roses. People stood in their nightclothes on front porches watching in shock.

Many more people, patients in pajamas and nightgowns, ran down the street past Alex and Jax. Police cars rushing in toward the hospital had to slow in places for the throngs to part. He didn't know where all the people were running. They probably didn't, either. They were simply filled with fear and wanted to get away. Their terror over being awakened by fire and the uncertainty of what would happen to them now had many sobbing as they wandered aimlessly.

Alex kept a constant lookout over his shoulder to see if anyone followed them. So far he hadn't seen anyone who looked overtly suspicious. It was dark, though, and there were a lot of people flooding through the streets. He hoped that in the throng of people escaping the hospital they had lost the men chasing them, but he had no way to tell if any of the people in the darkness were from another world.

Alex turned down a smaller side street as he made his way toward where his truck was parked. He didn't know if they would be safer out on the streets with all the people, or if it would be better to cut through alleys and backyards.

Once they were off the streets, they wouldn't know their way. That would slow them down. Worse, they might find themselves trapped in a box canyon of fences when the men chasing them caught up. And cutting through yards would draw attention.

In the end, he decided to stay on the streets.

As they made their way along the broken sidewalk, Jax was becoming dead weight. Her legs kept giving out. Fortunately, they weren't far from his Cherokee.

Alex was having difficulties of his own. It took a great effort to focus enough to work past the drugs the nurse had gotten into him. His vision was blurred. He hoped he could see well enough to drive. He didn't know if his racing heart would ever calm down.

With everything that had happened he didn't think that he would have to worry about falling asleep—at least for the time being. But he did need to find them a safe place where they could both get much-needed rest.

If he felt dulled by the drugs, Jax was laboring under an even heavier dose. She hadn't been able to stop taking the Thorazine and pills the way he had; they had only reduced her dose enough so that she could feel pain and terror, yet not fight back. After her ordeal of hanging in the shower for over twenty-four hours, he was amazed that she could move at all.

"It's just down the block. We're almost there. Hold on."

She nodded. "I'm fine."

"Yeah, right."

She smiled a little. Her right foot was dragging. He wasn't sure she was even aware of it. He was holding most of her weight so she could keep going.

Alex kept thinking about his mother being burned up in the fire. Ben had burned up in a fire, and now his mother had as well. He couldn't stop wondering what would have happened if he'd gotten her out. He wondered if when the drugs wore off she'd have been able to communicate with him, talk about everything that had happened in her life, in his, or if her mind was long gone. Now he would never know.

At least she'd had the presence of mind to stop the nurse. In the end, she had fought back against her captors. In the end she'd won a battle against them. That was something.

"Here," Alex said. "We're here. Hold on. I'll have you inside in a minute and you can relax."

Jax forced herself to stand straighter as he unlocked the passenger door. "Don't let yourself get complacent, Alexander," she reminded him. "Carelessness with these people will get you killed."

That was why she refused to give up, why she forced herself to stay as alert as she possibly could. To relax was to die.

Alex helped her step up into the passenger seat. He folded her right leg up into the truck.

"Once we're away from the hospital, you could get some sleep."

"My knives. Please, I want my knives."

As Alex reached under the seat and pulled the bundle out, a horrific explosion shook the night. The sky lit with the orange and yellow fireball.

As Alex turned to the explosion, he saw an orderly dressed in white barreling at him out of the darkness. The man was huge, and he had a knife.

Without even thinking, Alex grabbed a handle of one of the knives in the bundle and pulled it out. Despite the adrenaline rush of his sudden alarm, the balance of the knife, the feel, made an impression somewhere in the recesses of his mind.

As the man charged toward him, with no time to do anything more than simply react, Alex thrust the knife straight into the man's center mass.

It didn't stop him. The big man crashed into him at full speed, knocking Alex back.

As Alex rebounded off the side of the truck, the man swung his own knife. Alex ducked, seized the arm, and took it with him as he circled around the orderly. Once behind him he rammed his blade into the man's lower back several times in rapid succession. He didn't hit anything immediately vital, and his stabbing only made the man angrier.

The man twisted around, driving Alex back with his feet as well as his fists. More than one connected, staggering Alex back. The man was a fury of nonstop lunges and slashes. With the drugs, Alex had difficulty focusing.

The man was a good head taller than Alex and must have been sixty or seventy pounds heavier. Despite his size, he was quick. Not only was he hard to handle, but his size seemed to help keep the knife wounds from slowing him.

Alex made another attack. The man threw him back. As he rebounded, Alex ducked under a swing, threw a shoulder block into the man, and at the same time grabbed a leg. He pulled with all his strength, upending the orderly. The man landed flat on his back, but bounded back up as if on springs.

His arms seemed to be everywhere at once. Alex was having trouble keeping track of the furious attacks. He picked his openings and cut whenever he had the chance. One slashing cut across the man's thigh halved the muscle, making him stumble.

Alex used the opening to dive in to try to finish the fight. He seized the man's knife-wielding arm and stabbed again, but the man was strong enough to push him back. Alex felt like a child trying to fight a grown man.

When the man spun around, pulling out of Alex's grip, his arms were spread in an angry fighting stance. He looked like a bear on its hind legs about to charge. Seeing the opening, Alex used all his strength to drive his knife like a punch straight into the middle of the orderly's throat.

He felt the blade sink in and hit bone.

The furious fight seemed to freeze in place.

Then the man started to corkscrew toward the ground. As he collapsed, his weight pulled him off the blade.

Panting, catching his breath, his exhausted arms hanging, Alex tried to gather his wits. He was so drained, so bone-tired from the fight, that he was ready to drop.

Jax was suddenly there beside him, putting her arm around him, holding him up.

"Almost there," she reminded him. "Hold on."

He smiled at her words, words he had used to encourage her not to give up.

Alex felt like he was watching himself in a dream. He realized then, by the way Jax was bent over, that he was on his knees. He didn't remember going to his knees.

"Stay still," she said.

Jax turned away to the open door of the truck for a moment. She was frantically doing something. He couldn't figure it out. It finally dawned on him that she was ripping cloth. It was the rag the knives had been in. She was tearing off a long strip.

She put the strip around his upper left arm, wrapping it tightly around several times. She used her teeth to split the end and then tied a knot. She made another knot and drew it tight.

"What are you doing?"

"He cut you. I'm tying a bandage around your arm to keep the wound closed. I need to stop the bleeding."

Alex only then realized that blood was dripping off his fingers. He wondered how bad it was. He didn't really feel any pain, but at feeling a warm, wet sheath of blood running down his arm he suddenly began feeling sick.

"It's all right," she assured him. "You'll be fine."

By the way her voice sounded, though, he didn't know if he believed her.

"How bad is it?"

"It's dark. I can't tell," she admitted. "But I don't think it's too bad. Can you move your fingers?"

Alex tried. "Yes."

"Then you're fine. As long as your arm still works, it can't be too bad."

"Thank you," he said in a numb voice. "I don't understand why he was trying to kill me. If I'm dead they can't get the information they need."

343

"He wasn't trying to kill you. He was trying to capture you. If he had wanted to kill you I think he could have."

"Well, from my side of it it sure felt like he was trying to kill me."

She only smiled as she adjusted the bandage on his arm. Alex liked the feeling of her taking care of him. It made him feel calm, feel like everything would be all right.

She gently took the knife out of his hand. "I don't ever let anyone use my knife. Not this one."

Alex saw in the dim illumination of the dome light in the Jeep that it was the knife with all the elaborate engraving on the silver handle. Now it was covered in blood as well.

"It seemed rather important at the time," Alex said. "Do you think you could make an exception to your rule this one time?"

"Well," she said, glancing down at the dead man, "I guess that, in this case, I could."

With a concerned, gentle look, she smoothed the hair back off his forehead. Her face warmed with the special smile she gave only him. Her hand cupping the side of his face made everything better.

"Considering who used that knife," she said in an intimate voice, "I guess it's all right. You're welcome to use it anytime you'd like."

Alex swayed on his knees. "I think I'm going to throw up."

"Do it in that direction, will you? I need to send him back to my world."

Alex was going to tell her not to bother, that they could just drive away and leave him. But as his mind started working again he realized what a bad idea it would be to leave a body lying in the street. With so many people around, the man would be discovered in short order. Alex could see people off in the darkness. Fortunately they didn't see what was going on.

The dead people they had left in Mother of Roses would be

burned up. There would be little evidence of what had really happened. But if they left this man's body out on the street it would look like murder and raise a lot of questions.

By the time he had come to the conclusion that Jax was right, the man had already vanished. Her knife was shiny and clean.

Jax put a hand under his good arm to help him up. "Come on. Let's get away from here before any of his friends show up."

Alex was regaining his senses. He helped boost Jax up into the truck. The adrenaline of the situation seemed to have given them both a shot of strength. He didn't know how long it would last. He ran around to the other side and hopped in.

When he turned the key in the ignition and the truck didn't start, he wasn't the least bit surprised. Trying the key had been nothing more than a token gesture. He had expected it not to start. That was just the way the world worked. For some reason it seemed that things tended not to work when you needed them the most.

Fortunately, he had planned for the eventuality. He'd parked on a hill, and he'd parked at the end of the block so that no one could park in front of him and block him in.

He turned the wheels away from the curb as he put in the clutch. The Cherokee started rolling, gathering speed. When it was going downhill at a good clip he let the clutch out. The engine turned over and caught. With a minimum of fuss, he had the truck running, but he was more determined than ever to get it fixed as soon as they got the chance.

Alex drove slowly down the hill through the residential neighborhood. There were no cars, but there were people wandering all over the place. Here and there a person in pajamas or a robe would walk out into the street without looking. In the darkness it was difficult to see them all. Alex kept a sharp lookout for any of the staff who might be hunting them.

When he turned right onto Sixteenth Street, traffic was moving slowly, pulling over at intervals for emergency vehicles. Fire trucks, ambulances, and police cars raced through the night toward the hospital.

Alex stayed in the right lane, pulling to the curb and stopping for every one of them. He didn't want to be stopped by police and have to answer any questions. At that moment, he couldn't imagine what he would tell them about what he was doing there at that time of night. He couldn't say he was visiting his mother, not at night.

He was too tired to think. Best to avoid the problem altogether.

When the traffic cleared, he stayed close to the speed limit of forty-five as he headed toward the interstate. The interstate would be the fastest way to put some distance between them and anyone who might be looking for them. The older part of town was quiet that late at night. He kept an eye on the rearview mirror, checking to make sure that they weren't being followed. The road behind was empty. Most of the people out that late were interested in seeing the fire.

Alex was sure that the fire department had shut off the gas to the hospital and that had minimized the explosion. It had been bad enough, but not anything like it could have been. He hoped everyone had gotten out safely. He guessed he knew that not everyone had.

Jax was slumped in her seat, leaning against the door, her hand resting on her leg. He reached over and squeezed the hand.

"We're safe now. If you want you can crawl in the back seat to lie down and go to sleep."

She pulled her hair back off her face and hooked it behind an ear. "Where are we going?"

"I want to find us a motel or something, some place we can rent a room for the night. We're near the interstate highway. It shouldn't take long to get safely away from here before we stop. We both need rest and time to let these drugs wear off."

"I'll wait, then," she said. "Before we sleep, though, I'm going to need a needle and thread."

"What for?"

"To stitch up that gash on your arm. It needs to be closed up."

Alex nodded, but he didn't like the thought of having her sew on his arm, at least not without some kind of local anesthesia. He didn't want to stop in at an emergency room, though. They would have questions. He wasn't in the mood to think up answers to questions.

He tested his injured left arm a little. It was beginning to ache in earnest. The pain throbbed with each beat of his heart. He couldn't hold the wheel with his left hand alone. The pressure needed to turn the wheel hurt.

He glanced in the rearview mirror to look back at the fire.

Just as he did, there was a soft thud to the air that Alex felt as a thump deep in his chest. He'd felt that thump before.

In the mirror he saw a dark smudge swirl in the air behind them in the back seat. As soon as he saw it, the indistinct, dark swirl of night changed into a vortex of vapor.

The vapor condensed into a shape.

A man in a dark leather vest and no shirt lunged at them from out of the back seat, from out of another world.

42.

THE MAN IN THE BACK SEAT threw an arm around both Jax's and Alex's necks at the same time, pulling them back against the seat, choking them both. His bare arms were massively muscled. Alex's vision dimmed down to a narrow, dark tunnel. The powerful arm was cutting off his blood supply as well as his air. Out of the corner of his eye he could see Jax's arms and legs flailing and he knew the man was hurting her even more.

Alex tried to reach the steering wheel. The way the man's arm had him around the throat, pinning him back to the seat, Alex couldn't pull away. Try as he might, he couldn't reach the brake, either.

He was only able to sporadically get his fingertips on the steering wheel. The truck slowly started taking an arcing course across the road, toward oncoming traffic. As Alex brushed the wheel with his fingertips, it started back the other way, toward the right side of the road. He struggled to correct with the wheel to keep them from crashing into a light pole.

He couldn't get a breath. He tried to twist enough to steer with his left hand and pull at the arm with his right, but the fingertips of one hand weren't enough to steer. Alex used his knees to steady the wheel and switched to using both hands to try to pry the arm away. He reached back, trying to get ahold of fingers, but couldn't reach them.

His lungs burned for air. He was starting to have difficulty focusing his vision. He knew that if he didn't do something, and soon, he would lose consciousness. If that happened, it was all over—they would have him.

He could hear strangled sounds coming from Jax as she desperately struggled to breathe. Out of the corner of his eye Alex could see her face turning red. He could also see that her arms were hardly moving anymore.

The powerfully built man growled with the effort of keeping his arms clamped around them both. In the position he was in, Alex had no chance to gain the advantage.

He tried again but couldn't reach the brake. He couldn't reach the gas pedal, either, but since they were going down a slight grade the truck wasn't slowing.

In his rush to get away from the hospital, he hadn't retrieved his gun. He had figured that once they were safely away he would then get it out from under the seat. He had thought that if any of Vendis's men tried to stop them he would have enough time to get the gun out. He hadn't figured on a man materializing in his back seat.

He could think of nothing else but to try to reach under the seat for his gun. Try as he might, though, he couldn't get to it. It might as well have been a mile away.

He abandoned his attempt to get the arm off his throat. He pushed back against the man behind them to force him to change his hold a little. Just as the man loosened and moved his arm a bit to improve his hold, Alex lunged forward with all his strength.

Alex managed to grab the steering wheel with both hands.

He immediately cranked the wheel to the right. They were going slow enough that the front tires stuck and the truck cut violently to the right, hitting the curb and going up over it.

Between the sudden right turn and bouncing up over the curb, the man was thrown hard to the left. He probably didn't know anything about riding in a truck; it didn't appear that he was prepared for such a maneuver. He had such a hold on Jax that as he was thrown to the left he took her with him, pulling her by the neck, half between and half over the seats.

As he slid across the back seat, his head slammed into the metal of the door along the bottom of the window. The blow caused his stranglehold around both of them to loosen a little. He didn't let go, but it was enough that they both could at last get desperately needed air. He could hear Jax gasp several times.

Being pulled up out of her seat as she was, and with enough air to regain her wits, Jax was at last able to reach around and pull a knife from the small of her back. When the man had fallen over to the left, he not only pulled her back, but turned her a little, facing more toward Alex. She brought the knife around and sliced cleanly through the upper ligament of the biceps of the arm holding Alex. Their attacker cried out in pain and rage as his slack arm slipped off Alex.

Alex immediately slammed on the brakes. The man, already off balance, slid off the seat, down onto the narrow floor area. He lay sideways, stuffed into a space that was too small for him, but despite everything, his beefy arm remained locked around Jax's neck.

Pulled over as she was on her back, between the seats, and held by the throat, she was unable to maneuver. He had pressure on her throat again, cutting off her air. Her movements slowed as she started to lose consciousness. The man was obviously intent on breaking her neck, but being on the floor with her partly on top and somewhat behind him, he was having trouble accomplishing that task. He appeared perfectly willing to simply strangle her.

As the man fought to gain his balance and get up, Alex yanked the syringe from his pocket and popped the cap off with his thumb. In one swift movement he turned and thrust the needle down into the side of the man's bull neck. He pushed the plunger home.

The man kicked and bellowed in rage, struggling to get up. Alex stabbed the gas and slammed on the brakes, jerking the truck to keep him off balance. With his injured arm, he still managed to grab Alex's hair in his fist. Alex could tell that he was slowing from the drugs, his movements becoming less coordinated.

Still, Jax was in desperate trouble. She, too, was hardly moving as she lost consciousness.

Alex stripped the silver knife out of her hand. He pulled away from the fist holding his hair, turned, and leaned over the back of his seat to stab down at the man. As the man came up from the floor he met Alex's blade on its way down. Alex added all his strength to thrusting the knife through the side of the man's throat.

By the sudden spurts of blood, Alex knew that he'd hit an artery—the same one he'd managed to hit with the syringe. By the sounds of the man's breathing, he knew that he'd also hit the windpipe. The heavy volume of blood pumping from the severed artery flowed down into the deep gash and into his lungs as he gasped for air. The man started drowning in his own blood.

In the grip of the drugs and the throes of death, he finally let go of Jax. She gulped in air. Even as she was gasping and regaining consciousness, she took the knife back from Alex. As the man's arm flailed weakly about, his hand trying to grab her, she stabbed it. He reflexively, slowly, pulled the hand back and pressed it against the gaping wound in the side of his neck and throat. It appeared he was trying to stop the bleeding.

Alex was sickened by the messy act of killing a human being. It was a difficult, gruesome task.

As the man's struggles slowed, Jax began cutting symbols in his forehead. She wasn't waiting until he was dead. He managed to get out a gurgling curse as she gouged the lines of the design into his flesh.

Alex turned his attention to getting the car off the grass and back on the road before anyone came to see what was happening. With all the police cars in the area that was all too real a risk.

He didn't see what Jax did, but the burbling curses died out in muffled grunts.

In mid-grunt, it suddenly went silent inside the Jeep. A glance back between the seats confirmed what he thought: The man was gone, along with all the blood.

Jax let out a huge sigh as she flopped back into her seat. She held her throat as she coughed.

"Dear spirits, that hurt," she said in a hoarse whisper.

Alex had the Jeep back up to speed.

"Stop!" she suddenly cried out. "Stop the truck right now!"

Alex, surprised by her screamed command, slammed on the brakes. The Cherokee slid to a stop. He pulled off the road onto a thinly graveled parking area on the shoulder.

"What? What's the matter?"

"I'm an idiot!" Jax growled.

"What are you talking about?"

Jax reached up, grabbed the rearview mirror, and twisted it until it ripped off the windshield.

"What the hell are you doing?"

She threw open the door and heaved the mirror into the bushes. "Saving our lives."

She retrieved her silver knife from the floor and used the pommel to smash the glass in the side mirror on the truck door. The glass broke into a spiderweb of cracks. She bashed at it over and over with the butt of the knife handle until all the pieces of glass were knocked out. A black socket with an adjustment cable was all that remained.

She ran around the front of the truck and did the same thing to the driver's-side mirror. When she had finished she rushed back around and got in.

"Let's go," she said as she slammed the door shut. "Get us away from this last spot they saw us! Go, go, go!"

Alex checked over his shoulder and then dumped the clutch, spinning the wheels in the gravel as he pulled the Cherokee back out onto the street.

"You think they found us by the rearview mirrors?"

She slumped back in her seat, comforting her neck. "How else?"

He turned to look out the back window to make sure they weren't being followed.

He saw a big man in a leather vest running after them from the graveled parking area.

With a cold wave of shock, Alex realized that the man must have arrived in this world right where the Jeep had been only a moment before. She had told him once, in the driveway of his house, that they usually arrived in pairs. That was the partner of the man they had just killed and sent back.

Alex stepped on the gas. The next time he looked back, they were too far away for him to see the man. He would never be able to follow or find them on foot. Alex let out a sigh of relief. He gripped the steering wheel tighter to try to stop his hands from shaking.

Jax, also watching the man vanish in the distance behind, looked over at Alex out of the corner of her eye, as if to ask if he understood, now.

"That was close," he admitted. "But how am I going to drive without mirrors?"

"Would you rather drive with new passengers arriving from my world every few minutes?"

"I guess not," he admitted. He glanced over at her. "Are you all right, Jax?"

Her brow wrinkled as she fought back tears while rubbing the muscles in her neck. "I think I will be after I get some sleep."

"Close your eyes," he said in a gentle voice. "I'll wake you when I get us a room. Sleep until then."

She didn't answer. He didn't know if she'd fallen asleep or if she had passed out.

Alex looked back over his shoulder. The road behind was empty. He wasn't much comforted.

43.

ALEX LEANED TO THE SIDE A LITTLE, trying to balance Jax's weight with his right arm and hip as he used his aching left arm to try to unlock the door. In her semiconscious state, Jax did her best to stand, but her legs kept giving out, making his hand pull away from the keyhole. He at last managed to turn the key in the lock. The door swung open.

He used his foot to shut the door, then swept Jax up in his arms and carried her into the room, following the well-worn track across the beige carpeting. It hurt his injured arm to hold her like that, but he figured it would be easier than trying to get her up off the floor if she passed out completely.

In her groggy state, she let out a soft moan as she put her arms around his neck. She laid her head against his shoulder as he carried her into the dark room. It made him imagine the innocent, feminine little girl she once had to have been.

A long rectangle of light from signs for the truck stops shining in through the window beside the door fell across the double beds.

An older TV sat on the long counter where it could be watched from bed. A tiny table with two wooden chairs sat under the front window beside the door. It smelled a little musty, but he wasn't about to complain. At that moment the small room looked like a presidential suite to him.

Outside, semitrailer trucks constantly rumbled past on the interstate. He could hear a TV on in the room beside theirs. Still, it was a relief to have what appeared to be a safe place to stop, a place hidden away from all the people hunting them.

Alex gently laid Jax on one of the two beds.

"The mirrors, Alex," she mumbled.

"I know, I know."

He went into the bathroom, flicked on a buzzing fluorescent light, and draped the white bath mat over the mirror. He brought a towel out and hung it over the mirror on the wall beside the TV. He adjusted the towel to make sure that not the tiniest part of the mirror could peek through. He felt like his mother, draping things over mirrors.

Alex pulled the cord, closing the heavy, ugly blue drapes, shutting out the garish light of the truck-stop signs. Once the drapes were closed, he turned on the lamp on the taller section of the long counter. The dark fake-wood veneer was chipped along the edge of the counter from people hitting into it as they lifted their suitcases up to lay them open. The bedspreads were the same blue as the curtains, with bands of burgundy designs that matched the valence above the window. It was tacky and cheap-looking, but it was a place to stop, to rest, to hide from the people hunting them, and for that reason Alex was delighted with the room, already thinking of it fondly as home, at least home for the night.

Jax sat up, blinking slowly at him, as if the single lamp he had turned on was too bright.

"Lie down," he told her.

"I can't. My bladder is going to burst."

"Oh. The bathroom is right there," he said, pointing.

He put a hand under her arm and helped her up. Using her legs after the stress of stretching up on her toes all night to breathe followed by the heart-pounding escape left standing almost more than she could manage. Without the spur of terror, her muscles were giving out and her legs wobbled unsteadily.

As he was helping her to the bathroom, she said, "I need a needle and thread. I need to sew up your arm."

He left her at the doorway into the bathroom. "We'll worry about that tomorrow."

She gripped his shirt for support. "Now, Alex. We need to wash it and do it tonight or it will become infected."

Alex sighed. He had an idea.

"All right. You go use the bathroom. Wash up for bed if you want. I'll go get what we need and be right back. I'll leave you the gun."

"No. I'm hidden inside. You will be out there where people can see you. You have no way of knowing who might be looking. You take the gun. I have my knives."

He couldn't imagine that she could fight very effectively in her condition, but he didn't want to argue and she did make sense. "I'll be right back. I'll knock twice, pause, and knock twice again before I open the door so that you know it's me coming back."

Alex locked the door and checked it before jogging across the parking lot. It was starting to drizzle. The inky blacktop reflected the bright light of signs off its slick surface. The spotlights pointed up at signs for interstate travelers illuminated the otherwise invisible mist drifting past.

The cross street was busy, even late at night. People were coming off the interstate for gas, to get something to eat, or to stop for the night. Trucks were pulling in and out of a nearby truck plaza.

The convenience store had half a dozen truckers and other travelers inside. Alex carefully checked each one for potential threat as he picked up a basket and went to the coolers. A memory of the first time he'd met Jax flashed through his mind. She had looked at everyone that same way, checking for threat. Now he understood it so much better.

He pulled a handful of packaged turkey slices off a peg in the cooler and threw them in the basket. He grabbed some ham as well, along with a variety pack of sliced cheese. He picked up a couple of six-packs of bottled water and a variety of other small items he thought they might need.

As he kept an eye on a big guy with long, greasy black hair and a beard, he stopped at the section with first-aid supplies and picked up the things he needed. As far as Alex was concerned, the man looked a little too much like a pirate. But in the end it seemed he was buying far too much beer to be a tracker from some distant world hunting the last Rahl.

Nonetheless, it was comforting to have a Glock only a twitch away. After the brawl in his truck had ended, he had quickly retrieved the gun from under the seat. It was a relief to have it handy. The next time someone from another world showed up, he vowed to be ready. They had been fortunate and survived a number of surprise attacks. He didn't want to be caught unprepared again.

At the checkout counter he asked the clerk for two of the prepaid cell phones on the rack against the back wall. Alex paid for everything with one of the hundred-dollar bills Sedrick Vendis had used to buy Alex's six paintings.

That seemed not only like a lifetime ago, but like a different life. Maybe it was.

When he got back to the room, Alex knocked with his special signal to let Jax know it was him. When he opened the door, he saw her sitting cross-legged on the end of the bed staring at the TV. There was a talk show on.

"What are you doing?" he asked as he set the plastic bags on the small table.

Jax looked rather alarmed. "I saw one of these things where they held us. I was drugged so I couldn't pay much attention to it. But they have one here as well, just like at the crazy house. I saw a button that said 'on,' so I pushed it." She pointed. "These pictures appeared."

Alex thought that having a TV in a "crazy house" was rather appropriate.

The host on the TV was fawning over an actress who thought she was brilliant because she happened to have been born beautiful and read lines written by other people. It amazed Alex what qualified a person for being worthy of adulation.

"Why are you watching this?"

Jax looked up again. He could see that she was so sleepy that she could hardly keep her eyes open.

"This is something like watching this world through mirrors." She gestured to the TV. "I wanted you to see this."

"I've seen TV before." Alex switched it off. "You mean to say that this is what it looks like when you saw me through the mirrors in my studio?"

She made a face as she considered. "Not exactly, not this clear, but in some ways it looks much the same. I was astounded when I saw this."

Her gaze drifted away. "It . . . reminded me of home."

Alex understood then. "Oh."

He took off his jacket and for the first time, because they were finally in the light, saw that his shirtsleeve was completely caked with dried blood.

Jax patted the bed beside her. "Come sit."

She used her knife to cut the sleeve away from the rest of his shirt. Once he had his shirt off, she cut the length of the remaining sleeve and helped him pull it away from his skin. On his way to the bathroom to wash the wound, he set the security latch on the door.

As sleepy as she looked, Jax followed him into the bathroom and helped him undo the bandage she had put around the wound. Her concern for him seemed to have given her a second wind as she worked. She washed the blood off his arm and then, being as careful as she could, she cleaned the wound while he held his arm over the sink. Washing it made the pain flare up, and made it start bleeding again. He winced against the pain.

When Alex really saw the cut for the first time, he cursed under his breath. He wondered if maybe he really should go to an emergency room. He quickly decided against it.

"Here," he said, "put this antibiotic in the cut."

"Did you get the needle and thread?" she asked as she drizzled the brown liquid in the wound. It stung like mad.

"I got something better," he said as he opened a package of superglue, getting it ready.

"What could be better?" she asked as she dabbed his arm dry with a towel after it stopped bleeding.

"Just hold it closed and I'll show you."

She used both hands to do as he asked, carefully aligning the sides of the wound. With two fingers, Alex pressed the top layer of the cut tight together. With his thumb and third finger he squeezed the tube of superglue, spreading it generously down the length of the cut. He went back over the places where it hadn't closed completely and added more glue on top of the cut.

"What are you doing?" Jax asked in astonishment.

"Superglue."

"Superglue?" It sounded like an exotic foreign word when she said it.

"Yes, good old superglue. Bonds skin instantly. They use it in surgery now."

He waited a few minutes just to be sure, then took his fingers away. The deep wound stayed tightly closed.

"See? Easier than stitches."

She gently tested it with a finger. "I think you're a big baby and are afraid to have me stitch your arm."

"Just wrap it with that gauze, will you, please?"

Jax smiled at his annoyance and wound the gauze snugly around the arm, not trusting the glue to hold. After that, he had her wrap it with the tan stretch bandage. When she had finished, he moved the arm, testing it. The bandaging wasn't too tight, but it was tight enough to cocoon the wound and protect it. He thought that it ought to heal fine, wrapped as it was.

Seeing her eyes keep closing, he helped her out to the other room. He turned down the bed for her and got an extra pillow out of the tiny closet to add to the two thin pillows on the bed.

She sat on the end of the bed and pulled off a boot. "Did you see? They have a bathing tub in there. A real bathing tub."

Alex smiled at her amazement. "In the morning we'll flip a coin to see who goes first."

She looked at him out of one eye. "Didn't your mother ever teach you 'ladies first'?"

"I guess that our worlds share some important things."

When she saw his smile fade, she said, "Sorry."

Alex nodded. "I know. Me too. I wish . . . well, I'm just glad that she was there to help us when she did. If not for her, I think they might have had us."

Jax nodded as she put her leg up onto her knee to pull off her other boot. "Wake me at dawn."

"I need you well, Jax. You need rest now or you're going to end up worse off. We're safe here for the time being."

She stared into his eyes a moment. "I know, but we need . . . we need . . ." She squinted as she tried to think. "Something . . ."

"We need your mind working or we're sunk, that's what we need. You're the one who figured out what they want."

"The gateway," she mumbled as her eyes started to close. Her hand had stopped with the boot only half off. She looked too exhausted to complete the task.

Alex pulled her boot the rest of the way off, then helped her lie down. He pulled the covers up over her. "I paid for two nights so that we wouldn't have to worry about checkout time in the morning. I hung the 'Do not disturb' sign on the doorknob. We can get up and leave whenever we want. You need to rest."

"But . . ."

He knelt beside the bed, gazing into her half-closed brown eyes. "I need you, Jax. I need you well and alert. You need rest. Do this for me?"

She reached out and cupped the side of his face. "Thank you, Alex—for everything. You need sleep, too."

"I know. I think we'll be safe here. Sleep and get strong for me."

"I don't want to stop looking at you," she whispered. "I'm so relieved that you're safe. I was so afraid for you. . . ."

Alex smoothed her hair back as he smiled at her.

And then he leaned in and gently kissed her. Her lips felt better than he had ever imagined. Her hand came around to lightly hold the back of his head for a moment as she returned the gentle kiss. It was a simple act of quiet joy, saying more than words ever could have how relieved they were to have each other safe.

As he got up to get into the other bed, she softly called his name. He turned back and knelt again beside her bed.

"What is it?"

"Alex . . . I was so afraid there, at that place."

"I know. I was terrified for you."

"I thought I was going to die alone, like so many others Vendis has gotten his hands on. I thought my life was at its end." Her eyes welled up with tears. "I was so afraid. It hurt so much and I was so afraid. I'm so far from home. I don't know if I will ever see home again. I feel so alone."

Alex gently squeezed her hand. "I know."

When he started to get up, she pulled him back down by his hand. "Alex, would you lie close to me so that I don't feel alone tonight? Just lie by me so that I'm not alone?"

Alex smiled. "Sure."

He kicked off his shoes, turned off the light, and lay down on his back beside her. He pulled the bedspread up over them both. Jax nestled close to him.

"Hold me? Please? Just hold me?"

Alex didn't say anything, fearing to test his voice. He would have given anything, paid any price, just to hold her.

As he slipped his arm around her, she laid her head on his shoulder. With his other hand he gently smoothed her hair.

If she noticed how fast his heart was beating, she didn't say so.

Alex kissed the top of her head. "Sleep well."

Her breathing slowed and evened out almost immediately. She was asleep in mere moments.

Alex stared at the ceiling in the near darkness, not wanting to go to sleep lest he miss a moment of the simple bliss of holding her in his arms.

But he didn't last long before he drifted off, the whole time thinking of the precious woman so close to him, safe, for the moment.

44.

WITH A FINGER, ALEX OPENED the curtains just a crack to peek out, looking for anything out of place. It was a heavily overcast, gray day, but it wasn't raining. The Cherokee was parked right outside their room. He didn't see anyone out in the parking lot who looked suspicious. He reminded himself that Dr. Hoffmann, the nurses, and the orderlies at Mother of Roses had never looked suspicious to him.

They didn't all look like pirates.

Alex felt wide awake, truly awake, for the first time in what seemed like days and days. He was foggy on exactly how many days it had been, but he knew that the whole ordeal at Mother of Roses hadn't been more than a few days. Some of the things that had happened didn't seem real. The reality of how many people had died—how many people he had killed—was hard to wrap his mind around. It felt like he was coming out of a long, dark dream filled with endless terror.

He felt a profound empathy for his mother's years of being lost in that living limbo. He was saddened that she had never been able to escape that private, lonely hell, that she never had a chance to live her life. He was heartbroken and angry that people from another world had come here and done that to her—stolen her life—and in the end had murdered her.

The worst part of that entire nightmare, though, had been seeing Jax hanging helpless in the shower at Mother of Roses, seeing her struggle to breathe, fearing what horrific torture they would subject her to, dreading that she would eventually suffocate as she hung there all alone, like so many others that Vendis had had in his clutches.

Now, after twelve hours of sleep, the drugs had largely worn off. He had escaped the nightmare, some of it, anyway. Jax, too, for the most part looked like she was almost back to normal. He had no words for how relieved he was to see her eyes so bright and alive again. She was sore and bruised, but she was alive. That was what mattered.

He heard the tub finish draining, and in a few minutes she came out dressed in fresh jeans and a red top. The color looked stunning with her blond hair, even if her hair wasn't dry. She rubbed it with a towel, drying it as best she could.

He gestured to the little refrigerator under the counter. "You want something to eat?"

"No, not now. I'd rather get going and then eat."

She went back to toweling her hair dry.

"You could use the hair dryer and have it dry a lot quicker."

She gave him a blank look. "The what?"

Alex smiled. "Here, let me show you."

He took her into the bathroom and lifted the hair dryer off its rack. He turned it on high and played it over her hair a moment before turning it off.

"See?"

"That's amazing," she said, taking it from his hand and looking it over. "I can do a similar thing with magic, but magic doesn't work here. I didn't realize you would have technology to match it." She handed the hair dryer back. "Do it some more."

Alex switched it back on and directed the warm air around on her hair. She turned her back to him and let him work at blowing her long fall of wavy blond hair dry. When he had finished, she turned back around and looked him over.

"How come you look clean?"

"I took a shower while you were still asleep."

"Oh," she said, going back out into the main room. "I thought that we agreed that ladies go first."

Alex smiled. "I win any way I can, even if I have to break the rules."

She gave him a meaningful smile. "I'm glad you do."

"How do you feel?"

"Like a new woman."

"Well, you look as beautiful as ever."

She smiled. "So do you."

"If you're feeling better, then I'd like some answers," Alex said, turning serious. "Before we were ambushed and the lights went out, my mother said that they asked her all the time about the gateway. When you heard that word—gateway—you said that you had fig-ured it out, that you knew what they wanted."

She nodded. "They want the gateway."

Alex rolled his eyes. "I got that much of it. But I don't know what it means."

"Well," she said as she started folding her dirty clothes and pack-ing them into the duffel bag they'd bought back at the outlet mall, "do you remember when I told you about how I tried to take the painting you gave me back to my world to show to people?"

Alex nodded. "You said that on the journey back it simply vanished. You said that you didn't know what happened to it, but that the experience confirmed what people had suspected, that things couldn't be taken back from this world to yours."

"So, if nothing can be taken back to my world, why would people from my world come here? Why would Radell Cain have been sending so many people here for so long? What could they possibly want, if they can't take anything back?"

"Knowledge, maybe?"

"Well, I suppose that's not out of the question, but I think that Cain wants something more basic. They're after something specific and they've spent a long time and a lot of effort trying to get it. Why do you suppose they kept your mother prisoner all that time? Why do they want you?"

"Obviously, I guess, they want the gateway. But I don't know what that means." Alex opened his hands in a gesture of frustration. "What the hell is a gateway? Why would they want it?"

She tucked her folded jeans into the duffel bag and then straightened. "It has long been speculated in some quarters that ever since our worlds were separated, some form of connection remained between them. It's always been an obscure theory, though."

Alex eyed her suspiciously. "So what does this obscure theory say?"

"Well, do you remember me telling you how the Lord Rahl banished all those people to this world to end the war?"

"Yes. You said that they didn't come here the way you did, that it was thought that the worlds were for an instant joined at the same place and time and when they separated the people who wanted to live without magic were left in this world and your people in that one."

"That's right. That's why it's called the separation event. Not a lot is known about what happened back then, but it's thought that Lord Rahl somehow bridged the void between our worlds, brought them together for a spark in time in order to send the people who didn't want to live with magic here."

"You mean he sent them through a gateway?"

"No, but according to this theory, there had to be an actual place of connection, a small breach in the void of nothingness between the worlds, an opening through time and space, that allowed everything to remain in balance while the worlds were brought together and then the separation was taking place. The fact that we can come here and return is claimed to be proof that the connection still exists; otherwise, they say, we couldn't cross the void between our worlds.

"The gateway, some theorized, was a side effect of the separation event, an anomaly, an artifact, that remains to this day.

"Other believers in this gateway say that it had to be created by Lord Rahl to balance what he was doing, or the separation event could not have taken place."

"Seems to me to be a pretty important event. Why is this all just speculation? Why isn't more known?"

"At one time there were records, but the long period of the Golden Age ended in wars that resulted in the destruction of many of our most treasured records. It was a dark time. After it ended, we were left without much of our history."

Alex sighed. "So you think this separation event left a conduit between the two worlds? A wormhole of some kind?"

Jax shrugged. "I don't know what a wormhole is. A conduit is a little simplistic, but I guess you could look at it that way. A better way to think of it is as a kind of vent, a balance needed between the profound forces on each side."

"Do you think this connection, this gateway, is a fact, or is this simply people making wild guesses about things that may or may not have once happened?"

"It's been inferred by some from what little is known about the separation event. At least, it's inferred by the few people who actually subscribe to this 'Gateway Theory.'"

"Why didn't you ever bring this up before? Why is it such a surprise? This whole gateway thing sounds pretty important."

"It may seem so now, but it's actually an obscure, fringe theory. To be quite frank, Gateway Theory has always been considered a crackpot notion. It never entered my mind that this whole thing with Radell Cain could have anything to do with such a crazy idea until I heard your mother say the word 'gateway.'

"That they would use that specific word to your mother suddenly made everything that's been happening all come together for me. It suddenly all made sense."

"But even if this gateway once existed, in the beginning, do you think it still exists?"

"I don't know. But Radell Cain apparently thinks so. His people kept questioning your mother about it, didn't they? They asked me about it. I'm sure they must have asked you, too."

"They did," Alex admitted. "In fact it was the only thing they wanted me to talk about."

"Your mother gave me the answer I've been looking for, the answer to why they're coming here and what they want. Radell Cain wants the gateway."

Realization dawned on him. "The land I'm inheriting. The gateway must be somewhere on the land that was left to me."

Jax was nodding. "You were right from the beginning. All along it's been about the land."

"But why would they need my mother? Or me? If they suspect the gateway is located there on that land, then why not simply go there? The place is primitive and remote. They could have the gateway to themselves and no one would likely even know that they were there or what they were up to."

"Maybe they already went there and found it, but they couldn't use it for some reason. Maybe that was when they became interested in the Rahl line here in this world."

Alex hadn't thought of that. He paced to the window and back as he thought about it. He wondered what part the Daggett Trust played in the whole thing.

"If they did go there and couldn't make the gateway work, what makes them think that I could?"

"A Rahl separated the worlds. If in so doing he also created this gateway between worlds, and it still exists, then maybe it has failsafes and it takes a Rahl to open it again."

"But that was him, not me. Even if I am a descendant of this Rahl line from your world, I don't have those kinds of abilities. How the hell am I supposed to open a gateway between worlds? I never even knew another world existed. I'm the last person on earth to go to for answers about a gateway."

"Not really," Jax said as she shrugged. "The Law of Nines names you as central to it all. You would be the very person to go to."

"The Law of Nines? How can that have anything to do with a gateway?"

"I don't know, but Radell Cain wants the gateway, and the Law of

Nines leads him directly to you as being central to the whole thing. He sent Sedrick Vendis here, his most trusted man, to secure both the gateway and you."

Alex paced as he thought. "But like you just said, they're coming to this world. They can already come here and go back. What more is the gateway going to do for them that they can't already do?"

Alex paused in midstride as the answer to his own question suddenly became clear. "Except that when they come here they can't take anything back with them." He met her gaze. "Could they take things back through a gateway?"

She was smiling in an unsettling way. "According to the theory, a lifeline isn't needed in the gateway, so objects could be taken back through it."

"What would they want to take back through the gateway?"

"What's the weapon they're using to conquer and control people in my world?"

"The ability your world has but this one doesn't, weapons of magic."

"Right. And what is it Cain wants to eliminate from our world?"

"Magic."

"So, what happens if they succeed?"

Alex felt the hair on his arms stand on end. "Dictators always seek to take weapons away from people so that there can be no effective opposition to their rule. If they eliminate magic, they will eliminate the weapon that people could use to resist tyranny.

"But in taking it away from the people who might oppose them, they will also be eliminating it for their own use. So, if they eliminate the weapon everyone on both sides is using now, they will need some other kind of weapon to replace it."

"That's right," she said. "There is a kind of balance of power now. Both sides have access to the same kinds of weapons. If they eliminate magic, that would leave the balance of power static—neither side would have it. So, if they want to seize rule they will need to replace their lost weapons with some other kind of weapon. That would tip the balance their way."

"Technology," Alex whispered. "They could use radios to communicate, drugs to control people, and guns to kill anyone who tries to resist them."

Jax was nodding again. "And who knows what else. For all practical purposes, technology is interchangeable with what we can do with our abilities—they do the same kinds of things. When the tools created with the use of magic are suddenly gone, people will be helpless."

"Those with technology to replace those lost tools will be able to rule the world."

"Exactly." Jax swept an arm out. "There is a whole world of technology here for the taking. Last night you went out and bought that magic glue—"

"Superglue."

"Right, superglue. We use magic to heal in a similar way, knitting wounds closed much like you did. But if our ability to do that is gone, we will have no way to heal the wounded. Imagine the advantage Cain's side would have with something that simple. How many people would give in to his side just to be healed with the technology only Cain could provide?

"But there is a great deal more. There is a whole world here full of things we wouldn't have. They could walk into a store and buy things that would be invaluable in my world, if everyone in my world were stripped of their abilities. They could take that technology back through a gateway. Cain would be the sole source of the things that people needed to live, and only he would have weapons to enforce his rule."

"But do you think this Gateway Theory is really right? That people could take things back through it to your world?"

"I imagine that Radell Cain must have reason to believe so."

Alex sat down on the edge of the bed. "What is it I've heard you say . . . ? 'Dear spirits'?"

"Yes, if things are bad enough."

Alex rested his elbows on his knees and put his head in his hands. "Dear spirits, they want a gateway to run guns to another world."

"Any ideas?"

"Sure, let's call in ATF."

"Who?"

"Nothing," he said, waving off his flip remark. "That still doesn't really explain my part in this. I've never even heard of a gateway. What would I know? What do they think I can do?"

"You're a Rahl—a Rahl specifically identified by the Law of Nines. It was a Rahl who created the gateway. I think that if they could simply find the gateway and use it they would have done so ages ago. Since they haven't, that means they can't. For some reason they need you."

"Do you honestly think that they intend for me to open this gateway for them? Do you really think they believe I can?"

Jax let out a long sigh. "I don't know, Alex. Do you have any better explanation?"

"I guess not," he said.

"So what now?"

He went to the desk and retrieved one of the phones he'd bought the night before. "I think I had better call Mr. Fenton, the lawyer for the land. I think we need to get ourselves to Boston, take title to the land, and then go up to Maine and have a look for ourselves."

"I agree. It's our only lead now."

45.

ALEX DIALED THE NUMBER. "I'll put it on speaker so you can hear," he told Jax.

"Lancaster, Buckman, Fenton. This is Mr. Fenton."

"Mr. Fenton, hi. It's Alexander Rahl."

"Mr. Rahl, I'm so relieved to hear from you." The man sounded like he meant it. "I was beginning to worry. Is everything all right? I mean, it's been over a week since you had said that you were going to call. I was beginning to get concerned."

Alex hadn't realized that he'd lost track of that much time drugged up in Mother of Roses. "I apologize. I was distracted by some things for a few days, but I'm free now."

"That's good to hear. Say, I've been seeing on the news about the big fire you had out your way, at Mother of Roses. Do you know anything about it?"

Alex wasn't sure what he should say, so he decided to be vague. "Some. Why?"

"Well, the thing is, one of my associates, Mr. Buckman, took ill earlier this year. His doctor thought that he was possibly suffering a breakdown of some sort, and as a result had fallen into a rather severe psychosis. They couldn't seem to get to the bottom of it, so Mr. Buckman was sent out your way to Mother of Roses Psychiatric Hospital for extended care. I guess they specialize in that sort of thing. It's a private care facility where he has been receiving special-ized evaluation and treatment."

Alex's mouth went dry. "Treatment? From who? Do you know his doctor's name?"

"The specialist in charge is Dr. Hoffmann. I was just wondering if you knew anything more about the fire. You know how unreliable the news can be. I haven't been able to find out anything about Mr. Buckman. I don't know if he's all right or not. The news reports said that a number of patients died in the fire, most of them on the ninth floor. That's where Mr. Buckman was confined."

Alex shared a look with Jax. "I'm terribly sorry. My mother died in the fire at Mother of Roses. She was on the ninth floor."

"Dear God." He was silent for a moment. "I'm so sorry. I didn't realize. You have my deepest sympathy, Mr. Rahl."

"Thank you."

"I remember very well your mother not being able to take title to the land because she fell ill, but I had no idea that she was at Mother of Roses. What a strange coincidence that Mr. Buckman was at the same institution, and on the same floor."

"Yes, that is quite the coincidence."

Alex didn't generally believe in coincidences. His mind raced as he tried to fit the pieces together.

"Have you tried contacting the authorities here in Nebraska to find out if Mr. Buckman might have been one of the people who escaped the blaze? I've heard that it was quite a chaotic scene but most of the patients did manage to escape."

"I heard the same encouraging news. I've tried to get more information, but there seems to be quite a lot of confusion right now. Being a lawyer, I was able to get ahold of the state hospital authority, but no one can even find a patient register."

"Are there other records?" Alex asked.

"I was told that the records at the hospital were destroyed in the fire. There were supposed to be backups of all the patient files kept off-site but there was apparently some kind of problem with the backup—they said it might have been a computer virus or something. No one knew about it until they went to retrieve the information and discovered that it was corrupted beyond recovery. So, the authorities there are in the dark even about how many people might have been under care at the facility. That makes it even more difficult to determine how many may have died.

"—Oh, I'm sorry. Here I am going on about Mr. Buckman and side issues when you lost your mother there. You probably need to get back to making arrangements."

"No, it's all right. There aren't really any arrangements to be made. I don't have any living relatives. My grandfather died a short while back. Being confined in a mental hospital all these years, my mother didn't have any friends or really even know anyone. There's actually nothing to be done. I will have to wait for any remains to be found—if they ever are. The fire was pretty intense. For now, there's really nothing I can do."

"I see. Are you headed here, then?"

Alex thought that he detected an odd tension in the question. "Yes. I will need to look into what flights are available. I'll try to get the earliest flight we can going to Boston."

"We? You have someone with you?"

"My fiancée."

Another pause. "That's wonderful. Congratulations."

"Thank you. You'll get to meet her. She's a wonderful person. She has been helping me get through the loss of my mother. Her name is Jax. She's here with me now. I have you on speaker if you would like to say hello."

Jax leaned in at Alex's urging. "Hello, Mr. Fenton."

"How do you do? I'm so sorry to hear of your unexpected trouble."

"Thank you. We're doing the best we can."

"I look forward to meeting you soon, then."

"We can't get there fast enough," Jax said.

"I'll let you know as soon as I have a flight number," Alex put in.

There was a long pause. "Mr. Rahl, I suggest that you not fly."

Alex's antennae went up. "Why is that?"

Again a pause. "Mr. Rahl, may I be honest with you?"

"I wish you would."

"I fear that certain people may be watching the airlines, trying to find you."

Alex's blood went cold. "Certain people?"

"It's possible that you could be in danger from these people. They might be expecting you to head here. They may be watching airports and bus stations—any kind of place you would go to take public transportation. I don't mean to alarm you, Mr. Rahl, but I believe that these people could possibly be dangerous."

"I think I know what you mean."

Another pause, longer this time, as if the man was considering what to say, or maybe how much to say. "Have you been approached, or . . . threatened by anyone?"

"I think we're talking about the same people. I've run into them already."

"Are you all right?" he asked in a rush. There was genuine concern, even alarm, in his voice.

"Yes. Right now I think it best if I get there as soon as possible. I have your address—"

"No."

"No?"

"Well, the thing is . . ." There was another pause before the man went on. "I fear that these same people might be watching my offices. I don't really have any way to tell. I'm sorry—I don't mean to alarm you unduly. It's possible that I'm simply being paranoid."

Alex took a deep breath. "Mr. Fenton, this is too important for us to keep up this pretense. You were honest with me, I'm going to be honest with you. You need to listen to me and listen carefully. These people are killers."

Alex didn't know if the man would scoff, or hang up.

"I'm listening, Mr. Rahl."

Alex thought that it was a good sign that the lawyer didn't try to minimize the danger. In fact, the man sounded concerned, even frightened.

"First of all, I'm Alex."

Alex could imagine the man smiling with relief. "My first name is Myron, but if you call me by that name I'll sue you for pain and suffering. Everyone calls me Mike."

Alex smiled. "I have enough on my plate without a lawsuit. Mike it is. I know it may sound far-fetched, but you need to trust me about all of this. I know what I'm talking about. I need you to do exactly as I tell you. First thing, does this number show up on your phone?"

"Yes. I'll have it in the caller ID memory."

"No, you won't."

"But my phone—"

"I don't want you using any phone you have now. These people can somehow track you with your phone. From now on I don't want you to touch any phone you presently have. Don't use your cell phone. Don't even take it with you. Do you understand?"

"Yes."

Alex thought that it was promising that Mr. Fenton wasn't freaking out or recommending that he see a shrink, and even more significantly, he wasn't arguing. "Memorize this number. Don't say it out loud. Don't write it down. Memorize it."

"Done."

"Good. It's possible that the phone I'm talking on is now compromised because I've called your regular phone. I'll have to throw this phone away after I hang up. I have another. Add one hundred forty-three to this number and you will have the number of the new phone. After you leave your office, buy a disposable cell phone and call me back on my new number."

"All right."

"Are you married? Do you have family?"

"No. Not close family, anyway. I have . . . good friends that I will need to talk to."

"All right, but don't take any phone that you have now with you. Best to get several cell phones. Use one of those others to call your friends. Make up some excuse—tell them that you will be away on business or something for a while. After you talk to them, throw that phone away; it could become compromised by calling them and then the people you're worried about could use that new phone to track you."

"All right. What else?"

"We'll need a place to meet. Don't say it now. Wait until we talk later. I know that these people have the ability to track people through phones, but I don't know if they can listen in on conversations. I don't want to find out the hard way that they can. I'd rather be too cautious than spend eternity in my grave wishing I'd been more careful."

"I understand. I will pick up some phones and call you then."

"When you leave your office, go home and pack a bag. You need to stay away from any place you are known to frequent. Don't go stay with a friend. Don't stay at your office or at a club if you're a member of one. You need to go somewhere that you don't frequent, a place you've never been. Make sure you aren't followed. Once there, don't go back to a known location or these people could be spooked enough to pick you up right then and there."

"I understand." There was a pause. "Alex, are you sure that such extreme measures are necessary? I mean the staying away from any known locations and all?"

"The fire at Mother of Roses was set deliberately. They murdered my mother and I would bet that they murdered Mr. Buckman as well. They killed a number of innocent people just so that they could destroy any records of what they were up to."

"Dear God. You really think so?"

"I don't think so, I know so. I was there. I saw Dr. Hoffmann set the fire to cover their tracks."

Alex waited for a moment, trying to guess at the silence.

"I must tell you, Alex, you have just confirmed my worst fears. We've been trying to gauge if the danger is real. You have just answered a lot of our questions for us."

"Who is this 'us'? Who are you talking about?"

"I think you're right," Mike said. "It would be best if we talk later."

"You're right. That makes sense."

"I'm going to be leaving my office immediately. I will take all the title documents with me. I will have everything we need to transfer the land into your name. I realize that it may seem like a silly formality in the middle of all of this other business, but I assure you, it is vital that it be done."

"I'd like it taken care of myself. I want that land in my name."

"Good. I'm glad. I think it best if I not go home, though. I think the risk has now become too great. I'll buy whatever I need. I will pick up some phones, as you suggest, and call you."

"Good. Please be careful."

"I will. Thanks, Alex, for leveling with me."

"Jax always says that it's best to tell the truth."

He chuckled. "I'll call you later today. I'll also make arrangements so we can meet and take care of everything."

"Mirrors," Jax said.

"Oh yes. I know this sounds crazy, but you need to stay away from mirrors. If you stay someplace with a mirror, cover it immediately."

"I haven't had any mirrors in my office or house for years."

Alex and Jax again shared a look.

"In fact, it's been so long since I've been near a mirror that I'm not even sure what I look like anymore."

"Do you have a rearview mirror in your car?"

"Yes, of course."

"That's a mirror. You need to break the rearview mirror off the windshield and break out or remove the outside mirrors. If you break the glass out, make certain that every speck of mirror is gone."

"Is that really necessary?"

"I found out the hard way that it is. You may not be as lucky as we were. Take the mirrors out of your car."

"I've always been so careful with mirrors, and all this time I never thought about the rearview mirrors in my car. This explains some things. I'm glad you're so thorough. I will remove them before I start the car."

"I think we're going to have a lot to talk about when we get together."

"More than you know, Mr. Rahl."

"Alex."

"Right. I will call you later, Alex. And I especially look forward to meeting you, Jax."

"Stay safe," she said. "And be careful."

"I understand. Good-bye."

"Good-bye," Alex and Jax said together.

He closed the cover and then dropped the phone in a plastic cup full of water.

"Well, what do you make of that?" he asked as he slipped the other new phone, the one he hadn't used yet, into the pocket of his jeans.

"It's obvious he knows something."

"I wonder how," Alex said. "I guess that the sooner we get there the sooner we'll find out. We'd better get going."

"How are we going to get there?"

"I don't see that we have any choice. We'll have to drive. If we flew we could be in Boston in a day. But by the time we can get on a flight it's liable to be two days, maybe even longer on such short notice. Driving will take close to three days, but if we drive, Cain's people won't know where we are or when we'll show up. I want to keep them in the dark as much as possible."

"Me, too."

"Just as well, anyway," he said as he put his jacket on to cover his gun. "I wasn't comfortable with the idea of giving up our weapons in order to fly. Airports have metal detectors, like at Mother of Roses. They won't let you take a weapon of any kind onto a plane—not even a small pocketknife.

"We'd have to pack our weapons in the luggage. If anything happened they would be useless to us locked away in the baggage compartment, the same as they were useless to us when they were locked away in the truck. Besides, the luggage could be lost, or stolen, especially if Cain's people are watching, trying to catch us flying. They would probably snatch our bags to make sure we were unarmed."

Jax pulled the silver-handled knife from behind her back. She twirled the blade through her fingers and caught it by the tip. She held it up, the handle before him. It was then that he noticed, for the first time, that the ornate scrollwork formed the letter R.

"There is no way I'm giving up this knife just so that they will let me go up in the sky."

Alex's gaze moved from the knife to her eyes. "Why is there an R on the handle?"

"It stands for the House of Rahl. It's an ancient weapon, an exceedingly rare weapon, a weapon carried by only a very few people now."

"Why do you have it?"

"For the same reason I volunteered to come to this world. Because I believe you are the one to stop this madness. Because I believe in you, Alexander Rahl.

"This is the knife I was sharpening when I made the test cuts on that tree in the painting you made. You painted those test cuts in your painting, those test cuts made with this knife as I was sharpening it in preparation for coming here. You are connected to this blade in more ways than one, just as you are connected to everything else."

"Are you positive, Jax?"

She smiled. "I'm as positive of it as you are, and you're dead certain of it."

Alex smiled back. "It's scary how well you know me."

He pulled the phone out of the glass of water, then opened it and broke it in half. He handed the broken pieces to Jax. "Here. There's a dumpster across the lot. I'll put our things in the truck. You throw this away."

"Gladly."

46.

THEY HAD JUST FINISHED filling the Jeep with gas and grabbing a quick bite to eat at the Amana Colonies along Interstate 80 in Iowa when Alex's phone rang. He didn't have to guess who it could be.

"Hi, Mike," he said, looking back over his left shoulder at the traffic coming up behind him as he merged onto Interstate 80.

"You still all right, Alex?"

"Fine. We're on the road, headed your way. I have you on speaker."

"I've followed all of your instructions to the letter."

"And you didn't use the phone you're on now to call anyone?"

"No. This is the only call I've made with it since I unwrapped it."

Alex was relieved that the man was taking everything so seriously. He did wonder why, though—what kind of encounters he could have had that would make him go along so willingly.

"Good. Thanks."

The other thing that concerned Alex was that it seemed certain that Cain had to know about the land. Why else would they have taken Walter Buckman to the ninth floor of Mother of Roses, where he would be under the thumb of Dr. Hoffmann? One way or another they would have gotten all the information out of Mike Fenton's partner—and God only knew who else.

If Cain's people were watching airports and bus stations to see if they could catch Alex and Jax, then they surely would also be waiting and watching the land up in Maine. After all, they had to know right where it was. They had to know that sooner or later Alex would end up there. Everything was funneling them right to that one place.

Of course, if Cain's men could snatch them in an airport, he and Jax would be unarmed, which would make it a lot easier for them. That was probably what they were hoping. They wanted to capture Alex, but they surely would kill Jax on sight.

At least if they ran into Cain's people up in Maine, he and Jax would be armed and expecting trouble.

"I'm not sure how long it will take us to get there," Alex said when Mike asked. "I think it must be about thirteen hundred miles to Boston. We got a late start today, so I imagine we'll be there by day after tomorrow—late in the day."

"Since I suspect that my office was being watched, I feel uncomfortable having you come to Boston for us to meet. I think it would be best if we met closer to where the land is located, and to where some of the others are."

"You have a place in mind?"

"Yes. I've made reservations, if it's all right with you and Jax. If not, I can change the location. It's farther up beyond Boston, but it's on the way to where you're headed, so it would be convenient and it wouldn't lose you any time."

"Well, I guess we are most interested in getting to the land."

"That's what I thought."

"So, where do you want us to meet you?"

"In Bangor, Maine. I'm at a motel just outside Boston right now. I'm going to be heading up to Bangor in a day or two, after I finish taking care of some legal details. I already made reservations for you as well in the name of Hank Croft."

"How'd you pick the name?"

"Stuck my finger in a phone book. It seemed like an easy name to remember. I'll be staying at the same place."

"Hank Croft. Got it. But when you check into a motel they usually want to see a driver's license or some kind of ID."

"That's one of the reasons I'm still in Boston. I've been taking care of that. You would be surprised how easy it is to get those kinds of documents. It's easier than going to the DMV. As long as I was at it, I picked up an ID for Mrs. Jenna Croft—they gave me a quantity discount. It will all be on your bill. I had the IDs say you were married. I figured that, just in case, it would make it easier."

"Jenna Croft. That's good thinking," Jax said, leaning toward the phone in Alex's hand. "You mentioned 'where some of the others are.' Who are these other people?"

"They're from the Daggett Trust. They need to sign off on the transfer of title to the land into Alex's name."

"And do they know you're coming?" Jax asked. "Know that we're coming? And where we're all to meet?"

"Yes."

Alex gripped the steering wheel in his fists and gritted his teeth, but tried to keep his voice calm. "Mike, they could be followed. They could do any one of a number of things that could compromise us."

"I told them your instructions. They will follow everything you told me, do everything the same as I'm doing."

"How can you be sure that they will take all of it seriously enough?" Jax asked. Alex could hear a thread of anxiety and anger in her voice.

"These are very cautious people. They're the ones who originally told me about mirrors."

Alex shared a look with Jax.

"You told them about the rearview mirrors in their cars as well?" Alex asked.

"I did. They were quite embarrassed that they hadn't thought of that long before now. They were mortified, in fact. They're in the process of retracing their tracks over the last few years to try to identify anything that could have been put at risk because they hadn't considered the mirrors in their cars."

"Who the hell *are* these people?" Alex whispered to Jax.

She frowned and shook her head as if to say she couldn't imagine and shared his concern.

"I have to tell you, Mike, it worries me that there are other people involved, other people who know our plans. It creates opportunities for trouble to find us."

"Alex, I trust these people with my life."

"Good for you, but I don't know if I'm willing to trust them with mine, or Jax's."

"I can understand your concern, but I assure you, these people can be trusted."

"Maybe so, but why can't you take them the papers after I sign them? Why do you have to bring them in on this meeting?"

"Because these people are the board of directors of the Daggett Trust. The Daggett Trust has a large stake in this. The directors have to be there in order to make this happen. While the technicality is written in convoluted legal terms, what it boils down to is that they have to, in essence, approve of the title to the land going to you."

"What do you mean, they have to approve it? I thought that if I meet the conditions of the inheritance, which I do, then the land goes to me."

"Yes, that's right. But their approval is one of those conditions, as is payment of the legal fees. You do recall me telling you about the fees, don't you?"

Alex thought it an odd thing to bring up. "Yes. How much?"

"I don't have the final figures on the expenses, yet, but it will be a little under ten thousand dollars."

Alex thought the legal fees were pretty hefty, but he didn't say so. He didn't know how much work was involved or how much lawyers were supposed to cost in such matters. Throwing in the danger element, he supposed that it didn't sound so out of line.

"What if they don't approve for some reason?"

"Alex, believe me, these people are looking forward to you having the land in your name."

"Why?"

"Because the inheritance of this particular piece of land has cast its shadow over a number of people for centuries before it finally settled on you. They know that the land is meant to go to you."

"How would they know that I'm the one who is supposed to have it?"

There was a long pause before the man answered.

"Because of the Law of Nines."

Alex almost dropped the phone. Jax's face lost a little color.

The tires droned on against the pavement and made a rhythmic thump at every expansion joint in the road. Alex couldn't figure out how the Daggett Trust fit into it all, or how these people would know anything about mirrors, much less the Law of Nines.

"Well?" he whispered to Jax.

She shrugged as she shook her head, as if to say that it made no sense to her, either.

"Alex, are you there?"

Alex cleared his throat. "Where is it you want to meet Hank and Jenna Croft?"

"At the Downeaster Motel in Bangor. The fastest route that will take you in the direction of the land trust is Interstate 95 up through the state. I thought it best to make the stop along that route, in Bangor. I figured that Bangor is a big enough place that it won't be easy for them to watch as it would be a smaller town closer to the land."

"That makes sense."

"The Downeaster Motel is just off of Interstate 95 on Hammond Street, right there in Bangor. I'll give you exact directions and the address when you get closer, but it's not hard to find, just a right turn off I-95 north and go up a short distance."

"All right. Don't use the phone you're using right now to call anyone else. Use it exclusively to call us. I see the number on the caller ID. I'll call you along the way to let you know how we're doing. If anyone but me calls you on that phone, destroy it and buy a new one and then call me immediately."

"How long do you think it will take?"

"I don't know. It's starting to get dark here now. Probably close to another three days. I want to be careful and not draw attention to us. I also don't want to show up exhausted and half asleep, either. Not being alert can get you in a world of hurt with these people. I'll be able to give you a better arrival time as we get closer."

"Call anytime, day or night. I will have this phone on me all the time."

"Same here. If anything smells fishy, I want to know about it."

"You've got it. I can assure you that we're all being extremely careful."

"What about the other people in your office? Does anyone else know about the land or me?"

"I am the office."

"What do you mean?"

"There was only me and Walter Buckman. Mr. Lancaster died a number of years back in a car accident."

That's what had happened to Alex's father, but he didn't say so.

"You and Mr. Buckman handled everything with all your clients by yourselves? No secretaries? No assistants?"

"No, none. We only have one client: the Daggett Trust."

Alex lifted an eyebrow to Jax.

"You need to consider everything that Walter Buckman knew and assume that they now know it all," Jax said. "These people are perfectly willing to use any means necessary to get answers. Assume that if he liked salt on his eggs, they know how much."

"We have already made that same assumption. We've taken efforts to close off any avenues his knowledge would have opened for them."

"Let's just hope that it's not too late," she said.

"All I can tell you is that we've done everything we can think of to minimize the risk. As you've said, these people are dangerous. We can't entirely eliminate every single threat, but we've done what we can. Unless you have any other ideas?"

"No," Jax said. "We know quite well how dangerous these people are, but we don't know how many people they have, what they've been up to, or the specifics of what their plans are."

"Other than knowing that these people are dangerous, we're largely in the dark as to what's going on," Alex added, not completely, one hundred percent convinced that the man was not somehow connected with Radell Cain and trying to suck them into a trap. If Mike Fenton was on Cain's side, Alex didn't want to give the man the idea that Jax and he could provide answers he didn't have. "You probably know more than we do. We're hoping that when we meet, you can fill us in on just what this is all about."

"Let's stay in touch," Mike said. "Keep me updated as you get closer."

"I will. Good-bye for now," Alex said.

"Good-bye."

Alex flipped the phone closed. He glanced over at Jax. "What do you think?"

"I don't know." Jax shook her head. "The Law of Nines is something from my world. It has to do with how things work in my world. I don't see how anyone here could know about it."

"It's involved in my world now, too," he reminded her. "So you think it's another ambush?"

Her mouth twisted in thought as she considered for a moment. "I don't know, but the man seems to ring true to me."

"He could be conning us. I never suspected Dr. Hoffmann of working for Cain, or those nurses and orderlies being from your world."

"The only thing I know for sure is that Cain would like nothing more than to capture you," she said. "We can't allow that."

"What do you say we hope Mike Fenton and the others are on our side, but be prepared for them being on Cain's."

"That's all we can do."

47.

OOK, THERE," JAX SAID, POINTING. "Hammond Street, two miles."

Alex glanced over at the green sign in the mist as they sailed past it on their way north. It was late in the afternoon. Traffic was getting heavier as rush hour approached.

He looked over his shoulder to make sure the road was clear as he pulled into the right lane. He had just gone by a woman in a small car who looked to be terrified by the weather conditions. It was annoying not having a rearview mirror, but to get over his annoyance Alex had only to recall the desperate fight when a man from Jax's world had appeared in the back seat of the Cherokee. Alex saw that the woman he'd just passed had a death grip on the wheel. Her eyes stared unblinking straight ahead as she single-handedly created a traffic snarl, so afraid of danger that she had become danger itself.

Jax pointed. "Hammond Street, one mile."

Over the long drive, Jax had developed into a good navigator. It had only taken her a short time to overcome her uneasiness at traveling at highway speeds. She was now an old pro.

She was good at reading maps and had good eyesight, so she was adept at picking out signs in the distance for different highways they had needed to take on their way east and then north. She also kept a look-out for any cars—or pirate plumbing trucks—that might be following them. Several times they had taken exits and detours to be certain that cars that stayed on their tail were not really following them.

Jax had been amazed at the size of some of the cities they had gone through and couldn't get enough of the sights and changing scenery as they crossed the country. She was a tourist in a strange land. Her childlike wonder never failed to make Alex smile.

They had stopped at night only long enough to get the sleep they needed to keep going. Alex knew that they both were still working the drugs out of their systems. Jax especially still needed rest to recover from her ordeal. Given the nature of the people after them, they knew that they had to stay alert. It was also fatiguing to constantly remain on the lookout for anything that might be suspicious.

Alex had been able to persuade her to cover herself up with a blanket in the back seat and get some sleep along the way. He could tell how much she still hurt because he didn't have too difficult a time convincing her to rest. She hated missing all the sights, and she didn't like leaving him to be the lone lookout, but she needed the rest and she knew it.

As they drove up through the seemingly endless woods of Maine, she looked to finally be a lot better. She had stared longingly out the window at the passing forests. He knew that they reminded her of home.

Alex turned on the windshield wipers as he took the Hammond Street exit. From his brief look, the city of Bangor seemed old and tired. Some of the houses did look grand, but in a bygone-era sort of a way. It looked like a peaceful, low-key place to live, a place where people made do with what they had, and not a whole lot ever changed, except with the slow rot of time.

He followed Mike Fenton's directions and in short order they saw the red glow of the sign for the Downeaster Motel. There were a lot of cars in the front parking lot. The portico in front stood at the head of two parallel sections of rooms running back from there in a U shape.

As he drove slowly through the lot, he scanned the cars for license plates from Massachusetts. He saw a number of them here and there. Maine being a tourist destination, there were plates from all over. Some of the cars were packed full with belongings pressed against rear windows. Some of the trucks had kayaks or bicycles attached to their roofs.

Alex drove around to the far wing of the two-story building that extended back to end at a small area of residential woods. A lot of cars were parked for rooms up closer to the office, but farther down the side was mostly deserted except way at the end, where there was a cluster of cars. By the room numbers on the doors he knew that was the place he was looking for.

When he reached the end he made a U-turn and parked on the slight slope at the back of the broad lot so that if he had to he could get the Cherokee rolling downhill to start it. So far, on their trip east, it had behaved itself, failing to start with the key only once. He supposed that if someone had been chasing them it would have failed to start more often.

Parking as he had also put the driver's side closest to the room.

"You ready?" Alex asked as he watched for any activity.

Jax carefully scanned the whole area, appearing to take note of every detail. "This makes me nervous."

"I can't say that I disagree."

Jax took his hand and squeezed it, offering reassurance. They'd made it through tough situations before.

Alex hooked a magazine pouch on his belt on his left hip. It held two seventeen-round magazines. He double-checked to make sure the magazines were placed in the pouch with the bullets facing forward so that if he got in a gun battle and had to draw them to reload, he could use the index finger of his left hand to feel the tip of the hollow-point round at the top of the magazine to help guide it into the gun in his right hand for fast, blind reloading. He lifted the Glock from its holster and held it in his lap, his index finger lying along the slide.

Alex opened the phone and hit Redial with his left thumb. Mike Fenton answered.

"This is Alex. We're outside."

Alex watched and saw the drapes open a crack as the man peered out.

"I see your truck. We're so glad you're here, and that you're early. Come on in. Everyone is dying to meet you."

"How many of you are there?"

"Including me, nine."

"I want all of you to come out of the room. Leave the door wide open. I want everyone to move away from the door, toward the woods at the back. Stay in plain sight. Jax is going to go in and check the room."

"Alex, I can understand that you would be a little nervous, but we—"

"If any one of you does anything threatening, I won't hesitate to shoot them."

Mike went silent.

"Do you understand?" Alex asked.

"I do," Mike said. "I don't blame you for being cautious. You're right. We're happy to do as you ask."

"Thank you."

Alex closed the phone.

"If you hear any gunshots, hit the ground," Alex told Jax. "Understand?"

"Yes. I think they're sincere."

"I hope so, but I'm not going to take any chances. You be careful in there, will you? If you have any problem I'll be there in a flash."

Jax nodded. "Just don't miss if this turns out to be an ambush. There's two of us and nine of them."

Alex offered her a smile. "It's their tough luck to be at such a terrible disadvantage."

She squeezed his hand as she returned the smile.

Alex watched as the people started filing out of the room. They strolled casually, talking among themselves so that it wouldn't look suspicious to see that many people standing around in the parking lot. There were seven men and two women. They were all dressed casually, similar to but perhaps just a little better than most any tourist traveling up to Maine for a vacation.

"The trees smell so good," Jax said to herself.

"What?"

"Nothing. Just thinking of home. The balsam trees remind me of home."

As Alex watched the group amble off into the lot closer to the trees and out of the way of the open door, he squeezed Jax's hand again. "Be careful."

She winked at him. "You too."

He watched her walking across the lot, mesmerized by the graceful shape of her, by her fall of long blond hair, by how beautiful, how precious she was. There was no other woman in the world like her.

How he wished she was from his world.

He knew that if they ever accomplished what they needed to

accomplish, accomplished what she had come to his world to do, and they found the gateway and somehow were able to make it work, she would have to go back to her own world.

Along their long trip east, when she had told him what she knew about the gateway and how it could be used to take things back to her world without a lifeline, he had asked if it was possible for him to go through the gateway, too.

Jax had said that that was one thing she was certain of: no one from his world could ever go to hers. Lord Rahl, the man who had separated the worlds, who had sent people to this world, had made certain that that could never happen.

She could come here, but he could never go there.

Alex didn't know how he would be able to endure her leaving. Without her in his world—in his life—his world would be dead.

The group of people all took in Jax without looking obvious about it as she walked toward the room. She disappeared inside.

None of the people looked concerned. Alex thought that was a good sign. He hated to be so melodramatic about the whole thing, but he'd been fooled by Cain's people before. He wasn't going to take chances if he didn't have to.

After a few minutes, Jax reappeared in the doorway. She gave Alex the all-clear. He holstered his gun and hopped out of the truck, pulling his jacket down over the weapon. Jax started ushering the people back into the room, then stood just outside the door, waiting for him while she watched them like a sergeant at arms.

As Alex joined her, she put an arm around his waist. "They don't look like a dangerous lot," she whispered.

"That's what we're hoping."

"But that doesn't mean they aren't."

"I know."

48.

AS ALEX STEPPED INTO THE ROOM behind Jax, all eyes were on them. The two-room suite was larger than the typical motel room. The two beige couches forming an L at the corner of the front showed discoloration from heavy use. A round table with half a dozen chairs sat at the back.

None of the furniture was especially elegant, but it was comfortable-looking. There was a wet bar beside a TV in a tall cabinet opposite the couches. Through double louvered doors that stood open to the right he could see the edge of a bed in the other room.

The nine people standing in a cluster in the center of the room were all grins. They looked like devout worshippers about to meet the Pope.

"I'm Mike Fenton," a rather thin man said as he stepped forward, thrusting out his hand.

He was shorter than Jax, balding, and wearing jeans that still had the fold marks in them from coming right off the rack. His gray-and-blue-striped, long-sleeved shirt likewise looked to have been freshly unwrapped. He was grinning from ear to ear.

Alex shook the man's hand. "Alex. It's nice to meet you face-to-face, at last."

Still gripping Alex's hand, Mike swept his free arm around, indicating the rest of the people in the room. "We're all so relieved that you arrived safely. And you would have to be Jax."

"I am," she said as she shook his hand. He held her hand respectfully, gazing into her eyes as if welcoming an alien from another planet to his world. Alex supposed that he was.

Alex was so focused on evaluating everyone as Mike introduced them that he knew he wouldn't remember all their names. None of them looked like a pirate. They were all wearing new clothes that to a greater or lesser extent still bore new-clothes folds. They had apparently followed Alex's instructions and had not gone to their homes or any place familiar.

Mike gestured to the table in the back, where papers were neatly laid out. "How about if we get business out of the way first? Get the title to the land taken care of so that everything is finalized and legal?"

"I'd like that," Alex said.

"Do you have the fee?"

Alex pulled an envelope from an inside pocket of his jacket. He handed it to Mike.

"There's ten thousand even."

"It came to ninety-six hundred and seventy-five dollars."

The man opened the envelope and counted back three one-hundred-dollar bills. He then fished around in his pocket and came up with a twenty and a five. He handed them over as well.

"There. Paid in full."

Alex folded the money and slipped it into a pocket. "If you don't mind my asking, what's going on with this money issue?"

Everyone chuckled self-consciously.

"Well, it's rather hard to explain, and there are much more important things to deal with, but briefly it has to do with traditions involving this land and the way it has been deeded. The simplest way to explain it is 'value for value.' Stipulations having to do with the title require conventions that can seem a little odd at a time like this, but they have a serious purpose and must be followed to the letter. Payment for services is one of those stipulations."

Alex was in a way only too happy to use the money that Sedrick Vendis had paid to buy his paintings just so that he could deface them. It seemed like ironic justice to use that money to pay for the legal fees to get the land that Vendis and Cain so badly wanted.

"But now that the fee is out of the way," Mike said, "we can get on with it."

At the man's urging, Alex sat before a stack of papers and folders. Jax stood behind him, her back to the wall. Mike sat beside Alex as all the others gathered round to watch. It had the feeling of a grand ceremony.

The lawyer opened the top folder. "All of these need to be signed where I've indicated with little red stickers."

Alex eyed the inch-thick stack. "Shouldn't I read all of these?"

"You're welcome to do so, and as a lawyer I must advise that you do, although I can assure you that I've been over everything, personally, and it's all in order. I'd be happy to explain any of it you find difficult to understand."

Alex picked up the pen. He scanned the first and second pages that were stapled together. They had to do entirely with identifying the parties involved in the rest of the paperwork. It took two pages to say that he was Alex Rahl and that the Daggett Trust was the Daggett Trust.

Alex started signing his name.

Mike Fenton lifted away each page after Alex had signed it. He scanned the next page, really only looking for anything that stood out as odd. Everything looked like what he imagined normal deed transfers would look like. With people wanting to run guns through a gateway to another world, the legal technicalities of the land where the gateway sat didn't seem overwhelmingly important, but Alex scanned them anyway just in case.

But then he started coming to pages having to do with the Daggett Trust. Those pages had nine signatures on them—the nine trustees. Each page awaited Alex's signature.

"What's this?" Alex said, frowning at the trustee agreements.

"In essence, it puts you in charge of the Daggett Trust, making you the lead trustee to the land involved in the Daggett Trust—all of it."

Alex looked up. "What do you mean, all of it?"

"Well," Mike said, "the part you inherit, and all the rest of the land associated with it—all the land controlled by the Daggett Trust. It all belongs together. This puts you in charge of all of the land as a single entity."

Alex stared at him. "All of it."

"Yes, that's right."

"And how much land is that?"

"Altogether? Nearly sixty-five thousand acres."

Alex was still staring at the man. "And what do you mean that it puts me in charge of the land?"

404

Mike Fenton folded his fingers together on the table. "Well, for all practical purposes, it all becomes yours once you take title to the key piece. You become the lead trustee. For all practical purposes, this makes you the Daggett Trust. You have to uphold all of the deed stipulations, of course, but it's all yours."

"Deed stipulations. You mean like how I can't build on the land?"

"Well, actually, as lead trustee you can build a place for yourself on the land, seeing as how the property is your responsibility and you will be overseeing it all."

"And I can't sell my portion except to the trust."

"Right."

"But you said that this, in essence, makes me the trust."

"That's right."

"So, if I wanted to sell—but believe me, I don't—where would the money come from?"

"Well, let me show you . . ." Mike said as he started shuffling through the file folders.

One of the women, the older, boxy-shaped one, leaned in to help. When Alex looked up at her she smiled.

"I'm Mildred—the accountant for the Daggett Trust. I'm the one who takes care of this aspect of the trust. I'll be at your disposal, of course, to help with everything."

"You will find Mildred indispensable," Mike said.

Alex didn't want to have to find an accountant indispensable. He simply wanted to keep Radell Cain from using the gateway to take technology to Jax's world.

Mildred quickly found the file and pulled it out, opening it before Alex.

"Here it is," he said. "This is the financial area of the trust. Over the entire time that the trust has existed, its funds have been invested in only the most stable, safe areas. None of the trustees throughout the history of the Daggett Trust has ever taken any risks with it, so it's grown quite slowly, but steadily."

"So how much is in there?"

She pointed to one of the lines of figures. "A little over sixty-three million dollars."

Alex blinked. "Sixty-three million?"

Mike nodded. "Yes, that sounds about right—not including the accrued-five-year-interest account. Most of it is in numbered overseas accounts. You aren't allowed to touch the principal, of course. That's one of the stipulations. But as the lead trustee you are entitled to use any and all the interest it earns. After expenses, of course."

Mike scratched his nose as he flipped through the papers. "Let's see . . . last year, for example, after trust expenses, that was about nine hundred thousand dollars—but interest rates last year were at a record low. It's usually higher. You are also entitled to any unused interest from the last five years—that's the accrued-interest account I mentioned—so altogether you actually could draw just a little over five million, if you wanted to."

Alex was still staring at the man. "You mean to say that I could take all that interest, nine hundred thousand dollars—and all the rest of five million if I wanted—and spend it all on lobster dinners?"

Everyone chuckled.

"Yes, if you want," Mike said. "Any money you don't take out simply stays in the accrued-interest account. Any you don't draw down from that portion within the five-year limit is rolled back into the trust account as it reaches that five-year maturity. It then becomes part of the principal. Once it flows back into the main trust account after five years, you then aren't allowed to touch it for personal use. Of course, it will earn additional interest, along with all the rest, which you can draw out."

"If there is all this money for trust expenses, then why on earth would you be so concerned with me paying the legal fees?"

"It's more than simply a part of the bylaws of the trust. It's part of the stipulations of the inheritance. It's all part of making sure that the person the lands goes to is the right kind of person, that they are responsible and take obligations seriously.

"You were not yet the owner of the land or the lead trustee. You had no legal right to the trust's money. You had to pay for the services I provided having to do with the inheritance without resentment of the debt and without trying to dodge the obligation. It's just one little way that the trust verifies integrity. Now that you've paid the fee, though, you not only own the land but you become lead trustee and have complete access to the interest from the trust accounts, so I'm sure you can see why it's vital to the safety of the trust that it have someone responsible at the helm. Mildred can help you keep track of it all."

"What expenses? What expenses does the trust have?"

Mike gestured around. "Well, besides our fees for the work we do on behalf of the trust, the largest expense is security."

One of the men stepped forward, extending his big, weathered hand. "Hal Halverson, Mr. Rahl. I'm head of security for the property."

While he wasn't especially big, he was the kind of man Alex would not want to have to wrestle. Hal Halverson was perhaps in his late forties, but looked like he only became stronger and tougher with every year he gained.

"How many security people are there?"

"We have twenty in all. Me, seventeen men, and two women officers. Because of the way the land was set up as a special conservation
area, we have legal status as game wardens and full law-enforcement
powers. By law, we're employed and paid by the trust alone. Our
land is technically situated within parts of several counties, but the
trust is an entity unto itself. The state and counties don't have juris-
diction over us, so they can't do things like reassign us to other law-
enforcement duties. As head of security I alone recruit and hire our
security force."

With a thumb, he lifted out the lapel of his brown sport jacket.
"I usually wear a uniform. The uniforms help to make people take
us seriously so that we can keep everyone off the land. We generally don't wear our uniforms off the trust property, and, well, your
orders meant that I had to pick up this to wear. And if I may say so, I
was especially pleased by your grasp of the importance of security."

"So you can carry weapons?"

The man lifted out his jacket to reveal a large-frame Glock. "Like
I said, we have legal law-enforcement status. Only we in the trust
can recruit our officers, but they still have to pass state law enforcement tests and extensive background checks."

"Which reminds me," Mike said as he opened another folder.
"Here is your identification in the name of Hank and Jenna Croft,
should you need it. Sign it here, if you would, please. Jax, you too."

She leaned in beside Alex and signed her full name on the incomplete driver's license. One of the other men had her stand against a
wall so he could take her picture. He snapped Alex's photo as well
and then took the licenses to the bar sink, where he began working
with some small equipment. Alex assumed he was placing the photos onto the licenses.

"Here is a State of Maine permit to carry concealed firearms,"

Mike said, sliding it across to Alex. He looked up. "This one is in your real name. We assumed that you would be armed and need a CCW for Maine. Just in case, we have one for Jax as well. We'll put the photo on them, too, after you both sign."

"You people are pretty thorough," Alex said as he and Jax signed the licenses. When he was finished, Mike handed them to the man working at the bar sink with the photos.

"We're very careful in how we look out for the trust," one of the others said.

Alex wondered why and where they had developed such care. At Mike Fenton's direction, Alex went back to signing papers. At a few places the man stopped and explained details of the trust.

It seemed to Alex that he was taking on a huge responsibility he didn't really want. Originally, he had just wanted to take title to the land in order to have a place to paint in peace.

Now, though, he needed to secure the gateway and prevent Radell Cain's people from using it. He supposed that this was all necessary in order to do that. And, should he need them, it did give him a lot more authority and resources to help him accomplish that task.

When he finished looking over and signing the stack of papers, Alex leaned back in his chair and let out a sigh.

"It's done," Mike said. "At long last. We can't tell you what a relief this is."

"All right, as lead trustee, I'd like to know what this is all about. What's going on? What's really behind the Daggett Trust and the land? What's the connection?"

49.

SOME OF THE PEOPLE LAUGHED NERVOUSLY while others cleared their throats. Alex stood and pushed the chair in so that he could stand beside Jax and see all the smiling faces. He didn't join in the smiling over the title transfer being concluded. A lot of people had already died because of the land, people close to him. He waited patiently for them to explain about the Daggett Trust.

Picking up on Alex's sobriety, Mike turned serious as he went on to explain. "Those of us here in this room, along with the security staff who are on property, are members of an ancient society. It's a small and very secret organization. We are the protectors of this land. Now, you are as well. Us by choice, by passion, by belief, and by dedication. You, Mr. Rahl, by birth as well as by choice."

Alex looked around at all the suddenly serious faces watching him. "You mean you're like high priests, or the last Knights Templar, or something?"

"In a way, yes," one of the other men said.

Alex was a little surprised that they didn't dismiss such a

suggestion out of hand. Since learning about Jax coming from an-other world and seeing some of the things he'd seen, he was pretty well past being shocked, though. But he was concerned that the inheritance of a piece of land had ended up pulling him into the middle of some kind of secret organization.

Alex glanced around at the faces watching him. "So just what kind of secret ancient society is this? What's it for?"

"It's a long story, with a very long history to it, and at some point we will fill you in on all the details," Hal Halverson said. "But for now I don't like all of us here in one place together. It's not how we usually do things. There is no telling if some of the people who are causing trouble might somehow know about us all being here. For all we know, any one of us could have inadvertently led that trouble here. To protect the trust, we rarely get this many members together all at once."

"Where are the others?" Alex asked.

"The security people are all members," Hal said, "and there are a few more members scattered around Europe. Other than the rest of the security people, though, this is most of us right here in this room."

"Hal is right," Mike said. "We'll give you the quick version and leave the details for later."

"This ought to be interesting," Jax said under her breath as she folded her arms.

"Ages ago—"

"How long ago is that?" Alex interrupted.

Mike waved off the question. "We're not sure, exactly. Well over a thousand years, we believe. Anyway, back then, ages ago, is when the Daggett Society was formed. It was, from its inception, a highly secret organization. There's not a lot in the way of written records, other than the accounting and deeds. Most of our history and such is passed down orally. The people who formed the Daggett Society were risking their lives. Revealing its existence to anyone likely would have meant death."

"What was so important about founding this secret society that they would risk their lives?" Alex asked.

"It was founded on the belief that at least some people in this world resettled here from another place."

Alex looked around at all the faces. "You mean some space aliens flew people here in flying saucers?" he asked, still not completely ready to let them know that he knew exactly what they were talking about.

Alex didn't like deceiving these people by playing dumb or by making it look like he was deriding them. He thought they were on his side. They seemed sincerely interested in protecting him, and they seemed devoted to protecting the land where the gateway was located.

But too much was at risk to worry about hurting their feelings. His life, Jax's life, and the lives of other people from both worlds were at stake. People had already lost their lives. People close to him had lost their lives. He wanted to know exactly what these people knew before he was willing to let them in on everything he knew.

"Not exactly," Mike said. "The book simply says—"

"What book?" Jax asked as she straightened, her arms coming unfolded.

One of the other men leaned in toward the two of them. He was the only African-American in the group. He appeared to be in his early fifties and in relatively good shape. He had a shaved head and wore small, thin-rimmed glasses. He had on khaki pants and a red plaid shirt, but he looked like he belonged in a herringbone suit.

He extended a hand. "I'm Ralph Overton, I'm the one in charge of the book."

Alex shook his hand. "Like Jax asked, what book?"

Ralph adjusted his glasses. "Back at the time the society was formed, a book was compiled containing a variety of information, some of it sketchy. It isn't an elaborate book like monks of the time would make. It's more homemade, more crude than that. It's the only written record we have.

"It appears to partly be a record of events, and partly an attempt to set down broader information related to those events. The book has always been an underlying element of the Daggett Society. According to the book, it seems that at least some of the people in this world came from another place."

When Alex and Jax didn't say anything this time, he went on.

"The society was formed to be the keepers of this secret knowledge, to preserve it so that it wouldn't be forever lost, wouldn't be entirely forgotten, as the people who put the book together believed would happen to everyone who had resettled here. Yet they had sound reason to believe that secrecy was necessary to protect the safety of the people in that other world, those brothers and sisters who are still there in that home place."

"And how is this secret society supposed to protect the safety of these other people?" Alex asked.

"Well, you see," Ralph went on, leaning in toward them both, "the book contains a prediction that a time will come when someone from this world will have to save that other world. That is the central founding reason for the book, and the reason the society was formed. The members of the Daggett Society were meant to be the keepers of this knowledge until that time came."

"The members of the society," Mike said, "are the keepers of this knowledge and prediction so that when the time comes they can help that person. Those of us in this room had for years all studied obscure historical clues spread across centuries and different cultures. That passion eventually led us to others like ourselves in the Daggett Society. We are the keepers of this knowledge, believers in the purpose of the book and the founders of the society. We believe that there is this other world somewhere out there."

Alex frowned around at the faces watching him. "So this is like a religion, a religious belief?"

"No," Ralph said, shaking his head emphatically. "Not a religious belief. We are not worshippers of this other world. You might say that it is akin to a spiritual belief in this other home world, but it's not a religion. For us, for all present and past members of this small society, it's a deeply held interest, a common passion, an absolute conviction, a vital purpose to our lives. It's based on this book, the clues culled from history, and the things that have been passed down from older members to new members over the centuries."

"Sounds like a religion to me," Alex said.

Ralph shook his head again, along with everyone else. "The society was formed to keep this knowledge until the day it would be needed. That is our purpose, not adoration or deification. We don't worship this other world, or its people. It's simply an acknowledgment of the fact that we have a common ancestry, that we are both, us here in this world and those in that place, individuals who are all part of the greater noble race of mankind. We are one, in that life itself is what matters."

Ralph lifted a finger for emphasis as he made his point. "We want to stand ready to make sure that when the time comes, the individuals in that other world do not lose that precious gift of life because we failed to act on knowledge only we have. We would hope that those in that other world would have the same reverence for our lives, and not let innocent people here die needlessly."

Alex glanced over at Jax. She also appeared taken by the man's words. It was how Alex felt about life and how precious it was. He remained silent, though, as Hal Halverson put in a word.

"Countless people have been born, grown up, become lifelong members of the society, and died without ever seeing any of the things we believe in come to pass."

"Over the centuries," Mike said, "the members made every effort to secure certain things having to do with the book. The most important thing, the thing the Daggett Society searched hundreds of years for, was what they believed would be the place of connection to this other world. In the late seventeen hundreds it was found by an explorer named Léon Deforce, who just happened to be a member of the society. He carried word of his discovery back to the society in Europe." He gestured to Ralph. "You know the most about that part. Why don't you tell them about it?"

Ralph nodded and took up the story. "The members of the Daggett Society, having found the connection they had long believed to exist, emigrated from Europe to the New World. They brought the book with them and settled in New England, mainly in Boston. At first many of them merely lived in the area to protect the wild place they had found, the place that matches the drawing in the book."

"Drawing?" Jax asked. "What drawing?"

"The early members didn't know where the place mentioned in the book was located, but there is a rough sketch in the book showing what it should look like. Léon Deforce, being a member of the society, had carefully studied the drawing in the book, so when he was on an expedition and saw the place, he knew immediately what it was. That's how he originally discovered its location—with the help of the drawing."

"Over time," Mike said, "they came to realize that with ever more people settling in New England, more was going to need to be done to protect such a singular place in this world. The society eventually bought up the area they were able to identify as central to everything, the place drawn in the book.

"They eventually also acquired additional surrounding acreage to encircle and better buffer the crown jewel at its center—the original, larger part that you inherited, Alex. They set up the trust to further protect it. The inheritance was established as a way of fulfilling the Law of Nines and telling when the predictions of the book were coming about.

"Over the years since, as members passed away and new members came along, they worked to ensure the continuation and protection of the society and the land we hold so precious. They invested their own money to create the trust for the benefit of the land."

"You see," Ralph said with a smile, "the Law of Nines is from this ancient book, tied to it, tied to the land, and tied to you. From the beginning, the members of the society have all studied it. Over the intervening centuries, the conditions it sets out never came to pass. The society remained vigilant, though, waiting for that time to come."

"We are the first members of the Daggett Society," Mike said with great care and emphasis as he gestured around the room at his fellow members, "to actually have the things in the book come about in our lifetimes. We can't tell you what this means to us, Mr. Rahl."

"That's quite the story," Alex said into the sudden silence. "How much of it do you all think is true?"

A few members of the Daggett Society shared troubled looks.

"Show them," Ralph finally said.

"Show us what?" Alex asked.

Hal Halverson went into the other room while Ralph went on with his explanation. "We didn't dare to bring the book. Considering all the things that have happened recently, we deemed it far too dangerous. The book is kept in a safe-deposit box in a bank vault in Boston, along with the thing we brought. Besides the danger of bringing the book here because of the people causing us all trouble, the book, as you can imagine, is extremely fragile. We rarely dare to handle it."

"I see," Alex said.

"We brought something else, in its place," Ralph said as he scratched an eyebrow. He readjusted his glasses as he waited. "We are hoping that this will mean something to you, since it's a little more directly connected with you."

Hal Halverson came out of the other room with a narrow box not quite a foot and a half long. It was made of wood that was so dark with the patina of age it was almost black. He set it carefully on the table.

Ralph stepped in close. "From the beginning, this has always been kept with the book. It actually predates the book, and is part of the reason the book was written, and the society created."

He gently opened the cover of the box.

Inside sat a silver knife that looked to be the twin to the one that Jax carried.

Ralph reverently, lightly, touched a finger to the silver handle lying in a bed of purple velvet. "From the book, this letter R is said to identify the House of Rahl. The book says that this was brought from that other world, and in that world it was once carried by elite protectors of the Lord Rahl."

"Dear spirits," Jax whispered as she stared at the weapon lying in the box.

As the roomful of people watched, she drew her own knife, spun it through her fingers, and then set it on the table beside the one just like it resting in velvet.

Everyone stared in shock at the identical weapons bearing the letter R.

One of the men in the back fainted.

50.

THE MEMBERS OF THE DAGGETT SOCIETY stood frozen in shocked silence, staring at the identical knives. Alex, facing all the people, saw the eyes of the man in the back roll up in his head. Alex sprang forward to try to grab the man as he toppled back, but he wasn't close enough.

When the man hit the floor they all suddenly came to their senses at the same time and turned to help. Sounds of concern filled the room as everyone offered advice at the same time.

"Tyler, just stay there," one of the men said, kneeling down as the supine man started coming around. He gestured into the confusion. "Get a pillow to elevate his feet." He started taking the supine man's pulse in a way that looked to Alex like he knew what he was doing. "You'll be fine, Tyler. Just lie there and let the blood get to your brain."

"No, please, I'm all right now," Tyler said, looking embarrassed as he lifted his head.

As someone pushed a pillow from the couch under Tyler's legs, the man over him put a hand on his chest to hold him down.

"I was just so shocked, that's all. I'm fine, Doc." Tyler started sitting up. "I'm all right," he insisted, if weakly. When he started to stand, some of the other men reached in to steady him.

"Maybe you'd better lie down," Alex said as he gripped the man's upper arm in case he keeled over again.

"Yes, he should," the doctor said.

"I'm all right now," Tyler said, his voice still sounding weak. "It's just that when Hal was opening that box to show you the knife that the society has held in safekeeping for over a thousand years, I was thinking of all the generations of members who have lived for this day without ever seeing any of the things they believed in and waited for, and here I stand, seeing a prediction in a book over a thousand years old come to life right before my very eyes. But then when I saw the other knife . . ."

Everyone started talking at once. Jax took the opportunity to retrieve her weapon and return it to its sheath as she came around the table to see about the man.

The doctor told Tyler to lie down on the couch and put his feet up. The man, embarrassed by the attention, didn't want to, even though he still looked wobbly on his feet. People spoke up, telling him that he should follow the doctor's orders.

Out of the corner of his eye, on the other side of the knot of people, Alex saw a hand reach out and snatch the knife from its velvet bed in the open box.

In a blur of movement, the middle-aged man with the knife elbowed a woman back out of his way as he dove for Jax.

Jax saw him at the last instant and jerked back, but not fast enough. The blade caught her with a glancing blow as she spun away from the surprise attack.

Hal was close. He crashed through the chairs toward the man

and deflected his arm as he again drove the blade in toward Jax. By then, Alex was also flying into the melee. The woman who had been knocked out of the way by the knife-wielding man screamed.

Other people yelled, "Fred, no!" at the attacker.

Ignoring the cries for him to stop, Fred slashed wildly. Jax drew a knife as she dodged the attacks. As he lunged for her again, Hal kicked the arm of the knife-wielding man away from her. The blow whirled him around so that his back was to Alex.

As he raced in, Alex twisted to add momentum and power as he used all his strength to smash his elbow in against the back of the man's neck. The impact was enough to crush his vertebrae. The man went limp and in a sinuous movement collapsed, sprawling onto his back as frightened people scrambled out of the way.

The doctor went to a knee beside him, putting fingers to the side of his neck. "He's still alive, someone call—"

Using a foot to boost herself, Jax leaped over a toppled chair, knife in hand. She landed beside the downed man and, with both fists around the handle of her knife, drove the blade down through the center of the prostrate man's face. It slammed in far enough to hit the back of the skull.

"Now he's not," Jax growled.

Alex saw blood down the front of her white blouse, but other things had suddenly taken priority. He grabbed Jax by the arm, lifting her. She held on to the knife as he hauled her up. The bloody blade abruptly came unstuck and drew back out as she pulled it with her.

Alex shoved her back toward the wall behind the table. As she was still stumbling back and hitting the wall, he rounded the table and drew his gun. He used the table as a physical barrier to maintain space as he brought the weapon up, pointing it at the people before him.

"Everyone on the ground!"

They froze in shock.

"On your knees! Now! Or I'll start shooting!"

People dropped to their knees in a panic.

"Hands behind your heads! Lock your fingers!"

"I'm a doctor," one of the men said. "Jax is hurt. Let me help her."

"On your knees or you're dead! Understand?"

The man nodded reluctantly.

"Jax?" Alex asked over his shoulder without taking his eyes off the people lined up on the floor. "How bad is it?"

"Not bad enough for you to put down your Glock."

Alex didn't find her words all that encouraging, since he knew that she believed he was more important to stopping Cain's plan than she was. At least she was talking.

Alex gestured with a tilt of his head. "Hal, take a look, will you please?"

Hal, to the side on one knee with his hands raised, rushed to do as Alex asked. Alex focused on the task at hand, on watching everyone in case there were accomplices to the man who had attacked Jax. He didn't know if there was another traitor among the society. For all he knew this whole thing was an elaborate trap. He didn't want to panic into pulling the trigger, but he had to be ready in case it became necessary.

As Alex kept the gun leveled on the cluster of people kneeling on the carpet in the middle of the room, he saw Hal rush over to the wet bar and grab a towel. He heard the towel being ripped.

"Hal—talk to me."

"Dead Fred there caught her arm with the knife. Fortunately it hasn't been sharpened in a thousand years or it might have done more serious damage. I'm not a doctor, but I'm sure she's going to need stitches."

Alex let out a sigh of relief.

"What's the plan, Alex?" Hal asked as he walked Jax over to the wet bar, pressing a towel against her forearm the whole way.

"The plan is not to have any more surprises."

"That was a pretty big one," Ralph said from his place on the floor. "I've known Fred Logan for years and I never thought him capable of anything like that. I don't understand what's going on."

"That makes two of us," Mike Fenton said.

Alex kept his finger alongside the barrel of the gun as he sighted through the iron sights, fearing to hold his finger against the trigger lest something make him flinch and cause him to accidentally press it. He knew from countless hours of practice that from where they were on the floor no one could beat him to his gun before he could twitch his finger down to the trigger.

Hal cursed under his breath. Out of the corner of his eye Alex saw him leading a somewhat wobbly Jax around behind.

"That damn bar sink isn't big enough to wash a grape," Hal said. "I need to take her into the bathroom and use the sink in there, or the tub."

"How bad is it?" the doctor asked.

"It didn't seem to cut any veins. She's lucky."

"Right, lucky," Jax growled.

Underlying the sarcasm, Alex could read the anger in her voice. He was relieved that she was angry. That meant it wasn't as bad as he'd feared at first.

"I have a kit in my car," the doctor said.

"You just do as Alex asked, Doc, and stay right there for the moment," Hal said.

"Well, wash around it good but don't get soap in the laceration, then wrap it tight enough to put compression on the wound to stop the bleeding."

"Will do," Hal said, his voice echoing from the bathroom as he flicked on the light.

"Mr. Rahl?" Mildred said, unable to take her eyes off the bloody corpse sprawled on the floor in front of her. "I think I'm going to be sick."

"Mildred, look at me." The frightened woman looked up at him. "You're going to be fine. Don't look at him, look at me. You're not going to be sick. You're a member of the Daggett Society. You're going to be strong."

That seemed to buck her up a little. She took a deep breath and kept her eyes on Alex. He hoped she wasn't in on it.

"I don't understand," Mike Fenton said. "We've all known Fred Logan for years."

"Don't feel bad," Alex said. "I've been fooled by these people as well. They're good at what they do. You knew Fred here for years. I've only known most of you for hours. There is a lot at stake. I hope you understand why I can't take any chances."

Most of the people nodded.

Alex was glad to see Jax coming out of the bedroom. Her left forearm had a makeshift bandage made of strips of motel towels.

She drew her knife as she knelt down beside Alex. "I'm fine," she whispered. "I'm just angry with myself that he caught me off guard like that. I feel stupid letting him cut me."

"Now you know how I felt," Alex said.

A number of the people watching from only a few feet away gasped when Jax leaned over and started cutting symbols into the dead man's forehead. The beige carpet was soaked with blood all around his head. Yet more trickled down as Jax cut.

Finished, Jax sat back on her heels. Alex concentrated on trying to stop his hands from shaking as he sighted down the gun at people he hoped he wouldn't have to shoot.

"Jesus H. Christ," Hal said under his breath. "He's vanished."

Alex glanced down and saw that the dead man was indeed gone. The carpet was clean. Jax's knife was clean.

"He was from my world," Jax said to the people watching in wide-eyed shock. "I sent him back."

Everyone began asking questions at once.

"Quiet!" Alex shouted. The room fell silent.

"What now?" Jax whispered to him.

"Now," he said so that everyone could hear, "we're going to test all of these people to see if any of them vanish and go back like Fred did."

People gasped in fear. Alex gestured with one hand to quiet them down.

"Don't worry, we're not going to use a knife."

Struck with a sudden worry of his own, he glanced over at Jax and whispered, "You don't need to cut the skin, do you?"

"No. I only use a knife because I want to send their people a message, a message delivered in blood. I can use anything that will make marks."

"Hal," Alex said, gesturing with his gun, "frisk them. I want to know if any of them are armed."

Hal apologized as he went from one person to the next, doing a thorough job of looking for hidden weapons. When finished, he stood.

"No hand grenades, no rocket launchers."

"Good. Can you get Jax a pen off the table there, please?"

Hal stayed out of the line of fire and walked around behind to hand Jax the pen.

Jax crooked a finger at Mike Fenton, then pointed at the carpet a few feet in front of her. "Stay on your knees and come forward."

Mike moved forward, keeping his fingers locked behind his head. He looked up at Hal, as if pleading his case.

"Just do as they ask, Mike. After what happened with Fred, Alex is making sense. We have to check everyone out."

"Why not you?" Mike asked.

Hal heaved a sigh and knelt down in front of Jax. He tapped a finger against his forehead. "Test me first."

Jax nodded and started drawing the symbols with the stubby motel pen. When she finished she sat back on her heels and rested her drawing hand in her lap. Hal turned and showed off the symbols on his forehead.

"See?" she said to the group. "I'm drawing a trigger that will activate a lifeline to take anyone from my world back there. If Hal had been from my world, he would have gone back just like that dead man, Fred, did."

Everyone nodded that it made sense. They all looked considerably less worried. They came up one at a time and let Jax draw on their foreheads with the pen. It looked bizarre to see a roomful of people on their knees, all getting strange symbols drawn on their foreheads.

Mildred went last. She didn't vanish. She looked relieved, though, as if she had feared she somehow might.

"I wish I could somehow preserve it," she said to the group as she looked at all their foreheads. "We're the first members of the society to see something from that other world since the book was first written."

"Now what?" Hal asked, concerned with more important things than preserving a design.

"Now we let the doctor see to Jax's arm," Alex said.

"About time," the man grumbled as he stood and came forward.

On his way by, Hal grabbed the man's shirt at his shoulder. "Don't you be that way to Alex. Fred's the one who tried to kill Jax. Alex didn't have to come. He didn't have to take the land and he doesn't have to be a part of any of this. Don't begrudge him being afraid for his life, and the life of this young lady, here. It was one of the people we asked him to trust who attacked her."

The doctor sighed. "You're right, Hal. Sorry, Alex, Jax. I guess I just feel guilty because we let one of them into our midst. We could have ruined everything, and it would have been our fault."

Other people nodded.

"Like I said, they fooled me, too," Alex said. "But just because you all passed the first test, that doesn't mean that I'm satisfied yet. Jax and I were almost killed by a doctor from this world who was working with them."

Hal looked surprised. "Seriously?"

"Serious as a heart attack," Alex said.

"This is going to need stitches," the doctor said as he unwrapped Jax's arm.

"Can't you use magic glue?" Jax asked.

When the doctor frowned up at her, Alex said, "She means superglue."

"Oh. Well, I could."

"I have some in my truck. Hal, you want to get it?"

"Wait." The doctor tossed Hal his keys. "Get my bag out of the back seat of my car instead, will you? I've got superglue but it's medical grade. It's more flexible and works better."

Hal hurried out. He shortly returned with a black bag.

The doctor gestured to the table. "Over there. Let's get her over there so she can lay her arm on the table."

The two of them guided Jax over to the table. The doctor warned her that the glue would feel hot and sting. If it did, she didn't voice a reaction. Alex didn't hear a peep out of her as he kept his eye on the group on their knees before him. A few of them were getting tired and sat back on their heels.

It seemed to take forever, but when the doctor was finished Jax reappeared at Alex's side sporting a tightly wrapped arm below the rolled-up sleeve of her white blouse.

"I have blood all over me," she said. "I need to get some other clothes or I will draw attention."

With a quick glance, he saw that she looked like she'd participated in an ax murder. "You're right. Hal, would you go out to my truck with her? Watch her back?"

Hal caught the keys when Alex tossed them. "Sure."

After they had returned, Jax hurried into the other room to change. It wasn't long until she came out of the bedroom wearing the red top and different jeans.

"What now?" Hal asked.

"Now," Alex said, "we're leaving."

"What about all of us?" Mike asked. "We have so much more we need to talk about."

"We'll have to talk later. I'm going to let Hal do the second half of the testing first, to see if any of you were in cahoots with your dead Daggett Society member from another world."

Alex kept the gun pointed in the general direction of the group as he took Jax by the arm and backed toward the door.

51.

ANY IDEAS WHAT WE SHOULD DO?" Jax asked on the way across the dark lot toward the Cherokee.

Safely out of the room, Alex scanned the area and at last holstered his gun. "I don't see that we have a lot of options. We can go after them or we can run."

"If we run they will hunt us down."

"Then I guess that answers your question."

He looked back over his shoulder to see Hal come out of the motel room and turn to tell everyone to wait there and that he would be back shortly and they would discuss it all then. Hal shut the door and started across the lot after them.

He was carrying something under an arm.

"We came here to get to the land and see what we could figure out," Alex told Jax in a low voice. "I think it's about time we do so."

"That makes sense," she said as she watched the shadows at the edge of the lot. "But I don't think we're going to be able to get to it in the middle of the night."

"And it's still a long drive to get there. We'll probably have to get a room somewhere along the way, grab a little sleep, and then first thing in the morning collect some supplies and head up toward Castle Mountain."

Hal Halverson caught up with them as Alex was unlocking the Jeep. Hal set something dark on the hood of the truck. Even though it was hard to see in the dark, Alex thought that he knew what it was.

"So I've got to ask, why did you trust me in there and no one else?"

"Two reasons," Alex said. "First, you were the one who kept Fred from doing worse to Jax."

Hal shrugged. "Makes sense, but I could still have been party to it."

"True, but you were the only one in that room who has had a background check. You and your security force have all had extensive law-enforcement background checks. I'm sure they must be quite thorough."

Hal smiled. "That's pretty good."

"That's the second part of the test—run those background checks on everyone in there."

"You think there was someone working with Fred? Someone from this world in on it?"

"I'd bet on it. From what I've seen, these people from the other side try to find people here to help them. I'm not sure what they offer but they can probably come up with any wish or want."

"Anyone in particular you suspect?"

"Tyler."

Hal nodded unhappily. "That's what I was thinking. He provided the diversion for Fred to make the attack."

"That was my thought, too," Jax said.

"It may not be him," Alex said. "In fact, it may not be any of them.

But you need to do the most extensive background check you can and see if anything troubling turns up. If it does, it could indicate that the person would be susceptible to being turned against us."

Hal nodded. "I was FBI before I came on board with the trust. If any of them didn't wash behind their ears in the third grade I'll find out about it."

"Keep in mind that the people we're dealing with are killers," Jax said. "Be as quick about it as you can. If one or more of them are working against us, then the rest of those people in there are in great danger. Any traitor among them would be able to point assassins right toward them."

Hal let out a deep breath. "They're good people. At least the clean ones are. They've given up a great deal for their belief in the purpose of the society. They've devoted their lives to protecting the people in your world. They're in there now, cleaning up Jax's blood to avoid any kind of trouble."

Jax nodded. "All the more reason to take measures to protect them. None of us wants good people to get hurt."

"Do you want me to help you two find a place to stay tonight? It was a long drive from Nebraska. In the morning we could get back together and you could ask them about any other information on the land that might be helpful."

"We've done what we needed to do," Alex said. "The deed to the land is transferred. It's now legally mine and I'm signed off on the trust as well. The requirements are fulfilled."

In the faint illumination of a light that lit up the lot closer to the building, Alex could see the man smile a little. "That's what I would do. Safer to be on your own, without being around people who know you."

Alex frowned as an idea came to him. "This book that the society keeps, it doesn't have any information about something called a gateway, does it?"

"Gateway?" Hal shook his head. "No. Never heard of it. There is one place, though, that says that the one identified by the Law of Nines will know the secret. Maybe they were talking about the gateway.

"But listen," Hal went on, "there is one other thing from the book that we weren't able to get to because of the attack."

"What would that be?" Alex asked.

Hal slid the object sitting on the hood of the truck toward Alex. "The knife we showed you. We didn't get the chance to tell you that the book says this must go to you, that you will need it."

"Are you sure?" Jax asked.

Hal nodded. "In a way, the whole purpose of the book, the whole part with the Law of Nines, and all the rest, is just a long involved way of finding the person this knife needs to go to."

"And what am I supposed to do with it? What purpose does it have?"

Hal shrugged. "Sorry, but the book is mute on that topic. It insists that you must have this, but doesn't say why. In a way, the whole purpose of the Daggett Society is to make sure you get this knife."

Alex lifted the lid to look at the silver knife lying in the box. Faint light on the side of the building reflected off the ornate scrollwork that made up the letter R.

Alex sighed. "Then they've carried out their part in all of this— for the time being, at least. It's up to me now.

"Besides, I don't want to stick around long enough to give other people a reason to snatch those people and torture them for information about us. They don't have the mind-set to deal with the likes of those who are after us."

"They're good people, but you're right, they don't think like we do. Most people aren't good at being properly paranoid. I'm thankful that you seem to have the knack."

Alex smiled. "You'd be paranoid, too, if people were after you."

"Guess so," Hal said with a laugh. He pulled some papers out of his inside jacket pocket and laid them on the hood of the Jeep. He brought up a small flashlight.

"Here are some maps I thought you could use." He shined the light on a state map as he opened it. "I've outlined the property, since it isn't identified on any map. This highway here is the best way to get up that way. Then take this road here, through Westfield."

Hal tapped a thick finger next to the town. "Most people go through Westfield on their way to Baxter State Park. It's a tourist town that has become a destination in and of itself. A lot of art, crafts, antiques, that sort of thing.

"Instead of heading on toward Baxter State Park, though, you take this small road that cuts off here, right after Westfield. Then follow it up this way," he said, tracing the road with his finger. "It will eventually take you all the way to the property, right here.

"It's about a two-, two-and-a-half-hour drive from Westfield to the property. It only gets more remote the farther you go. If you want any food, supplies, or gas, you'd best get it in Westfield, because there isn't anything between there and the property except woods."

"Are there any roads on the property?" Alex asked.

"Yes, if you have four-wheel drive. Your Jeep is ideal."

"Good."

Hal pulled out a paper from under the map. "I drew this out for you. It shows the state road, here, that's on the regular maps, and then here I drew in the private road that isn't. This takes you onto the property. Here's the combination for the locks. We keep the gate locked at all times to keep people out.

"These roads, here, on the property, are only accessible by four-wheel drive. You can only drive into the land for a short distance, and then you have to hike the rest of the way to Castle Mountain. That's here," he said as he tapped the homemade map. "I marked it for you."

"Thanks," Alex said. "This will be a big help."

The man extended his hand. Alex and Jax shook it in turn.

"I'll call my people and tell them they can expect to see you out there sometime probably late tomorrow morning," Hal said. "I'll give them a description of your truck and the license number so that they won't get spooked when they see it."

"Good idea," Alex said.

"I'll tell them to watch your back, and make sure you aren't followed once on the property."

"Thanks, but I'm afraid that won't do a whole lot of good. These people can show up out of thin air."

Hal sighed heavily. "I suspected as much." He handed Alex another piece of paper. "Here's my number. It's a new phone, never been used. Call if you need anything. If need be I'll come with guns blazing."

Alex smiled. "Will do." As he gathered up the maps he saw a small envelope. "What's this?"

Hal frowned as he took it from Alex's hand. "I don't know. I had the maps sitting on the table earlier, before you two arrived. I must have picked it up with the maps without seeing it."

He turned it over. Both sides were blank. He ran a finger under the flap, tearing it open. He unfolded the piece of paper that was inside and stared at it a moment, reading.

"All it says is, 'Hamburg, Germany, seven-fifteen a.m. local time. London, England, six-thirty a.m. local time.'"

Alex took the paper and looked it over. The words were hand-written with precise care. He handed it back.

"Any idea what it is?"

"Not a clue."

"Well, we have a long drive tonight. We need to be on our way."

As Alex and Jax climbed in the truck, Hal came to the driver's door. "You be careful, Alex." He ducked down so that he could look over at Jax in the passenger seat. "You too, and please take care of him for us?"

"That's why I'm here," she said with a smile.

"We all have been waiting a very long time for you to finally come to the property, Alex. We'd all hate it if you got yourself killed on our watch."

Alex didn't want to tell the man what he thought of his chances of success. "You be careful, too, Hal."

Alex turned the key as Hal nodded.

Nothing happened. Alex sighed.

"Hal, could you give me a little push, please, to get us rolling. The starter has a dead spot in it."

Hal put a hand against the windshield pillar. "If this happens once you get out on the property you're going to be in trouble. You can't roll the truck to get it started on those rutted dirt and rock roads. Listen—I assume you planned on grabbing some sleep in Westfield tonight?"

"That's the plan," Alex said. "Unless you have a better place."

"No," Hal said, shaking his head. "Not a lot of choices going that way, unless you'd like to sleep in the truck, but I don't advise that, not out all alone where unfriendly eyes could look in and spot you sleeping. Kind of dangerous. Better to stay in a room."

"I thought the same thing."

"A lot of people up that way drive four-wheelers. Westfield has a small Jeep dealership. You ought to stop in first thing in the morning and let them fix the starter while you get any supplies you need."

"Thanks for the tip. You wouldn't believe how long I've been putting off getting the starter fixed."

"Take care," Hal said as he leaned his weight in and pushed. "As soon as I run the background checks I'll head out to the property to be close if you need me," he said as he trotted along beside the truck, pushing.

As they picked up enough speed, Alex let the clutch out. The engine turned over and started without a fuss. Alex waved good-bye to Hal, then rolled up the window as he made his way out of the lot back toward Hammond Street.

"You can take a nap if you'd like," he said to Jax.

"I'd rather keep a lookout. Cain's people are waiting for us somewhere out in that darkness."

52.

"AY I SEE YOUR DRIVER'S LICENSE, PLEASE?" the young woman behind the counter asked as she entered information into a computer.

Alex glanced out the side window, keeping an eye on Jax to make sure she was all right. The blue "Vacancy" sign lit up the side of her face as she sat in the idling Jeep just outside watching him. Tired as he was, he reminded himself that he had to remain vigilant.

Alex tossed the license that said "Hank Croft" across the counter to the woman. Displayed under the glass that covered the counter were brochures for sightseeing tours, kayak rentals, a logging museum, and nearby places to visit. Menus from several local restaurants were also on display.

Alex didn't know if the phony name would do any good in throwing their pursuers off track. To get to the land he had to drive in from Westfield or come the long way around from the other side of town, or come in from way north. Those were the only three possible routes to get to the road onto the land, or to even get close to the remote property. He was sure that there had to be people watching for him and Jax on all three of those routes. Those people would have a description.

Unless he dropped in from the sky, Alex had no real hope of sneaking onto the land unseen. Cain's people had the advantage of knowing right where he and Jax were headed, while they, on the other hand, had no way of knowing who was from another world and might be watching them, ready to pounce at any moment.

For all Alex knew, the Westfield Inn could be run by people from another world just like the ninth floor of Mother of Roses had been. He and Jax could be ambushed in their sleep. He wondered if he was starting to be too paranoid. Given everything he knew, he wondered if that was even possible.

The young woman handed his license back. "Thank you, Mr. Croft. Here's your key and your receipt." She leaned forward to look out the screen door as she pointed to the right in an exaggerated manner. "Down the drive to the end of the building, follow it around to the second entrance. The room is inside to the left."

"Thanks." Alex picked up the key and papers. "Can you tell me where the Jeep dealership is?"

"Sure." She pointed in the opposite direction. "Just keep going down the highway into town. It's only a tenth of a mile or so. You can almost see it from here. It will be on your right. You can't miss it." She snorted a little laugh to herself. "It's not like Westfield is very big."

Alex drove through the fairly crowded lot and found their room without any difficulty. He took the box with the knife in with him. He was afraid to let it out of his sight.

Entering the room, he flicked on a small light over the door. He saw by the glowing red numbers on the clock on the nightstand that it was well past midnight. He was dead tired and falling asleep on his feet. He kept his hand on his holstered gun as he checked the small closet and the bathroom.

"How's the arm feel?" he asked, after clearing the room and quickly covering the mirrors.

Jax looked equally sleepy. "It's fine."

"Liar," he said as he closed the drapes over the small window that looked out into darkness. He imagined eyes out in that darkness watching, waiting.

Jax looked around at the small room, then tossed the duffel bag on one of the beds. The room smelled like pine-scented cleaner. The color scheme of the cheap decoration was blue and brown. As sleepy as Alex was, the bed looked wonderfully inviting.

He felt discouraged to be this close to their destination without having yet come up with any solid idea of what they needed to do. It was daunting to be at the center of so many things all leading to him, all depending on him. He felt like a fraud, a nobody appointed by fate to do the impossible.

He turned to Jax when she put a hand on his shoulder, as if she were reading his mind and offering silent comfort.

He brushed a lock of blond hair back off her face. "Any ideas come to you yet about how to stop Cain?"

"Sure, one."

He squinted suspiciously. "What would that be?"

"Only you can make the gateway work for him. I could kill you and then theoretically the gateway would be useless to him."

Alex couldn't help but smile. "Then why don't you?"

She slipped her arms around him and hugged him close, laying her head against his chest. "Because then the world would be a lonely, empty place."

439

If she ever left it, it certainly would be.

Alex was so tired he could hardly stand. After a long day of traveling, the heart-pounding terror of the events with the people back in Bangor and his fear that she had been hurt or worse had drained him. The long drive through the night after that had completely sapped any remaining energy he might have had.

It seemed that even his spirit had abandoned him, leaving him feeling nothing but despair at what lay ahead. In the back of his mind, he couldn't help but think that the only thing that really lay ahead for them both was death.

He sat down on one of the double beds. Jax sat with him, one arm still around his waist. When he lay back on the bed, she went with him. Together they both moved up to put their heads on the pillow.

In such a remote, lonely place, on such a desperate, lonely mission, their only comfort was with each other. In the shelter of each other's arms they both silently shared an understanding of the enormity of the task before them and felt at least momentary refuge from its unknown terrors.

They came together in a soft, gentle kiss. Jax was so warm and alive in his arms that it made life itself seem to have a point and a purpose. Her kiss felt as perfect, as compassionate, as any kiss he could imagine.

Somewhere over the course of events since Jax had first come into his life back in Nebraska, she had come to be at the center of his heart. It seemed a mystery exactly when that had happened. In a way, it seemed like he had always known her, always known that he never wanted to be with anyone else but her. There could be no one else.

By the way she kissed him back, he knew she felt the same.

Right then, right there, that feeling seemed complete. There could have been no better comfort in the face of all the difficulty they faced. No matter what happened, they were together. Somehow, that seemed more important, more wonderful, to him than anything else.

In a loose embrace, still fully dressed, they fell asleep.

Alex woke with a start. Jax, still in his arms, woke up when he did. In the muted, mellow light, it took a moment to remember where he was. Weak daylight leaked in around the curtain. The small light over the door around the corner of the bathroom was still on. He looked over at glowing red numbers on the clock on the nightstand. It was a little past seven.

Alex yawned. He wanted to go back to sleep. He wanted to keep holding Jax.

But he couldn't. He needed to get the Cherokee over to the dealer and see if he could talk them into doing a rush job of replacing the starter. He figured that if he gave them a big tip up front it might help persuade them to hurry.

"Do I have time for a bath?" Jax asked.

"Sure, go ahead. I'll run the truck down the street and leave it to get the starter fixed. That should give you plenty of time. We're going to need to go out and pick up some supplies and hopefully by then the starter in the truck should be fixed."

She rolled over on top of him. "Do we have time for another kiss?"

He pulled her into his arms in answer. Her hair slipped forward over her shoulders to fall around his face, as if even her hair wanted to be close to him. After a long, luxurious kiss she pushed back.

With a finger she brushed his hair back off his forehead. "I've never cared this much for anyone."

"I know. Me neither."

"Not even Bethany?" she said with a mischievous grin.

"Especially not Bethany," he said without smiling before he pulled her back for another kiss.

When it ended she pushed back again. "What are we going to do about us?"

"What do you mean?"

She shrugged as her eyes turned away. "Well, I'm not from here. If I can find a way, I have to go back."

She had just touched the agony that tortured him. Alex knew that he couldn't ask her to turn her back on the people who were depending on her. He didn't know what or who she was in her world, but he knew that she was someone important there, and that people needed her.

"What if there was a way for me to go with you?"

She sighed. "If only . . . but you can never come to my world. There is no way that can ever happen. Without the spark of the gift that those of us there all carry, you can't make it into my world. You would only die in the attempt. If you can work the gateway, you can't use it. I can. With the gateway I would have a way to return home. I must . . ."

Alex swallowed at the painful thought of her leaving his world, leaving him. "Maybe I won't be able to figure out the gateway."

"No hope of that," she said with a sigh. "You're Alexander Rahl."

"Well, who knows. We may never have to worry about it."

Her brow bunched together. "What do you mean?"

"If Cain has his way we'll both die before then."

Her smile returned. "You have a way of making me smile even when my heart is breaking."

"Then you should at least give me another kiss."

She did. It was a kiss that made the kisses before seem less than meaningful. It took Alex away, made him forget everything but her. It made him feel complete, as if he had never really been alive before that moment. In that moment he felt, for the first time in his life, sheer, perfect bliss.

Finally, she pulled breathlessly away. Alex didn't think he would ever get enough of looking at her. She was the most perfectly feminine creature he had ever known. She was so beautiful it made him ache for her.

"So," she whispered as she looked down into his eyes, "do we have time for more than a kiss?"

53.

LEX HAD BEEN correct—a hundred-dollar tip to the service writer got him an eager promise of prompt attention. Fearing to give the man the phony license because the registration for the Jeep was under his real name, he handed over his real driver's license instead.

"All right, Mr. Rahl," the man behind the small podium in the drive-in entrance said, "we'll have you fixed and back to your vacation in no time. Is there a number where I can reach you?"

"Sorry, I forgot to recharge my cell phone last night. I'll just check back with you after a while."

"Give us a few hours and we should have it taken care of." He pointed with his pen. "You can wait in the lounge, if you like, and I'll come get you when it's finished."

"I have some errands to take care of. I'll check back."

"We'll be here. You can get out the same way—through the lounge."

Alex thanked the man and made his way past the line of

other trucks waiting to be taken in for service. Out the open overhead door the leaden sky seemed like it was descending to smother
the town.

As Alex went through the lounge the word "Hamburg" coming
from the TV stopped him cold in his tracks.

The morning news anchor on the TV was giving a report about a
massive fire at a hotel in Hamburg, Germany. The alarm system in
the hotel had reportedly malfunctioned and the firefighters had problems getting adequate water to the site. Dozens of deaths were feared.

"Fifteen minutes later, in London," the announcer said, "another
tragedy struck when a runaway truck crashed into a crowd of people
outside a busy train station. Sources say that as many as eleven people
were killed with a number of others seriously injured. The driver fled
the scene. Police are searching for him and hope to have him in custody
soon. Authorities say it is the worst such accident in recent memory."

Alex stood frozen, his mind racing, as he watched the international news for a few minutes more, waiting to see if they would
say anything else, but they went on with stories about a global sum-
mit on world economic growth that leaders from the industrialized
nations were scheduled to attend in Japan in the coming days.

Alex remembered the note that Hal had found with the maps
in the room back in Bangor. It had listed two cities: Hamburg and
London. The times written on that note had been for that morning,
and they had been fifteen minutes apart. He knew without doubt
that it was not a coincidence.

He hurried up the street, suddenly feeling the urgent need to get
back to Jax. He rushed into the room and found her pacing. She had
an envelope in her hand.

"The phone rang. I answered it. The person said that there was a
letter at the front desk for Hank Croft. So I went to the office. They

wanted identification. I showed them the thing that Mike Fenton made for me that shows my image and says I'm Jenna Croft. They gave me this."

Jax handed him the envelope. On the outside was written "Mr. Hank Croft."

Alex tore it open. Inside was a single folded piece of paper. He recognized the precise handwriting. It was the same as the handwriting on the paper Hal Halverson had found.

Jax bit down nervously on her lower lip as she watched him reading. "Well, what is it?"

"It's a list of cities—Springfield, Scranton, Raleigh, Tampa, Mobile, Indianapolis, Fort Worth, Grand Rapids, Denver, Bismarck, Winnipeg, Provo, Sydney, Boise, Eugene, Mexico City, Bakersfield. It says 'Now' at the bottom."

Alex's hands shook as he lowered the paper.

"Do you know what it means?" Jax asked.

"I think I do, but I hope to hell I'm wrong."

He switched on the TV. The images of confusion and screaming people hit him like a blow.

"Breaking News" ran in a big band across the left corner at the top of the screen. The second line underneath said "Terror Attacks Rock the Nation." The news crawl rolled slowly across the bottom of the screen, listing cities where attacks were reported—all cities that were on the list in Alex's hand.

"As these reports are just now coming in, the president has promised a statement sometime within the hour," the anchorwoman said. "We're also just getting word that mayors and governors across the nation . . ." The woman glanced to the side to someone or something off camera. She looked rattled.

"We're getting news from Florida." She cleared her throat.

"Sources are reporting that Hamilton High School in Tampa, Florida, is the scene of a large fire. We have a live report from our local affiliate there in Tampa."

They switched to a man in a gray suit holding a microphone. In the background a column of smoke rose into a blue sky.

"The county school administrator here in Tampa, Loretta Dean, has just issued a brief statement saying that the fire is confined to the Hamilton High School auditorium. Other, unnamed sources tell us that students were assembled there as they arrived at school to be counseled in dealing with the frightening news of the knife attacks at schools in Raleigh and Indianapolis. It was during that assembly that fire broke out.

"The size of the fire—as you can see in the background—is extensive. Several students we've spoken with who managed to escape the blaze tell us that when they tried to get out of the auditorium, they found the exit doors were locked. They say that the people inside panicked and students were trampled in an attempt to escape. Unnamed sources are telling us that the doors were all heavily chained and that over three hundred students and teachers were trapped inside until firefighters were able to use the jaws of life to cut the chains. School officials insist that they have never used chains on school doors. Firefighters were not able to determine how many students may have been overcome by smoke and died before they were able to gain entrance."

The reporter went to news footage that showed mass panic, with parents screaming and crying as they arrived on scene.

Alex switched the station. A man was reading from papers in his hands. "These knife attacks in Mobile and Springfield were all on schools or preschools, while the ones in Scranton and Eugene were at local hospitals. The Winnipeg and Boise attacks took place at early-morning church services. Authorities confirm that the patients and workers who died at the retirement home in Springfield were also victims of knife attacks, but they declined to give the number of dead.

"Unconfirmed reports say that, as in the other attacks, the throats of all the victims had been cut, linking all the attacks in the methods used.

"At the school in Grand Rapids, police cornered the two knife-wielding assailants in an upstairs library after they had reportedly managed to gain entrance to a classroom and murder an undetermined number of middle-schoolers before the police arrived on scene. The SWAT team conducted an assault on the library, where the suspects had barricaded the doors. Unnamed police sources say that when the SWAT team entered, the assailants had vanished. An extensive house-to-house search is under way."

"They will never find them," Jax whispered to herself as she stared at the TV. Tears ran down her face, dripping off her jaw.

"We're also getting sketchy reports of an attack in Mexico City. Terrorism experts we've been able to talk with are shocked by this latest development in what over just the last few minutes has developed into an international crisis, with Mexico only the latest country reporting similar attacks along with Canada, England, and Germany. Unconfirmed reports of attacks are also coming in from Australia."

The camera switched to another reporter at a fiery scene. "There is mass confusion in Denver right now at a plant that produces components for wind turbine generators. Plant officials say that there were over a hundred third-shift workers trapped in the main assembly building when fire broke out.

"The surprise attacks and killings of workers leaving their jobs a short time ago at Easton Fabrication on the outskirts of Denver has only added to the strain on emergency services, as have the fires at two of Denver's hospitals. Those fires are now said to be contained. While many people are calling this a deliberate act of terror, officials are cautioning people not to jump to conclusions.

"Yet across the world this morning, the death toll from all of these incidents is expected to reach well into the hundreds. In every instance, it seems, the attacks have been carried out in the most gruesome fashion possible, with victims either being trapped in burning buildings or, in other cases, with victims reportedly having their throats cut.

"So far, no group has claimed responsibility.

"Moments ago, the president issued a brief statement calling for calm amidst a growing cry for retaliation. He also said that his heart goes out to the families of victims.

"As of yet no terrorist group has taken responsibility or been linked to the attacks. Officials have insisted that none of the attacks bear resemblance to the pattern of any known terror group, except in their deadly nature and brutality, and of course in the way in which they have targeted innocent people.

"Military officials we spoke with, who wish to remain anonymous, say that the attacks are at a level of coordination and focus never seen before. In response to comments made by a number of people, Homeland Security undersecretary Robert Franklin said that it was too early to say that the nature of the attacks appears to be intended as a message of some sort. He went on to promise that those responsible would be caught and brought to justice."

Alex switched off the TV.

With trembling fingers he folded the paper listing all the cities and put it in his pocket.

"Let's go."

54.

A S THEY LEFT THE MOTEL and walked quickly down the sidewalk toward the center of the small town of Westfield, Jax put her hand on his back in silent compassion. Neither of them spoke. Both of them were in a state of shock at the unexpected turn of events.

Radell Cain had just turned everything upside down. Before, Alex hadn't known what to do, but the task had at least seemed straightforward. Now he felt a numb sense of paralyzing shock and dismay. It no longer simply seemed a matter of preventing Radell Cain from getting access to the gateway. In light of such chaos everything had just gotten far more complex.

The heavy overcast seemed to match their mood. It made the day feel quiet and somber.

"I'm ashamed that people from my world have come here and done this," Jax said as they walked past a bakery.

Alex shifted the duffel bag to the other side so that he could take her hand as they hurried along the sidewalk.

"Don't take on guilt for murders just because they came from where you live. You came here to stop these people. You're risking your life to stop them. You have no reason to feel ashamed."

She squeezed his hand in appreciation of his words. He could see another tear or two run down her face.

"I'm the one who should have done something," he finally said into the silence. "From the beginning you've been trying to tell me how brutal these people are. You tried to do something; I didn't listen. If I had believed you in the first place, acted sooner, maybe this wouldn't be happening."

"Don't you now blame yourself, Alex. Radell Cain is responsible."

"But maybe I could have—"

"No, you couldn't. Don't let him make you fall into the trap of second-guessing yourself. He's been watching you and making his moves based on what you do, not when you did it. Had you acted sooner it would only have prompted him to make his move sooner.

"He's sending us a message. There is nothing either of us could have done to stop him. If we had gotten here sooner he would have only carried out these attacks sooner.

"I've seen him do this sort of thing before. This is the way he thinks. He will kill as many people as he has to in order to get what he wants. It never occurred to me that he would bring his ruthless methods here, to this world. It was foolish of me not to realize he would."

Alex raked his fingers back through his hair. "I don't get it, though. I don't get the reason for murders all over the world. He's been trying to get his hands on us since the beginning. He left that note for me, so he obviously knew where we were. He could have stormed the place and had us last night while we were asleep. Why do this instead? What does he think this is going to accomplish?"

"I'm afraid that he's changed his tactics." Jax glanced over at him. "He gave you that note to let you know that he knew the fake name the Daggett Society had made up to protect you. He wanted you to know that you can't hide from him, that there is nowhere safe where he can't find you.

"He told you the places of the attacks so that you would know that he was responsible. He wanted you to know his reach."

Alex scanned the tourist traffic and dump trucks making their way along the congested, narrow road through town, checking to make sure that none of them looked imminently threatening.

Alex heaved a sigh. "I guess you're right. It was all an elaborate, bloody show just for me. We've slipped through his fingers in the past, like back at Mother of Roses. This is retribution for being able to avoid him. He's telling me that if I don't do as he wants, he can kill innocent people by the thousands."

"I'm afraid so. Those killers he sends don't have to worry about being captured and punished. They can kill innocent, helpless people while they have the advantage, and then if it looks like someone might stop them, they can activate their lifeline and vanish in a heartbeat."

Alex shook his head in disgust. "But how can any human being do such things to innocent people—to children?"

"Their minds are poisoned by years of indoctrination. They believe what they're told. They see it as doing good. I'm sure that when they get back, Radell Cain will give them rewards for their bravery and great work in advancing their cause. They will feel only pride, not revulsion, for what they've done. Cain likes giving awards for killing women and children because he knows that that kind of thing strikes mindless fear into his enemies."

"Well, it's working," Alex said under his breath.

They fell silent with brooding thoughts as they made their way down the street. The town of Westfield was a typical small New England tourist town. All the clapboard buildings were old, crooked, and crowded together. The two-lane highway through the three-block-long center of town was slowed and backed up by tourists turning out of side streets and trying to find places to park. Small buildings had been converted to restaurants, gift shops, and art galleries. One picture window they hurried past had photos of houses and land for sale.

Alex and Jax went into one of the wilderness outfitters to pick up what they might need for hiking into the land and sleeping outside. Together they grimly went about the business of equipping themselves.

Jax knew exactly what was needed. Alex converted her list into what his world had to offer. When she said that they would probably need bedrolls, he showed her sleeping bags. They selected a small, compact tent for two that took up very little space strapped under a backpack. She was impressed with the quality and innovation of the backpacks and other equipment and was able to minimize what they would need.

All Alex could think about as they quickly went about selecting various equipment was all the people who had died such horrific deaths that morning and all the traumatized survivors and all the lives that would be forever altered. Everyone in the shop was talking about the terror attacks. A number of people thought it was the work of Islamic fundamentalists, while two older women argued that warring drug cartels had been responsible.

Everyone feared what it could mean. The mood was one of dread and expectancy that they were yet to see the true dimension of the coming shadow of a cataclysm. Some people seemed to think such violence would soon swoop in to visit even the little town of Westfield.

Everyone feared what would happen next.

Alex guessed that what happened next depended on him.

After they left with their purchases, they stopped in a small market and bought food to pack in, then went to see if the truck was done. The service writer told Alex that it was almost finished and suggested they wait in the lounge for a few minutes. The TV was on in the lounge, carrying details of the killings. Alex didn't want to watch it. Besides, his mind was racing too fast for him to sit still. He needed to walk.

As they went outside, he spotted something hauntingly familiar in an art gallery directly across the street from the Jeep dealer. After two huge log trucks rumbled past, he took Jax by the hand and, in a break in the traffic, ran across the street.

On an easel, where it would show prominently through the front window of the gallery, was a large painting dominated by angry slashes of red paint. It reminded Alex of a frenzied, bloody, murderous temper tantrum.

He slowly approached the window, looking in at the painting on display as if it were something threatening, something deadly. He stood frozen, staring at it. He recognized the style.

The precisely made signature on the painting was *R. C. Dillion*.

"What is it?" Jax asked, frowning over at him.

He couldn't find his voice. It suddenly all made sense.

"Alex . . ." Jax called after him, hurrying to catch up as he swept into the gallery. "What's the matter?"

Inside, Alex stopped in front of the painting. The random collection of red slashes dripped red paint down the face of the canvas.

"What?" Jax said.

Alex pulled out the piece of paper and handed it to her. "Look at the handwriting on the paper. Don't read the cities, just look at the handwriting."

She studied the list of cities for a moment, then looked up at him again. "What about it?"

"Look at the signature on this painting."

Jax squinted at the muddy-white, precisely done *R. C. Dillion.*

"Dear spirits," she whispered. "They're the same hand."

"R. C. Dillion," Alex said as he finally looked over at her. "R.C.—Radell Cain. He's been right under my nose the whole time. He's been there watching me, playing with me."

"Quite a stunning piece of work, isn't it?" a woman in a tightly buttoned dark gray suit said as she came up to them, smiling, clasping her hands before herself.

"You can't imagine," Alex said.

"He's an up-and-coming midwestern artist who is becoming a national figure at the forefront of a new reality in art."

Alex recognized the words Mr. Martin, the gallery owner back home in Orden, had used to describe R. C. Dillion. He wondered if R.C. himself had given them that description.

"A new reality," Alex repeated in a flat tone. "Yes, so I've heard. How much?"

She was a little taken aback that he so immediately demanded the price. She fingered the small white collar folded over the suit at her throat as she ran figures through her head.

"It's well worth—"

"How much are you willing to sell it for? Cash. Right now."

The woman smiled. "R. C. Dillion has recently arrived in town for a little rest and seclusion, he told me, and only just placed this with us. We're honored he allowed us to offer one of his pieces. The price is twelve thousand dollars."

Doing his best to contain his rage, Alex pulled one of the fat envelopes stuffed with cash from his pocket. He started counting out one-hundred-dollar bills as the woman stood in mute shock to see him paying cash on the spot.

It was the money from the settlement for the fire that had destroyed his grandfather's house. Alex thought that Ben would have approved of what he was doing.

When he had handed over the whole twelve thousand dollars, he asked, "Do you have a black magic marker? The fat kind, with permanent ink?"

A little confused, she half turned and gestured toward an old oak desk sitting behind a furnace grate, back against the white plastered wall. "Why, yes, I believe I have one like you're talking about. It's the kind of marker we use to write signs for the window. Is that what you mean?"

"Yes. May I borrow it, please?"

The woman went to the desk and searched through a couple of drawers until she found the marker. She returned, her heel strikes echoing off the warped, wooden floor, and handed it over.

Alex picked up the painting he now owned and in big letters across it wrote "R.C.—I will be at the gateway. Come and get me." He signed it "Lord Rahl."

He handed the painting to the stunned woman. "Please give this to good old R.C. when he returns, will you? My treat."

The woman stood slack-jawed and speechless as Jax and Alex walked out.

55.

AFTER LOCKING THE GATE, Alex walked back to the truck. Beyond all the official signs on the other side of the formidable gate warning people not to enter the property, it felt as if he were standing in the narthex leading into a grand cathedral. In the uncanny quiet he looked around at the gloomy shadows, searching for any eyes that might be watching back.

The highway was too far away for them to hear any traffic, if there was any. The remote road had been virtually deserted on the way up from Westfield. Once past a few clusters of camps and some logging roads, they had seen only a few trucks.

Standing in the silent, ancient forest, Alex felt as if he were in another world.

He could see by what lay ahead that the road into the property was hardly what he was used to thinking of as a road. It looked like little more than a cut though primordial woods. Here and there trees crowded in tight right up to the edge of the road. Out ahead lay an open chamber cast in the gloom beneath the big pines. The thick overcast and mist only added to the sense of foreboding.

Immense trunks of monarch trees rose up through the underlying regions of the forest where only muted light penetrated. It was as if there were two worlds: the open, lush vegetation on the forest floor, and the world of the towering pines overhead. Nurseries of small, waist-high spruce huddled in clusters here and there in the understory. Swaths of ferns nodded under falling drops of water combed from the mist by the pine needles above. The ferns creating feathery beds in places throughout the quiet forest floor lent an exotic, spicy aroma to the place.

Alex climbed back in the Jeep and shut the door. Jax carefully watched out the side windows for any signs of trouble.

"Can I ask you a question, Alex?"

He turned the key and the Jeep started without him holding his breath, for once. "Sure."

"When you wrote on that painting, why did you sign it 'Lord Rahl'?"

Alex shrugged as he eased the truck ahead into the woods. "I don't know. I thought it might rattle Cain, maybe distract him. For some reason it just felt like the right thing to do. Why?"

"I just wondered, that's all."

"Does it bother you, because of what it meant in the past?"

"No. I don't care so much about what went on in the past. I care about what's happening now and what's going to happen."

"I know," Alex said, thinking about all the helpless, innocent victims who had died that day because of Radell Cain and his people.

As they crawled along, moving ever deeper into the somber woods, Alex wondered what Jax was brooding about. Since it didn't seem like she was going to say anything, he finally asked.

"What's going through your head, if you don't mind my asking?"

She stared out the side window for a time. She finally answered without looking at him.

"I was just weighing the worth of worlds."

Alex glanced over at her. "What does that mean?"

"I came here for a reason. I came to fulfill prophecy, to save the innocent people in my world from the threat looming over them."

Alex shrugged. "Go on."

"I don't know if I can do that anymore."

"What do you mean?"

"A lot of people died today, Alex. What do you think I mean?"

"You mean you're thinking of quitting?"

"I know what Radell Cain has planned next. I've seen him do things like this before. He's going to make you responsible for the deaths of innocent people if you refuse to help him. He's going to force you to choose."

Alex stared ahead as he inched along the rocky ruts. He had considered such questions in the back of his mind. He hated to bring them to the front, to dwell on them, to contemplate having to make such a choice.

As they drove on deeper into the woods, they eventually passed two side roads that were on the map that Hal Halverson had drawn for him. Those roads essentially circled the entire property. The road he was on was the only one that went deeper in toward what the people of the Daggett Society called the crown jewel of the property: Castle Mountain.

They had long since left the buffer property that he controlled through the Daggett Trust, and were now on the land that he had inherited. It seemed surreal to think that he actually owned everything he could see.

Another hour and a half of tough going finally brought them to a circular spot that had been cleared so that vehicles could turn around. Off to the left side was a brook that came from farther into the property. Beside the brook Alex saw a trailhead. He circled the Jeep around and parked.

As he got out and shut the door, Alex noted that the brook rushing over rocks created a lot of noise that would mask the sound of anyone who might be sneaking up. He scanned the woods before he lifted the tailgate so they could get their gear out. The dark wooden box with the knife was sitting in the back, seeming to wait for him.

Underneath the velvet he found a black leather sheath trimmed in silver that looked just like the one Jax had. He threaded the sheath onto his belt, placing it on the left side behind the pouch holding two spare magazines. He had the other four spare magazines in an easily accessible pocket on the side of the backpack. He had also packed a number of boxes of ammunition in the backpack. Ammo was heavy, but he wasn't about to leave it behind.

Ben always told him that you could never have enough guns or ammo. He wished now that he had taken the time to get another gun. He was thankful to at least have one and to know that it was as dependable as a rock.

Jax lifted the silver-handled knife out of the box. She pulled hers out to look at them together. The one from the box still had her blood on it.

Alex gestured at the weapons lying in her hands. "It's mind-boggling to think that those two knives haven't been together for probably a thousand years or more."

"That's what I was thinking," she said.

When she handed him the knife, he started to wipe the blood off. Jax stopped him. "No, leave it."

Alex frowned at her. "Why?"

"These blades were made to draw blood. It should have a taste to wake it from its long sleep to its purpose."

Alex gazed into her resolute eyes for a moment, then slid the knife, still stained with blood, into its sheath on his belt.

He and Jax silently went about the task of getting their gear together. It was already early afternoon. Fixing the truck and the drive up had taken most of the morning. He knew that there was no way they would make it all the way in to Castle Mountain that day. They would have to set up a camp and make it the rest of the way to their destination the next day.

He supposed that Radell Cain, Sedrick Vendis, and Yuri the pirate could simply pop in at Alex's destination without having to go through the effort of a long hike. He certainly had no doubt that they would show up.

Alex was looking forward to finally meeting the visionary artist who was creating a new reality. His blood boiled with rage in anticipation of meeting him.

Jax looked like she knew what she was doing with the camping gear. She got her pack together quickly and efficiently, then hoisted it up onto her back and buckled the waist strap. Alex did the same. Their packs had collapsible water containers and they also had water bottles hooked on utility belts.

As they left the Jeep and started into the woods the calls of birds echoed through the trees. Walking along side by side in the more open areas, they shared a couple of packages of rolled-up meat and cheese. They had preserved food, but the meat wouldn't keep, so they ate it all as they made their way deeper into the gloom.

Farther in, the trail became less defined, but it wasn't difficult to follow. The security people probably used the trail into the interior of the property, and over the time that the Daggett Trust had protected the land the trail had become a reasonably well-defined route. Besides the roads, Hal had also marked such trails on the property. There weren't a lot of them, but they provided access to just about any corner of the land. As he walked along, Alex could see that there were deer trails that could probably be followed if need be.

As the afternoon wore on, the land began rising. At first it was gentle slopes, but it soon began to get rocky and more difficult to climb. They were both breathing hard as they ascended a series of ridges, having to go down the back side of each one before going up again to get over the next.

After the ridges, the trail took switchbacks up a steep area with a series of cliffs. Each of the rock faces wasn't all that high, but negotiating them was difficult, especially carrying all the gear they had. In some of the places Jax's legs weren't long enough and Alex had to lie on the upper trail and reach down to help pull her up so that she wouldn't have to take time to climb around. Other than that, he was having a hard time keeping up with her.

As they went higher, the mist thickened. It felt cool on Alex's sweaty face. The land finally leveled a little. The trail wound its way up through trees with gnarled roots clinging to seams in areas of exposed granite ledge. Leaving the ledges behind, they plunged back into thicker woods. Moss underfoot made it a quiet walk.

"It won't be long until dark," Jax said back over her shoulder. "With the cloud cover there won't be any moon or stars. It's going to be a pitch-black night. Hiking in this kind of terrain after it gets dark is dangerous. You could walk off a rock face, or break a leg in a hole. We're going to have to think about setting up camp pretty soon."

Alex sighed. He was weary from their pace, but he hated to have to stop. He had wanted to get closer to their destination, but he knew that she had a lot more experience at this kind of thing and so he took her advice seriously.

"How about if we keep pushing for just a little longer. We can always use flashlights to help us set up camp."

She agreed, but told him that it wouldn't be long until it would be too dark to push on. Everything soon began losing its color, making the trees look gray. Darkness was falling quicker than he would have thought.

And then they came out of the closed trail to a small opening in the woods that for the first time gave them a view into the distance. They halted together, surprised by the unexpected sight.

Silhouetted against the fading gray sky while at the same time lit a little from the obscured sun setting to the left stood Castle Mountain, rising up before them from the undulating, rolling landscape.

It didn't really look at all like a castle to Alex. It looked more like a plateau rising up out of the surrounding forests. Its top wasn't flat, though, instead looking somewhat crenellated with irregular rock outcroppings rising and falling across the surface of the top.

"Dear spirits," Jax whispered.

"What? What's the matter?"

"I don't believe it."

"What don't you believe?"

"It looks very much like a place in my world called the People's Palace." She shook her head. "I can hardly believe what I'm seeing, but I guess, when I think about it, I've somehow expected all along to see it."

"Sure doesn't look much like a castle to me. What's so special about the People's Palace?"

"It's the place where our worlds were split apart. Up there, at least up there in my world, is a place called the Garden of Life. From there, at the end of a long struggle, people were banished to this world. It only makes sense for that to be the place of connection, the place where the gateway would be."

The enormity of such a concept gave Alex pause.

She pointed. "Can you see that line rising up diagonally from the bottom left toward the top right?"

Alex squinted into the gathering darkness. "Okay, I see it now."

"It looks like a narrow, angled ridge. In my world that's a road up the plateau to the palace at the top." She let out a sigh. "From here it's probably a hike of four hours to get there. We'd better look for a place to camp and get some sleep."

56.

THE TRAIL SOON TOOK THEM BACK into the shelter of the woods. They found a place that Jax liked for a camp because there was a rock overhang to protect them in case it started to rain. In the gloom they quickly set up their tent and unrolled the sleeping bags.

"Tonight we should stand watches," she told him as she used rocks to make a fire ring around an area she had quickly scraped clear of forest litter. "A fire could possibly be seen, but it's more important that we can see them—and not die of exposure."

Gathering wood nearby, he looked back over his shoulder. "You think that watches are necessary?"

"I hope not," she said. "But being this close I wouldn't want both of us to be asleep and have Yuri and his friends show up in the dark."

Alex built kindling up in the center of the fire ring and lit it with a match. He had been about to argue the point of a watch, but her words gave him pause. "All right. But only if you will take the gun on your watch."

She said she would. He handed her a foil pouch and a plastic spoon. In the dark he wasn't sure if he had pulled out meatloaf or roast pork. His was meatloaf. They ate in silence, listening to the coyotes in the distant mountains. It was a spooky sound to hear all alone so far out in the woods.

When they were finished Jax said that if it was all right with him she was really tired and would rather sleep first and take her watch the second half of the night. Alex agreed. She found a comfortable place on a flat rock just out of the ring of light from the fire and told him that it was a good place to keep his eye on things without being blinded by the fire. She told him to make sure to keep wood on the fire.

She rested her arms on his shoulders and clasped her fingers together behind his head. "Come wake me when it's my turn."

Before he knew it, she was kissing him. It was a lonely, desperate kind of kiss. It was wonderful only in the sense that they at least had each other. He understood her emotion, and how it came out in the embrace. They were both dispirited by the killing of innocent people earlier that day. The kiss wasn't passion so much as it was meant to be comfort.

Alex helped her get into her sleeping bag, since she'd never seen one before. When she was settled in, he went to the rock and sat, resting his gun in his lap.

The mist came and went, but at least it didn't rain. He checked his watch every once in a while and waited longer than half the night to let her have a little extra sleep.

When he woke her, she put her arms around his neck and hugged him tight. It felt like a fearful, lonely hug.

He put more wood on the fire for her; then, when she sat on the rock, he put the gun in her lap. On the long drive from Nebraska to

Maine he had explained how it worked in case she ever needed to use it. At night he had taught her to switch magazines and clear a jam. She was familiar enough that he didn't feel he needed to give her another lesson.

Jax put her arms around his neck again and pulled him close. "Alex, you do know how much you mean to me, don't you?"

Alex smiled in the darkness. He pulled back to gaze at her face. Firelight sparkled in her beautiful brown eyes.

He thought about that morning back at the motel in Westfield. He smiled to reassure her. "You made it quite clear."

"I would do anything for you. I hope you know that. You won't ever doubt me, will you?"

He smiled. "Never."

Her eyes brimmed with tears. She put her hands to each side of his face as she gazed into his eyes. "Alex . . . would you do anything for me?"

He frowned a little. "What is it you want me to do?"

"To say you love me."

Alex had wanted to say it a thousand times. He guessed he had always been waiting for the right time. That morning had been the right time. In his whole life, nothing had made him happier than when he'd heard those same words from her lips.

"I love you, Jax Amnell."

"I love you, Alexander Rahl, defender of man."

She kissed him softly, then pulled back just a little.

"Promise me," she said as she looked at him from inches away, "promise me that you will never doubt that I love you, that you will never doubt that I will always love you as long as I draw breath."

"Jax, are you all right?"

"I will be if you promise me."

467

Alex ran a hand tenderly down her hair. "I promise—as long as you promise the same."

"I do," she whispered before kissing him again.

She let out a reluctant sigh. "You had better get some sleep. It will be light sooner than you think."

Alex lifted an eyebrow. "Now you want me to try to sleep? After that, you think I will be able to sleep?"

She smiled a strangely sad smile and gave him a quick kiss. "Yes. You need to sleep. I want you to be strong tomorrow."

"For you, anything."

Alex crawled into his sleeping bag and tried to go to sleep. His heart seemed to be beating too fast for him to ever be able to sleep. He could think of little other than those precious words from her.

Yet his mind started drifting to the dangers she faced. What with alternating between fear and rage at those dangers, it was difficult to try to sleep, but somewhere in that wild swing of emotions, as thoughts of her filled every part of him, he was so overcome with exhaustion that it carried him into a sound sleep.

When he woke up, it was just getting light. He yawned, wondering why Jax hadn't woken him up sooner.

As he turned, he saw the gun lying not far from his head.

Alex sat up in a rush, staring at the gun, trying to make sense of it.

"Jax?" he called out from the tent as he picked up the gun.

She didn't answer. She should have been close enough to hear him.

He untangled himself from the sleeping bag and raced out of the small tent.

The fire was dead.

Jax was gone.

57.

ALEX FRANTICALLY SEARCHED AROUND THE CAMPSITE, hoping against hope that he was wrong and that Jax was actually close at hand. He screamed her name as he looked. Panting in panic, he realized that he wasn't mistaken. She was gone.

He searched the site, looking for the footprints of intruders. He didn't see any. At the trail, he found a partial print left by her boot. It was headed in the direction of the mountain.

With a sinking feeling of icy dread, Alex knew what she had done, and why.

He snatched up his pack and threw it on. He left the tent and the gear they had gotten out. He took time only to grab the water bottles. Her pack was leaned up against the rock where she had been sitting. He left it and took off up the trail.

Before he had gone far, a man suddenly appeared directly in front of him in the trail. He was big, perhaps in his early twenties. He looked like he belonged in a biker gang. His matted brown hair didn't appear to have ever seen a brush. Alex froze. The man grinned wickedly.

"Radell Cain has a message for you," the man said in a deep, gravelly voice.

"I have a message for him," Alex said as he drew his gun.

He put a bullet in the center of the man's chest.

Birds took to wing at the resounding bang.

With a look of stunned shock on his face, the man crumpled to the ground, groaning. The sound of the single gunshot echoed through the woods to reflect back from the mountain up ahead.

Ben had taught him to quickly fire two or three rounds into the center mass of a threat, and if warranted, more. The man was seriously wounded. There would be no help for him out in the middle of such remote woods. The only thing that would find him would be the coyotes. Alex had a limited supply of ammunition; he wasn't going to waste any on a man who clearly wasn't going to present further threat or last long.

He stepped over the gasping, dying man and hurried up the trail.

As the morning wore on, Alex only pressed on harder. Instead of climbing down and then up to cross small gullies, he bounded across. Instead of climbing down short drops, he jumped down. He knew that he had to be careful or he could break an ankle and then he would be helpless, but he couldn't make himself slow down. He knew that he was in a race to stop Jax before it was too late.

He kept thinking of her asking him to promise that he would never doubt that as long as she drew breath she would always love him. He felt a lump rising in his throat as he ran. The limbs and brush he flew past turned to a watery blur.

He was furious at himself for not catching on to the things she'd said. He'd thought that it was because she was upset at hearing about all the deaths that morning. He should have known it was more. Having been sleepy was no excuse. Excuses couldn't undo it if he lost her.

A few hours of grueling effort brought him to the base of the plateau that rose up out of the forest. Catching his breath, he looked up the rugged series of cliffs toward the top. Squinting into the iron gray light, he couldn't see anything beyond the edge other than the wispy limbs of trees.

Jax had said that the ascending rift in the rock was in her world a road up the side of the cliff to the top. While not a road, the trail led to the craggy edge of rock that looked like a natural formation, yet went up along the face of the cliff at a steep angle. It looked like it might go all the way to the top. If it didn't, if the lip of rock ended, he was going to find himself awfully high up with nowhere to go.

Alex couldn't see that he had a choice and so he didn't give it a whole lot of thought. He simply started climbing.

There were places along the way that at first looked impassable. In each case, though, he quickly found a way to pass. In other spots he had to climb over gaps in the narrow outcropping, but along much of the sloping, weathered rock ledge it widened to several feet, and in spots at least six or seven feet, where it presented no trouble at all, except that it sapped his strength to climb so fast at such a steep angle. His thigh muscles burned from the effort. He panted for air as he pressed on, refusing to slow for anything.

In a little more than an hour, he was getting near the top. As he came around a protruding rock face, two burly men were waiting. Alex took a hurried step back, at the same time drawing his gun. Without hesitation he fired at the closest man charging toward him. The bullet must have gone through his heart, because the man faltered and dropped.

The second man put a boot on the downed man and leaped over him, diving toward Alex. Alex pressed the trigger twice in rapid succession. He didn't know if his bullets found their mark or not, because the man was still crashing in on him. As the man's arm came out to tackle him, Alex dodged aside, seized the man's hair, and used his forward momentum to help heave him out over the edge. The man stumbled, trying to stop, but he was moving too fast. He screamed all the way down.

Gun held in both hands, Alex pressed his back against the rock wall, catching his breath. He looked out over the edge and went weak in the knees at how close he had been to going over the side with the assailant.

The man on the ground wasn't moving. Alex didn't like the idea of not having the gun fully loaded as he went into an unknown but definitely hostile situation, so he quickly pulled a box of ammo out of his backpack. With his thumb he forced four more shells into the magazine, filling it to capacity. Seventeen rounds in the magazine plus one in the chamber gave him eighteen rounds in the gun plus the rest of the loaded magazines if he needed to reload in a hurry.

While eighteen rounds sounded like a lot, he knew that if there were enough men coming at him even that many shells wouldn't last long. He didn't know what choice he had.

Gathering his wits, he hurried the rest of the way up the trail to the top, where it flattened off considerably. Even so, it wasn't exactly flat. Beyond an expanse of forest, jumbles of rock rose up to make the top of the massive plateau a series of rocky layers.

While from a distance it might have looked flat on top, up close the stacks of ledge, the sheer granite faces, and the squared-off breaks in the stone had a hauntingly man-made look to them, even though the plateau was obviously entirely natural. A person with a good imagination could make more out of it than layers of rock. With some imagination it looked almost like an extensive, complex structure.

Now that he had made the top, Alex wasn't sure what to do. He searched around the area where the sloping rock ledge had emerged on top, but there was no man-made trail. While the trail below was used by the security force to get to the mountain, they apparently rarely or never climbed to the top. It didn't look to him like anyone had ever walked across the delicate pale lichen and deep green mosses.

He finally decided to follow the exposed ledge that created a natural trail through the woods. In one low, damp place, he spotted Jax's boot print. Deeper in, he came to a curious depression leading into the rock jumble.

Before going into the narrow chasm, he pulled a box of ammo and four magazines from his pack. He put the box of ammo in the front pocket of his jeans and the spare magazines in his back pockets. As he moved into the tight opening in the rock, he found that it wound into gorges that eventually rose perhaps a hundred feet in places.

The natural trail through the rock led him into a narrow cleft. High above, he could see that the smooth sides revealed only a long slash of leaden sky. Alex went in deeper. The rock overhead that must have once stood taller yet had toppled over in the distant past, possibly during earthquakes, so that it now lay across the cleft and acted as a roof. The deeper Alex went, the gloomier it became.

The farther in he went, the more the jumbled, weathered rock turned into a dark labyrinth. Alex stuck a hand into his pack, searching blindly for a flashlight. He found it and pulled it out.

When he switched on the light and pointed it ahead, a man was standing in the narrow passageway through the rock. Alex went for his gun.

"If you want to see her alive, you need to follow me."

Looking at the man through the iron gunsights, one eye over each of the two outer dots and the center blade of the front sight rock-steady over the bridge of the man's nose, Alex hesitated.

But for only an instant.

He pressed the trigger. The gunshot inside the confines of the rock passageway was deafening.

"I don't negotiate with murderers," Alex said under his breath as he stepped over the corpse and made his way deeper into the maze of rocky crags.

"Seventeen left," he counted to himself as he hurriedly followed what was becoming like a cave running deeper into the mountain. With his flashlight he had to check that each side branch he came to was clear. He stuck to what seemed the main crevice running through the mountain. In places the huge slabs of granite had shifted over millennia or even tipped and fallen, leaving many spots a tight squeeze to get through. In other places he had to climb over rubble from when the rock overhead had collapsed.

Alex didn't know how long he had been running when he realized that up ahead he saw natural light. As he continued on, the light grew steadily brighter.

When he rounded a slight bend in the fissure through the mountain, he spotted something out ahead in that area of light. He rushed ahead, trying to make it out.

His heart came up in his throat.

It was Jax.

58.

ALEX COULD SEE JAX STANDING in the middle of a broad area of white sand. The place looked to have once been a cavernous dome but the center of the roof seemed to have eroded away and partially collapsed over time to leave a room that was open to the sky. Here and there boulders that looked possibly to have once been part of that domed ceiling sat littering the room.

Jax, standing in the center of the sand under that opening, watched him come. He could tell that her hands were tied behind her back. Tears stained her face. A trickle of blood ran from the corner of her mouth.

With his gun held in both hands and at the ready, Alex inched into the open area. As he emerged from the passageway through the rock, hundreds of men came into view. They stood silently around the outside near the walls or in other caves and cracks leading into the room. They were all watching him. None made a move.

They were dressed in clothes that would be familiar anywhere—mostly jeans and oversized T-shirts with words on them. A number of them wore baggy, knee-length shorts and sandals, just like a typical guy at the mall or out getting a pizza. Alex spotted what looked like knives under the shirts of some. He was sure that all of them had weapons concealed somewhere on them.

Despite their ordinary dress, they weren't especially well groomed, with ratty hair and scraggly beards or stubble. Alex supposed that even that wasn't too out of place anymore with their everyday outfits. They all had hard eyes and wore grim expressions. They looked like thugs. That, too, was a rather conventional look that seemed to be cultivated by many men and had become accepted.

Walking down the street these men wouldn't warrant a second look from most people. Any one of them, carrying a knapsack, could walk unnoticed through any airport. Seeing them gathered all together as they were, though, on a remote wilderness mountaintop, looked bizarre in the extreme, as if they had all been transported there from the bleachers of a basketball game.

Alex knew that they were chameleons, killers intended to fit in and be unseen—until they struck. That, in itself, was what was so frightening about them. They would be invisible out among innocent people.

A glance back showed that the way he had come in was now blocked by dozens more men just like them.

"Alex," Jax said in a shaky voice, "give them your gun."

"No."

"Please . . ."

"I'm not—"

"You can't hope to change things," she said. "Don't make it any more difficult than it already is. Please?"

The audience of killers all silently watched. Alex knew that even if he hit his target with every round, and he managed to reload with every one of his spare magazines, he wouldn't have enough bullets to take out all the men gathered. When he ran out of ammo, they would have him. But he knew that in reality it would never come to that. They would all simply rush him at the same time. They'd be on him before he could empty the magazine in his gun.

"Talk to me, Jax. What's going on?"

"Give them your gun, or they'll just hurt me until you do, or take it away from you after you run out of bullets."

As if to demonstrate, one of the men heaved a fist-sized rock. It struck Jax in the back of the shoulder. She cried out as she went to a knee, bent by the pain of the blow.

Alex put two rounds into the man, dropping him almost instantly. None of the other men so much as flinched at the loud sound or the flash.

Dozens of other men all around the cavernous room lifted rocks to show him that he had no chance to change the outcome. Jax staggered back to her feet. If all of those men threw those rocks she would be stoned to death before he could do anything effective to stop them. Alex's vision was red with rage. He wanted to strike out at all of them.

But he knew that doing so would only get Jax hurt.

Violating a rule that had been drilled into him from the first time he had learned to shoot, he squatted down, laid the gun on the ground, and slid it across the granite toward Jax. It stopped right before the area of sand.

Ben had always told him that you never give up your gun. But a gun was merely a tool of self-defense. If it couldn't defend him, or protect Jax, then it ceased to be a tool and became nothing more than a useless hunk of metal.

Alex was enraged that he had no choice but to give up the weapon.

He was ashamed of himself for not thinking of something to keep it from coming to that.

He reminded himself that it wasn't over yet. He might have had to give up his gun, but he wouldn't quit as long as he had breath in his lungs.

Sedrick Vendis stepped out from behind some of the men in a dark cave opening to the left and walked out to retrieve the weapon. He picked it up and stuck it in his waistband.

"That's better, Alex," he said with a smirk. "Sorry I missed the show at the hospital. I hear it was quite the event."

Alex ignored him. "Jax—what's going on?"

"I'm saving your world," she said in a voice choked with emotion.

Alex had thought as much.

He strode to the edge of the sand, close to her. Sedrick Vendis casually backed up a few steps to stay out of his immediate reach. Somewhere inside it pleased Alex that, even alone and without a gun, surrounded by hundreds of men, they considered him dangerous.

He intended to prove their fears warranted.

To Alex's left, another man stepped out from the darkness beyond the men watching. He was tall, with slicked-back blond hair and thick features. He wore dark slacks and a simple white pullover shirt with short sleeves and an open collar. He looked like he might be about to go out for a game of golf. He was maybe forty, but looked to be in good shape, as though he could take care of himself if he had to.

If Alex had his way, he was going to have to.

As he approached, the man's piercing blue eyes never strayed from Alex. He stopped ten feet away, smiling at Alex in a knowing manner.

"How nice to meet you at last, *Lord Rahl*."

He emphasized the title in a way obviously intended to mock Alex for having written it on the painting.

Alex was pleased to know that the title had hit a sore spot. "Get to the point."

"Ah, the direct approach." He shrugged. "Very well."

Alex was distracted by another man coming out from the shadows to stand not far from Jax. It was Yuri. The pirate was still wearing the same dirty clothes and a grin that showed his yellow teeth.

"I'm Radell Cain," the tall man said, drawing Alex's attention back. He swept an arm out, indicating the area where Jax stood. "This is the gateway, in case you hadn't guessed." He crooked his fingers. "Come, have a look if you would be so kind."

As Alex followed the man, Jax's eyes tracked him the whole way. He stopped where indicated, at one of the boulders sitting before the area of sand. The flat top of the rock, several feet square, was angled toward him. It was smooth although somewhat weathered-looking, as if it had sat in that spot exposed to the elements for a thousand years.

Alex was startled to see that it had what looked to be a petroglyph drawn on the flat area of the light-colored granite. The darkish lines had a reddish cast to them. It almost looked like it might have been done with blood.

Alex was even more shocked to see what that drawing was. It was a simple scene of a forest, composed of ten trees, much like the scenes Alex liked to paint.

Below the drawing was a small slot in the stone.

Alex was beginning to understand.

"Rather like one of your quaint little paintings," Cain said, smiling without amusement as he gestured dismissively at the drawing on the stone.

"What do you mean?"

Cain shrugged. "Rather outmoded, passé—as opposed to the new reality my vision is ushering in."

"If you have invited me here to discuss art, I'm afraid that you aren't qualified to speak on the subject."

"No, I don't care what you know about art, I only care about what you know about the gateway."

Alex shrugged. "Not much."

Cain's humorless smile returned. "Well, since you wanted me to get to the point, here it is. I want this gateway functioning, and I want it functioning right now. I've followed your family long enough, waiting for the right time to come. With you, it finally has. The Law of Nines is now fulfilled. I'm through waiting.

"Yesterday I gave you a small sampling of what I can do if I need to. If you don't cooperate, I'm going to rain death and destruction down on this world the likes of which you can't imagine. Yesterday, where I killed one, tomorrow I will kill thousands. I can send men into schools, shopping centers, hotels, restaurants, workplaces, sporting events, and . . . well, I think you get the idea."

He swept his arm around as if introducing the hundreds of men watching. "These are but a few of my legions that I will send into the most secure, secluded places you can imagine. Do you know that we have the ability to show up in, say, the bedroom of your president? The bedroom of every world leader? We can eviscerate your leaders, your police commanders, your army generals. Why, I have an entire staff of people who have nothing better to do than think up ways in which to kill the unsuspecting people of your world.

"If I want, I could even set nations against each other and launch your world into war. I could have my legions carry out the most brutal attacks to partially bring down the ruling government of Israel, for example, and goad them into launching a nuclear attack against surrounding nations. If I want, I can light the fuse that will ignite a holocaust."

"Alex," Jax said, "listen to him. He's not bluffing. He will kill innocent people in the thousands."

Cain turned to her. "Don't be insulting. I will kill the people here in the tens of thousands—the hundreds of thousands—if I have to."

Alex felt dizzy. He knew that Jax was right, that Cain wasn't bluffing.

As if to prove his point, Cain looked around at all the men watching. "If *Lord Rahl*, here, does not give me what I want, you will all receive my order to carry out the instructions you have already been given."

The men all bowed their heads.

"I'm not giving you what you want," Alex said.

Cain turned a cold glare on him. "Then the killing will continue until you do. If I have to reduce this world to a sea of blood, I will."

"Alex," Jax said, drawing his attention again. "Please, do as he asks. You alone hold sway over all those innocent lives. You alone can prevent this from happening to your world."

Alex stepped out onto the sand, closer to her. "Why would you turn yourself over to him? Why are you doing this?"

"Because I know that as long as I'm free you would never give up. As long as I'm free you would fight no matter what. I can't let you put your love for me above all the people who will die if you keep fighting him. I had to remove myself from the equation.

"To let this happen, to let him unleash his wrath on your world while I stand by and watch, is a violation of all that I value and believe in—of everything I've been fighting to preserve. I couldn't let your world pay the price for the people in my world.

"We are lost. Our war is done. Don't let it come down on your world, too. Please, Alex, do what he says. Don't let any more people here die needlessly.

"There is nothing you can do for me now. I am lost. Let me go. Only you can do something to save all the people in your world who will otherwise die. Please, Alex, don't allow the sacrifice of my life to stand for nothing. Do as he wants and think of your own people now."

"Yet more outdated moral drivel," Cain said in a contemptuous tone. "Hardly the kind of strength exhibited by the strong, by true visionary leaders. No wonder you're losing." He turned to Alex. "Still, you should listen to her, if for no other reason than because you are just as weak as she is and you will want to spare the people in your world all the pain and suffering I will unleash on them."

Alex looked away from the venomous glare of Radell Cain, back into the eyes of the woman he loved more than life itself.

"These people are from my world," she said softly. "We must suffer them. You must not let this place suffer them as well. That is your highest responsibility. I gave myself up because if I didn't my life would be lived at the cost of the lives of thousands of innocent people. I can't live with that."

"I don't negotiate with murderers," Alex said.

"You aren't negotiating," she whispered, "you are making a choice. You can't win by wishing it was other than it is. This is what is before us. We have to choose or the choice will be made for us and others here will suffer because of it."

"You should listen to her, Alex," Cain said. "She's a smart lady. That's why I can't allow her to run free."

Alex swallowed at the lump in his throat. He could think of no argument that could change things. He had nothing to fight with. If he held out, then all the suffering and death that Cain promised would come to pass.

"Let her go first."

Cain heaved an irritated sigh. "I grow weary of this." He turned to the men watching. "You all have your assignments. Go, now, and await my orders. If you get my command, then you will unleash war on these people tomorrow. If he cooperates by tonight, and you don't receive orders from me to attack, then return home at once to prepare for the transition to the new reality in our own world, where we must be ready to rule."

Men all around clapped fists to hearts in salute. In so doing they also vanished almost all at the same time. Where hundreds had stood, there was only darkness and stone. Only a few dozen men remained behind.

Radell Cain turned back to Alex. "They will be in place by tonight, out among the people of your world—death stalking among the unaware and unprepared. If you don't open the gateway for me, then by morning I will give them the order to start killing on a scale you can't imagine.

"What's more," he said with a growing smile, "I will hand Jax over to Yuri to do with as he will. If you cooperate, I will instead have her beheaded—put to death quickly. If not . . ." He shrugged.

Yuri pulled out a knife, displaying it for Alex. It was Jax's silver-handled knife. "Don't you worry, my men and I will keep her alive for a good long time. When we finally tire of her feminine charms, then I'll start in cutting on her."

Jax closed her eyes at the terror awaiting her.

Alex knew that he'd run out of options, and time.

He gazed into her beautiful, sad eyes as they opened. In those forlorn eyes he could see his world ending.

"You know, don't you? I can see it in your eyes," she whispered to him. "You figured it out, didn't you?"

He nodded.

"Then don't let me down, Alexander. The time has come to defend mankind, here, in your world. Open the gateway for him."

"All right," he whispered back to her, "I'll do it."

59.

ALEX GESTURED TO JAX to move off the area of sand. Yuri seized her arm and roughly pulled her back against the stone wall.

Alex went out onto the white sand and with his arm smoothed the footprints out, leveling the sand. He began drawing the symbols that he had learned from Jax to activate a lifeline, only on a large scale. He needed to buy a little time to think things through, to put together all the things Jax had told him, and the things the Daggett Society had told him about what the book said. He made a job of carefully laying out the designs as he put all the pieces together in his head.

"That's not going to open the gateway," Sedrick Vendis snapped.

Alex looked up at the man. "Since you seem to know so much, why don't you tell your boss how it's done?"

Vendis glowered but finally folded his arms and fell silent.

When he finished drawing, Alex stood and faced Cain. "I will have to trust that you will keep your word she won't suffer at the end."

Cain's smile was bone-chillingly evil. "I'm nothing if not a man of my word."

"Since this is the end for Jax and me, I want to tell her a few private words of good-bye before I finish this for you. I want to have a moment alone with her. Then I will open your gateway for you. If you won't grant me that simple human decency, then I may not believe that you're an understanding man who will keep his word about granting her a swift death."

Alex gave the man an iron look. "I may have second thoughts."

Cain glared for a moment. He finally held out his hand. "The knife first."

Alex pulled the silver-handled knife out of the sheath behind the two magazines on the left side of his belt. He held it by the blade still stained with Jax's blood and placed the handle with the House of Rahl symbol in the man's hand. Cain looked down at the knife in his hand as Alex stood with his own hands in his pockets, waiting.

Cain finally gestured with the knife. "All right, if it will end this pathetic emotional drama, go ahead."

"Alone," Alex reminded him.

"Leave them be, Yuri."

The greasy pirate moved away to stand beside Sedrick Vendis as the three of them watched Alex go up to where Jax, her hands tied behind her back, stood all by herself against the stone wall. She looked forlorn and resigned.

Vendis asked Cain something in a whisper. The men leaned in, discussing it among themselves as Alex stepped up close to Jax. Her chin trembled as she finally looked up at him.

"I'm so sorry, Alex."

As he put his arms around her she put her face against his shoulder and started to cry.

"Don't be sorry, Jax," he whispered, "be strong."

Alex placed his open pocketknife that he had palmed into her hands behind her back.

She went still when she realized what it was.

"The blade is razor-sharp," he whispered into her ear. "Be careful when you cut the ropes. Keep your hands together as if they're still tied and wait. You'll know when."

"Alex—"

"Jax, I'd rather die trying than let them have what they want. You can't bargain with evil. You can't appease it. You can't compromise with it.

"Giving in to them will only lead to endless suffering and death in the long run. How long until they return here deciding they want more from this world and start to kill again to get it? I have to try to stop it now. You're the one who came here to stop this evil. You came here to do a job. It's not finished. Are you with me? Are you willing to try?"

He knew what he was asking of her. Yuri stood not far away leering hungrily at her. They both knew the consequences if they failed, not merely for her, but for everyone.

She nodded against him, putting on a show for the men watching. "You're right. If we have any chance, we have to take it. I was so afraid for the people of your world, so afraid that I had come for your help only to end up causing harm, that I forgot who I was for a time. Dear spirits, can you ever forgive me for being so weak?"

He reached up and held her tight, smoothing her hair as he held her head to him. "That's the Jax I love. You're anything but weak. You're the strongest person I know. In case this doesn't work, just know that I love you more than anything."

"You are a devious man, Alexander Rahl." She kissed his neck. "I love you anyway."

"I learned it from you."

"Enough," Cain growled.

Alex kissed her quickly, then turned to his task.

60.

ALEX HELD HIS HAND OUT. "I need the knife."

Radell Cain's eyes narrowed. "Why?"

"To open the gateway."

"And how is the knife going to do that?"

"Opening the gateway requires the person named by the Law of Nines. Right?"

Cain studied his face for a moment. "Go on."

Alex spread his hands. "So how the hell is the gateway supposed to know it's me, know I'm the one named by the Law of Nines? Do you think that because it's me I can simply say 'Open sesame' and the gateway will recognize me as the one and open? There is no magic in this world, so how is the gateway to know that I'm the one that is able to open it?"

"I give up, how?" Cain asked with clear distaste for the game Alex was playing.

"Blood."

"Blood?"

"Yes. It needs my blood to recognize that I'm the one who is able to open it."

"Well," Cain said, "now you have my interest."

He handed the silver knife kept by the Daggett Society for a thousand years back to Alex, the one named by the Law of Nines as the only person who could open the gateway.

Alex drew the weapon across his forearm. As dull as it was, he was still able to cut himself enough to bleed liberally. In the back of his mind, Alex realized that the cut on his left forearm was very much the same place, direction, and length as the cut on Jax's forearm from when the man who had infiltrated the Daggett Trust had attacked her.

Alex wiped the blade in the blood running down his arm. The cut stung, but he was already lost in his own world, in what he had to do. He turned the blade and wiped the other side until both sides of the steel were red and blood dripped from the tip.

Radell Cain seemed to be quite caught up in the ritual to open the gateway.

Alex went to the rock that had the flat spot with the petroglyph. He held the knife over the rock, slanting it down just a little. He let a few drops of blood drip off the tip into the slot.

With a thud to the air all around, a faint glow of light ignited over the sand.

Men watching oohed at the strange, charged feeling to the air and the light from nowhere shining before them. It was beautiful, entrancing, inviting.

"All right, I need some people to send through the gateway."

"What for?" Cain asked with an angry frown.

"It doesn't just open," Alex insisted. "You can't load cargo on the sand in the center and transport it. It needs people to work. It's people that are the core of its function, so the gateway needs people to open.

The more people the better it works—the wider the gateway opens to accommodate them. In that way, the more things—the more supplies and cargo—the gateway will support going through it."

Radell Cain thought it over. He seemed to understand that it made sense.

Everyone else stood staring in amazement at the slowly twisting shaft of light hovering over the sand before them.

"Well?" Alex asked. "You wanted the gateway opened. It's opened. But to make it actually work, we need to send people through it."

Radell Cain, finally grinning in triumph, gestured some of his men forward. "Come on, then. Let's have some of you go tell them that we've succeeded."

Half a dozen men rushed forward. Alex was surprised that they seemed so eager. He guessed that in their world they were used to such things and accepted them.

The men gathered out on the area of sand. They held their hands out as if showering in the light. By their reaction it appeared to tingle pleasantly. They all looked up into the sky as if looking up into the source of the warm light. Like kids about to go on an amusement-park ride, they all wore big grins.

Radell Cain stepped forward to the edge of the granite before the sand, fascinated by the light show and the way it began to sparkle with the presence of the men. Sedrick Vendis as well stepped up to get a closer look.

"All right," Cain said to Alex, gesturing with an arm as if urging him to levitate the men, "go on, open it fully. Do it."

Alex held the knife in his fist above the slot. "Ready?" he asked the men in the light.

They were all grins and nods.

Alex shoved the blade charged with his blood into the slot.

In an instant, the men were drawn upward without their feet leaving the sand, elongating them into columns of flesh ripping apart into an explosion of blood and gore that shot skyward. They never had time to scream, but the sound of their bone and muscle coming apart was horrific enough.

All the men watching stood frozen in shock.

In that instant in time when none of them moved, Alex and Jax did.

Jax spun. The pocketknife in her fist scythed diagonally across Yuri's face, laying it open. As he bent back from the slicing blow, she kicked him in the groin. As he doubled over forward, she pulled her knife from his belt, reached under, and cut his throat open.

Alex yanked the knife out of the stone and went for Cain.

The men all descended out of the sides where they had been watching to defend against the sudden attack. Cain backed a few steps as he pulled out his own knife.

Jax was a whirlwind. Her blade cut into the men as they charged in. Several died before they had even drawn their own knives.

Alex dove to the side when he saw Sedrick Vendis draw the gun that he had in his waistband. Vendis started shooting. By the way he handled the gun, Alex could tell that he didn't have any experience. But if he got hit, Alex knew that wouldn't be any consolation. Bullets ricocheted off rock and splattered against the far wall. Even Cain had to dodge to keep from being accidentally shot.

Vendis turned the gun on Jax, firing wildly in a panic. Jax dodged and ducked past men, using them as shields. Several of the men were hit, but the bullets missed Jax.

Alex dove in past Cain's own knife, coming up and ripping his leg open. Cain fell back with a cry of surprise, pain, and rage. Vendis turned the gun on Alex to protect Cain. He fired wildly, and again Alex had to dive away to keep from getting hit.

When the gun went empty the slide locked back. When pulling the trigger no longer did any good, Vendis looked at the gun briefly and then tried pulling the trigger again. When the empty gun still wouldn't fire, he growled in anger and threw it at Alex.

Alex caught the weapon as it flew at him. With his thumb he pressed the release behind the trigger and dropped the empty magazine. He shoved a loaded magazine home. When the slide slammed forward it stripped the top round off the magazine and chambered the round, loading the gun.

Vendis was coming for him with a knife. Alex fired two rounds into the man's chest and then put one in his head.

Alex looked up and saw that Jax had just caught Cain before he could get his balance. Men were racing in from every direction to protect Radell Cain. Alex started firing, taking them out as fast as he could before they could get to Jax.

He could see out of the corner of his eye that she wasn't paying any attention to the men trying to get to her. She was lost in a rage of her own, hacking away at Radell Cain. The two of them were covered in blood.

One of the men charged at Alex just as his gun ran out of ammo. As the man lifted his knife to stab at Alex, Alex slammed his foot into the center of the man's chest. The man fell back. Alex pressed the release, dropping the empty magazine, and rammed a full one home.

He fired a round into the man as he was scrambling to his feet, then swiveled and fired once at a man to his left. He immediately turned and fired at two men going for Jax. The first one dropped, the second spun around once but kept going. Alex, his heart hammering, planted the sights on the man and pressed the trigger. It ended the charge.

He looked around but saw no more men coming for them. He stood panting in a state of wide-eyed shock. It had seemed like it had lasted an hour, but he knew that it had probably been little more than seconds.

Jax was still slamming her knife wildly into Cain's bloody corpse. Tears ran down her face as she furiously stabbed the dead man.

"Jax. Jax. It's over."

She lifted her arm again but stopped with it raised, her silver-handled knife held tightly in her fist, her teeth gritted with determination, blood splattered across her face and through her hair, tears running down as she gasped in fury.

"Jax . . . it's over."

She stared at him a moment, almost as if she didn't recognize him; then her face softened as she fell sobbing into his arms.

"We did it," she cried. "We killed the bastard. I can't believe that after all this time, after everything he's done, after all the people who have died, after how long we have worked, we finally killed the bastard."

"You killed him," Alex corrected softly.

"I killed him," she wept. "I killed the monster. I did it."

She finally pushed back to look at him as her sobs turned to tears of joy.

"You're a bloody mess," she said, half laughing.

"You should see yourself in a mirror," he said with a smile.

Jax hugged him as if she feared he would float away.

61.

AFTER A TIME, she finally allowed herself to part from him.

"I don't get it, though," Alex said. "Why didn't they activate their lifelines and escape?"

"A few of the men did—the ones back out of the way. Vendis and Cain feared to try."

"Why would they fear to try to vanish and escape?"

"It's not as simple as you make it sound. It takes a moment of concentration to do it. It's not long, but for an instant when they would be doing it they would be totally defenseless and vulnerable. They obviously feared to stand there naked to our blades and bullets for that instant for fear we would have had them. They're also used to being in control and killing others at will. They had confidence that with their numbers they could get control of the situation."

Alex sighed. "They were wrong. They underestimated you."

"They underestimated both of us," she said, "but they especially underestimated a person from this world without their abilities." She laid a hand on his chest. "I made the same mistake."

"You did what you had to do. You were fighting for life." Alex smiled as he touched her face. "I love you and you're safe. That's all that matters to me."

Jax looked around at the carnage. "We need to send them back. We need to let everyone know that Cain and Vendis are dead."

"If you activate their lifeline won't their bodies go back to their people, to their side?"

She nodded as she wiped her nose on her sleeve.

"What about the Garden of Life in your world?" Alex asked. "Who controls that place at the other side of the gateway?"

She looked up at him suddenly. "We do."

"So if we send them through the gateway, they will go to your side instead. Then everyone on your side will know of the victory won here today."

She blinked. "Well, that would be wonderful, but . . . you mean you can really make the gateway work? For real?"

Alex smiled. "Of course. Isn't that why you came here? All that Law of Nines business?"

"Yes, but . . . I don't understand."

"I did what was needed to open the gateway, but I only did part of what is necessary to make it work properly. I think it has a fail-safe."

"How would you know about that?"

"About what?"

"A fail-safe. Things of magic, things that are dangerous, usually have a fail-safe. Radell Cain thought that the fail-safe was your blood, the blood of the one named by the Law of Nines. But sometimes a more subtle fail-safe is integrated into dangerous things so that only the right person can use it."

"Well, this fail-safe is pretty simple, but I guess that sometimes simple things are the best."

Alex took her hand and led her to the stone where he had put the knife to activate the gateway. She slipped her arm around his waist.

"Look here," he said.

She frowned as she looked down at it. "It's a drawing of trees. It's kind of like the picture you gave me. It's something like the Shineestay place you painted." She trailed her fingers across the drawing. "Except that this one has all the trees."

"And how many trees does it have?"

Jax touched the trees as she counted. "Ten."

"And if I'm the one named by the Law of Nines, how many do you suppose it ought to have?"

She puzzled up at him. "It should have nine. It has one too many."

Alex nodded. "For the gateway to work, for the one named by the Law of Nines to activate it, for his blood to work, for it all to ring true to the fail-safe, one of the trees has to be removed, just like I removed one in that painting I gave you."

Jax was frowning in earnest. "How are you supposed to know which one to remove?"

"Easy. You take out the one that doesn't fit the composition." Alex laid a finger on one of the trees. "This one spoils the composition of the drawing. It doesn't belong. An artist would know that. I knew it the instant I first saw it. Radell Cain didn't see it because he wasn't really an artist. The Lord Rahl who put this there was."

"You mean to say that if that tree is erased, the gateway will function?"

"I'd bet my life on it."

Jax looked around. "Then let's send them back. Let's try it."

Together the two of them gathered up the bodies and piled them in the center of the sand. The white sand turned red as it soaked up all the blood still running from the corpses. They laid the bodies of Radell Cain and Sedrick Vendis side by side on top for all to see when they arrived.

Alex used his thumb, wetted with his own blood from the cut on his arm, to erase the tree that didn't belong. When it was gone, he slid the knife into the slot.

With a thud to the air, the light instantly ignited above the sand, sparkling around the pile of corpses. The bodies vanished in a blink. No fading away, sparkling swirls, no nothing, just gone. The sand was again white.

Alex and Jax looked at each other. All of the blood from the men was gone off them as well. All that remained was their own.

Suddenly alone, they looked into each other's eyes for a moment before coming together in an embrace and then a kiss that was filled with joy and relief.

As they sat together close under the soft light coming in from above through the open roof in the center of the room, she said, "You really are Alexander, defender of man. You were true to your name."

They sat in silence for a time, just letting the peace and quiet settle in as they held each other close.

"I know what you're thinking," he finally said.

Jax, her head against his shoulder, glanced up at him. "You do?"

Alex nodded sadly. "You're thinking that your part isn't finished yet. You're thinking that you are the defender of your people."

A tear trailed down her face. She swallowed as she looked away from his eyes.

"I wouldn't love you, Jax, if you were willing to abandon them without at least preparing them for you to leave them on their own."

Her smile returned. "You wouldn't?"

497

"No," he whispered.

"You understand?"

He nodded, having difficulty finding his voice. "Even though it will break my heart to have you gone from my world, I understand that I have to let you do this."

She laid her hand on the side of his face as she rested her head against him. "Only for now. I promise it will only be for a while." Her lips trembled as she held back tears. "But I have to go back while we have the chance you have just given us. You've saved our world, if we act quickly. I need to see to it that we use what you have just done to make sure we strike while we have this chance to end it."

"I know," he said as he looked away, unable to bear it.

She reached up and turned his face down to look at her. "I swear, Alex, I'll be back as soon as I can. My life is yours now. Even if I'm not here, I'm yours. Now and always."

Tears ran down his face as he kissed her, never wanting it to end.

62.

ALEX MADE HIS WAY ALONE through the forests that were now his. He was in a daze.

Tears running down his face mixed with the gentle rain that felt as if the sky were reaching out to gently touch him in sympathy.

It all seemed surreal.

He was in love with a woman from another world. He had just fought a battle between worlds. He had just saved his world from killers who would have murdered people in the thousands.

He wondered if he really was nuts.

He wiped his nose on the back of his hand as he looked up at a patch of sky he could see through an opening in the trees. He imagined Jax's world out there somewhere.

She was out there, somewhere.

He didn't even know where "somewhere" was.

He walked on without seeing anything. His mind saw only her. He thought only of her. He wanted only her.

His world was empty without her.

Alex sighed. Life would have been so much simpler had he fallen in love with an Earth girl.

He smiled, then, thinking that she must be thinking something rather similar.

After she had gone, he'd spent the night alone in the place of the gateway. He hated to leave the last spot he had seen her. They both wished she could have stayed for a while, stayed longer, stayed the night, stayed the week, the month, the year.

Forever.

But she couldn't. She had to strike while they had the chance to end it. She had to press that advantage now if her people were to live, to have the chance to be free of the sorrow Radell Cain had set loose on them and her world.

Alex was proud of her. She was strong. It would have been easy to stay. But she was strong. Her people needed her.

At least for a while.

Along the way back, Alex had come across the bodies of the men he had killed on the way to get to Jax and the gateway. He didn't want their bodies lying about in his woods. He activated their life-lines and sent them back.

Near the end of the day Alex finally reached his Cherokee, parked beside the stream. He was tired from the long hike back from Castle Mountain.

There was a white pickup parked there as well. On the door it said "Daggett Trust."

He was somehow not surprised that Hal Halverson would be there waiting for him. The man was sitting on a rock nearby. He rose up when he saw Alex coming, stretching to look back up the trail. His face was a picture of ferocity colored with alarm.

"Where's Jax? Is she all right?"

PRIVATE ARCHITECTURE
Masterpieces of the Twentieth Century

ROBERTO SCHEZEN

Introduction by Peter Blake • Text by Susan Doubilet

THE MONACELLI PRESS

I will return to the Villa Savoye in a moment, and to the other twenty-nine houses of the twentieth century. But first a word or two about the collection as a whole.

What is so amazing about this collection of houses is how *different* they all are from each other. In most historic collections, there is a distant resemblance: a resemblance of period, of style, of detail, and of place. Most Japanese houses of the Heijan period, for example, have an unmistakable family resemblance, even though they were constructed over a period of some four hundred years—as do most Tudor houses of the fifteenth and sixteenth centuries, most stuccoed Mediterranean villas of almost any period, and most classical and neoclassical residences of the past and of the present.

But most of the houses photographed by Roberto Schezen seem to have much less in common, although they were all built over a period of almost exactly one hundred years: Frank Lloyd Wright's "organic" fantasies have virtually nothing in common with the Villa Savoye—or with Mies van der Rohe's house for Dr. Edith Farnsworth. Pierre Chareau's Maison de Verre shares almost nothing with Adalberto Libera's Villa Malaparte on the island of Capri. (Actually, the Maison de Verre really seems more "modern" than Libera's red stone fortress on Capri—which is odd, since the Maison de Verre was in fact constructed some ten years earlier!)

Even two houses that seem to be almost identical at first glance—like Philip Johnson's Glass House in Connecticut and Dr. Farnsworth's house outside Chicago—turn out, upon closer inspection, to be very different: the first is entirely symmetrical on all of its exteriors while the latter is determinedly *a*symmetrical (and hence presumably more "modern"); the first is firmly planted on the ground, while the second seems to float in midair, several feet above terra firma!

Why are these houses, and most of our houses, so different from each other? The reasons are fairly obvious: there is really no excuse for two houses, designed by different architects, for different clients, on different sites, with different budgets, in different climates, using different materials, and responding to different programs—to mention only half a dozen variables that govern most sensitive designs—to be anything but superficially alike. And since humanity has built vastly more houses in the past century than ever before in a comparable period, it has been possible—indeed, unavoidable—to build in vastly different manners or styles.

Yet, despite their enormous differences, these houses seem to fall into two or three distinct categories: there are those that are works of high technology, at least in intent and in spirit; there are those that are works of romance, works of humanism, works of nature—again in intent and spirit. And there are those that fall in between.

The Villa Savoye, on the cover of this book, is an abstraction, a mathematical composition of great beauty and precision, an intellectual exercise; whereas Fallingwater, Frank Lloyd Wright's masterpiece at Bear Run, Pennsylvania, is a romantic poem, a symphony in praise of nature. No two buildings could be more different in spirit and in intent.

The Villa Savoye is a modern, twentieth-century reinterpretation of the Athens Acropolis: a work of pure geometric art, raised against the sky like a modern Parthenon. But Wright's Fallingwater is as much a part of the rocks and the forest and the cliffs and the water as humanity could possibly make it. It is not an imposition on or invasion of nature but a perfect fusion of building and earth. The landscape of Bear Run would seem incomplete without Fallingwater—and vice versa; whereas the Villa Savoye could be built anywhere—and, in fact, Le Corbusier proposed to build a suburban cluster of *twenty* Villas Savoye near Buenos Aires! (Fortunately, nothing came of that project.)

To understand how intimately Fallingwater relates to its landscape, it is not quite enough to look at photographs of the residence afloat above the waterfall; one should visit the place, discover for oneself how the house relates to its natural setting through the views from various spaces *inside* the building to the exterior. There are expanses of glass that Wright designed, very carefully, to focus upon a beautiful tree or an expanse of nearby forest; and there are interior spaces that begin to "sing," almost literally, when the patterns of sunlight and shade spread and move across walls and flagstone floors. The house is not merely an object to be admired from the outside—it is a natural phenomenon that enriches the lives of those who live inside.

The Villa Savoye is a very different sort of animal: it is a political, urbanistic pronouncement about the nature of modern cities as Le Corbusier saw them. The house is raised off the ground on what its architect liked to call "pilotis"—columns that open up the ground floor of the urban scene to vehicular and pedestrian traffic. Its next level, one flight up, is not merely an enclosed living space—it is also a walled, private garden, a patio that in effect doubles the space of the enclosed rooms within. And the roof is what Le Corbusier liked to call the "fifth facade"—a recapture, for pedestrian use, of the footprint of the building. The roof, largely flat, becomes a great public space, accessible from the enclosed living areas below, with views into the distance, and with days of sunlight and breezes. The villa is really an abstraction of what Le Corbusier called his Ville Radieuse—Radiant City—a small-scale diagram of his vision of humankind's future habitat. One gathers that M. Savoye may not have seen it in quite that way—he thought Le Corbusier's Maison de Week-End was much too expensive, and preferred to stay in Paris. Madame was a little more sympathetic.

▲▼▲

"Form follows function"—a dictum usually attributed to the architect Louis Sullivan—does not seem to apply to many of the buildings in this collection. Almost every one of the houses documented here was designed for one specific purpose and for one specific client, but subsequently underwent some remarkable transformation in purpose and ownership. The Tugendhat House in Brno, in what used to be called Czechoslovakia, experienced more changes in function (though just barely in form) than most structures of the twentieth century. It was designed by Ludwig Mies van der Rohe in the late 1920s, for Fritz and Grete Tugendhat, whose families had been involved in the textile business for several generations. The Tugendhats lived there for seven or eight happy years until the Nazis invaded Czechoslovakia; the family fled to Venezuela to escape Nazi persecution.

I first visited the house in 1962, when it had become part and parcel of a determinedly Stalinist utopia. The residence had by this time been transformed into a gymnasium for handicapped children; their doctors occupied the lower level of the house, using the servants' quarters as examination rooms. Prior to that, the house had been used for a great variety of purposes: it served as the home of Albert Messerschmidt, the German aircraft manufacturer for German troops (who cooked on an open fire inside the residence), and, like the Villa Savoye, as a stable during the German occupation. Subsequently, the building became a ballet school, and it was also used as a studio for photographers. After Czechoslovakia had become democratic again, it was used as a conference center; leaders of the Czechs and the Slovaks met there to plan their amicable political divorce. Today the Tugendhat House is an officially designated historic landmark, and it is being restored with great care by authorities, with help from various sources in many parts of the world.

The restoration of the house/ballet school/gymnasium/conference center is not without problems. The Germans and the Soviets who occupied Brno before, during, and after World War II did not treat the building with the respect it deserved: some of the beautifully detailed partitions had been removed; the dazzling white linoleum floor in the living areas had been painted red; and the huge, sliding glass walls had been replaced with rather more conventional steel-framed sash. But the elegant cruciform and chrome-plated steel columns looked as perfect as they must have looked on day one, as did the specially designed and fabricated door hardware and much else.

When I returned to the United States from my visit to Czechoslovakia, I showed Mies the color slides I had taken of the Tugendhat House in its new guise as a gymnasium. "I guess they had to paint the floor red given the political situation," Mies said. It didn't seem to bother him all that much. The freestanding onyx wall in the living area was in perfect condition. Most of the Mies-designed furniture, largely freestanding, had been removed and much of it sold; it has been replaced, in recent years, with identical chairs and tables. Fritz Tugendhat, according to his wife, Grete, was a "passionate photographer," and his photographs documented many of the original details and furnishings of the house—they have been helpful in restoration.

The glass houses—both Mies's and those inspired by his drawings—fall between Fallingwater and the Villa Savoye—between romance and technology—in spirit. They are precisely geometric in their linear configurations, like twentieth-century diagrams, and they relate to the surrounding landscape in dramatic ways. Even so, these relationships to nature clearly differ from each other: as pointed out earlier, the Farnsworth House is raised off the ground and divorced from it, whereas Philip Johnson's Glass House, though hardly Wrightian, tightly hugs the earth, as if there were no tomorrow. There are other differences as well: the Glass House reflects the trees and the bushes around it, and sometimes disappears in the reflections of its natural habitat—visually, at least. The Farnsworth House, meanwhile, reflects the sky, which makes it seem even more "afloat," more divorced from the ground.

Aside from the reflective surfaces and the steel bones that characterize the Farnsworth and Johnson houses, and give them a familial resemblance, something else makes the two structures siblings under the same glass skins: both houses are shaped by repetitive spaces between columns and beams. This structural module is something that has characterized much of modern architecture from its very beginning—and, indeed, has characterized much formal, classical architecture from its earliest days in every part of the world.

The buildings designed by Louis Kahn adhered to a similar repetitive rhythm. But in addition to the modular, structural discipline found in the work of Mies van der Rohe and others, Kahn offered something entirely new: he introduced a repetitive, spatial pattern that was much more closely attuned to the way people use his buildings—a repetitive system of three- or four-dimensional modules closely related to the spatial experiences of people as they progressed through his buildings.

Kahn's Fisher and Korman houses, both in Pennsylvania, are shaped not so much by structural discipline as by repetitive "servant spaces," which usually contain support functions—bathrooms, kitchens, stairs, and so on—and make the much larger spaces between them habitable. Kahn made these servant spaces into highly visible, repetitive accents (often towers) that can double as structural points of reference. Such a design puts Kahn on the technology side of the scale—though the romantic qualities of his work cannot be denied.

Frank Lloyd Wright was committed to a high degree of structural discipline as well, and to an expression of different kinds of functional spaces. But he was primarily committed to an architecture in intimate harmony with nature—so much so that several of his buildings are clearly reminiscent of organic, natural forms. The Guggenheim Museum, in New York, for example, is a great concrete snail, and several of his unbuilt projects suggest seashells or the leaves and petals of flowers in their details and overall forms.

It is not clear whether Wright ever saw any of Antoni Gaudí's buildings around Barcelona—or if he was even aware of them. (In any event, he was not likely to have given credit to Gaudí's genius or to that of anyone else as a possible influence on his work!) But Gaudí, quite openly, gave credit to the forms of nature in the shaping of his own work; and the Palau Güell, in Barcelona, is a lovely example of the way its architect created his buildings in harmony with the natural forms he found in his native Catalonia.

When I first saw Gaudí's buildings, I was staying in a little town called Cadaqués, on the Costa Brava a few dozen miles north of Barcelona. Not far from Cadaqués there is a small harbor, called Port-Lligat, and I discovered by chance that Gaudí used to spend many of his summer holidays here, on one of the pebbly beaches of the Mediterranean. Those pebbles were unlike any I had seen elsewhere along this coast—they were either curvilinear and plastic in form, as if created by the sculptor Henry Moore, or they were jagged and distinctly hostile in configuration, like the kinds of fragments one might find in a volcanic crater. Both of these distinct elements kept appearing on Gaudí's buildings, including the house he designed for the Count Eusebi Güell, a textile manufacturer who became a close friend and constant patron.

Güell commissioned Gaudí to design a half-dozen buildings and parks for him—all of which continue to enhance their sites in the Catalan capital. The count's house, Palau Güell, became a major cultural center for Barcelona, a meeting place for artists and politicians, poets, clergymen, and musicians. The building was completed in 1889, and it was the first of several important structures Gaudí designed and built for Count Güell, most of which are still in place in Barcelona and are universally admired. Several of the artists whom Gaudí met and worked with in the course of designing the Palau Güell collaborated with him on later projects, including the curvilinear Casa Milá and the fantastic Church of the Sagrada Familia, a building whose design and construction occupied most of his life and one that is still being completed—more or less in the spirit of Gaudí—as this is written.

Although Gaudí's later buildings became more sculptural than the Palau Güell, this residence has certain dramatic interior spaces that seem almost theatrical in character; its later service as Barcelona's Theater Museum may thus be seen as well suited. The building is not only remarkable as an early work by a young designer (Gaudí was thirty-four years old when he began to work on it); it is remarkable, too, for its extraordinary use of beautiful woods and metals, put together with exquisite workmanship. Gaudí's father had been a metalsmith, and Gaudí had learned from him how to create the most elaborate grilles and railings. These, plus other decorative fantasies on the roof of the building, made this villa one of the most memorable apparitions in the city.

The most intricate examples of ironwork in the Palau Güell are the grilles that fill the two front doors (one an entrance, the other an exit). These doors are framed by parabolic stone arches, a shape that Gaudí seems to have adopted throughout his life as symbolic of modern structural engineering. The parabolic arches—in place of more conventional frames of Euclidean configuration—became a trademark of much of Gaudí's work, all the way to the Sagrada Familia. In the entrance and exit doors of the Palau Güell, and in the domed ceiling of the tall living room, Gaudí's infatuation with parabolic arches became most evident. "The Catalans," he said, "have a natural sense of plasticity." This house is a perfect example.

▲▼▲

Most of the other houses in this collection relate, in one way or another, in their sense of romance and their sense of technology, to the architecture of Wright, Le Corbusier, or Mies van der Rohe—or to all three: Libera's Villa Malaparte, though very Mediterranean in spirit, obviously owes a great deal to Wright's love affair with nature; Alvar Aalto's Villa Mairea, about a hundred miles northwest of Helsinki, close to the west coast of Finland, owes something to Mies van der Rohe's court-house projects, and something to Wright's infatuation with natural forms. But most of all the Villa Mairea owes its special mix of remarkable qualities to the poetic genius of Alvar Aalto, who had a great talent for blending seemingly diverse concepts into coherent works of art.

Aalto was an extraordinarily sensitive designer: all of his buildings responded, in every detail, to the ways in which he thought people would use and enjoy them. The Villa Mairea, built in the late 1930s, contained many interior and exterior surfaces of wood, naturally finished. But in this case, the wood slats on the walls and floors and even on steel columns were not only soft textures to please the eye; they were thought of as surfaces that would be soft to the human *touch*. The clients for whom this summer villa was designed—Maire and Harry Gullichsen—enjoyed having friends over for dances, and so Aalto selected a Norwegian beech flooring for a part of the villa's living area (rather than flagstone, which he used elsewhere), so that guests would have a softer wood surface to dance on. As in other Aalto buildings, the steel columns that formed the structure of the villa were wrapped in caning—but only where people might touch them, not above or below.

There is a distinct sense that this villa was walked through—mentally—by its architect as he designed it, and that he thought of every aspect of the experience of living in and enjoying the place as he drew up the plans. The Gullichsens were very close to Aalto in several respects—they owned the Artek Company, which manufactured Aalto's curvilinear, laminated-birch furniture; and they assisted the architect in the installation of some of the exhibits he designed for World's Fairs and similar events. The Artek furniture is still being manufactured, and it is considered among the most innovative design of the century. The Gullichsens' house became known as the Villa Mairea in honor of Maire Gullichsen.

The humanism that was conveyed in all of Aalto's work differs markedly from the "machine for living" attitudes expressed in Le Corbusier's and Mies van der Rohe's houses. Le Corbusier would have painted the columns white, or left the surfaces unfinished, in what he referred to as "béton brut." And in Mies's houses, the columns would have been (and were) chrome-plated. Aalto's work also differed quite markedly from the humanism of Wright's buildings. Wright, one of the century's most interesting egomaniacs, considered humanism in architecture a quality that would please and celebrate one particular human—himself; Aalto's humanism was clearly an expression of his clients' needs and interests above all.

That does not mean that Aalto's work was not an expression of his own special talents. In every Aalto building there is a special quality that is rarely found in the work of others: the sense of touch. Surfaces on walls and floors and in surrounding gardens are not merely collages to please the eye; they are there to be touched, to be experienced in all sorts of ways by those who use the buildings. There is a kind of dialogue between the architect and the clients that one rarely senses in houses designed by others; and in the Villa Mairea the dialogue often lapses into poetry. Not bad for a mere building! And possibly the perfect midpoint between technology and romance.

Readers of this book—a collection of remarkable photographs of remarkable houses—may notice that, oddly, none of the pictures shows any people. It struck me as strange at first, but then it became clearer that if human beings had been in evidence, their presence would almost certainly have been staged. So the absence of human beings, in a sense, adds to the realism of the images; for the way these houses have been photographed suggests that you—the reader and observer—are invited to enter into the picture and into the architecture. And you should do so—especially since nobody else seems to be in residence at the moment.

In fact, some of the houses appear almost as beautiful stage sets, inviting us to participate and to perform. It would be hard to imagine a more extraordinary stage set than Luis Barragán's Gilardi house with its pool and dramatic, cantilevered staircase leading down to it. One can easily imagine a procession of swimmers skipping down those steps, as in a scene from a Broadway musical. And one can easily imagine Dr. Edith Farnsworth making a dramatic appearance via the terrace at one end of the Farnsworth House—as indeed I saw her appear one weekend in the 1950s, before the house was bought by that extraordinary "collector" of architecture, Peter Palumbo, who will see to it that the house—and all its polished coats of pure white enamel—is preserved in all of its glory in perpetuity.

And one can also imagine Richard Neutra in what may be his best house, the multilevel Lovell House in Los Angeles. He was quite an actor himself, and he designed the residence in 1927, perhaps in anticipation of a wonderful movie set such as *The Shape of Things to Come* or some other futuristic production. In other words, these houses—all of them—relate to a significant experience in some part of our century—and they celebrate that experience in ways that no other medium can match. They are "dream houses," because all of them convey a sense of magic, of unreality that a more pedestrian architecture is never likely to achieve. And they all depict architecture at its most fantastic—after all, who in his or her right mind would build and live in a house that is all glass, or in a house that sits on a waterfall?

And yet these wonderful houses *were* built, and they *were* inhabited; and they continue to excite those who still live in them, and continue to excite the young students of architecture who visit them, and who can barely imagine that such things happened in the real world.

And yet they did, and will again.

NOTES ON THE HOUSES

SUSAN DOUBILET

WE WHO LOVE TO LOOK AT ARCHITECTURE—VIA PICTURES OR THE real thing—often note with fascination how the greatest architecture-gazers of all, namely architects, learn from one another in countless ways. It is an aspect that has become increasingly valid and nuanced as the twentieth century has progressed, with advances in photography, international travel, and the exchange of information. This very idea—concepts borrowed and transformed, often into totally different contexts—constitutes one of the themes in the texts accompanying this book's photographs. A thread can be observed, for example, extending from Frank Lloyd Wright's open plan ideas, known to European architects through the Wasmuth publications of his early work, to Adolf Loos's *Raumplan* principle, Le Corbusier's free plan, and Mies van der Rohe's flowing spaces.

Another discernible theme is the selection of building materials by each of the architects to underscore the concept of the house. Pierre Chareau, for example, chose his materials for their functional effectiveness—though the end result was full of style. Richard Meier, like Le Corbusier in his Purist period, uses materials for their planar emphasis. Frank Lloyd Wright chose his from the natural resources of the region, as an expression of "organic" architecture. Eliel Saarinen used materials that would reveal the craftsmanship of the artisans who worked for him. Mies van der Rohe and Philip Johnson used glass and steel similarly, and yet quite differently. The list, of course, goes on.

In attempting to understand the forces of design at work in some of the houses, certain details about the clients can provide insight: Malaparte's peculiar character, for example, must have had an impact on Adalberto Libera's designs for the villa. In the case of the Villa Noailles, the client made sure that artist friends from his circle were involved in the realization of his house by Robert Mallet-Stevens. The Franks' needs, in contrast, were largely ignored by Peter Eisenman; even their name was omitted in the identification of their house, which was called House VI. These stories can help give substance to the story of a house's creation.

Finally, the reader who takes time to understand the floor plans will be well rewarded. When the plans are studied in combination with the photographs, the mind's eye can begin to reconstruct the three-dimensional experience of walking through the houses. Nothing, of course, replaces reality, but superb images coupled with imagination are a worthy substitute.

My thanks go to Suzanne Stephens, for her advice and assistance over the years, to my friend and colleague Daralice Donkervoet Boles, for her always inspiring observations, and to James Elliot Benjamin, my insightful researcher.

PALAU GÜELL

Barcelona, Spain
1885–1889

ANTONI GAUDÍ

1852–1926

THE ORNATE, ALMOST PHANTASMAGORIC CREATIONS OF THE
Catalan architect Antoni Gaudí seem to emerge uniquely from their
creator's rich fantasies. Undulating, apparently irrational forms are
clad in colorful crushed tiles and elaborated by imaginative, sinuous
ironwork, particularly at the roof, where outcroppings appear to
foreshadow monstrous evolutions of natural creatures. At the basis
of the work, however, are numerous external influences, including
the nineteenth-century French theorist Eugène-Emanuel Viollet-le-
Duc, whose principles of Structural Rationalism called for forms to
emerge from regional factors and natural, rather than conventional-
ized, structure. Gaudí's curvaceous constructions incorporate both
the traditional technique of the Catalan vault—corbeled layers of
thin tiles held together with thick mortar, eliminating the need for
formwork—and the equilibrating, stiffening form of the parabolic
arch. The voluptuous roofs of the entrance pavilion at Gaudí's Parque
Güell (1903–14), for example, are hyperbolic parabolas; the colorful

Opposite: View up into cupola over salon.

Above: Salon windows overlooking street.

Opposite: Detail at entrance.

Overleaf: Parabolic entrance arches.

DANA HOUSE

Springfield, Illinois
1902–1904

FRANK LLOYD WRIGHT

1867–1959

O F ALL THE ARCHITECTS CONSIDERED "MODERN," FRANK LLOYD
Wright was probably the most influential. For architects, his open
spatial plan was nothing short of revolutionary, especially in Europe,
where his drawings were assembled in a portfolio issued by Wasmuth
Publishers as early as 1910. The Wasmuth edition influenced virtually
every knowledgeable European architect of the time. And in the realm
of the ordinary builder, an everyman's model that combined the horizontal thrust and natural materials of Wright's Prairie house and the
one-story-with-carport economy of his Usonian house was reproduced
across America, particularly in the West, and became known as the
ranch house.

Among the images now most commonly associated with Wright
himself—along with the more abstract Fallingwater of 1936 (page 198)
and the far more abstract Solomon R. Guggenheim Museum of 1943—
is that of the Prairie house prototype, whose wide roofs hover close

Opposite: Detail of art glass.

Above: Seating area.
Opposite: Galleria.

Above: Passageway.
Opposite: Billiard table.
Overleaf: Entrance facade.

HILL HOUSE
Helensburgh, Scotland
1902–1903

CHARLES RENNIE MACKINTOSH
1868–1928

HILL HOUSE REFLECTS THE DICHOTOMY WITHIN ITS DESIGNER: his deeply felt Scottish roots and his cosmopolitan, startlingly brilliant, modern outlook. As the house is approached, it is seen rising from the landscape of suburban Glasgow like some severe Celtic castle. Yet as it is entered, it reveals itself as open, delicate, and fresh.

Charles Rennie Mackintosh's star rose meteorically and then fell quickly; his architectural commissions, though greatly influential, were limited in number. In the mid-1890s, while still a student, he founded (with his future wife, Margaret Macdonald, and her sister and brother-in-law) the Glasgow Four. The group's achievements in graphic and furniture design were published and exhibited nationally and internationally, exerting a major influence on supporters of the Vienna Secession movement, among others. Mackintosh's work, which incorporates sinuous surface decoration inspired by forms from nature, is identified with the Art Nouveau style; at the same time, these stylized organic forms, in

Opposite: Inset detail.

combination with patterns of straight lines and small squares, are applied with restraint and within a framework of plain, rectilinear surfaces. His most important project, the Glasgow School of Art, spanned his years of greatest productivity, between 1896 and 1909, bearing witness to his rich artistic development. The first stage of its construction, with its E-shaped plan and flexible arrangement of spaces, demonstrates the architect's fundamental Gothic Revival training; the second stage, the west wing and the double-height library, revealed his increasingly refined originality. The aesthetic for which Mackintosh is best known, however, contrasts with the dark, austere forms of the art school and the more intensely colored work of his final years, and is reflected in his 1903–4 designs for the Willow Tea Rooms in Glasgow, characterized by glowing white surfaces that are decorated sparsely but with sensuous motifs.

Hill House, dating from 1902–3, reveals Mackintosh's Gothic Revival roots as well as his signature style, but the two aspects are seen side by side, not merged. The house's roughcast exterior appears to be a simplification of a traditional baronial mansion, reflecting the medievalist, regionalist approach of the English Arts and Crafts architects of the preceding generation. In contrast, the interior, designed (like most of Mackintosh's projects) down to the last detail of fabric and furniture and created in association with Margaret Macdonald, is startlingly original. From the great hall, rendered dramatic by dark-stained wood beams and paneling, one enters a series of white rooms whose starkness is enlivened by the syncopation of small squares and softened by gently curved details and touches of violet and silver. The furniture—for example, the still-popular ladder-back chair—has an architectural function, as is usual in Mackintosh's work. While the pieces are simple individually, they function as screens and create a complex system of spaces within spaces.

Overleaf: Living room.

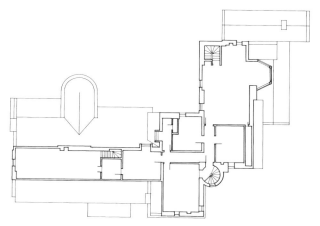

THIRD FLOOR

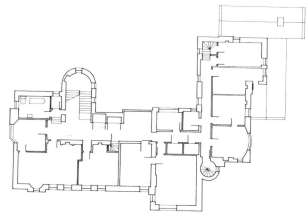

SECOND FLOOR

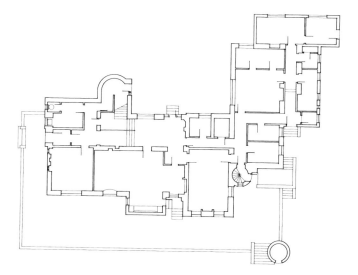

FIRST FLOOR

0   3 m

0   10 ft

49

Above: Fireplace and wardrobe doors.
Opposite: Fireplace in living room.

Above: Dressing table in bedroom.
Opposite: Bedroom.

Above and opposite: Hall.
Overleaf: South facade.

Above: View down from second story of oval entrance hall.

Opposite: View from entrance hall to exterior.

Above: View to ceiling of entrance hall.
Opposite: Upper level of entrance hall.
Overleaf: Stair hall.

Above: Library alcove.
Opposite: Library.

Above and opposite: Marble bathroom.

GAMBLE HOUSE

Pasadena, California
1908

GREENE AND GREENE

C. S. Greene, 1868–1957
H. M. Greene, 1870–1954

For the brothers Charles Sumner Greene and Henry Mather Greene, as for many Americans around the end of the nineteenth century, California offered opportunity, refuge, and inspiration. The brothers, who had studied architecture at the Massachusetts Institute of Technology, visited Pasadena when they were in their mid-twenties, and, enchanted, stayed on. To the foundation of their classical training were added new influences: the inspiring oasis landscape and the honest simplicity of expression of Spanish mission architecture. These influences were reinforced by the Greenes' close study of the construction methods and philosophy of two far-flung sources, the American Arts and Crafts movement and Japanese design. As a result, the brothers developed an architecture that eventually influenced residential design throughout the region and across the country, and became known as the California bungalow style. Among the features of Greene and Greene's houses were broad sloping roofs, overhanging eaves, projecting rafters, and stained board-and-batten wood siding. Contrasting

Opposite: Tiffany stained-glass window.

VILLA SKYWA/PRIMAVESI

Vienna, Austria
1913–1915

JOSEF HOFFMANN

1870–1956

JOSEF HOFFMANN, ONE OF THE MOST BRILLIANT OF OTTO
Wagner's academy students, joined the anti-academic Vienna Secession
group in 1896 and soon became its leading architect. Within a few
years he moved away from the organic curvilinearity of the Secession-
ists toward a more sober and eventually classical mode. With fellow
designer Kolo Moser, he established the Wiener Werkstätte to produce
not only architecture but also furniture and decorative objects. His
objects and his buildings, such as the Purkersdorf Sanatorium of
1903–5 and his masterpiece, the Palais Stoclet in Brussels of 1910–15,
were revolutionary in their cubic abstraction. Classical in their proportions and symmetry, they made almost no explicit allusions in their
details to historical models.

The Villa Skywa/Primavesi of 1913–15 was in some ways a throwback.
Designed for a social class and lifestyle that with the dissolution of the
Austro-Hungarian monarchy would soon disappear, its expression is

SCHINDLER/CHASE HOUSE

West Hollywood, California
1921–1922

R. M. SCHINDLER

1887–1953

R. M. SCHINDLER'S VISION OF ARCHITECTURE WAS LIFE ITSELF:
a pragmatist, he designed as much on the construction site as on the
drafting board. As one of Otto Wagner's students in Vienna, he learned
to express distinctly each of a building's elements. From his experience
as a painter, he developed a sophisticated understanding of flattened,
non-perspectival cubist space and composition. And as a young employee of Adolf Loos, he was introduced to the open planning ideas of
Frank Lloyd Wright and the structural expression of the Chicago
School, and became attracted to the United States. In 1914, he made
his way to Chicago, where he was disappointed by the bottom-line
myopia of commercial architects. From there, as an employee of
Wright, he moved to Los Angeles. In that city of hospitable climate
and open lifestyle Schindler, like his compatriot Richard Neutra a few
years later, came into his own.

Schindler's designs represented a most Californian brand of mod-

Opposite: Concrete wall panels with glass infill strips.

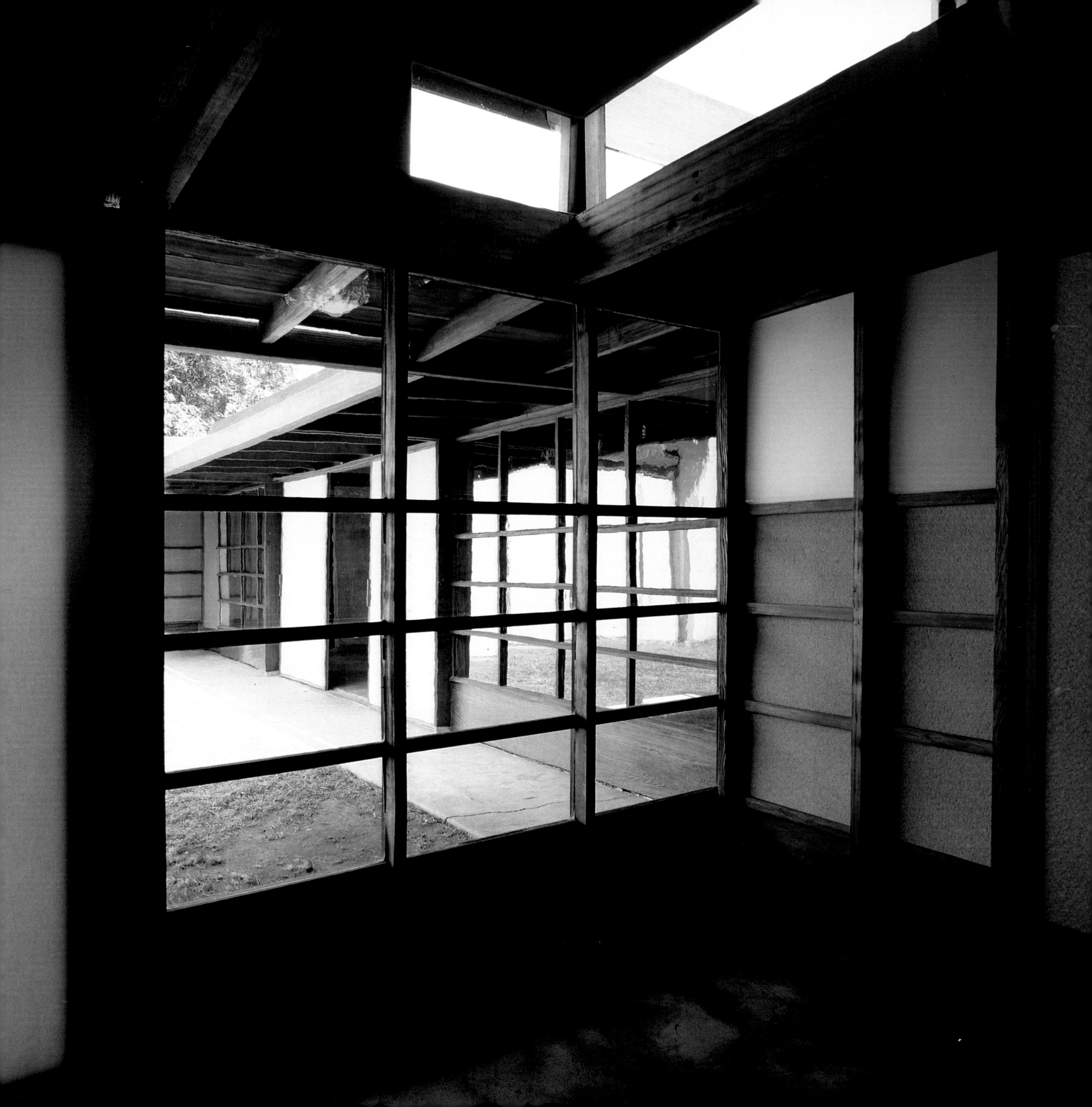

Above: Corner detail.
Opposite: View from living space to patio.
Overleaf: Patio.

VILLA NOAILLES

Hyères, France
1923–1926

ROBERT MALLET-STEVENS

1886–1945

THE FRENCH-BORN ROBERT MALLET-STEVENS HAD A TALENT
for recognizing interesting new ideas in art and architecture and
synthesizing them in glamorous, sophisticated works. As the son of an
important art dealer and the nephew of Josef Hoffmann's client for the
Palais Stoclet, the young Mallet-Stevens—a student at the progressive
Ecole Spéciale d'Architecture—moved among the artists and architects
of Europe. He turned for inspiration first to the Secession and then to
cubism and the de Stijl and Art Deco movements. His ability to create
boldly sculptured geometric buildings was revealed by his work in the
mid-to-late 1920s, which included the five concrete houses on the
Parisian street named for him. But in 1923, when he was hired to
design a villa on the Mediterranean for the Count de Noailles, he had
no completed buildings to his credit, only interiors and movie sets.

The count, who had rejected Le Corbusier for the commission because
of his brusque personality, was able to manipulate the inexperienced

Opposite: Francis Jourdan clock.

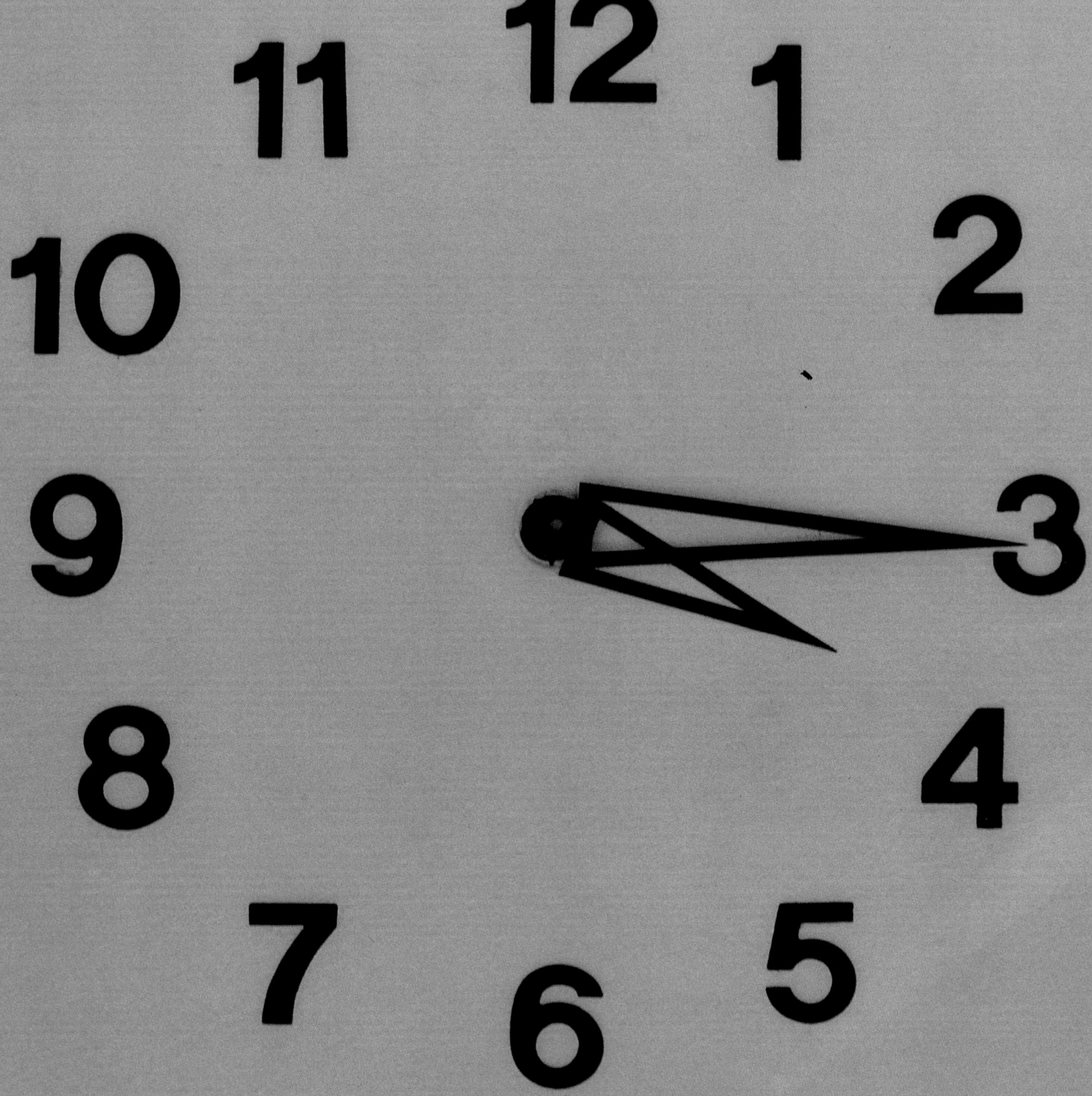
12
1
2
3
4
5
6
7
8
9
10
11

Mallet-Stevens easily. He used him or replaced him by other architects at will, as the commission grew during construction from a small country house to a large aggregation of wings and pavilions to accommodate the Noailles circle of socialites and artists. But Mallet-Stevens made a number of intelligent decisions in the design, and was able to incorporate the work of many of his artist friends. The first decision involved the preservation of some vestiges of the convent, château, and retaining walls on the hilly, four-acre site. The retaining walls created natural terraces across the site, above which Mallet-Stevens organized the building in long, relatively unobtrusive rectangular layers facing south toward the sea. A tower designed to create a vertical counterpoint was shortened by the client, who stressed functionalism over drama. The house was built traditionally of masonry, then stuccoed to resemble the reinforced concrete the architect would have preferred.

Among the talented contributors to the house were Pierre Chareau, who designed a glass-enclosed open-air room featuring a bed hung from the ceiling; Theo van Doesburg, whose design for the walls of a small flower-arranging room was inadvertently executed upside down; and Gabriel Guevrekian, who laid out a geometric garden on a triangular, prow-shaped plot. The nautical metaphor was carried throughout the house, with long corridors, cabinlike rooms, and identical clocks by Francis Jourdan in every space. Louis Barillet designed stained-glass skylights for the windowless "pink salon," and Mallet-Stevens himself, Marcel Breuer, and Eileen Gray provided furniture designs. The villa was always thought of as a modern-day château, and in 1928 it provided the setting for Man Ray's film *Le Mystère du Chateau de Dé.*

Overleaf: Gabriel Guevrekian garden.

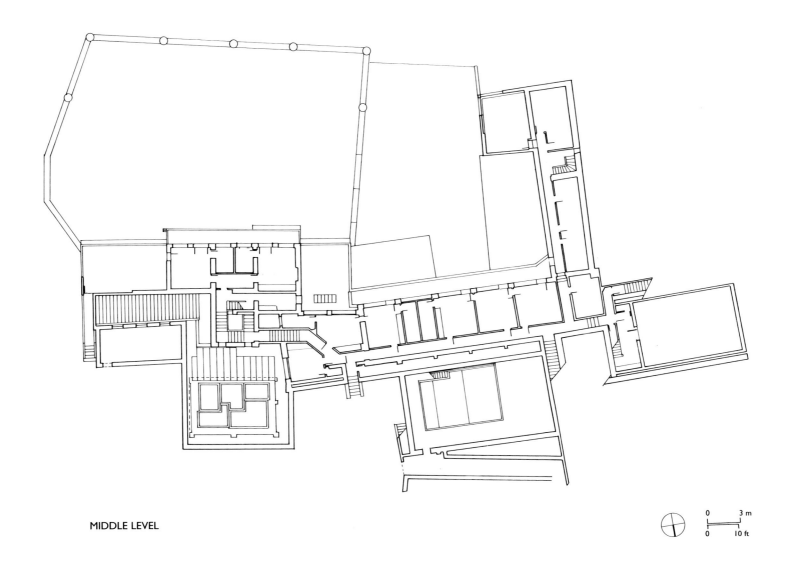

MIDDLE LEVEL

109

Above: Flower-arranging room.
Opposite: Stairhall.

Above: Pink salon.
Opposite: Louis Barillet skylights in pink salon.

Above and opposite: Garden views.
Overleaf: Entrance facade.

WITTGENSTEIN HOUSE

Vienna, Austria
1926–1928

LUDWIG WITTGENSTEIN

1889–1951

LUDWIG WITTGENSTEIN HAD ALREADY PUBLISHED HIS masterpiece of philosophy, *Tractatus Logico-Philosophicus,* when in 1926 his sister Margarethe asked him to participate in the design of her house. Their father, Karl Wittgenstein, one of the wealthiest people in Vienna, was a steel manufacturer and art patron who underwrote, among other projects, the construction of the Secession building. But the brilliant thirty-seven-year-old son was in a tormented state; he had given up his philosophy pursuits, given away his inheritance, and taken on menial jobs in the years after his World War I service. Margarethe's offer, then, was intended as a kind of therapy for her brother, who had some engineering knowledge but no architecture experience. He agreed to assist the commissioned architect, Paul Engelmann, and soon took over the design completely.

The cubic forms of the house's exterior are reminiscent of the work of Wittgenstein's compatriot Adolf Loos. The organization of the house

Opposite: Entrance and stair to central hall.

Above: Doors from dining room to terrace.
Opposite: View to entrance vestibule.

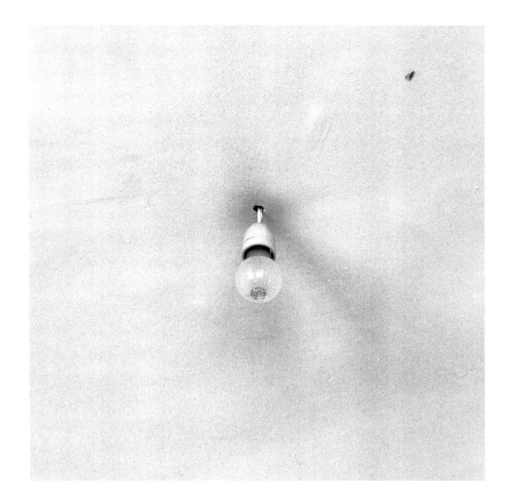

Above: Light fixture.
Opposite: Main stair.

LOVELL HOUSE
Los Angeles, California
1928–1929

RICHARD NEUTRA
1892–1970

Richard Neutra, born in Vienna, early on came to revere the United States and its machine-based culture, as did his mentor Adolf Loos; unlike Loos, he eventually realized his dream of moving permanently to America, where he soon achieved success. His first stop, Chicago, disappointed him. The modern steel skeleton, meant (he felt) to be celebrated and expressed in the manner of the Chicago school, was being buried under layers of fashionable Beaux-Arts detail. Los Angeles offered him his chance: moving there in 1925, he soon opened his own practice and was able to combine his love of industrial materials with his penchant for classical harmony, developing an architecture that was at once light, elegant, and creative.

In Los Angeles, Neutra began working alongside another Viennese émigré, R. M. Schindler, first as an employee of Frank Lloyd Wright and then independently. In 1927 Neutra wooed away a Schindler client, Dr. Philip Lovell, and built for him the house that was to bring the architect

Opposite: Stairway from upper level to living room on middle level.

Above: Stairway.
Opposite: Living room on middle level.
Overleaf: Built-in seating in living room.

SAARINEN HOUSE

Bloomfield Hills, Michigan
1928–1930

ELIEL SAARINEN

1873–1950

ELIEL SAARINEN WAS A SYNTHESIZER RATHER THAN AN innovator, but he had a clear and humanistic vision of the network that tied together the built world. His own house at the Cranbrook Academy of Art is a glowing microcosm of the bigger picture of both his life and his work. Built while he served as architect and director of the academy, the house was his family's residence, his work studio, and a meeting place for colleagues, students, artists, and clients. In this way it represented Saarinen's ideal of the home-centered artistic life, as did Hvritträsk, his house in his native Finland, which he left when he was almost fifty years old. Demonstrating the continuum of the human-made environment, the artifacts are integral to the house, which is a unit within the Cranbrook complex, itself designed following planning principles applicable to the larger world. Cranbrook, founded by newspaper mogul George Booth to raise the standards of arts and crafts in the United States, includes school buildings, dormitories, a museum, and a library, all designed by Saarinen.

Opposite: Stained-glass panel.

Above: Dressing table.
Opposite: Dining room.

Above and opposite: Master bathroom.
Overleaf: Rear facade.

MAISON DE VERRE

Paris, France
1928–1932

PIERRE CHAREAU

1883–1950

THE FRENCH ARCHITECT PIERRE CHAREAU HAD A NUMBER OF practical problems to resolve in the design of the Maison de Verre: the resulting solution—which was to constitute Chareau's primary claim to fame—was nothing short of extraordinary. His clients wished to construct a private residence and a ground-floor gynecology office on their urban lot; however, the third-floor tenant in the property's existing town house refused to move. Chareau proposed shoring up the tenant's quarters, keeping it intact, and inserting a new, structurally independent three-story unit under it in the original two-story space. This technological problem and a further one—how to introduce sufficient light into the relatively narrow site—dominated the design. Chareau and his associate, Bernard Bijvoet, approached the problem as a piece of industrial design. In doing so, they hoped to advance the state of construction by introducing new materials and fabrication methods, a goal pursued in diverse ways by many architects, from Le Corbusier to Buckminster Fuller to Norman Foster, throughout this century.

Elevator door.

To provide both privacy and luminosity at the front and back facades, the architects considered but rejected bland panes of frosted glass, finally hitting upon a variety of glass block known as the Nevada-type lens. Glass block had been used in limited expanses for floors as well as walls, but the extensive use of it for exterior facades was untried, and the manufacturer would not guarantee it. Undaunted, the architects concluded that panels four glass blocks wide by six blocks high (about seven by ten feet) would be structurally sound and easy to handle, and could be inserted into a steel grid to make up the facade. They concluded, as well, that a steel frame for the building's overall structure would provide the necessary stability and flexibility of design. On the rear garden side, clear glass could replace some glass-block panels, and terraces could cantilever freely. The frame structure allowed interior partitions to be arranged independently. Two-story spaces, extending from the ground-floor office to the doctor's second-floor study, and—most dramatically—from the second-floor salon up to the bedroom level on the third floor, demonstrate the architects' ability to manipulate space as well as their interest in avant-garde design.

The seven-by-ten-foot module was used throughout the interior, for sliding screens, bathroom fittings, and storage cabinets, which were executed in unusual materials—tin-plated steel, for example, since aluminum was rare at that time. While the architects' goals were exalted, their methods were artisanal: specific solutions were devised with crafts-people on the spot, few construction drawings having been prepared beforehand. By and large, technical solutions for the house proved not to be generally applicable; some of them were outdated as they were being executed. Nevertheless, even beyond its undeniable aesthetic achievement, the Maison de Verre continues to stand as a brilliant model for conceiving rationalized design.

Overleaf: Main stair from first floor to second floor.
Second overleaf: Front alcove of grand salon, with glass-block panels.

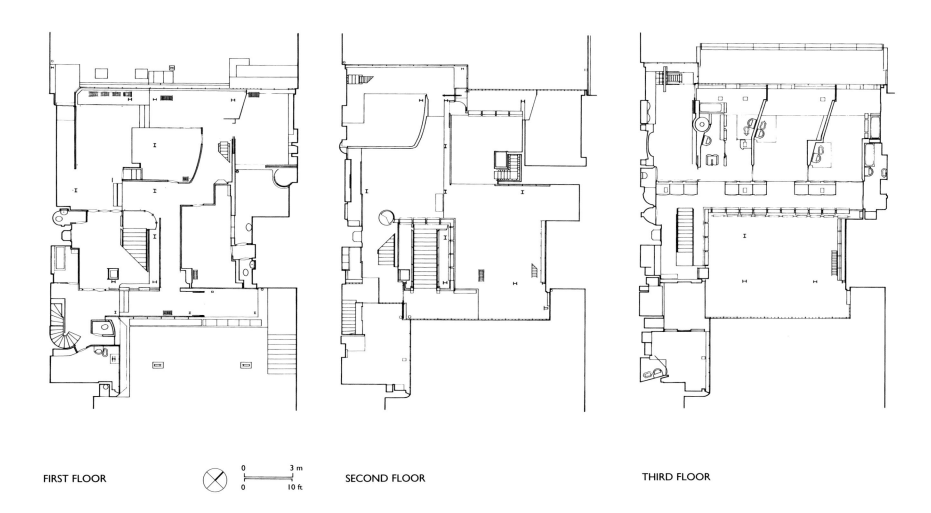

FIRST FLOOR

0   3 m
0   10 ft

SECOND FLOOR

THIRD FLOOR

VILLA SAVOYE

Poissy, France
1929–1931

LE CORBUSIER

1887–1965

THE SCULPTURAL VILLA SAVOYE, ONE OF THE MOST influential houses of the twentieth century, is the repository of the myriad ideas Le Corbusier had absorbed and transformed in the first four decades of his life.

Le Corbusier, born Charles-Edouard Jeanneret in La Chaux-de-Fonds, Switzerland, learned as a youth that structure—of objects in nature as well as buildings—was the key to form. This idea was reinforced, while his focus changed from Structural Rationalism to classicism, in subsequent jobs in Paris and Berlin, where he was introduced to modern-day technology, notably Auguste Perret's specialty, reinforced concrete. Travels through Mediterranean countries aroused his deep appreciation of the purity of ancient Classical forms. Art movements in Vienna and Paris awakened him to the idea of a new age, in which objects would be machine-produced and would, in turn, reflect technology by their very forms.

Opposite: South facade.

Above: Bathroom.

Opposite: Corridor on living level.

Above: Living room.
Opposite: Terrace.
Overleaf: View of ramp from terrace.

MÜLLER HOUSE
Prague, Czechoslovakia
1930

ADOLF LOOS
1870–1933

Adolf Loos's radically new way of conceiving interior space, known as the *Raumplan,* was first used in the 1910 retail/residential building now renowned as the Looshaus, a structure considered at the time more shocking for the plainness of its facade than for its revolutionary layout. The *Raumplan* concept was only fully developed by Loos in a series of houses built in Vienna and Prague toward the end of his career. One of the last of these was the Müller House of 1930.

In the *Raumplan,* the building is considered a volume within which spaces are freely arranged, uninhibited by the traditional assumption of continuous floor levels. The cubic exterior itself, abstract, screenlike, and modulated only by a cubic balcony and bay window, suggests this idea of the building as a volumetric container. Unlike other Loos houses, which have a mute front but more open sides and back, this

176

Opposite: Bench at entrance.

house presents a severe expression on all four sides due to its location: sited on a hill and entered from the rear, it is relatively open to view.

Inside the Müller House, a variety of stairs and split-level rooms on the second floor are tightly and ingeniously packed together and intertwined—almost like a Rubik's cube. The thirty-six-foot-wide living room, which is thirteen feet high, shares a common ceiling level with the other rooms on this story, but the floor levels are raised from one room to the next, as room heights are tailored to their use. The ceiling over the sitting area in the dining room is not as high as in the living room, where one is likely to stand and talk, and the cozy seating alcove in the ladies' sitting room, or boudoir, is even snugger. Circulation from the ground-floor entrance, where one encounters a built-in, almost sepulchral bench, through the second floor is complex: a central Z-shaped stair on the ground floor takes one up to the living room. From there, eight steps lead up laterally to the dining room; then, a corner is turned and eight more steps lead back along the central axis up to the library at the rear and to the ladies' boudoir on the side. Several steps lead back *down* from the library's entrance to its main space and from the boudoir's seating alcove to its main level. Openings provide views from the dining room and the boudoir alcove to the living room, and from the alcove across the skylit central staircase through to the dining room and its bay window, revealing the spatial relationships and relieving the density.

Finishes are rich and varied. Green Cipollin marble faces the living room's dado and piers. The dining room has a ceiling of mahogany; its granite table was designed by Loos. The library is clad in mahogany and furnished with English-style furniture, which was much admired by Loos. The boudoir is paneled in yellow satinwood.

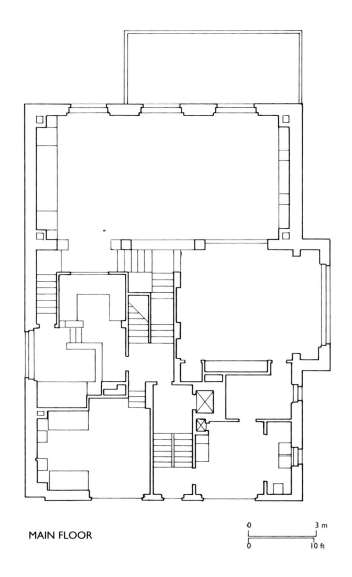

GROUND FLOOR

MAIN FLOOR

0   3 m
0   10 ft

Above and opposite: Details of marble in living room.

Overleaf: Living room looking toward main stair and dining room.

Second overleaf: Built-in sofa at one end of living room.

Above: View to skylight over stair.
Opposite: Dining room.

Above: Stair overlooking dining room.
Opposite: Boudoir.

TUGENDHAT HOUSE
Brno, Czechoslovakia
1930

LUDWIG MIES VAN DER ROHE
1886–1969

LUDWIG MIES VAN DER ROHE, CONSIDERED WITH LE CORBUSIER and Frank Lloyd Wright a founder of the modern movement, was born and spent the first five decades of his life in Germany. There he led a creative and successful professional life and served as the last director of the Bauhaus. As such, he tried to accommodate the Third Reich until freedom of expression became impossible. In 1938 he immigrated to the United States, where for the next three decades he taught and practiced prolifically. The Tugendhat House is among his early, defining designs.

Whereas Le Corbusier's Purist buildings represented the *idea* of the machine age, with white, scaleless surfaces that suggested modern efficiency but eliminated the architectonic materiality, Mies van der Rohe's work combined both materiality and intellectual rigor. Schooled practically, initially in his father's stone masonry business, and subsequently in Peter Behrens's architecture office in Berlin, Mies believed in the funda-

Opposite: Entry.

mental, philosophical beauty of refined, clearly expressed structure such as found in the neoclassical buildings of Karl Friedrich Schinkel. At the same time, he was deeply interested in the abstract sensibility of the de Stijl artists and architects, as well as in the open plans of Frank Lloyd Wright's houses. He first brought together his interests—in material, structural expression, and abstraction—in two astonishing buildings, the German Pavilion for the World Exhibition in Barcelona in 1929, and, a year later, the Tugendhat House. In both cases, the building is conceived as part of a larger spatial continuum; its roof, floor, and walls define only a portion of this continuum.

The Tugendhat House, located on a sloping site, is entered at its upper, bedroom level. A staircase leads from this level to the lower floor, which is designed as an open space whose major functions—living, dining, and study—are defined only by planes and a grid of columns. As in the Barcelona pavilion, the columns are cruciform in plan and are finished in chrome, reflecting, on the one hand, the fluting of a classical column, and, on the other, the modern, machined steel element—albeit custom-made and carefully hand-polished. The living area is divided from the study only by a flat onyx plane, and the dining area is delimited only by a curved wall of ebony-faced plywood. The furniture, designed by Mies, is placed to form part of the spatial definition. The long glass wall that defines the space's garden edge underscores Mies's idea of the continuity of space beyond the building itself: the wall can be retracted to disappear below the floor. Nevertheless, while the space is continuous from inside to outside, the floor level is well above ground level. The house is designed in harmony with nature, but it represents humanity's rational side, and as such is distinct from the natural world.

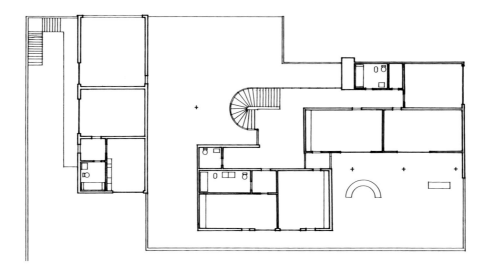

ENTRY LEVEL

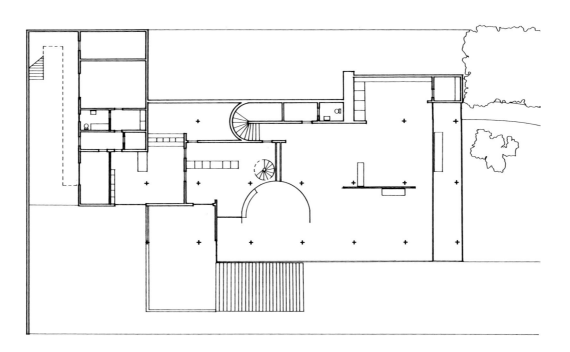

LOWER LEVEL

0   3 m
0   10 ft

193

Above: Glazed entrance hall.
Opposite: Living area.
Overleaf: Dining area.

FALLINGWATER (EDGAR J. KAUFMANN HOUSE)

Bear Run, Pennsylvania
1936

FRANK LLOYD WRIGHT

1867–1959

EVEN TODAY, FRANK LLOYD WRIGHT'S FAMED HOUSE Fallingwater epitomizes for many all that is modern and American. Totally original, it sprang full-grown from one mind and challenged all preconceived notions of architecture. The house celebrated nature yet seemed to defy a fundamental law of nature, namely gravity. It seemed almost to be alive, having lost not one iota of its spontaneity in the translation from sketch to concrete reality.

America was still suffering from the deprivations of the Great Depression when Edgar J. Kaufmann, a department store magnate, offered Frank Lloyd Wright the commission to design a four-bedroom weekend retreat (later to be augmented by a guest wing) in a forested area some miles from Pittsburgh. Kaufmann's favorite spot, and the most arresting place for the house, soon became apparent: by a waterfall within the woods. When Wright sat down to sketch his ideas, the whole design, from concept to major details, came pouring out in a

Opposite: View of cantilevers from below.

matter of hours. The house's floors took the form of concrete trays stretching out *over* (not beside) the waterfall; the trays were pinned back into the rock escarpment by means of tall fieldstone walls. The basic organization for the house grew from the Prairie house concept (an open, centrifugal plan, natural materials, and outreach into the landscape), but the mix was shaken up and reassembled for the hilly, wooded terrain. At the same time, it was executed in more modern materials—large, steel-framed plates of glass and poured concrete, the limits of which Wright pushed to the utmost. The architect, whose work had been omitted from the Museum of Modern Art's celebrated International Style exhibition of 1932, seemed to spew out the design in a fit not only of inspiration but also of revenge. If the elitist East Coast architects wanted flat roofs, he would give them flat roofs. If they wanted modernity, he would out-modern them all.

As unanticipated as Fallingwater's form was, at the same time it is so startlingly appropriate that its existence seems somehow inevitable. Tied to the land, its materials are culled from the region and its form patterned after—or so one can believe—the structure of the surrounding trees, with its vertical stone core representing the trunk and its trays the outstretched branches. The rocks on the site are allowed to break through the floor to form interior outcroppings, notably at the hearth, rendering the interiors almost cavelike. At the same time, the overall impression the house projects is *not* naturalistic, although it is rooted in nature. It provides new insight into the term *organic* as used by its largely self-taught, iconoclastic creator: each part is shaped deliberately and expressly for its use and its site, intentionally jettisoning irrelevant conventions.

Overleaf: View from south.
Second overleaf: View from northwest.
Third overleaf: View from northeast.

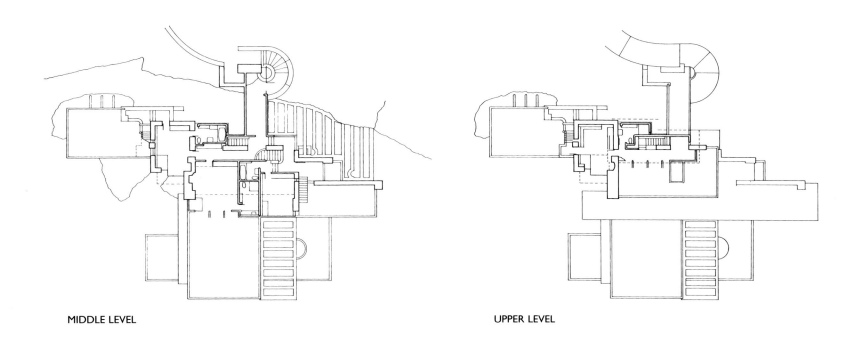

MIDDLE LEVEL

UPPER LEVEL

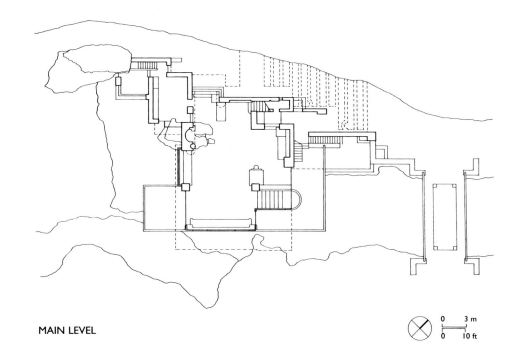

MAIN LEVEL

0   3 m
0   10 ft

Above and opposite: Open stair leading to platform above waterfall.

Overleaf: Living room.

Above: Dining area.

Opposite: Living room with fireplace.

Above: Corner desk.
Opposite: Passageway.

VILLA MAIREA

Noormarkku, Finland
1937–1939

ALVAR AALTO

1898–1976

Alvar Aalto's designs were, above all else, sensitive responses to both human needs and the natural environment, even as they reflected with great intelligence numerous important trends in twentieth-century architecture. His training in Helsinki, from 1916 to 1921, exposed him to two contrasting traditions, the National Romantic teaching of the time, which tended toward regionalism and Art Nouveau fluidity, and Scandinavian neoclassicism. By the late 1920s, news of Rationalism and Functionalism had reached Scandinavia and influenced Aalto as well. Still, throughout his prolific practice (he built close to one thousand commissions), he never lost sight of his fundamental belief, to harness technology in order to create a humane environment. The Villa Mairea, one of Aalto's most significant early works, brings together many of these ideas in an unusually poetic synthesis.

The villa was designed for Aalto's friends Maire and Harry Gullichsen, owners of a forestry firm and manufacturers of Aalto-designed

Opposite: View from east.

furniture. They, like their architect, wished to reflect the benefits of industrialization and the emancipating role of modern architecture. The villa, located in a clearing on a wooded site, defines a precinct that is clearly human-made and that unites both rational and naturalistic forms. The courtyard, which focuses on an amoeba-shaped pool, is bound on two sides by the L-shaped house, and on the other sides by an earth mound and a traditional grass-covered log sauna. The main building features an integrated 2,500-square-foot living/art gallery/dining space, which harks back to the undifferentiated living space of the Finnish peasant house.

In Villa Mairea, Aalto and his collaborator, his first wife, Aino, used numerous tactile elements that relate to nature, modern production, or primitive construction, and combined them as if they were creating a collage. Spruce poles are bundled together to hold up the free-form entrance canopy, a composition intended to represent a cluster of trees. The principal stair is lined with a screen of slender poles, another forest reference, originally planned to be of bamboo to recall Japanese design. The floor of the large living space is tiled in the main seating area and finished in oak in the gallery/library. Columns in this space are steel, wrapped in cane at the midsection or, in some cases, faced in vertical strips of wood. Artwork is stored in cabinets that can be moved to subdivide the large area into more intimate spaces. The exterior of the building employs slate, whitewashed brick, tile, and teak, among other cladding materials. The second-story art studio is sheathed in vertical wood slats, reminiscent of the undulating Finnish pavilion Aalto was designing at this time for the 1939 World's Fair in New York.

Overleaf: View from courtyard.

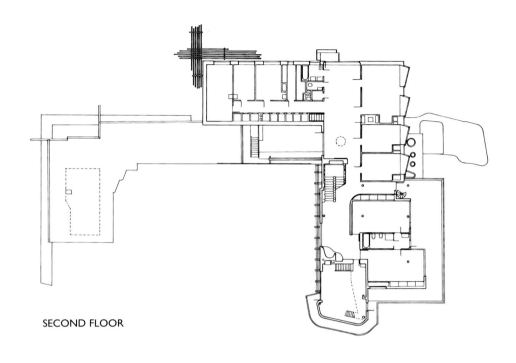

SECOND FLOOR

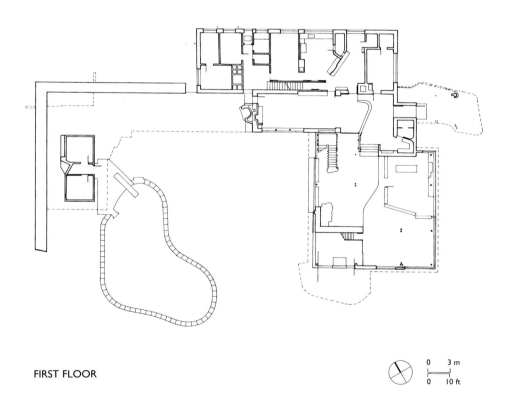

FIRST FLOOR

0   3 m
0   10 ft

219

Above: View from south.

Opposite: View from north.

Overleaf: View into wooded area from entrance canopy.

Above: Main stair.
Opposite: Living room.
Overleaf: Dining room.

VILLA MALAPARTE

Capri, Italy
1938–1940

ADALBERTO LIBERA

1903–1963

THE DESIGN OF VILLA MALAPARTE IS ASSOCIATED AS MUCH with its owner, the sometime-Fascist writer Curzio Malaparte, as it is with its sometime-Fascist architect, Adalberto Libera.

Malaparte was a chameleon, but a flamboyant one. Born Kurt Suckert, he adopted the name Malaparte and liked to claim a relationship with Bonaparte—the family's "bad side" (*mala-*), as opposed to its "good" one (*bona-*). He claimed, at times, to have designed his villa himself; he called it "Villa Come Me" because he identified closely with it. Among his fabrications was the assertion that General Rommel had been his guest at the villa. He embraced Fascism for some years and served as editor of the Fascist newspaper *La Stampa,* possibly allowing his concocted stories to mingle with the truth. He became a Communist in 1944, but did not refrain from writing for mass-circulation capitalist newspapers. When he died in 1957, he was found to have bequeathed his villa to the Chinese Communist Writer's Union.

Opposite: Giant staircase leading to roof terrace.

As to Libera, he was a Rationalist, a member of Italy's Gruppo 7 (which strove to combine futurism and traditionalism), and a founding member of the short-lived official body, the Movimento Italiano per l'Architettura Razionale. The Italian Rationalists managed to tread a line that traversed classicism, modernism, and romanticism, and accommodated to the Fascist regime. Among Libera's major commissions was the Palazzo delle Esposizione in the EUR Garden City outside Rome. Its rear facade features a daring bow-trussed curtain wall, while its front presents the city with a more compliant face, characterized by a long, quasi-Doric colonnade.

Yet not a shred of compromise is seen in Villa Malaparte, even when weighed against its powerful, uncompromising landscape. A rocky headland jutting into the Bay of Naples, the site possesses a presence by which almost any architectural form would have been cowed. Not the Villa Malaparte. A solid rectangular block fused to a long stepped pyramid, it might have been carved out of the very rock from which it appears to emerge. The funnel-shaped stairway leads to the top of the rectangular block, from which one can survey the unequaled view, protected, if at all, by a simple curved wall. Seen at close range and from the side, the building is surprisingly plain; its windows and a scarcely noticeable doorway are cut directly into the stuccoed stone wall. Inside the door, a stairway leads up to the main floor, which contains a sequence of connected rooms: a long living room, followed by two bedrooms (one for the mistress of the moment, one for the owner), followed finally by Malaparte's private sanctum, his writing studio at the edge of the promontory. The rooms are sparsely furnished, as the views are paramount. Even the fireplace is backed with glass.

Overleaf: View from above.
Second overleaf: View from roof to approach.
Third overleaf: Living room.

232

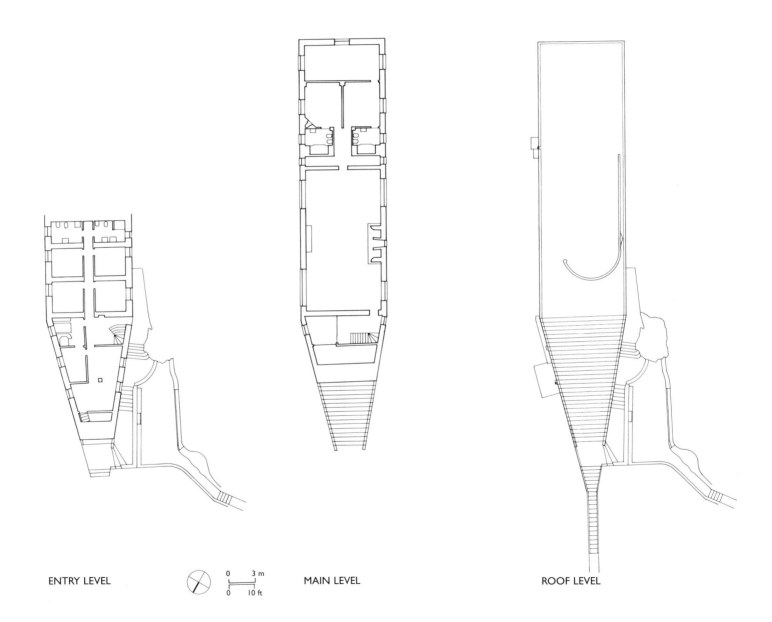

ENTRY LEVEL   MAIN LEVEL   ROOF LEVEL

0   3 m
0   10 ft

Above: Living-room furniture.
Opposite: View from living-room window.

Above: Bookcase-lined study.
Opposite: Bedroom.

FARNSWORTH HOUSE
Plano, Illinois
1946–1950

LUDWIG MIES VAN DER ROHE
1886–1969

LUDWIG MIES VAN DER ROHE CLOSED THE BAUHAUS SCHOOL in 1933, and in 1938 left his native Germany for America, where the directorship of the architecture school at Chicago's Illinois Institute of Technology (as it was soon renamed) awaited him. In his practice over the ensuing decades, he continued to refine the expression of the steel frame structure, always as the manifestation of the true challenge to architects as he saw it—namely, to portray reason in harmony with nature. He designed scores of skeleton buildings, among them the Lake Shore Drive Apartments in Chicago (1948–50) and the Seagram Building in New York (with Philip Johnson, 1954–58). He also conceived several clear-span one-story buildings, the first and arguably most beautiful being the weekend house for Dr. Edith Farnsworth.

Three tales surround the building of the house: the first, while interesting, is unexceptional from today's vantage point, but the other two are significant as cautionary notes. The first concerns the scandal of

Opposite: Terrace.

the architect-client relationship, which devolved into a personal and then a litigious one. The second involves the abuse of the design for reactionary political ends—the house was one of a number of modern buildings denounced by *House Beautiful* as being un-American. The third concerns an environmental problem—the glazed house was too hot or too cold most of the time. Mies, however, had a vision to pursue.

The house Mies designed was a temple *for* modern times, celebrating the harmony of humankind, architecture, and nature. It was also a temple *of* its time, realized in plate glass and steel in a way never before envisioned. Two steel-framed planes, the floor and the roof, are held nine feet six inches apart by eight wide-flange steel columns. Mies used these elements to express the continuity of space in various ways. He raised the floor slab five feet three inches above ground level
(a physical necessity as well, since the site was in a floodplain), so that space passes under the building. He cantilevered the slabs at the two ends and subordinated the enclosing glass planes by recessing them behind the columns, so that space seems to flow unfettered through the steel skeleton. The sense of planes hovering within limitless space is further underscored by the unenclosed terrace at one end of the house, and by the additional plane that forms a stepping pad up to the house. Within the house, divisions are suggested by two asymmetrically placed freestanding units: the kitchen/bathroom/hearth core and the closet, both of which, like the furniture designed by Mies himself, contribute to the sense of flowing space. Materials form a pale and elegant frame for the landscape—the steel, with joints carefully sanded, is painted white; the floor is paved in travertine; and the core faced in primavera wood.

Overleaf: Approach from south.
246
Second overleaf: North facade.

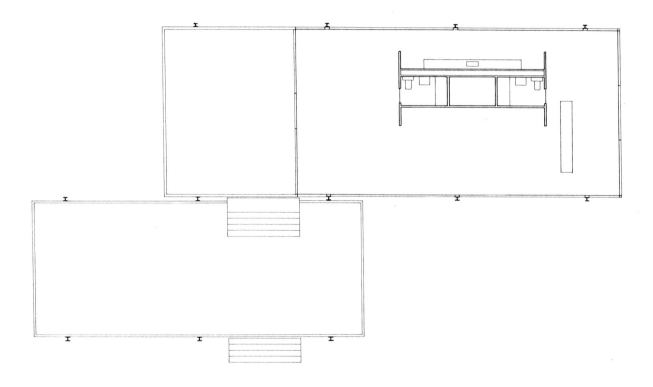

GROUND FLOOR

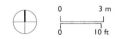

0   3 m

0   10 ft

247

GLASS HOUSE
New Canaan, Connecticut
1949

PHILIP JOHNSON
1906–

PHILIP JOHNSON IS NOW BEST KNOWN AS THE ARCHITECT of the AT&T Building and other postmodern high-rises. He began his career, however, as a modernist, co-organizing the Museum of Modern Art's International Style exhibition in 1932, practicing Miesian-type design, and eventually working with Mies on the design of the Seagram Building in New York. In 1949 Johnson decided to design his own house based on the all-glass concept suggested to him by Mies van der Rohe, whose Farnsworth House (page 244) was not yet built. Johnson's Glass House was to take on enormous importance, influencing the articulation of glass facades and profoundly changing the way architects thought about design.

The conditions surrounding the Johnson and Farnsworth projects—private, wooded sites, and single residents of means, who could use the houses part-time—made possible the exclusive use of glass. Furthermore, the designs shared basic characteristics: steel and glass, eight classically arranged columns carrying a flat roof, freestanding three-dimensional partitions, Mies-designed furniture, and a minimalist vocabulary. From there, however, the two designs diverged. Whereas Mies's

Opposite: Living area.

design implies the infinite nature of space and emphasizes the elongated frame, Johnson's stresses the Golden Section box. Johnson effected this difference by sitting the house directly on a brick plinth on the ground and by placing the glass outside the steel frame except at the inset corners. The position of the glass and the darkness of the steel's finish impart a sense of substance to the walls when viewed from the exterior, especially when the reflective qualities of the glass predominate; the shiny box then plays off the brick box of the nearby Guest House. The inset corners attract attention intentionally, as the house is approached obliquely, part of a landscape/siting strategy that Johnson has pursued on the site over the years. The brick of the floor, which is continued up around the fireplace/bathroom cylinder that pierces the roof, is a warm, populist choice compared to Mies's travertine. The focusing of the interior (when the landscape is draped in darkness) on the brick hearth is warm and earthy and is a move reminiscent of Frank Lloyd Wright.

Shortly after the Glass House was built, Johnson articulated the many other sources that influenced his design, including Karl Friedrich Schinkel, Claude-Nicolas Ledoux, Theo Van Doesburg, Le Corbusier, and the Acropolis as analyzed by Auguste Choisy. In so doing, Johnson revived historical models long shunned by the modern movement and placed them alongside modern ones. Questioning the traditional notions of cause and effect and of progress in history, Johnson and, in the 1960s and 1970s, his younger followers argued that architectural history could be foraged for concepts—or forms, for that matter— that could be shorn of their original associations and applied at will, an approach that produced some controversial results. Johnson himself made a virtue of inconsistency in designs across America and on his own New Canaan estate, where he built additional pavilions in disparate styles. As a result of this chain of events, the Glass House, an icon of modernism, helped spawn the postmodern movement.

Overleaf: Living area.
Second overleaf: Night view.

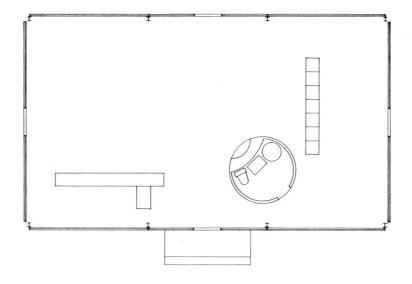

GROUND FLOOR

0   1 m

0   3 ft

VILLA PLANCHART

Caracas, Venezuela
1954–1955

GIO PONTI

1891–1979

GIO PONTI'S SUNNY, INCLUSIVE DESIGN PHILOSOPHY, BEST exemplified by his residential work, was disseminated by the Italian magazine *Domus,* which he founded in 1928 and directed for the better part of fifty years. In the magazine he put forth his vision of the light-filled, joyous house and the decorative objects that would fill it. His own design work spanned the gamut, from paintings, graphics, cutlery, ceramics, furniture, and theater sets to houses, churches, museums (including the Denver Museum of Art), and office towers and even to town planning. His endeavors to merge classicism and Rationalism were inspired in part by the Wiener Werkstätte, but he had his own, Italian vision, a "poetry of precisions," as he called it, that blended spirituality, fantasy, and reason. His early work, which used a pared-down Classical vocabulary, identified him as one of the Milanese Novecento architects, but by the mid-1930s, as his commissions grew in size, he turned to a more modernist approach. His best-known large-scale building is the Pirelli Tower in Milan, designed with Pier Luigi Nervi in 1956.

Opposite: Entrance facade.

The unadulterated joy Ponti could express in design is seen in the Villa Planchart. The house embodies both meanings of the word *light,* being both light-filled and seemingly light in weight. Terraces are notched into the building at several points along its perimeter as well as at its center, where a two-story atrium cuts through the roof. The soaring, butterfly roof appears to float above the exterior walls, while the walls themselves appear separated from one another and from the ground, perching ever so lightly on the inset stone foundation. The glowing, floating effect is intensified at night by a kind of backlighting, as strips of light above, below, and behind the walls complete the sense of detachment. Inside the house, the open, spacious planning permits views in virtually every direction.

Ponti called the Plancharts ideal clients, "happy" ones, and he was given freedom to design all aspects of the house. Within the bent-rectangular perimeter of the generous structure he placed sitting rooms and dining rooms, some enclosed and some open-air, with decorative objects designed by him or by artists he selected. The living room has a luminous ceiling, and connects visually by an internal window to the colorful *comedor,* or outdoor dining space. The central stairway is decorated with ceramic pieces by Fausto Melotti, as is the adjacent plant-filled atrium. For the house, Ponti designed porcelain dinner services, produced by Richard Ginori; cutlery; and furniture, including adjustable tables for a variety of uses and a marble table for the *comedor.* The stuccoed ceiling of the entrance hall depicts the sun and the moon, references to his generous clients, whose foundation now maintains the house and its furnishings as a museum.

Overleaf: View from under entrance canopy.

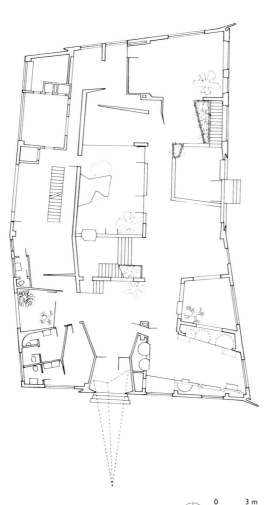

FIRST FLOOR

0   3 m
0   10 ft

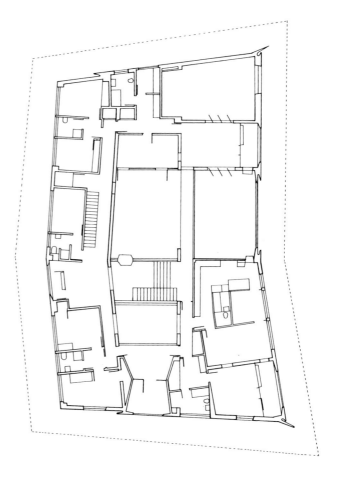

SECOND FLOOR

263

Above: Decorated ceiling.
Opposite: Stairway with sculpture.
Overleaf: Living room.

Above: Living-room alcove.
Opposite: Comedor.

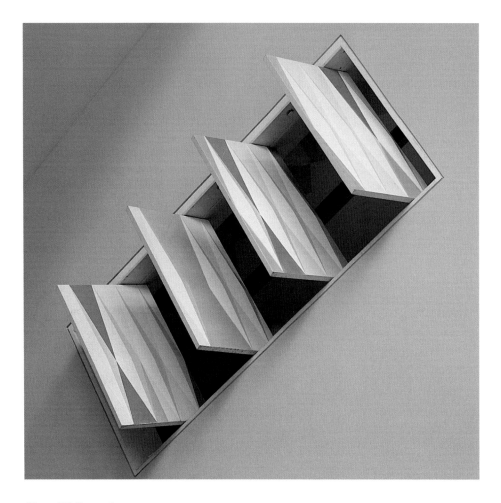

Above: Wall panels.

Opposite: Sitting area.

MAISONS JAOUL

Neuilly-sur-Seine/Paris, France
1951–1955

LE CORBUSIER

1887–1965

So great was the range of Le Corbusier's seminal designs that later modernists of many kinds—formalists and technocrats, Purists and brutalists—have claimed his patrimony. The Maisons Jaoul, a pair of houses for a father and son, seem to represent, for example, a startling change in approach by the architect who had, twenty years earlier, designed the Villa Savoye (page 162). In fact, during the 1930s Le Corbusier had begun expanding his vocabulary beyond the machine-age geometries of Purism. This reexamination occurred not only because he found the white finishes of his 1920s Purist buildings weathering poorly but also because he sought new ways to interpret the ideas of regionalism, which had been fundamental to his early training, and of primitivism. Primitivism, which had figured in the architect's Purist designs, implied not only a simplicity of form but also a coexistence with nature; primitivism and regionalism, then, came together in "vernacular" architecture. As it happens, Le Corbusier had several commissions during the 1930s for rural sites where a white

274

Opposite: Shared courtyard.

Above: Stairway.
Opposite: Pipe system.

FISHER HOUSE

Hatboro, Pennsylvania
1960–1967

LOUIS KAHN

1901–1974

LOUIS KAHN'S ARCHITECTURE IS BASED ON PURE GEOMETRIC forms, endowing the plainest of commissions—the public bathhouse in Trenton, New Jersey, for example—with a timeless monumentality. At the same time, the modesty of the materials, details, and proportions, and the clarity of expression, allow even the grandest of his commissions—governmental buildings in Dacca in Bangladesh, for example, and synagogues—to communicate a sense of intense simplicity. Kahn, born in Estonia but brought up in the United States, came to this balance of grandeur and plainness by transforming, over the space of decades, the formalism of his Beaux-Arts training, received at the University of Pennsylvania and in the office of Paul Cret. By asking of every design program, space, and material, "What does it want to be?," he produced buildings that seem both artless and universal. One of the major ways in which he clarified an architectural problem was to separate the expression of the "servant" element (circulation spaces, such as stairways, or ventilation spaces, such as exhaust flues) from those that were "served" (the main rooms in a house, for example).

Opposite: Bridge approach to house.

KORMAN HOUSE

Fort Washington, Pennsylvania
1971–1973

LOUIS KAHN

1901–1974

ONE OF LOUIS KAHN'S MOST IMPORTANT CONTRIBUTIONS TO architecture was his extension of the concept of Functionalism, in a way that gave energy and order to design. By distinguishing areas with specific functions—separating "servant" and "served" spaces— he established a strong, even monumental hierarchical order that nonetheless incorporated compelling formal variety. In his renowned design for the Richards Medical Research Buildings at the University of Pennsylvania (1957–64), for example, he inserted circulation and mechanical services into brick towers that were distinct from the glazed laboratory towers. His houses, on the other hand, embody a complex interpretation of this idea.

The Korman House is the last of Kahn's residential designs and in some ways one of the most formal and intricate. Its formality derives not only from the structure's command of its seventy-acre site but also from the rhythmic regularity of its glazed two-story living/dining wing.

Opposite: View from entry side.

The complexity of the house, on the other hand, is the result of a certain amount of overlapping of the rectilinear zones that make up the residence, an overlapping that for Kahn reflects a relatively relaxed response to the complicated, if well-known, program of the private house.

The house consists of three rectangular zones, discernible in the floor plan. Two of the zones are parallel to each other, each comprising two levels of bedrooms with a circulation zone between them; while the third, perpendicular to the bedroom wings, contains the double-height living/dining block. The rectangle formed by these relatively simple areas is extended by servant spaces attached to its periphery: bathrooms, the kitchen, and fireplaces. These appendages are uncharacteristically asymmetrical. Even the two brick fireplace structures that bracket the living/dining block differ in their heights and the alignment of their axes. These differences reflect the components' disparate roles and the engagement of the overlapping zones. The westernmost structure ties the kitchen to the dining room; the easternmost connects the living room and the master bedroom suite. The latter, a two-story apartment with its own spiral staircase, is strategically located so as to function as part of both the living room zone and the bedroom wing.

Materials—wood or brick—are intentionally neutral in order to provide a backdrop for the clients' personal taste. Wood is used carefully to manifest the sturdy structure, on the one hand, and to form infill paneling on the exterior and in the interior, on the other. It is also used for fine detailing, notably in the stair hall. The brick structures, too, are clearly expressed as they enter and emerge from the house, most strikingly at the corner of the living room, where the large cubic fireplace incorporates an inglenook.

Overleaf: View of bedroom wing.
Second overleaf: View of living-dining wing.

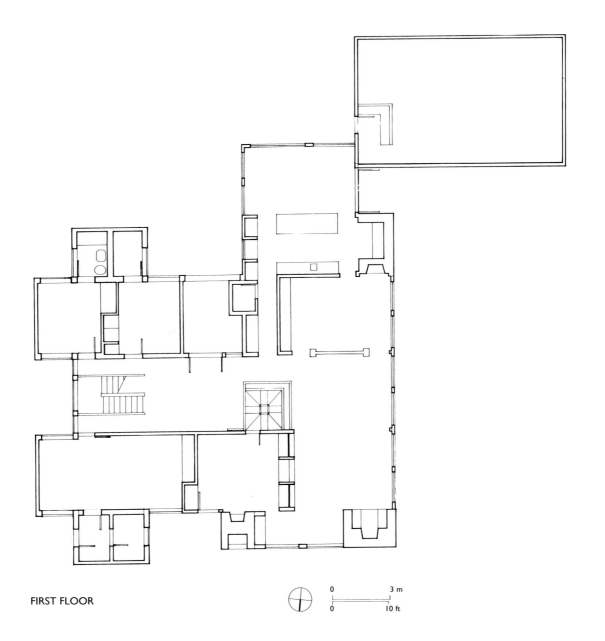

FIRST FLOOR

Above: View from top of stair.
Opposite: Stair in circulation zone.

Above: Bedroom landing.
Opposite: Spiral stair.
Overleaf: Living room.

BRION-VEGA CEMETERY
San Vito di Altivole, Italy
1970–1978

CARLO SCARPA
1906–1978

Upon THE DEATH OF GIUSEPPE BRION, THE ELECTRONICS
industrialist's widow asked Carlo Scarpa to design a small cemetery.
The cemetery was intended eventually to reunite the family members
on a site outside their hometown. In effect, it was to be a "house"
in which the inhabitants would spend their afterlife. With limited functional requirements, the design called for poetry.

The Venetian-born Carlo Scarpa was the appropriate choice, since his
work is remarkable for its abundant iconography expressed with great
visual richness. He used simple geometric forms, but overlapped them
and overlaid them with a variety of materials, contrasting heavily
textured masses with smooth surfaces. While he delighted in discon-
tinuous forms that meet and instantly separate, he also deeply respect-
ed the craft of building. Scarpa was active as well in restoration: his
approach was nothing short of breathtaking. He successfully managed
to insert bold, inventive new forms into centuries-old buildings while

Opposite: Path to chapel.

still giving primacy to the existing structure, as in his restoration during the 1960s of the Castelvecchio, the civic museum of Verona. He was also well-known for his exhibition design, and he acted as consultant to the influential Venice Biennale from 1947 to 1972. Apparently inspired by the architecture of Otto Wagner, Adolf Loos, and Le Corbusier; by Japanese design; and by the work of Frank Lloyd Wright—especially his dense, intensely sculptural designs—Scarpa integrated these sources within a highly personal vocabulary.

The Brion-Vega Cemetery (named for the family firm, which had been conceived under the star Vega) is designed as an L around the edge of the existing town cemetery. It is entered from the town cemetery through an inconspicuous gate, as if it were just another small mausoleum on the site. But it is from this very gate, half hidden by a weeping willow tree, that an extraordinary journey begins: organized as a narrative, it consists of symbols whose meanings, partly documented, are mostly in the eye of the beholder. Behind the gate, a short corridor leads to a wall featuring two large interlocking rings, which have been interpreted variously as eyes, wedding rings, or alpha and omega, the beginning and the end. At this point, the visitor can choose to turn right to the pond, in which stands a meditation pavilion, or left. Along the right-hand path, footsteps echo and passage is temporarily blocked by a sheet of glass that must be pushed down with force. The left-hand path leads first to the circular Brion tomb, containing two sarcophagi that lean toward each other under an arched roof, then past the family tomb and on to the chapel, which, like the pavilion, stands in water. Unlike the simple pavilion, the chapel is complex, replete with rich materials and square motifs that diagonally overlay other squares.

Scarpa died unexpectedly in 1978 while traveling in Japan. His remains, fittingly, are buried in the Brion-Vega Cemetery, at the crook of the L.

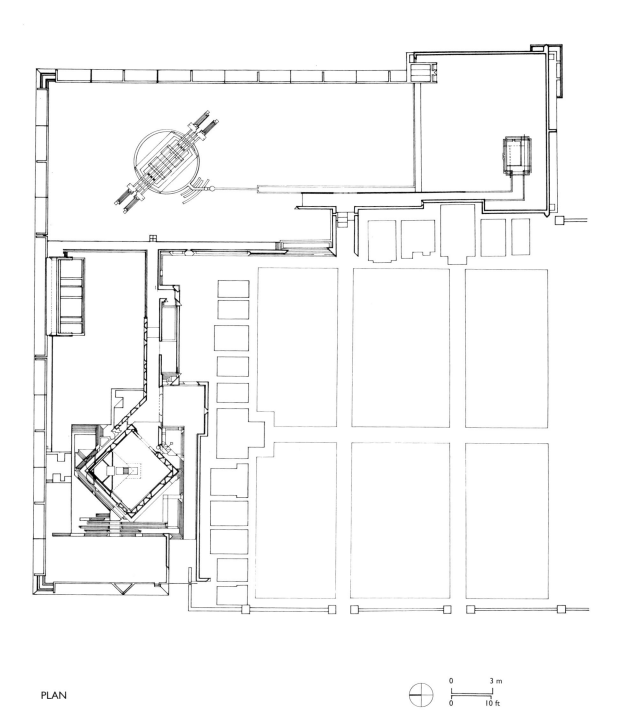

PLAN

0   3 m

0   10 ft

Above: Chapel interior.
Opposite: Corner of chapel.
Overleaf: Interlocking rings.
Second overleaf: Meditation pavilion.

HOUSE VI

West Cornwall, Connecticut
1972–1976

PETER EISENMAN

1932–

Whence Peter Eisenman designed this weekend house for Dick and Suzanne Frank, he was known internationally for his theoretical work, but had little built work to his name. His ideas were promulgated by the New York–based Institute for Architecture and Urban Studies, of which he was founding director, and by his exposure as a leading participant in the group known as the New York Five. The Five's small-scale but groundbreaking designs were exhibited at the Museum of Modern Art in New York and helped pave the way for postmodernism in architecture. Some of the Five turned to premodern sources for revitalization and some, including Eisenman, to early modern concepts.

Eisenman was interested in fulfilling the true modernist goal by moving beyond Functionalism, which he felt had falsely reflected the modern condition, to develop an architecture that was wholly self-referential. He based his designs on complex manipulations of geometries related in part to the early modernist de Stijl and Rationalist movements. Eisenman eventually abandoned residential work and has designed a number of large,

Opposite: View from southeast.

high-profile projects, including the Wexner Center for the Visual Arts at Ohio State University in Columbus (1989). Eisenman's later work involves some "contextual" references, usually of a cosmic nature (the Mercator grid or mathematical formulas) or a psychological nature (memories) or cosmic/psychological (memories as released by excavations).

The architect gave his houses numbered names rather than family names, an immediate clue to their experimental, objectified nature. House VI is designed around two stairways perpendicular to each other, one real (color-coded green) and one (painted red) embedded in the ceiling. The stairways are positioned tightly against two walls that slice through the building. In the design phase, the walls (or planes) divided the site into four quadrants, each of which was subjected to a possible "transformation" of the plane into a volume. The resulting house comprises volumes grouped in a spiral formation around the datum planes, ranging from zero volume, at the point of entry, to minimal volume (vestibule/closets) to largest volume (living/bedroom) and then decreasing to medium-sized volume (kitchen/bathroom). The largest volume—the quadrant subjected to the greatest transformation—consists of four cubes forming the living room on the ground floor and four additional cubes constituting the bedroom above. In order to demarcate the boundaries between the original component cubes, glass strips were inserted into the bedroom floor, on either side of which separate beds were specified. This design requirement, observed by the couple against their custom, surely constitutes the most flagrant anti-Functionalist move ever! That condition (which the couple only recently altered), in addition to a column alongside the dining table, kitchen cabinets too high to reach, and very leaky roofs, has led to a tough-love situation between owners and house. But they do love it, and it is easy, after all, to see why. The intellectual transformations have been realized in an object of great beauty, with dazzling two-story spaces intersected by gray/white (exterior/interior) beams and glazed and skylit volumes that glow from without and within.

Overleaf: View from west.

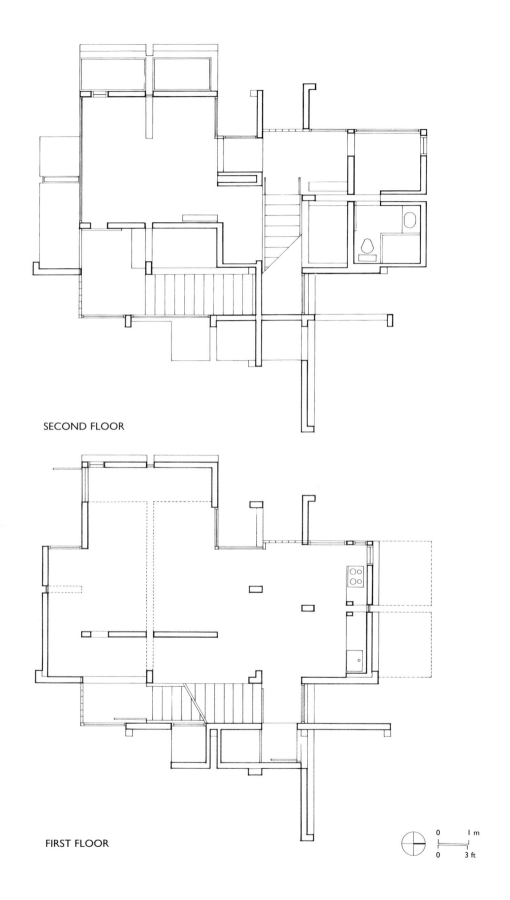

SECOND FLOOR

FIRST FLOOR

0   1 m

0   3 ft

Above: Red stairway embedded in ceiling.
Opposite: Green stairway to upper level.

Above: View to ceiling.

Opposite: Dining area under red stairway.

GILARDI HOUSE

Mexico City, Mexico
1975–1977

LUIS BARRAGÁN

1902–1987

T HE WORK OF LUIS BARRAGÁN, MEXICO'S MOST RENOWNED
modern architect, is suffused with a sense of poetry. The Gilardi House,
designed for a young art collector, reveals the architect's spiritual lean-
ings, but it also demonstrates an understanding of European modernism.

Barragán was trained in engineering. He supplemented this education
with stays in Europe, studying Moorish architecture in Spain in the
1920s and attending lectures by Le Corbusier in the 1930s. Most
significant to Barragán's development, however, were his deeply
empathetic observations of Mexican vernacular forms and landscape,
and his spiritualism. From these he evolved his vocabulary, austere in
fact but sensuous in effect: expanses of textured stucco walls painted—
or, as it would seem, drenched—in saturated colors, hovering concrete
slabs, rough-hewn wooden logs, simple, powerful gardens, and an almost
mystical use of water. Among his best-known works are the master
plan for the section of Mexico city called Los Clubes and the 1968
San Cristobal estate and riding stables within that section.

Opposite: View from central patio to front volume.

The Gilardi House, designed with Alberto Chauvet and Raul Ferrera, is located on a tightly defined lot in the Tacubaya section of Mexico City. The three-story front section of the house, with its cubic Loosian forms (but these are rose-colored!) and its almost unfenestrated screenlike facade, could nearly stand alone, architecturally and functionally: the entrance, garage, kitchen, and servants' quarters are on the ground floor, the living room and study/bedroom on the second, and the bedrooms on the third. This part of the house is contained in a rather square plan about thirty feet wide. Its major rooms occupy two opposite quadrants of the square, while a second-story terrace and a generous, skylit stair-cum-hall fill the remaining two quadrants.

However skillfully wrought the front section of the house, it is the interior of the site that is invested with Barragán's magic. The architect has imported a permanent sense of sun, sky, and water to this land-locked area. A one-story galleria connects the front of the house to the dining/pool pavilion at the back, leaving room for a patio that incorporates an existing tree at its center. The galleria is separated from the patio by a thick stucco wall into which vertical slots are cut. The inner side of the wall is painted a bright yellow, guaranteeing an impression of warm sun, no matter how weak or strong the daylight coming in from the patio. The galleria can be closed at either end; but when the door to the pavilion is opened, a world of water and color is revealed. Here, hues are used as if in reaction to their situation. Intense sky blue is found under the skylight at the corner of the space, and a red-painted column turns paler as it slices into the pool, as if discolored by the water. Barragán's architecture seems to project its own natural aura; it not only asserts nature's life-affirming qualities, it intensifies them.

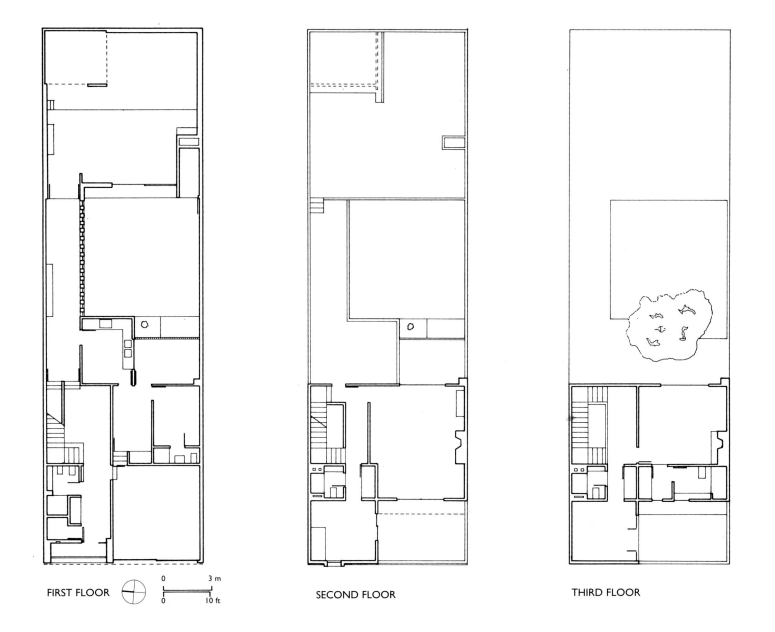

FIRST FLOOR 0 3 m / 0 10 ft

SECOND FLOOR

THIRD FLOOR

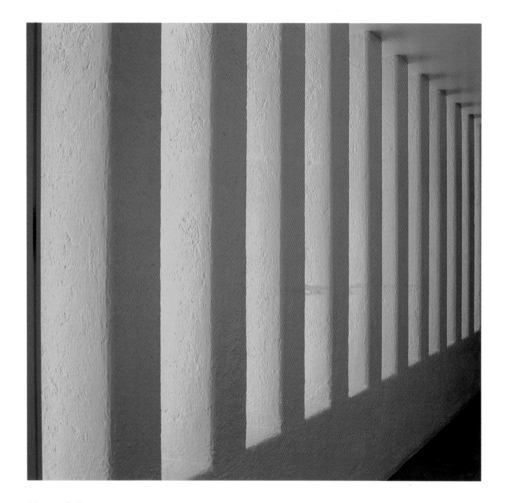

Above: Galleria interior.
Opposite: Pool in dining/pool pavilion.

SIRMAI-PETERSON HOUSE

Thousand Oaks, California
1983–1988

FRANK GEHRY

1929–

FRANK GEHRY'S SIGNATURE ARCHITECTURE HAS TAKEN SEVERAL
dramatic turns over the span of his career; however, the making of
form and space, as an expression of the culture of a particular place
and the personality of a given client, has always been paramount. The
buildings have been comfortable for their users, but the expression of
function and structure has nevertheless been subservient to artistic
expression. Gehry, born in Toronto, has been fundamental to the development of an open, art-driven architectural atmosphere in his adopted
city of Los Angeles.

After practicing commercial architecture for a few years, Gehry began
to engage his artistic interests, producing architecture that was related
to minimalist art and that explored the distortion of perceived space
in, for example, the trapezoidal house for artist Ron Davis of the early
1970s. He then embarked on a fertile period during which he experi-
mented with unexpected, inexpensive materials—corrugated metals,

Opposite: View from east.

chain link, bare wooden framing—and exploded volumes; an example is the startling renovation of the architect's own house in Santa Monica in 1979. In the early 1980s Gehry began fragmenting the volume by separating the component elements of the program into pavilions arranged around exterior spaces, as, for instance, in the Loyola College Law School building in Los Angeles and the Winton House in Minnesota. In the late 1980s and 1990s Gehry went on to create a far more expressionist series of buildings, featuring exuberant curved forms enclosing dramatic, Piranesian spaces, such as the Vitra Museum in Weil am Rhein, Germany, the American Center in Paris, and the Guggenheim Museum Bilbao in Spain.

The Sirmai-Peterson House belongs to the penultimate group, which features components separated into volumes around exterior courts. In the course of the design process, Gehry decided to have only the bedrooms function as freestanding pavilions and placed the main components under one roof. This multileveled "roof" culminates at the center in a "cupola" that bathes the middle of the space—notably the stove, positioned as an altar—in something like a holy light streaming from above. The architect, in fact, refers to the main volume as church-like: in the cruciform plan the living room acts as nave, the fireplace as apse, and the hall leading toward the bedrooms as side aisle. It is a rather barnlike church, highlighting exposed wood rafters. Gehry adds another metaphor to the mix (if there's a church, there has to be a town, perhaps) and refers to the exterior spaces between the stuccoed main house and bedroom pavilions as a kind of town square. The "town" now contains a lake, formed by damming the water that ran through the site and turning one of its drawbacks into an advantage. The house is located close to the edge of the site's ravine, and the jagged energy of the buildings plan—resembling a spastic Keith Haring figure with extended arms—seems to derive from the earth's rocky outline.

Overleaf: View from south.

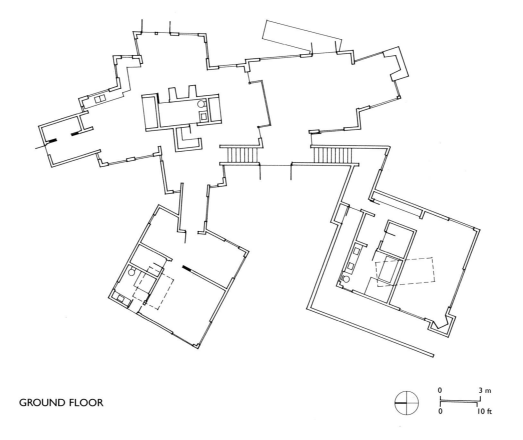

GROUND FLOOR

CRAWFORD HOUSE

Santa Barbara, California
1990

MORPHOSIS

Mayne, 1944–
Rotondi, 1949–

LIKE PETER EISENMAN, MORPHOSIS FOUNDERS THOM MAYNE
and Michael Rotondi have concluded that pure Functionalism does not
well reflect the condition of the contemporary world. For Mayne and
Rotondi (who now heads an independent office, RoTo), the inadequacy
of the Functionalist approach involves its inapt depiction of the unpre-
dictable, chaotic world, especially evident in Los Angeles, the city where
they are based. The undefined boundaries of American cities—indeed
the lack of a central urban focus in many regions of this country—
combined with a focus on individualism, relatively large sites, and the
balmy southern California climate, render European-inspired architectural forms irrelevant. Perched at the edge of the Western Hemisphere,
where periodic earthquakes, discordant human-made development, and
endless expanses of ocean inform the landscape, these architects—
like Eisenman—turn to geometry for order and connectedness. But
Morphosis, which has designed, among other projects, the restaurant
Kate Mantilini (1986) and the Cedars Sinai Comprehensive Cancer

336

Opposite: Lap pool.

Center (1985–87) in Los Angeles, seek geometries that clash, in order to create an architecture of fragments.

The Crawford House is located on a site dominated by a mesmerizing view of the ocean. The entrance to the house occurs along a slot that focuses on this view, a slot that ruptures the otherwise relentless structural system and is extended by a long lap pool. As if to underscore the divisive nature of the opening, the entrance takes the form of a wedge. To emphasize the center as void, the slot opens out to form a no-man's-land of terraces facing east toward the street, a dramatic if not quite comforting version of the outdoor California life. On either side of the slot, on the second level of the house, the only level visible from the street, are the main areas—the living/dining/kitchen wing and the bedroom wing. These spaces benefit from a continuous skylight that runs parallel to the house's main axis and defines the house's "cosmic" alignment with the earth's north-south lines of longitude. At the same time, the areas are insistently punctuated by a perpendicular grid, expressed by overlapping beams (which are supported by pylons at ground level) and a series of light monitors—the east-west ordering elements. At one end of the house is Joan Crawford's painting studio, and at the other end, separated from the main building and turned at right angles to it, is the knife-edged guest house. All the fragmented, gritty parts—oxidizing copper panels predominate in effect—are set into the hill and gathered together by a "boundary" formed by segments of a circular wall. The building's L-shaped plan is defined by a primary geometric perimeter, as is the case with the Villa Savoye; here, however, the pretext of closure is exposed.

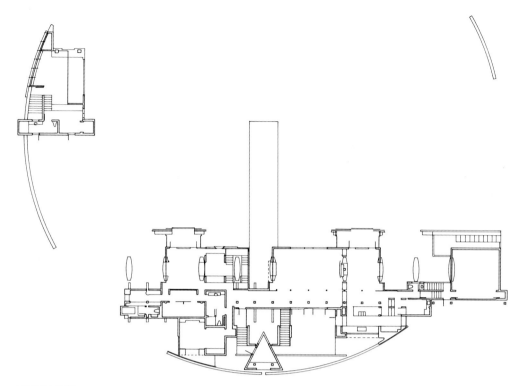

UPPER LEVEL

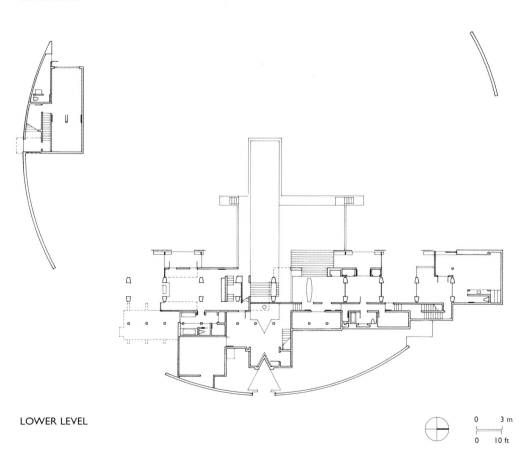

LOWER LEVEL

0   3 m

0   10 ft

339

Above: Corner detail.
Opposite: View from entrance to lap pool.

Above: Living room.
Opposite: Bathroom.
Overleaf: Partial view of facade.

RACHOFSKY HOUSE
Dallas, Texas
1991–1996

RICHARD MEIER
1934–

THROUGHOUT HIS CAREER, RICHARD MEIER HAS ENLARGED
on an aesthetic inspired by Le Corbusier's Purist period, a period that
produced, among other works, the Villa Savoye (page 162). From his
earliest days, Meier's buildings, such as the Atheneum in New Harmony,
Indiana (1978), the High Museum of Art in Atlanta (1980–83), and
numerous houses, have been characterized by stunning white prismatic
volumes that enclose dynamic spatial configurations. As his fame has
grown internationally and as awards such as the Pritzker Prize have
accrued to him, ever larger commissions have come his way. Some
projects, like the Getty Center in Los Angeles, completed in 1997,
have offered him the challenge of designing entire complexes as well
as individual structures.

The thirteen-thousand-square-foot Rachofsky house, designed for a
businessman and collector of major twentieth-century art, profits from
Meier's extensive experience in both residential and museum design.

Opposite: Front facade.

Rachofsky, a bachelor, wanted a house in which he could live with his collection, occasionally opening it for art or architecture tours. The house, accordingly, is almost all gallery. It has only one bedroom; even the planned guestrooms were eliminated in favor of another room for displaying artworks. Inside the entrance, a two-story gallery runs along the front of the house. On the next level up is the living room, a larger, two-story space that also serves as a gallery. The living room faces the pool and poolhouse on the interior of the site. On the top floor is the master bedroom suite, which overlooks and almost encircles the living room.

Like all Meier buildings, the Rachofsky House is extremely refined in concept and detail. Having been inspired by the white concrete surfaces that intentionally dematerialized Le Corbusier's Purist buildings, Meier went on to develop a more precise, sharp-edged realization of these surfaces, in many cases using enameled metal panels. In this house, the panels are aluminum plate. In a number of his earlier houses, Meier contrasted an opaque front wall with open, glazed walls on the more private sides, as did Adolf Loos, for example, in the Villa Karma (page 60). Meier repeats this strategy in the Rachofsky House, in which the wall facing the street consists of a large, seemingly independent, almost unfenestrated screen. The plan is carefully articulated, with spaces pro-portioned on the basis of squares and their multiples, or on the basis of Le Corbusier's Modulor, while stairways are given distinct expres-sion, in the manner of Louis Kahn. In most Meier houses, the ground itself forms the plane from which the building rises. In this house, a raised black podium finished in granite pavers provides the ground plane. Between the dining room and gallery is a wall that retracts into the floor to open up the space, a feature reminiscent of the exterior wall in Mies van der Rohe's Tugendhat House (page 190). While some of the parts of the Rachofsky House reflect concepts from selected modern masters, the whole is confidently, unmistakably, Richard Meier.

Overleaf: View from southwest.
Second overleaf: View from west.

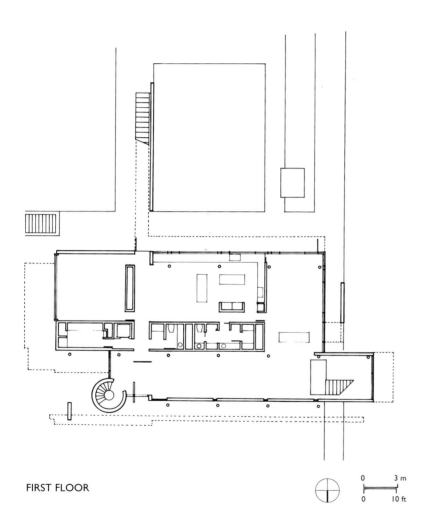

FIRST FLOOR

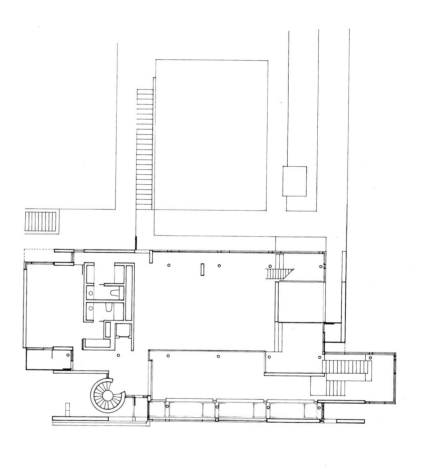

SECOND FLOOR

0   3 m
0   10 ft

349